DOWN TO YOU

SIXTH STREET BANDS #5

JAYNE FROST

SIXTH STREET PRESS

Edited by: Patricia D. Eddy — The Novel Fixer
Proofreading: Proofing With Style

Cover Design: Maria — Steamy Designs

Cover Photo: Storm Santos
Cover Model : Christopher Mason

Sixth Street Bands

The premise for this series began with a group of bands from Austin Texas, who rose to fame when *Damaged*, the original band from 6th Street, was cut down in a terrible accident. Through this tragedy, a new group of bands emerged to carry on the Damaged legacy. The media dubbed them The Sixth Street Bands. They became a family. And like all families, their lives, music, and day-to-day struggles became entwined. While each of the books in my series can be read as a standalone, you will see recurring characters woven into each story.

Reading order and a list of recurring characters on the next page.

Welcome to my band family!

TWIN SOULS MANAGEMENT

- Taryn Ayers (#4 Lost For You w/Chase Noble)
- Tori Grayson

CAGED

- Cameron Knight (#1 Gone For You w/Lily Tennison)
- Christian Seers (#2 Fall With Me w/Melody Sullivan)
- Sean Hudson (#3 Missing From Me w/Anna Dresden)
- Logan Cage (#5 Down To You w/Tori Grayson)

DAMAGED

- Rhenn Grayson —Deceased
- Paige Dawson— Deceased
- Tori Grayson (Rhenn's widow)
- Miles Cooper

LEVERAGED

- Dylan Boothe
- Beckett Brennin
- Zane Martin
- Conner Hart

REVENGED THEORY
Line-Up To Be Determined

DRAFTHOUSE
LINE-UP TO BE DETERMINED

Dedication

IN MEMORY

"And when you asked for light, I set myself on fire,"— CHRIS CORNELL

I didn't know you, but I loved you. Your music is the soundtrack of my life. Sleep well, find peace, and rock on.

And for Jeff, the love of my life ... all of my life.
If I'm the words, you're the music.

In the end ... it all came down to you

She started from perfect. A star who shone brighter than the rest.
But then fate took it all away.
Now she's broken.
A beautiful song with a fractured beat.

But I'm still on the rise.
Chasing a dream that she's already left behind.
If I'm lucky, I can find my redemption in the spotlight.

Destiny brought us together.
Put her in my path.

It started with a road trip. But somewhere along the line, it became a journey from here to there.

Maybe she can help me.
Maybe we can help each other.
Maybe music is enough.
Maybe.

Every story deserves a soundtrack.
And ours is *epic*.

PROLOGUE

Logan

Eight Years Old

Laurel sniffled and squeezed my hand as we followed the cop up the steps to the porch of the big house. Even though it was dark, and I couldn't see a thing, I knew it was nothing like our house. Our house didn't have a porch. And it was on wheels. Mama always said that one day we'd live in a house with no wheels. An apartment, maybe.

But not now.

Laurel squeezed my fingers. "Logan?"

I wiped my nose on the shoulder of my T-shirt before looking down at my little sister. "Yeah?"

Big blue eyes locked onto mine. "I'm scared," she whispered. "Where's Mama?"

Gone.

But I couldn't tell her that. Laurel was only four. She wouldn't understand. She wasn't big like me.

"Be a big boy. Watch your sister."

That's the last thing Mama had said before she jumped out of the car.

And then …

The bang exploded inside my head, and I shuddered, blinking hard to hold back the tears. Because eight-year-olds didn't cry. I wouldn't let anyone see me cry. Not even Laurel.

"She'll be back soon," I lied, pulling her closer when the porch light flickered on. "Just … be quiet, 'kay?"

Laurel nodded, turning those frightened eyes to the big man in front of us. With his hand on the butt of his gun, the cop leaned forward, whispering to the lady in the fluffy robe who answered the door. I only caught a few words.

Tragic.

No suspects.

Deceased.

"I really appreciate this, Tessa," I heard him say before glancing over his shoulder and motioning for us to enter.

I stubbornly held my ground, but not my sister. Laurel moved blindly, drawn to the lady with the kind smile and the smell of cookies that wafted onto the porch. Our trailer never smelled like cookies. Not even when Mama went to the store and bought one of those plastic tubes of dough and cooked it in the tiny oven.

"Please, Lo," Laurel whined, looking back at me as she tugged my arm. "Maybe she got some food in there."

My stomach turned, but I nodded at my sister. And then I hung my head and followed her into the house. Past the policeman with the sad eyes and the blood on his shoes. My mother's blood.

Sitting up with a start, I blinked and looked around the dark room. "Mama?"

And then it came back in a rush, and I knew she wouldn't answer. That she *couldn't* answer.

Squeezing my eyes shut, I gripped my hair, willing away the image of her lying on the asphalt. When the mattress dipped, I expected to find that Tessa lady, so I blinked in surprise when a girl swam into focus.

From her spot at the end of the bed, she stared at me with a crinkled-up brow. "Are you okay?"

I pressed my back against the headboard. "Get out of here," I growled. "Leave me alone."

I used my fiercest voice. The one that made all the other kids run. But she didn't move. Just tucked a strand of long, dark hair behind her ear and replied softly, "You were crying. I could hear you all the way from the guest room."

As my eyes adjusted, I could make out the shape of her face. It was like a little heart. She had a pointy chin. But I didn't tell her that. She probably knew.

Folding my arms over my chest, I tried not to sniffle. "I wasn't crying."

She sighed, running her hand over the flowered comforter. "Yeah, you were. It's okay. Lots of kids cry when they get here."

Since I wasn't sure where *here* was, I didn't acknowledge her comment. The last thing I remembered was Tessa tucking Laurel and me into bed after cooking us macaroni and cheese. Glancing at the empty spot beside me where Laurel should've been, my heart leapt into my throat.

"Where's my sister?" I hopped to my feet. "Where did you take her?"

The girl grabbed my arm. And for some reason I didn't knock her hand away.

"My dad works at night, so Mama let her sleep in her bed."

Suspicious, I narrowed my eyes and sank down next to her. "Why would she do that? Laurel's not kin to y'all."

She shrugged. "That's just how Mama is. My daddy's a cop, so whenever they need a place for kids to stay after an, um ... accident or something, they bring them here."

A tiny flicker of hope sparked in my chest. "Do the kids get to stay here?"

She smiled. "Sometimes. For a while at least."

I cocked my head. "Where do *you* sleep?"

Even in the dim light I saw her cheeks turn pink. "Here. This is my room. The bulb burned out in the guest room and Mama didn't want you to get scared if you woke up and couldn't turn on the light."

"I'm not afraid of the dark," I scoffed. "I'm eight. How old are you?"

"Almost ten." We stared at each other for a moment and then she asked, "So what happened?"

My heart stalled, because for the last few minutes while we were talking, I didn't think about it. But then it was there, and I could feel the sting at the back of my eyes. "None of your business."

Her shoulders straightened, and an apology crawled up my throat. But I didn't want to tell her what happened. Because then I *would* cry.

"Okay," she said as she pushed to her feet. "I'll leave you alone then."

"No!" I swallowed hard and looked down at my hands. "You don't have to go."

Please don't go.

I slumped when she walked toward the door. But instead of leaving, she stopped at the tall dresser. Levering up to her tiptoes, she opened a little box and music floated through the air.

Shuffling back to my side, she held out her hand. "Here."

I took the penny she pressed into my palm. "What is this?"

She lifted a shoulder. "My lucky penny. I think you need it more than I do."

I ran my thumb over the grooves, examining the coin. When I looked up she was gone.

As it turned out the penny wasn't so lucky after all. Because the next morning my dad showed up to collect us.

And nothing was ever the same again.

1

Logan

"Check this out," Mac said as he slid the bottle across the table in the private dining room at the Capital Grille.

Easing back in the leather chair, I turned the label toward me. Even if I could read what it said—which I couldn't—I refused to show any enthusiasm.

From the rich, amber color of the liquor, I'd say bourbon. And knowing Mac, expensive as fuck. On the band's first trip to LA, before we'd officially signed with Metro Music, Mac had wooed us with champagne that cost more than any of us made in a week—hell, a month. But that was a long time ago, and I couldn't be bought for the price of a bottle of booze. I couldn't be bought at all.

Then why the fuck are you here?

Ignoring the accusatory voice in my head, I gave Mac a bland stare. "I'm not signed with your label anymore. And I know you didn't fly all the way out here a week before I'm leaving on tour to discuss overpriced hooch."

Mac picked up the bottle and smiled. "This is Pappy Van Winkle Family Reserve. It's rare and hard to come by. Like loyalty in this industry." After that little dig, he twisted off the cap and poured three fingers into a crystal tumbler. "But you're right. That's not why I came."

He set the glass atop a neatly folded stack of documents, then slid the drink and the pile my way.

Disregarding the papers, I picked up the bourbon, but before I could lift the drink to my lips, Mac tipped forward. "First, take a look at the offer."

Offer?

Somehow, I knew that was the reason I'd been summoned. If Mac wanted to merely shoot the shit while he was in town we wouldn't be dining at the Capital Grille. The restaurant prided itself on discretion. And plenty of backroom deals were made right here. But hearing Mac say the words with that smirk curving his lips turned my stomach.

Still, I set my drink aside and unfolded the paperwork. I'd signed many contracts, so I was familiar with the look of them, even if the contents remained a mystery.

Functionally illiterate.

That was the term for someone like me. Not that anyone would ever guess.

Rubbing a finger over my lips, I pretended to peruse the pages, skimming over words and letters I couldn't decipher.

After a few moments, I tossed the mess on the table and let the games begin. "So?"

Mac chuckled and flopped back in his seat, shaking his head. "Look, I know you're pissed at me." With a sigh, he poured himself a drink. "But I'm really not to blame for any of this. Caged just got caught in the crossfire."

If I hadn't been a party to every sleazy legal maneuver he'd initiated over the past year, I might actually believe him. The conviction in his tone, the tilt of his head—all very convincing.

"Why should I listen to a word you say? Your legal team filed an injunction to keep my band from producing another album. And—"

"My beef is with Twin Souls," he interjected, impatient. "Tori

Grayson took my biggest clients. She may have had some luck as a manager, her and Taryn, but let's not forget she started her career with Metro. I made her band a household name."

Hearing Mac rewrite history reminded me of why I had a career to begin with. Nearly six years ago, Damaged was the only note-worthy client that Mac had. And when a bus crash took the lives of two of the founding members—Tori's husband, Rhenn, and Paige Dawson, her best friend—Mac didn't wait a hot minute to send every scout on his payroll to Austin to sign up their replacements. Caged was caught up in the wave, part of what the media now dubbed the Sixth Street Phenomenon.

I drained my glass. "Seems to me, without Tori you wouldn't have had any clients to begin with."

It was meant to be a parting shot. An inconvenient truth that Mac couldn't deny. And maybe a way for me to redeem myself for meeting with this asshole to begin with.

But Mac just shrugged. "Doesn't matter how I made it to the show. Point is, I'm here. You may not like me, Logan, but the deal I'm offering ..."

With the trip down memory lane, I'd almost forgotten about the papers in front of me. But it didn't matter. There was no way my bandmates were going to crawl back into bed with Mac. Hell, I needed a shower to wash off the stain from merely sitting across the table from him.

Shaking my head, I pushed my chair back. My ass wasn't two inches off the seat when Mac added, "You can't tell me the thought of a solo career never crossed your mind."

It took a minute for the words to register. *Solo career.* I sank back into my seat, stunned.

A slow smile crept over Mac's face. "You're a lot like me," he said, pouring us each another drink. "Friends are friends. But business is business. Do you think your new label's going to give you the oppor-tunity to strike out on your own?" He chuckled. "Of course not. Chase is going to look out for his brother. You may be the lead singer, but

Cameron writes all the songs. And he's almost as popular as you are." Mac sat back, lifting a finger off his glass and pointing it at me. "I'd say it's only a matter of time before Chase pushes you out."

Taking a long swallow of the smooth liquor, I shifted my focus elsewhere so Mac wouldn't know his words hit home. Signing on with the label my bandmate's brother formed was a no-brainer. Chase was a brilliant musician and he knew the business. Plus, he'd supported the band from the beginning. Hell, we still played a show a month at his club on Sixth. But now that Chase had hooked up with Taryn, maybe he had a different plan.

I scoffed inwardly at the thought. Chase was family. He'd never sell me out.

Returning my attention to Mac, I pinned on a self-assured smile. "Not going to happen."

He held his hands up in surrender. "Whatever you say. But it seems imprudent to put all your eggs in one basket." His gaze fell to the papers. "Look, I think you're the real draw in the band. And I'm willing to put my money where my mouth is. All of Metro's resources. You're going to get lots of visibility from the tour. I could have you in the studio the day after your last gig while your current label is still tied up in legal proceedings. Without a new album, Twin Souls is the only one who benefits from the tour, since they're doing this all them-selves." He tipped back his glass, then hissed air through his teeth. "And speaking of that ... how smoothly do you think this tour is going to go without a major concert promoter pulling the strings?" His brow lifted for the hundredth time. "Just sayin'. Something to think about."

After setting down his drink, Mac rubbed his hands together. "So what do you say? Shall we order dinner and discuss your options."

Options? Did I have options? Was *this* even an option?

Right on cue, the waitress appeared at our table. "Have y'all decided?" she asked, glancing at our unopened menus. "Or do you need a few more minutes?"

Mac tipped his chin at me. The choice was mine.

Hands curving around the arm of the chair, I willed my legs to work so I could get up and leave. But they didn't. Shrinking back against the leather, I took a deep breath.

"I'll take the rib eye," I told the server. "Make it bloody."

2

Tori

Flat on my back, I fidgeted with the string on my hospital gown as I stared at the ceiling in the radiology center. Despite my best effort, my legs shook, rattling the table.

Breathe.

My heart stalled when the lights flicked off, plunging the room into darkness.

The radiologist's voice crackled over the speaker. "We're about ready to begin. Are you comfortable?"

Comfortable?

I couldn't count the number of MRIs I'd had in the last five and a half years, but each one was worse than the last. And I was never comfortable.

"Fine," I choked out.

Shocked by the sudden jolt, my pulse rate kicked up as the table slid into the tube. Once inside the cylinder, I shrank from my distorted reflection on the metal ceiling. It looked like me—long, dark hair piled on my head, heart shape face, nose a little too narrow. But something was off. There was no life in my eyes. No spark in the amber hue. Before I fully adjusted, the machine whirred to life, the *clank clank clank* echoing in my head like cannon fire.

"Tori, try to keep still," came the voice again. "Just relax and don't fight the anxiety medication. We don't want to have to do this again."

If I closed my eyes it would be worse. But the sedative was already taking effect, and my lids were so heavy.

And then I smelled the rain. Felt it slick and warm on my skin. Or was that blood?

Gravel bit into my cheek, and somewhere in the distance, Rhenn called to me.

"Belle ..."

But I couldn't lift my head. I tried now, like I'd tried then. Nothing.

"Belle ..."

Drawn to the panic in his tone, I gave in and let myself slip beneath the veil of unconsciousness. And there, beyond the darkness, the worst night of my life waited to sweep me away.

"Shouldn't she be awake by now?" Taryn asked as I tried to pry my eyes open. "What did you give her, anyway?"

My best friend was a pit bull when she was angry. Or scared. Right now, she was both.

Because the doctor had prescribed a sedative to get me through the MRI, I'd asked Taryn to drive me to my appointment. But as I was coming out of my drug-induced haze, I knew that was a mistake. It was bad enough that I had to relive the trauma of that night. But I hadn't thought about Taryn.

Stupid.

Though my eyes weren't cooperating, I fought to push a few words out, but my mouth wasn't on board with the plan.

The nurse was in the middle of explaining when the door whooshed open.

Doctor Andrews's soothing voice floated to my ears. "Taryn ..." His tone was serene, and I imagined him rubbing her arm the way I'd seen him do so many times after the accident. "Tori's fine. I prescribed Halcyon, which is a relatively strong sedative, and—"

"Why?" Taryn's voice trembled despite the authoritative tone. "Why did you give her something that strong? She hasn't moved. It looks like she's in a ..."

She let out a staggered breath. But I knew the word on the tip of her tongue.

For two weeks after the bus crash that nearly ended my life, I'd lingered in a coma. And during that time, Taryn had never left my side. Hers was the first face I saw when I woke up. And she was the one who had to tell me that Rhenn was gone. And Paige.

A heavy weight descended, pushing in on me from all sides, and a little whimper scraped my throat. *That* was the drugs. Over the past five and a half years, I'd learned to control my emotions. My tears. The ache that had never truly gone away.

A hint of lavender and Taryn's warm hand on my cheek. "Tori?" When I didn't respond, she said firmly, "It's time to wake up now, Belle."

If she knew how much it hurt to hear her call me that name would she stop? I thought groggily. But I'd never asked.

With some effort, my lids fluttered open. "H-hey."

Taryn loomed over me, eyes wide and fearful. "There you are. It's about time you woke up." Over the forced humor, relief suffused her tone.

"How ..." I cleared my throat. "How long was I out?"

Doctor Andrews's smiling face appeared over Taryn's shoulder. "Not too long, champ. A couple of hours."

Hours.

Struggling to my elbows, my spinning head forced me back down to the pillow.

Taryn grimaced, and with a quick glance to the doctor she asked, "Is she okay?"

"I'm fine, T-Rex," I grumbled, and this time when I tried to sit up, it wasn't that bad. My throat was dry as hell, though. "Can you get me some water or something?"

Suspicion flashed across my best friend's face, like she knew I was trying to get rid of her.

"Um ... sure."

Reluctantly, she left the room, and once we were alone, I met Doctor Andrews' gaze. "So ... what's the verdict?"

His expression gave nothing away as he took a seat on the stool, but I saw it in his eyes, so I prepared for the worst.

"I've sent your films out for a second opinion," he finally said, grasping my hand when I exhaled a shaky breath. "But it's my recommendation that you never ..."

Once I heard the word "never," I tuned him out. Not on purpose. But the sound of a dream dying is louder than you might think. It starts with a crash that you feel to your bones, and then slowly takes over all time and space.

I watched his lips move, nodding like I understood. And when the roaring between my ears died down, I focused enough to catch the tail end of his explanation.

"So while it's technically possible for you to become pregnant," he said. "Carrying a child to term isn't advisable."

It was then that the girl I used to be decided to make an appearance. The one who still believed that anything was possible.

"But they make advances all the time," I said, my voice timid but hopeful. "I mean, I'm only twenty-nine. Maybe in the future there'll be some options."

Andrews shook his head, frowning. "The mesh we put in your abdomen during the initial surgery, it's become part of you. The tissue grew around it, so it can't be removed or modified. There just isn't enough give to withstand the pressure of carrying a child. Let alone labor and delivery. Then there's the matter of your hip. The pins holding it in place ..."

Enough.

Pressing my lips together, I nodded jerkily, and Andrews stopped explaining.

After a long moment, he said, "There are other ways to have a child, Tori."

I smiled. Fraudulent as hell. "I know. Thank you."

It was then I noticed Taryn just inside the door, holding the bottle of water in a death grip. Her eyes darted between the doctor and me, and I wondered how much she'd heard.

"Don't forget to keep up with your exercises," Doctor Andrews said as he hauled to his feet. When I looked down like a teenager who'd been caught sneaking in after curfew, he chuckled and pulled a prescription pad out of the pocket of his smock. "I'm ordering a couple sessions of physical therapy. Just so you can get into the routine of stretching."

Groaning, I flopped back against the pillow. "Ugh."

Unfazed by my melodramatic behavior, Andrews gave the prescription to Taryn, knowing that she'd stay on my ass and make sure it got done. Dropping my chart on the table on his way to the door, the doctor chirped, "See you in a few months, champ."

"Can't wait," I muttered as I sat up.

Taryn's fearful gaze latched onto mine as she shuffled over. "Is there anything wrong, Belle?"

She thought I was here for a routine exam, but given what she'd walked in on, I needed to reassure her. So I pushed my disappointment down deep. To the pit where there was no sun. And no air. And no hope.

I smiled. "Nope. I'm fine as frogs' hair. Just need to make sure I keep up with my stretching."

A pang of guilt shot through me for the lie. But then the tension lines around Taryn's mouth faded, the smile chasing the rainclouds from her eyes. And without a doubt, I knew it was worth it.

3

Logan

Cameron looked up from tuning his guitar when I strolled into the loft for rehearsal the next day. Narrowing his eyes, he tracked my movement, disdain curling his lip.

Fuck.

Cameron was as easygoing as they came. So I figured the sour look could only mean one thing: he'd found out about my meeting with Mac. And if Cam knew, everyone knew.

Squaring my shoulders, I dropped my backpack on the floor and sauntered to the mic.

Cameron followed, boots echoing off the high ceilings. "Seriously, bro? How could you do that?"

Jamming the cord for the amp into his Fender, he glared at me while feedback hissed from the speaker. The room fell silent as he turned the dial on his guitar, no one daring to make a sound.

Except for Sean.

Seated behind his drum kit, my best friend twirled his sticks, snickering.

I was about to ask what the hell was so funny when another muffled laugh floated my way.

Cutting my gaze to Christian, I found him adjusting the strap on his bass, trying desperately to bite down a grin.

"Dick move," he said to me, then quickly looked away, shoulders quaking and lips pressed together.

Confused, I turned back to Cameron, who was now beet red and glowering. "We all agreed," he growled, poking a finger at my chest. "No randoms in the dressing room."

"Random what?" I ventured carefully.

"Women!" Cameron roared. "How do you think Lily felt when she walked in and found some chick spread eagle on the couch wearing only one of your T-shirts?"

Behind us, Sean dissolved into a fit of laughter.

"It's not funny, asshat," Cameron shot back, glaring over his shoulder. "What if it was Anna?"

"If it was Anna," Sean managed between snorts, "she'd tell the girl to put her panties back on and quit hogging the couch."

Even I had to laugh at that one, but it was more from relief than anything else. Meeting with Mac was a stupid move. And one I planned on keeping to myself. Since our rendezvous, I'd done some asking around.

Turns out, a quarter of Metro's artists had jumped ship in favor of Twin Souls' new label. So it only made sense that Mac would be willing to cut a deal with someone he could use to fill the dead air.

Me.

I was the filler.

But the dude didn't count on my loyalty. Yeah, I was an ambitious fuck, but not completely without morals. And it was worth the price of admission to see the look on Mac's face when I'd told him to hang it out of his ass. After I'd sucked down all his fine whiskey, of course.

"I don't know which girl you're talking about," I said to Cameron, trying to keep a straight face. "Did Lily happen to take any pictures? I mean, I could probably identify her if I saw—"

"You're such a dog," Cameron replied, shaking his head. But he was smiling too. "Come on. Let's get this shit done."

Sliding his fingers across the fretboard, he launched into our first number. Sean and Christian joined in, and soon there were no more fucks to be given over my meeting with Mac. Time and space were reduced to the next note. The next lyric. The next beat.

Because in the end, it was all about the music.

4

Logan

With our last rehearsal out of the way, I decided to tie up a few loose ends before I got too busy packing and doing other shit in preparation for the tour.

The meeting was already underway when I slipped inside Classroom A at the Austin Recovery Center. Taking a seat in the back, I looked around for my sister.

Since completing her second stint in rehab a year ago, Laurel had faithfully worked her program. Meetings. A steady job. Family counseling. By all accounts, my sister was well on her way to controlling her addiction. Which eased a lot of my guilt. Not all of it. I couldn't buy back the years she'd spent in foster care. Or forget that it was my fault she ended up there in the first place.

When I didn't spot Laurel in the crowd, I made eye contact with her counselor, an aging hippy who looked to be about seventy, but in reality, was a good ten years younger. Breaking away from the skinny dude he was talking to at the refreshment table, Vaughn headed my way.

Noting the serious expression etching his weathered features, I pushed to my feet, a pit forming in my stomach. "Hey, Vaughn," I said in a shaky voice. "Is Laurel around?"

From my brief scan of the room, I knew she wasn't here, but still I waited for an answer. Any explanation that didn't include the word "relapse."

Vaughn cocked his head to the side, extending his hand. "Nice to see you, Logan."

Patience was never my strong suit, so ripping the answer from his throat crossed my mind. Instead, I slid my palm against his and held my tongue.

With the formalities out of the way, Vaughn rocked back on his heels. "Laurel isn't attending meetings here anymore. She didn't tell you?"

My natural inclination was to clam up. Handle this on my own. Laurel was my sister. My responsibility. But I'd failed miserably at this before.

When I found her in Nashville a year and a half ago, strung out and working the pole at a sleazy strip club, I sent her straight to the best rehab in the hill country. Luxury rooms. Private counseling. Massages and gourmet meals.

Mistakenly, I thought that would fix her. That if I showed enough support and gave her enough love, she'd walk the straight and narrow.

And then she'd relapsed.

Even though a second stint in rehab proved successful—and she was now eleven months clean—I lived with the knowledge that the peace my sister found might be temporary.

Shifting my feet, I looked down. "No, she didn't."

Vaughn squeezed my shoulder. "Let's step outside."

It was then I noticed a couple of people talking behind their hands and pointing.

"Yeah, okay."

We only made it as far as the front office.

"I don't think you should jump to conclusions, Logan," Vaughn said. "I've spoken to Laurel, and she told me she just needed to find a meeting place that was closer to home."

Which would make sense if I couldn't see the top of the building where she worked right outside the window.

"Do you know if she's found a place?"

Vaughn shrugged. "Meetings are anonymous. You know that."

Anonymous and completely at Laurel's discretion. He left that part out, but the subtext was there—I couldn't make her go.

Or so he thought.

I paid a good portion of my sister's bills. She lived in a nice loft, way out of the price range for a clerical worker. Her car, a late model Mercedes, was in my name. And I arranged to pay half of her grocery bill.

Yeah, Laurel needed to stand on her own two feet. But we grew up poor, without a mother, in a fucking trailer. And that's before she ended up in foster care. As long as my sister was doing her best, she'd never want for anything.

But what if she wasn't doing her best anymore?

"Thanks, Vaughn. I won't jump off the deep end."

He nodded, skeptical, but said nothing.

Affixing my sunglasses, I gave him a little smile and then strode out to my car. As soon as I was behind the wheel, I took out my phone and called my sister. And when she didn't answer, I pulled out of the parking space and headed straight for her loft.

"Answer the fucking door," I growled after ringing Laurel's doorbell for the second time. "I know you're in there."

My gut told me it was true. And if I had to knock the wood from its hinges to find out, I wouldn't hesitate.

My shoulders sank when the lock disengaged. Eyes wide with surprise, my sister peered out through a small gap in the door. "What are you doing here, Lo?"

Resisting the urge to push my way in, I locked our gazes. "Let me in. I'm not messing around."

As she contemplated, I searched her face. Aside from the tension lines bracketing her mouth and the pinched brow, she seemed fine. Except that she was hiding something. And that shit wouldn't fly.

When I moved to grab the door handle, Laurel jumped back. Stumbling over the threshold, I scanned the room. It took my brain a moment to register what I saw. Because it couldn't be true. But it was.

Jake Cage.

My father.

Even from the back, I recognized him. Pale blond hair, a shade lighter than mine. Broad shoulders. Imposing frame. Sitting in front of the big screen TV I'd purchased.

I didn't realize I was moving until Laurel stepped in front of me, small hand pressed against my chest. "Logan, you don't understand." Tearing my gaze from the back of Jake's head, I looked down into my sister's pleading eyes. "He's ... sick."

Truer words were never spoken. Jake Cage was the most twisted motherfucker I'd ever known. Sick didn't begin to describe the man. But then the haze lifted, and following my sister's line of sight, the air punched from my lungs when I spotted the wheelchair.

"What do you mean 'sick'?" I forced out, disgusted when my voice cracked.

Jake had no hold over me. I made sure he knew that the night I beat him to the ground in front of the trailer where we lived. Until then, I'd never fought back. Not in all the seventeen years of my life. But that day, when he'd signed over his parental rights and banished my sister to foster care, I won my freedom using my fists. And since violence was the only language my father spoke fluently, he'd let me go.

"He has early onset dementia," Laurel explained, gazing at the monster with soft eyes. "Most likely brought on by a traumatic brain injury from ..."

"All the people he tried to beat the shit out of who fought back?"

Any hope I harbored that I'd kept that last thought imprisoned behind clenched teeth faded when my sister flinched. "Yeah."

Ignoring her wistful tone, I shifted my focus back to our father. "How did he find you?"

That hint of a smile touched Laurel's lips once again. "He didn't. I found him. At the homeless shelter when I was dropping off canned goods from the food drive we had at work."

Of all the cards fate had ever dealt my sister, this was the cruelest. How many stars had to line up for Laurel to be in that exact place at that exact time? If I were Christian, I could probably form an equation to explain the odds. But I wasn't Christian. And my dad wasn't a mathematician. He was a bare knuckles brawler who made his living by driving men to the canvas with his fists. And once, I'd been his favorite punching bag.

Gut twisting from the memories, and drawn by some unseen force, I took a step. And then another. When I was parallel with Jake's chair, I fought the lump in my throat and replaced my spine with a steel rod.

"Hey, old man."

Until that moment, I wasn't sure if he was real. But then his gaze found mine. And something sparked in the pale blue orbs. I hated myself for leaning in just a fraction to hear what he was about to say.

"Jeremy."

My uncle's name fell from Jake's lips, hesitant. And it was like he'd punched me.

Laurel rushed forward. "No, Daddy." She gripped my arm, fingers digging in. "It's Logan."

Confusion clouded his features as he shifted his attention to my sister. "Beth?"

A tsunami of emotions battered me from the inside. Chaos and fury and a hatred so pure, I could barely speak. But I did.

"Don't you ever say my mother's name again," I spat, shaking off Laurel's hold. "Do you hear me?"

Jake blinked slowly. And for a second, I could swear he saw me. That he knew me. But then the light seeped from his watery gaze, and he turned back to the television. "I'm hungry."

My fury quickly gathered force, and I retreated a step, unsure if I could stop myself from wrapping my hands around his neck if I stayed that close.

Shooting me a cold stare, Laurel rushed to adjust the blanket on Jake's lap. "God, Logan."

But God had nothing to do with it. Because what kind of God would spare my father the torment of his memories? Of my mother's death? And my hatred? Finding no good answer for that, I stormed out, ignoring Laurel's pleas.

Propelled by a rage I hadn't felt in years, my fists clenched and unclenched as I rode the elevator to the ground floor. And as much as I despised the part of me that was exactly like my father, when I got into my car, I knew exactly where I'd end up.

Pulling the Rangers baseball cap low on my head, I kept my eyes downcast as I descended the stone stairs into the dank basement.

Straight into hell.

Smoke, sweat, and blood hung thick in the air, and I wrinkled my nose.

Spotting Dex's shock of black hair, I shouldered my way through the raucous crowd to where he stood at the side of the ring. Transfixed by the two men wailing on each other inside the ropes, he didn't notice me.

Dex had run the underground fight scene in Austin for as long as I could remember. Back to the days when my dad was a regular on the circuit. But Dex kept a low profile, and most people didn't know he was responsible for covering all the action.

I didn't care about the money, though. Not anymore. When Caged was still a struggling band, I'd pick up a fight now and then to make the rent. Or cover the cost of studio time. Or buy food.

Besides music, fighting was the only thing I was good at.

Dex finally turned his head, and looking up at me, his eyes widened. "Logan?"

It wasn't a question. He knew who I was.

I held out my fist for a bump, which he returned automatically. "Hey, man. Long time."

Brows drawn together, his gaze darted around the room. "Um ... yeah. What are you doin' here?"

Leaning a hip against the ring, I shrugged. "Thought you might be able to hook me up."

"With what?"

Were we really playing this game? Apparently so.

"A fight, dude. What else?"

Since I didn't look like some of the meatheads who frequented the circuit, I'd made Dex a lot of money from my fights. I was tall. But not overly muscled. Which drove down the odds. But I was also fast. And I liked the pain.

Dex contemplated for less than a minute before a laugh broke free. "Yeah, right," he scoffed and then took a drink of his beer. "What are you really doing here?"

Pulling some tape from my pocket to wrap my knuckles, I twirled the spool around my finger. "Send someone over with a shot. Bourbon, I don't care what kind. I'll be good to go whenever you are."

When I turned to find a dark corner to get ready, Dex's meaty paw curled around my bicep. "That ain't about to happen, Logan." I glanced down at his hand, and he pulled away, like he'd just touched a live wire. "Listen," he continued in a whisper. "I don't want no trouble. And I don't want any publicity. Whatever your game is, I can't help you. If I put you in that ring, it'll take about two minutes for someone to snap a picture or a video. And then where would I be?"

Following his gaze, I noticed a couple of people staring. Fuck. My days of being anonymous were long gone. Even in this shit hole.

Patting me on the back, Dex shook his head. "Just like your old man. Always looking for the rush."

His comment snapped me back to reality. Because even though it was true, I didn't want to hear it.

One of the guys in the ring hit the canvas with a heavy thud.

"Stay!" Dex shouted over the cheers that erupted. "Let me get you that drink."

Rooted to my spot, I watched blood drip from the loser's nose. Two of Dex's men hopped into the ring and pulled the dude to his feet.

This wasn't me. Not anymore.

"Some other time," I mumbled, pocketing the roll of tape. "See you around, Dex."

Without waiting for a response, I headed for the stairs. Busting out the door and into the dark parking lot, I took in a lungful of humid air to vanquish the acrid smell of blood.

Halfway to my car, I heard footsteps behind me. More than one set.

"Are you looking for a fight?"

Raising a hand, I waved them off without turning around. "No, I'm good."

And then I was on the ground with a knee in my back. "Well, I guess that's too bad," the stranger hissed in my ear. "Because I'm gonna whoop your ass, rock star."

Laughter. And three voices, maybe four, egging the dude on. But I'd learned long ago, the size of the audience didn't matter. Instinct took over and I grunted, flipping the clueless fuck onto his back.

Wide eyes blinked up at me, then shifted to my fist, cocked and ready to fly.

I eased up so he could wiggle free. Just enough to make it a fair fight.

And then I smiled. "Tell me, son. How bad do you want me to hurt you?"

5

Tori

Just before midnight, I parked at the edge of the sloping hill at the far corner of Oakwood Cemetery. Tomorrow there'd be a million people here. Singing. Crying. Celebrating.

But not tonight. Tonight was just for us. By design, I arrived before everyone else. Checking my reflection in the rearview mirror, I ran a hand through my long, dark locks. Normally, I wore my hair in a bun or a ponytail. But Rhenn liked it loose.

Before, I'd always worn it loose.

On nights like tonight, it was apparent my life was divided into before and after.

Before I was carefree. Fearless. Happy.

So fucking happy.

And after, I was none of those things. Troubles weighed me down. And my fears, too numerous to count. Living. Dying. Grief. And the void in my heart.

In almost six years, I'd never had one solid day of happiness. There were moments, even hours, of bliss. But always, the darkness came for me. And the worst part? Nobody knew it. Or they refused to see.

After the accident, my friends and family poured all the hopes and dreams they had for Rhenn and Paige into me. Like I was a vessel. When really, I was a sieve. *Broken.*

But still, time had passed. One year, then two. More. And every moment, I got closer to dead center, the day I'd wake up to the knowledge that I'd lived longer without Rhenn than with him.

He'd promised me forever. And I guess in some strange way he'd made good. I'd been his forever. And today, he would've turned thirty.

With a sigh, I stepped out into the Texas night, the pink box from Rhenn's favorite bakery clutched under my arm. A half-moon hung low in the starry sky, illuminating my path as I trudged up the grassy knoll. One hundred and thirty-seven steps. And then I was counting. At twenty paces my heart stalled as I took in the two granite headstones, one black and one white, gleaming in the sparse light. I sank onto the lush grass beneath the oak tree and set the box in front of me.

A wave of sadness rolled in like the tide as I ran my fingers over the inscription below Rhenn's name. A quote from *Beauty and the Beast*.

Take it with you so you'll always have a way to look back ... and remember me.

Wicking away the first tear, I whispered, "Happy birthday, baby."

A breeze picked up, and I smiled, my watery gaze shifting to the right where the other piece of my heart was buried. To Paige.

Taking the single rose from the pocket of my hoodie, I placed the flower on top of her headstone.

And then I sat quietly with my knees tucked to my chin, watching the wind rustle through the big tree.

A half hour passed before the first car door slammed. Another quickly followed. And then another. And soon, the warmth of my friends surrounded me.

Taryn knelt by my side and took my hand. "Hey, Belle. We're all here."

Smiling, I nodded, too choked up to speak.

If the paparazzi only knew that they could find the members of the three biggest bands in the country in the same place, at the same time, every single year, they'd have a field day.

Taryn took the cake from the box and then lit the single candle nestled in the center of the fluffy, white frosting. Then fourteen voices rose up, and we sang "Happy Birthday" so loud you could hear it all the way to heaven.

My phone alarm beeped promptly at eight a.m., and I rolled over with a groan.

We'd ended Rhenn's birthday celebration sometime after two. And when I got home, I came here. To his studio on the third floor of the house we'd built on Lake Travis. Even though construction was completed months before the accident, we'd never fully moved in. At the time, we were too busy. Touring. Recording. *Living.*

But this room, his room, we'd unpacked. And to this day, it remained exactly the same. Fifteen hundred square feet untouched by time.

Pushing off the couch, I looked around. Rhenn's guitar sat propped against the chair facing the window overlooking the shore, his favorite Dallas Cowboys T-shirt slung over the arm. On the table next to the notepad was a cup filled with pencils, erasers either chewed off or worn to the nub.

Shuffling to the console where Rhenn had spent hours mixing the band's last recording, I plopped down on the leather chair and picked up the page of sheet music with "Down To You" scribbled at the top.

It all came down to you ...

I'd read the single line a million times, wondering what it meant. Rhenn never left a song unfinished. Even if it took him all night.

A light knock at the door hurtled me into the present, and I dropped the paper back into its spot.

Schooling my features, I swiveled my chair to the door. "Come in."

Taryn peeked her head in, a strained smile tugging the corners of her lips. "Are you coming down?"

Are you coming in?

I didn't say that though. Because I knew she wouldn't. That she couldn't.

"Depends," I replied, hauling to my feet. "Did you make coffee?"

"Yep. And Dylan's cooking breakfast."

I faked a smile. It wasn't that I didn't want to see Dylan. But he was Rhenn's childhood best friend, and the two were so alike, it was almost eerie. Same gestures. Same slow, southern drawl. Same look in his eyes when he turned those baby blues my way.

I pushed that thought aside because I'd never go there. Not again. The one kiss we'd shared two years ago left me wrecked and Dylan ridden with guilt. And I had enough complications in my life without adding to them.

"Sounds good," I said. "I'll be there in a minute."

Grief marred Taryn's expression as she paused to glance over all of Rhenn's things. When our gazes collided, I saw the thought forming on her lips.

"Someday," I said in answer to her unspoken question.

Someday, I'd pack it all away. All the memories. The tokens of the life I once had.

But not today.

"Okay, Belle," she said softly. "I'll see you downstairs."

I waited until I heard her footsteps on the stairs, then made my way to the window. Gazing out at the grounds, Rhenn's voice rang in my head.

Look at that view. We're going to be so happy here.

And we were. For the twelve whole days we'd spent under this roof.

Fishing the key from my pocket, I headed to the door, and with one last look around, I stepped into the hallway, sealing my memories on the other side.

"Shouldn't you be packing?" I asked Dylan as I strolled into the kitchen. "You're running out of time, buddy. Four days and counting."

Frowning, he slid a plate of scrambled eggs in front of me as I eased onto the barstool. "It's not my first rodeo. I'll get it done."

Taryn and I exchanged a look, and she shrugged.

Picking up my fork, I pushed my food around my plate. "You know I appreciate this, Dylan," I said sincerely. "We couldn't pull this off without you."

In truth, I wasn't sure if we could pull it off at all. But we had to try. Metro Music had enjoined every group Twin Souls had signed to our new label in their bogus lawsuit. Originally, I thought the case would be dismissed in a month, but the proceedings had now dragged on for over a year.

I had no doubt that we'd prevail. But at what cost?

The smaller bands didn't have the reserves to withstand months and months of litigation. And soon they'd cut a deal with Mac and return to Metro. Which is why Twin Souls had organized the Sixth Street Survival Tour. To keep the money out of Mac's greedy hands and put it back where it belonged. With the artists.

But the whole plan was dependent on the biggest bands on our roster driving ticket sales. And Dylan's band was the biggest draw of them all.

"You don't have to sell me, Belle," he said wearily. "I know what's at stake."

As the words left his lips, his gaze flicked to Taryn, and she quickly picked up her coffee cup and turned toward the window.

Dropping my toast on the pile of eggs, I shifted my focus to my best friend. "Spit it out, Taryn. What aren't you telling me?"

She let out a little groan and gave Dylan the stink eye before meeting my gaze. "Skye Blue is out. Off the tour. I just found out this morning."

"What do you mean 'out'?" I snapped. "They can't be 'out.' They signed a contract."

Taryn scowled into her cup. "Apparently Mac offered Skylar a solo deal. And he's going to cover the legal costs if we decide to press the issue."

I let my head fall back. "Did we call our lawyers?"

"What's the point?" Dylan grumbled. "Metro's legal team will stonewall us for at least a few months. The tour will be over by the time a judge makes any ruling."

Suddenly it became clear why Mac had been spending so much time in Austin. I always knew he was a shark. But I'd never expected him to turn those teeth on me. My heart squeezed at the betrayal.

"Whatever," I said, tossing my napkin on what was left of my breakfast. "Nobody is paying to see Skye Blue. They want the headliners."

Taryn bit her bottom lip and looked out the window. "I'm not worried about Skye Blue. But how many other offers do you think Mac has thrown out there?"

Even with Leveraged, Revenged Theory, Drafthouse, and Caged sewn up tight, it would be difficult to pull off a festival of this magnitude if bands started defecting. And of course, Mac had waited until right before the tour kicked off to pull this shit. He didn't just want to win the lawsuit, he wanted to destroy me and everything I'd built since the accident.

My appetite gone, I took my plate to the sink. "We're golden," I said with as much conviction as I could muster. "Don't worry until there's something to worry about."

Taryn nodded, but it wasn't until her phone rang that she smiled for real. Only one person could make her grin like that. Chase.

"Hey, babe," she said, looking relaxed for the first time all morning. But as the seconds elapsed, her smile melted by degrees. "Oh, shit." Her gaze darted to mine. "Yeah, I understand. Let me talk to Tori first."

I set my fresh cup of coffee on the island to keep it from crashing to the ground when my hand began to shake. "Talk to me about what?"

Closing her eyes, she rubbed her temples. "It's Logan. We've got to go."

Dylan slid an arm around my shoulder. "Go where?"

Taryn hauled to her feet, lips pressed into a grim line. "To the courthouse. That idiot is in jail."

6

Logan

The shiny metal cuffs chaffed my wrists as the guard led me down the crowded hallway of the Travis County Courthouse. By the time I'd completed my walk of shame, I'm pretty sure at least three people had taken pictures. Or videos.

Not that I cared.

Despite my swollen knuckles and the blood staining my skin—the other guy's, not mine—I was innocent. The fact that I didn't have a scratch on me probably wouldn't go a long way toward helping my cause. And then there was the matter of my two prior convictions for drunk and disorderly and fighting from my dive bar days.

Yeah, I was fucked.

I didn't realize how fucked until I entered the small, windowless room marked Client Conference and found Trevor and not Chase.

The guard closed the door, taking any hope that he'd remove my cuffs with him.

"I was worried for a minute," I said to Trevor dryly as I dropped into the cracked vinyl chair across the table from him. "But I guess if I was in serious trouble, Chase would've called a real attorney."

Trevor's expensive suit and business haircut did little to tarnish the memories of him from the old days, drunk off his ass and passed out on the floor of whatever bar Caged happened to be playing at.

His bitter smile didn't reach his eyes. "And I'm guessing a real attorney might've let you cool your heels in the holding cell until your arraignment."

Arraignment. That got my attention.

"It was self-defense," I replied, my voice a little shaky. "The fuckers jumped me."

Clasping his hands on the marred table, Trevor scrutinized me with a narrowed gaze. "Before or after you left the fight club?" When I couldn't muster a response, he shook his head. "This is some serious shit, bro."

Pain shot from my knuckles when I flexed my fingers, and I dropped my gaze to the caked on blood in the cracks. "How serious?"

He shrugged. "I guess we'll find out. Chase is meeting with some friend of his. An assistant DA."

My mind jumped to the one thing I hadn't considered. "I have to get out of here. I leave for the tour in less than a week."

Trevor tossed his pen on the table. "Unless Chase can pull off a miracle, you're not going anywhere. Not without an ankle bracelet, at least."

Is that what was on the table? House arrest?

My head fell forward and, catching sight of my reflection in the steel cuffs, my father's words from long ago echoed from somewhere deep inside.

You ain't nothin' and you'll never be nothin'.

And for the first time, I let myself believe he might've been right.

A couple of hours later, the guard finally led me into the court-room. Bright sunlight poured through the windows, and I blinked, my lids like sandpaper over my bloodshot eyes.

The room was empty, my footsteps echoing off the ceiling as I shuffled to the defendant's table where Trevor sorted through a stack of paperwork.

"Where is everyone?" I asked as I took my seat.

Panic churned, crawling from my twisted gut, but I pushed it down. I didn't need anyone to hold my hand. Still, I wondered why none of my bandmates were here.

Trevor shoved a stack of documents in front of me. "I just talked to Chase about five minutes ago. They're posting your bond."

Thank fuck.

Hiding my relief, I pretended to scan the document while Trevor ran a distracted hand through his hair. "It's all in there. If you have any questions ..." His phone vibrated. "I've got to take this." Swiping a finger over the screen, he pushed to his feet. "Just read it," he mouthed, tipping his chin at the papers in my hand.

"Easy for you to say," I muttered to his retreating back as he walked away.

Refocusing on the documents, the letters formed their usual jumble. A thin sheen of sweat popped out on my brow as I tried to concentrate.

"Lo?"

Melting at the familiar voice, and the comforting hand on my shoulder, I blinked up at Anna.

"Hey," I said, and there it was again, that tremble in my tone. Hoping she didn't notice, I glanced around. "Where's Sean?"

"He's with Chase and Taryn." Her gaze darted to Trevor, holed up across the room with the phone cemented to his ear. "I thought maybe you might need me to, um … help."

A refusal coiled around my tongue, false pride stiffening my spine. But this was Anna. My best friend's girl had figured out my problem way back in high school. There was no use lying.

I swallowed hard. "Yeah."

One word—tinged with defeat. Shame. Soul-deep humiliation.

Smiling, Anna set down her bag, taking a seat in Trevor's chair. Rather than read me the document, she looked into my eyes. "Chase pulled some strings and got his friend to agree to a deal."

"What kind of deal?"

"Well, you still have to go to court. You wailed on that guy pretty good." She shifted her gaze to my mangled hand, and I got the urge to hide the evidence.

"It was self-defense," I blurted.

As if to argue the point, a memory of the guy's bloody face floated through my mind.

"Is that all you got, rock star?" he'd sneered.

And like a dumbass, I'd taken the bait, delivering a knockout punch straight to his jaw.

"Yeah, I know," Anna said. "I mean … I saw the tape. Those guys followed you out of the club."

My stomach dropped to my shoes. "There's a tape?"

She nodded. "Chase figured there had to be security cameras, so he paid the owner of the building a visit."

"Dex?"

"No. Dex just rents the place. The owner is a suit. He was reluctant to help at first. But Chase persuaded him to turn over the footage."

My shoulders slumped, and I closed my eyes. Chase was a land developer, and a well-respected business man. But he wasn't above using his muscle to protect those he loved. And that included me. But

39

I could fight my own battles. This was about Taryn—his girl—and what she stood to lose if there was a scandal.

Silence hung between us for a few beats, because Anna knew it too, how entwined our lives had become with Twin Souls.

"So you saw the tape." I crossed my arms over my chest. "The dude came after me first. Why am I here?"

"Diminished capacity," Anna replied softly.

I was vaguely familiar with the term. Anna was a law student, and she spouted more legalese than the average person by double. I guess I'd picked up on a little of it.

"I wasn't drunk." A rueful smile curved my lips. "My capacity was undiminished."

"Not you, Lo. *Him.* He was drunk or ... high ... or something. And the DA said you should've ..."

"Walked away?"

Anna dropped her gaze to her hands, nodding. She always looked for the best in people. Which sometimes led to disappointment where I was concerned.

A sigh parted my lips. "Well, we both know I didn't do that. So what does that mean?"

Straightening her spine, she looked me in the eyes. "It means that you're going to need to take anger management classes. And if you want to do the tour, you need to have someone with you."

I barked out a laugh. "Half the Twin Souls roster is on the bill. Plus, you're going to be there and the rest of the guys. It's not like I'm going to be alone."

"That's not enough. It has to be someone with a fiduciary," she paused, then amended, "a vested interest. Someone with money on the line. For your bond."

"I'll pay my own bond."

My tone had a hard edge that I didn't mean to direct at her.

Unfazed, she placed a hand on my arm. "You can't. And before you even ask, it can't be a member of the band. Or Chase. The DA said it was a conflict of interest."

Reality punched me hard in the chest, stealing my breath. She'd just named every person in the world with the means and the desire to help me.

The door creaked open, and Anna hauled to her feet. "Be nice," she warned.

Nodding weakly, I waited for Sean to yank me out of my chair. Or maybe Cameron or Christian would take the first shot. But it was Tori who slid into the seat beside me.

Fucking perfect.

Easing back in my chair, I crossed my legs at the ankles. "Come to watch the show, princess?"

"Get over yourself, Cage."

She snatched the plea agreement from the table, and I caught her wrist.

"Hey! That's none of your business."

Her amber eyes heated as she twisted out of my hold. "Really? I think it is."

Digging a slip of paper from her back pocket, she tossed it onto my lap. A receipt. With a hell of a lot of zeros.

Lifting it carefully, as if it were a bomb that could blow off a finger, I met her gaze. "What is this?"

But I knew. Even before Trevor ended his call and rushed over to keep the peace, I knew. Tori paid the bond. She was the person with the vested interest.

I locked eyes with my attorney. "Please tell me you didn't agree to this."

Trevor rubbed the back of his neck, looking more than fed up. "I can't agree to anything. It's up to you. But if you want to do the tour, this is your only option."

Tori didn't betray any emotion beyond irritation. But that was nothing new. The girl couldn't stand me. And the feeling was mutual. Sort of. When I wasn't thinking about wringing her neck, I did have the occasional fantasy about what she might look like naked.

"Will you sign the paperwork, already?" she snapped. "I've got things to do."

Whatever momentary bout of insanity had me considering the offer faded.

Wadding up the receipt, I lobbed it back at her. "You go ahead and do what you gotta do. Because I'm not signing shit."

7

Tori

Logan's bail receipt landed on the floor a couple of feet from the table.

"You can't do that." Panicked, I turned to Trevor. "Tell him he can't do that."

Shaking his head, the attorney threw his hands up. "You tell him. I'm done. Y'all need to work this out for yourselves." Briefcase in hand, he headed for the door. "I'll be in the hallway when you decide what you want to do."

Once we were alone, Logan laced his fingers behind his head and looked at me out of the corner of his eyes. "You really know how to clear a room, Grayson."

I discreetly dug my nails into my palms to keep from scratching his eyes out. But of course, he noticed. Logan was observant that way. At least when it came to me. He loved getting under my skin, like it was some kind of game. But today, I didn't have time to play. In the last hour, two more groups had dropped out of the tour. Taryn was on the phone with our West Coast attorney while Dylan was frantically making calls to the other down ticket bands, offering who knows what. That left me with one job: keeping Caged on the bill. And in order to do that, I needed their lead singer out of jail.

43

"Just sign the papers," I said, my tone even. "It's a good deal."

Quirking a brow, Logan tipped his chair back on two legs. "And why would I do that? I'm innocent. Or haven't you heard?"

"It doesn't matter if you're innocent. The only way you're getting out of here today is if you take the deal." I glanced over his dirty jeans and stringy hair. "Or would you rather stay in jail?"

A dry chuckle rumbled low in his chest. "You're going to have to do better than that, princess. They can't hold me longer than three days. And even if they charge me, which they *won't*, I can post my own bond and take my chances in front of the judge." All the humor faded from his features and the chair hit the floor with a loud thud. "So I don't need you."

He was right. I'd seen the tape. Even with the vicious beat down Logan had issued, he clearly didn't start the fight.

Tongue tied, I contemplated the demise of my business while Logan waited patiently for my next move.

Only I didn't have one.

Pushing out of my chair, I willed away the nausea churning in my belly. "Fine ... whatever," I snapped as I scooted around him. "It's your mess. You clean it up."

As I bent down to snatch the bail slip from the floor, a searing pain travelled from my hip to my pelvis. "Shit," I breathed, stumbling backward.

The ground came up fast, and I braced for impact. But Logan was out of his seat, hands molded to my waist, before I hit the floor. "I got you."

His heart beat soundly against my back, steady and reassuring. Which only added to my humiliation.

"I'm fine," I wheezed.

He didn't call me on the lie, but when I tried to move, his grip turned to iron. "Just stay still for a minute, will you?"

A mild protest crawled up my throat, but it took too much effort to force it out, so I just nodded. Heat rose in my cheeks when I realized my fingers were locked on top of his in a death grip.

"I'm okay now." Slanting my gaze to his, I blinked up at him. "You can let go."

Let go. Please let go.

Logan was one of the few people who didn't look at me like I was made of glass. And I'd do anything to keep it that way.

Unfurling his fingers from my waist, he took a step back. "What was that?"

Me.

Or what was left of me after the multiple surgeries and months of rehab. Rather than bore him with the details, I shrugged. "Just a head rush. I didn't finish my breakfast. One of my clients got thrown in jail."

He frowned, and for a moment I felt bad. But then I thought of my tour and I couldn't find the will to care.

"See you, Logan."

He caught my arm. "Wait."

Surprised, I looked down at his hand, then up to his face. For a moment we just stared at each other. His eyes, the palest blue, were so clear, a glacier reflecting the sky. Add to it the high cheekbones, full lips, and golden blond hair that fell just past his shoulders, and he was the full package. The quintessential rock star.

He finally blinked, then dropped his arm, and strode back to the table where he scribbled his signature on the plea agreement.

Relief flooded me, but quickly evaporated when he turned my way. "I don't need a babysitter, Grayson." Irritation threaded his tone. "Stay out of my way, and let me do my job. Are we clear?"

I wanted to tell him to shove it. To let him know he wasn't in a position to dictate terms. But I couldn't.

As much as it pained me to admit it, I needed Logan. So much that I was willing to do the one thing I swore I'd never do again: step foot on a tour bus.

Setting my jaw, I reached for the lifeline he offered.

"Are we clear?" he repeated, holding the papers aloft.

The asshole actually wanted me to say the words.

"Crystal," I bit out.

He thrust the documents into my waiting hand as he brushed past me. "See you in a few days, princess."

Dropping onto the closest bench, I wilted against the wood.

What did I just do?

8

Logan

I spent the next two days lying low at Sean's house out at the lake. And when I couldn't avoid it any longer, I drove into town to see my sister.

Laurel threw open the door, and despite how we left things when I'd seen her last, she flung herself into my arms. "Logan ... I saw the news. What happened?" She tipped her head back to look up at me. "And why haven't you returned my calls? I was so worried."

As much as I wanted to be angry at my sister, I couldn't do it. Especially knowing Jake was here. The man wasn't a physical threat any longer. Emotionally, I wasn't sure.

Searching Laurel's face out of habit for any signs of ... *whatever*, I tucked a curl behind her ear. "I'm fine. I've been at Sean's."

"I know. I talked to Anna." She looped her arm through mine. "Come in."

Silence swelled between us like an overfilled balloon as I held my ground on my side of the imaginary line. *He* was in there, tainting the air with every breath he took. But then, so was Laurel. For that reason, I crossed the threshold.

Lingering just inside the door, I shifted my feet. "Listen, I'm leaving tomorrow and I wanted—"

47

"Laurel!" My father's gravelly voice floated in from the living room, and it was like he reached inside and pulled me into the past. Right back to that trailer with the holes in the walls and the dirty dishes in the sink.

Every instinct told me to run. But I was frozen, my limbs like stone.

Laurel cast a nervous glance over her shoulder. "I'm sorry ... Let me see what he needs."

What he needed was to be gone. Out of this loft. And out of our lives. But my sister didn't seem to share my views on the matter, and she took off like a shot.

Get your shit together, you little pussy.

It may have been my thought, but it was Jake's voice in my head. And that was enough to peel my boots from the floor and follow my sister.

Jake inhabited the same spot in front of the TV as the last time. Deep crevices lined his face, and his mouth was slightly agape as he gazed up at Laurel with watery blue eyes.

Smiling, she rubbed his shoulder. "*The Price Is Right* isn't on right now, Daddy. How about some music?"

Affection glowed on her face. It was too much for me to take, so I wandered over to the window. My stomach bottomed out when Garth Brooks blasted from the sound system.

Laurel wandered over, brushing her hands on her jeans. "That should keep him busy for a while." Her smile dimmed when I turned around. "What's wrong?"

My traitorous gaze shifted to the old man. "This ..." I cleared my throat when my voice cracked. "This was Mama's favorite song."

Her lips fell into a frown. "I didn't know that. Sorry."

"Stop apologizing!"

Laurel's eyes darted to my fists, clenched at my sides. And in that moment, I knew what she saw. *Him.* Not the old man in the chair. The younger, lethal version.

Yanking the brochure from my pocket, I held it out for her to take. "This is a home. A facility. They specialize in Alzheimer's and brain disorders." Retreating a step, Laurel folded her arms over her stomach like I was holding a venomous snake. Prophetic. I shook the pamphlet. "I'll pay for it. And whatever else he needs. Just get him out of here."

Her face contorted in pain. "He needs *me,* Lo," she said softly.

"Maybe he should've thought about that before he signed you up for foster care."

Laurel wicked away the moisture on her cheeks, determination stiffening her spine. "That was a long time ago. I've forgiven him."

Didn't she understand? Forgiveness wasn't ours to give. Only one person could absolve Jake Cage. Our mother. And she wasn't talking.

My arm fell to my side. "Well, I haven't."

She lifted her chin, tears shimmering in her eyes. "I know."

My attention drifted to my father, staring at the black screen on the television, his fingers moving in time with the song. *Her song.* The one my mother used to sing to me every night before bed, about love that went on and on, even if tomorrow never came. It was like she'd known that someday I'd need those words.

I blocked out the haunting melody. "I'll see you in three months."

Laurel nodded, resigned, and for a second, she looked so much like our mother, I couldn't stand it.

Dropping the brochure on the table, I headed for the door before the past swallowed me whole.

9

Tori

Reporters descended on my car the minute I turned into my parents' driveway. Cameras trained on my face, they lobbed questions as I waited for the garage door to open.

"Tori, are you going to release a new album?"

"What about a Damaged reunion?"

"Care to comment on Logan Cage's arrest?"

The front door slammed with a loud bang.

"Y'all get out of here before I get my gun!" my daddy bellowed from the porch. A couple of the local reporters scattered, and I bit down a smile. If Daddy still had a gun, it was collecting dust somewhere. To my knowledge, he hadn't picked up a firearm since he retired from the Austin PD five years ago.

His distraction was enough to allow me time to slip into the garage. But that still didn't give me the courage to get out of the car. I'd put off giving my parents any details about the tour. They knew I was leaving in the morning, but I'd made it sound like I'd only be gone for a few days. But then the news went wide this morning on *Good Morning Austin*. And now the mainstream media was speculating about my reasons.

Grabbing my phone, I grimaced at the preview of the latest Google alert.

Ticket sales soar for Sixth Street Survival tour amid rumors that Belle Grayson will perform.

Blowing out a breath, I headed inside to face the firing squad. The scent of freshly baked cookies hit me the moment I stepped into the mudroom. Mama cooked when she was angry. And from the state of the kitchen, she was pissed.

Her dark amber gaze found mine, and then she returned to bludgeoning the half-mixed cookie dough with her wooden spoon. "It's about time you showed up, Victoria."

I don't know what bothered me more, her bluntness or the use of my given name.

Sliding a hip onto the barstool in front of the island, I clasped my hands in front of me. "Sorry. I meant to come by sooner. But then I got busy and ..." My mom had no patience for excuses, so I let the thought wither on my tongue. "Anyway, I'm here now."

Dumping a handful of chocolate chips into the bowl, she used the same fervor to fold the morsels into the mix. "Victoria ..." Shaking her head, she sighed. "I've got enough to worry about at the moment without you gallivanting around the country."

I stopped fidgeting. "Like what?" She ducked into the fridge without answering. "Mama?"

My butt rose from the stool, but a warm hand slipped around my shoulder. Slanting my gaze to my dad, the worry lining his brow did nothing for the pit in my stomach.

"Come on," he said quietly, inclining his head toward the door. "We'll talk in the living room."

I rose on wobbly legs, my eyes darting to my mom. She didn't look up, just continued to add nuts to the dough like it was her sole purpose in life.

"What is it?" I asked as I followed Daddy out of the room.

He stopped in front of the wall of framed photos in the hallway. Every child who'd ever come to this house—for a night, or a month, or longer—had a spot of honor. A home. Some of the kids I remembered, but most I didn't. The foster care system was far from ideal. And I wondered why my parents even bothered, considering the pain it had caused throughout the years.

Daddy straightened the frame encasing my sister's latest school picture. "We got a call yesterday about Courtney."

The name scratched the inside of my brain, and I crossed my arms over my stomach, fingers digging into my sides. "Who's Courtney?"

He took in a slow breath. "Zoe's mother."

"Zoe's *mother*?" I croaked. "Mama is Zoe's mother."

They didn't share DNA. But since the day my parents brought Zoe to this house, malnourished and frail, her eyes too wide and knowing to belong to any three-year-old, she'd been that to my mama—a daughter.

I was seventeen at the time, involved in my own thing. Music. Rhenn. The band. And I didn't want to get attached. I'd been down that road before. Sometimes it turned out well, but more often than not, when the kids found their forever homes, a piece of me went with them.

"It's been eleven years," I said when I found my voice. "What did she want?"

Daddy backed up and leaned against the wall, his eyes still on the photo. "It wasn't her. It was the case worker. Courtney's still in prison."

"Then why—?"

"Courtney wants to see her."

My jaw hit the floor along with my stomach. "Wait ... what? Courtney wants Zoe to visit her ... *in jail*?"

Another labored breath. "She's getting out soon, and the court wants to explore the possibility of a reconnection. We're going to fight it, but Zoe might need to speak to the judge and—"

A small sob floated down from the second floor—from Zoe's room—and Daddy looked up at the ceiling, anguish painting his features.

He called after me, but I was already halfway up the stairs.

Skidding to a stop at my sister's door, I looked around in shock. Clothes spilled from the dresser. The medals and trophies she'd won from her dance recitals littered the floor. It was like someone had turned the room upside down and given it a good shake.

"Zoe?" I stepped around the mess, knowing where I'd find her. "Zo ...?" I pulled open the closet door, and there she was in the corner, arms wrapped around her knees.

Blinking up at me with tears staining her cheeks, Zoe's face contorted. "Don't let them take me."

When I dropped onto the floor beside her, she practically climbed into my lap. Holding back my own tears, I kissed the top of her head. "Never."

"They're not going to take your sister," Trevor assured me as I paced in front of his desk. Leaning back in his seat, he steepled his fingers under his chin. "Chase was right about you. You're a little—" Stopping in my tracks, I glared at him. "Intense. Now have a seat and listen to me, will you?"

After giving him the once over, I reluctantly eased into the chair. "You don't know me well enough to order me around."

Until recently, Hollis and Briggs had handled all of my legal work. But I cut ties with the firm when I went into business with Chase. Trevor was his guy. But the kid looked a little wet behind the ears to me.

"How old are you, anyway?" I asked.

Trevor quirked a brow, a sexy smile curving his lips. "Twenty-eight. You?"

Jesus. Did he think I was flirting with him? Probably. The guy was devastatingly handsome in a GQ kind of way. Chestnut hair, a little longer on the top, fell over his brow, giving him a reason to rake the strands out of his eyes. Which were his best feature, really. The rich chocolate pools twinkled when he smiled, like he had a secret.

But not any secret I wanted to learn.

"Never mind," I said, digging my nails into the arm rest. "Tell me about Zoe. You really don't think there's anything to worry about?"

He pondered for an agonizingly long moment. "Depends on what you mean by worry. Do I think your parents will lose custody? No. Zoe is fourteen, and she has a say in where she wants to live. But, likely, she'll have to go through some kind of hearing if her mother pushes the issue."

"Courtney is not her mother," I growled. "She gave birth to her. That's it."

Trevor sighed, nodding. "I understand. But the court never severed Courtney's parental rights." He skimmed the file in front of him. "She's filed numerous petitions in the last nine years—"

"Nine years?" I tipped forward to glimpse the paperwork. "But Zoe's been with my parents for almost eleven years."

He shrugged. "Maybe the woman found religion or something."

But somehow, I knew that wasn't it. The timing was too much of a coincidence. Nine years ago my first album hit the charts, and my parents were swept into the Damaged media frenzy right along with everyone else. Including Zoe.

I swallowed over the lump in my throat. "You're sure that nothing is going to happen while I'm gone?"

Trevor took a sip of his bottled water. "Relatively sure. And I can always request a continuance. Legal aid is handling this matter, and they're always backed up."

Shoving to my feet, I slung my backpack over my shoulder. "My parents have your number in case something comes up. Whatever they need, whenever they need it, make sure you handle it."

"Sure thing." He snapped his finger as I turned to leave. "Wait, I wanted to give you this."

I took the file he offered. "What is it?"

"A loophole." While I thumbed through the papers, he continued, "Half of the anger management classes that Logan has to take can be completed online. Once he finishes those and takes the test, I'll petition the court to modify the terms of his agreement."

"What's that have to do with me?"

"If the judge agrees, she'll release you from the bond, and you can quit the tour."

My stomach uncoiled for the first time in three days. Hell, longer. "I'll make sure Logan gets it done, then."

Trevor arched a skeptical brow, but it didn't dampen my enthusiasm. Things were looking up. Finally.

10

Logan

Fun fact: every tour bus in the world smells exactly the same. A heady combination of diesel fuel, sweaty socks, pine air freshener, and something else that I could never put my finger on.

Nobody mentions it, though. Because it's too damn depressing to actually acknowledge that you're stuck inside a rolling toilet.

And the kicker? As fuck awful as it smells on the first day ... it only gets worse as the tour progresses. In another three weeks, after a thousand beers have soaked into the carpet, and a parade of fangirls have branded the sofa with cheap perfume, you long for the days when there was only one unrecognizable scent.

With that in mind, I slung my guitar over my back, took my last breath of unspoiled air, and climbed on board the silver beast. And holy fuck was I wrong. Stone floors. Granite countertops. And a kitchen that actually looked like you could cook a meal.

I was still taking in the wonder of my surroundings when a deep voice pulled me out of my revelry.

"Are you Cage?"

Turning with a start, I came face-to-face with a wall of muscle taking up half the aisle. My gaze flicked to the map in his large hand. With his short hair, neatly trimmed mustache, and starched white shirt, the dude didn't look like any driver we'd ever had. To top it off, I had to lift my gaze just a touch to meet his eyes. Unusual, since I was six four and the tallest guy in the room on any given day.

I offered my hand for a shake. "Logan."

Sliding his palm against mine, he squeezed, hard, his lips quirking into a half-smile when I returned the favor. "Paul."

Retracting my hand before I lost the use of my fingers, I fished my keys from my pocket. "Nice to meet you, Paul. The rest of the guys will be here in a bit." I tipped my chin to the window. "My bags are in the Mustang. Careful not to scratch the paint. I'm going to grab some shuteye."

Rocking back on his heels, a hint of amusement danced in Paul's eyes. "You do that, son."

Son?

Before I could reply, a familiar voice drifted from somewhere in the back. Tori. My body responded with the usual awareness. A residual effect from the days before we'd actually met.

"Shit," I muttered, dropping into one of the captain's chairs. "How long has the ice princess been here?"

Paul's brows drew together. "Ice princess?"

"Tori." I scrubbed a hand over my face. "Has she been here long?"

Paul glowered at me, but the sound of laughter caught his attention before he could speak.

Tori glided into the room, arm-in-arm with a little blonde. A teenager. The smile froze on her lips when she noticed me. And it was then I realized, I'd never seen her true smile before. The one that reached all the way to her eyes.

"Logan ... what are you doing here so early?"

I shoved my hands into my pockets. "Just figured I'd get settled before everyone else arrives."

A beat of silence passed, and then she shook her head and turned that pretty smile on the girl at her side. "Oh ... sorry ... this is my sister, Zoe." My stomach hit the floor when Tori flicked her gaze to the man who looked ready to introduce me to the pavement. "And I see you've already met my father."

Arms crossed over my chest, I leaned against my car, watching Paul stalk around inside the bus. Every few minutes, he'd stop in front of the couch where Tori sat, make a few animated gestures, and then resume his pacing.

Cutting my gaze to Tori's sister, kicking stones around the deserted parking lot, I chuckled. "I see insanity runs in your family."

My joke hit the pavement with a splat, and her lips parted, but then she dropped her gaze.

Well, shit. Somehow, I'd managed to alienate yet another member of Tori's family without even trying.

"I was kidding," I said, ducking my head to find her eyes. "I don't really think your sister's crazy."

Much.

Zoe gave a little shrug, then inched closer, running a hand over the quarter panel on the Mustang. "Solid car. It's a '69 Boss, right?"

More than a little impressed, I nodded. "Good eye."

She peeked in the window. "I like the '68 Shelby KR better, but this is nice too."

In most cases, I'd defend my baby to my last breath, but the kid had me dead to rights. The '68 Shelby KR was the shit. "Yeah, I wouldn't mind owning one of those myself someday."

She gave me the side eye, a sly smile lifting her lips. "Well, if you quit calling my sister names, maybe she'll let you drive hers."

I nearly choked on my tongue. Because, surely, I didn't hear the kid right. Somehow, I couldn't picture the princess tooling around the hill country in a muscle car built twenty years before she was born.

The look on my face must've said it all because Zoe pursed her lips. "What?" she growled. "You don't believe me?"

"Oh, I believe you. Lots of people collect classic cars." I rapped my knuckles against the metal frame. "I prefer to drive mine, though."

Zoe's indignation faded to a frown. "She used to drive it everywhere. Before ..."

It only took a couple of seconds for me to catch on. Two very long seconds where images of mangled wreckage, wisps of gray smoke, and a charred field in the middle of nowhere flashed in my head.

Before I could find my voice to offer an apology, the door on the bus slid open with a hiss. Paul lumbered down the steps, his gaze fixed on Zoe.

"I guess I'll see you later," she said. Not likely, but I smiled anyway. She took a step back, but then paused. "Take care of my sister, okay?"

The laugh caught in my throat when her blue-gray eyes locked onto mine. She was serious. I didn't have the heart to tell her I was the last person anyone would trust with that particular duty.

"I'll do my best."

My statement held just enough conviction for Zoe to offer her hand for a shake. Biting down a smile, I obliged. The kid was a little unnerving. All teenager, but there was something in her eyes. Wisdom, maybe.

Zoe held on for a long time, only letting go when Paul called her name. "See you, Logan."

I watched her retreating back for a second before sliding behind the wheel of my car. Paul had a good twenty-five years on me, but something told me the age difference wouldn't stop him from taking me to the ground if he had the chance. Better to remove the temptation.

When I heard his truck rumble to life, I chanced a peek, and found Zoe waving like we were old friends.

I waved back.

Once they were gone, I twisted around and did a quick sweep of the car, checking the floorboards and the backseat for anything I might've missed. After patting the dashboard one final time, I pushed the door open. Sunlight poured in, dancing off the surface of my lucky penny, suspended from a piece of twine on the rearview mirror. Out of habit, I rubbed the coin between my thumb and forefinger.

Years ago, I wore it around my neck. Until the night my dad ripped it off when he was trying to keep me from choking the life out of him outside the trailer. I didn't realize it was gone until I got to Sean's house. At the time, I thought the coin was the price I had to pay for my freedom. One penny, some cracked ribs, and a few dozen bruises. And strangely, I was okay with that.

But then a couple of days later when I snuck back to get my things, I found the penny in the gravel by the steps to the trailer. And though I should've been happy, all I could hear was my old man's voice.

"Your life ain't worth a red cent, boy. Don't you ever forget it."

Brought back to the present when someone touched my shoulder, I met Anna's wide eyes.

"What did you do?" she asked. My back stiffened in defense, a knee-jerk reaction. But then her fingers shot to my hair, sifting through the strands. "You cut your hair?"

I chuckled. "Oh ... yeah."

Sean and Cameron wandered up, bags in hand, wearing identical looks of surprise. Or horror. Probably horror.

"Dude," Sean said, wrinkling his nose. "Why would you do that?"

A smile wobbled on Cameron's lips. "You look kind of like my accountant." He cocked his head. "Do you do taxes?"

And just like that, the dark cloud lifted. Plucking the lucky penny from the mirror, I slipped the twine over my head and discreetly tucked the coin under my T-shirt. "Very funny," I said, unfolding myself from the seat. "Let's get this show on the road. We're burning daylight."

Two hours after everyone arrived, and we still hadn't moved. The delay only served as a stark reminder that nothing was in the band's control. This was Tori's show. And that was my fault, since I'd given her the power by signing the plea agreement.

But did she really think she could jerk us around like this?

The curtain on my bunk rustled, and Sean's five-year-old daughter peeked her head inside. Like always, it only took one look at Willow's little face, and the tension ebbed from my body.

"Come watch me pway, Unc Lo."

She tugged at her hearing aid, a habit she'd picked up recently. I wondered if she'd only just realized that they were there. Willow was born almost completely deaf, but for the last few months, her parents had been taking her for tests in preparation for the surgery that would restore her hearing.

"Sure, baby."

I let Willow lead me to the sofa in the common area where everyone was sprawled out on the two couches facing the big screen TV. Everyone but Tori. Curled up in a captain's chair with her legs tucked beneath her, she stared out the window like we weren't even here.

Two can play at that game, princess.

Plopping down on the sofa, I kept my back to her. Cameron set his phone on his knee and nudged me with his elbow. "What's the hold up?" he whispered. "Weren't we supposed to leave, like, an hour ago?"

"This ain't my barbecue." I flicked my annoyed gaze to Tori. "Ask our manager."

Cameron slanted his eyes in her direction, and I swear he shuddered. "Nah. I'll just call Chase. He'll give me the scoop."

He pushed to his feet, and I turned my attention to Willow. "Whatcha got there?" I asked when she thrust a CD case at me.

"Zewlda."

Glancing over the elf on the cover, I scratched my head. "O-kay." Making eye contact with her daddy when she skipped off to load the game, I lifted a brow. "No Halo?"

Sean chuckled. "She's five, dude."

"Anna confiscated all the war games," Christian chimed in. "We're stuck with Zelda, Mario, and Luigi."

I grabbed some chips from the bowl on the table. "Sounds kinky."

The guys pressed their lips together to keep from laughing, but Anna wasn't amused. I smiled at her innocently as Willow scooted onto my lap to begin her quest.

A few minutes later, Cameron reclaimed his seat. "The driver's held up," he said. "Could be another hour."

I tamped down my irritation, because really, where else did I have to be? Our show wasn't until tomorrow night. Settling back against the cushions, I watched Willow's avatar running through the forest. There were worse ways to spend the morning.

When lightning flashed outside the window, Christian turned his phone in my direction. "Check it out. We're going to catch the outer bands of that tropical storm."

Green and red swirls danced on the screen, cutting a swath across the southern half of the state. If we would have left on time we'd be ahead of it. "Perfect."

I turned to glower at Tori, but her chair was empty. Something about that didn't sit well with me, but I didn't know why. Slowly, I pushed upright and repositioned Willow on the cushion beside me. "Be right back, baby."

Under the guise of stretching, I stood up. And that's when I saw Tori, standing in the parking lot, fat droplets of rain soaking her hair and clothes. I was out the door in a second, splashing the newly formed puddles as I stomped toward her.

"What are you doing?"

She didn't answer. Didn't move. Just stood frozen with her face tilted to the angry sky, blinking the rain out of her eyes. Shaking off the heavy feeling in my chest, I gently took her arm. "Tori, what the hell?"

As if she just realized I was there, she jerked her gaze to mine. "It's raining." The words trembled as they fell from her lips. "It's not supposed to rain."

Another bolt of lightning flashed across the darkening sky, and a shudder took her whole. She shifted her gaze to the bus, and it was like watching someone's worst nightmare come to life.

Taking a step to block her view, I cupped her cheeks, forcing her to focus on my words. "You're all right."

I wasn't sure why I said it. Tori was about as far from all right as a person could get. But she nodded. And I nodded back.

Infusing as much calm into my tone as I could manage, I said, "We need to get out of the rain." Her eyes widened, and she shook her head, sending a torrent of tears sliding over my fingers. "Listen to me." I stroked her cheek with my thumb, and she stilled. "How about we sit in my car for a minute. Would that be okay?"

The tension in her jaw eased, and she found her voice. "Just for a minute."

Once I got her settled in the passenger seat, I crouched so we were eye level. Swept away by the torment churning in her amber gaze, I barely felt the rain that continued to lash at my skin.

"It wasn't supposed to rain," she said softly.

And I wasn't sure if she meant today or if she was locked in the past.

I tucked a wet lock behind her ear. "Sometimes things don't happen according to plan."

She nodded, a little color returning to her cheeks. Embarrassment replaced the desolation in her eyes, and I knew she was a moment away from shutting me out. Before she did, I needed a plan. An option that didn't include Tori on that tour bus.

"I'm going to grab a couple of towels," I said as I hauled to my feet. "Be right back."

Through the curtain of rain, I spotted Cameron eyeing me from the window as I trudged toward the silver beast. He met me at the door.

"What's going on?" he asked, following me to my bunk.

I slid the strap on my duffel over my shoulder. "The bus is too fucking crowded. I'm going to drive."

"Drive?" Confusion laced his tone. "What about Tori?"

After grabbing my guitar case and Tori's rollaway from the opposite bunk, I finally looked Cameron in the eyes. "The princess isn't letting me out of her sight. She already parked her ass in my car."

I didn't lie to my boys. Not usually. But what else could I do? Tori was only on this little adventure because of me. I owed her this bit of solace. Of privacy.

I patted Cameron on the back as I scooted past him. "Explain it to the guys. I'll see y'all in Oklahoma."

11

Tori

Shivering, I rubbed my arms. But it didn't help. The chill came from within, bred from my own defeat.

In the end, I couldn't go through with it. Not to save my business. Or preserve Rhenn and Paige's legacy. I'd have to leave the heavy lifting to Taryn. Again.

She'd offered to take my place on the tour, even if it meant leaving Chase for three months. But I'd refused, claiming that I didn't need anyone's help. I guess I was wrong.

As I pulled out my phone to tap a message to my best friend, shame settled over me as thick as the soot and ash that I could still taste on my tongue.

You were right.

Thumb hovering over the send button, I stared at the three little words. My white flag of surrender. The final nail in the imaginary coffin that kept me from moving forward.

The trunk slammed, pulling me from my thoughts, and I set the phone aside.

A second later, the driver's door opened with a creak, and Logan leaned in, water dripping from his chin. "Watch your head, princess."

I ducked in time to avoid getting beaned when he swung my rollaway over the seat. Sliding behind the wheel, he tossed a Caged T-shirt into my lap.

Confused and still a little dazed, I brushed my fingers over the lion's head logo. "What's this for?"

"Thought you might want to change out of your wet clothes." He finished adjusting the mirror, then looked over at me, his gaze falling to my chest. A slow smile quirked his lips. "On second thought ..."

I glanced down at the white blouse plastered to my skin, my sheer bra and erect nipples clearly visible through the sheer fabric.

My arms flew up to cover myself. "I'm wet." Logan's smile grew, and I felt the blush detonate on my cheeks. "I mean ... I'm cold."

He arched a brow as he fired up the engine. "If you say so."

As he slid the column shifter into drive, my hand darted out to grab his arm. I didn't need Logan to drop me off at Twin Souls like I was a defective product he was returning for an exchange. "I can get my own ride."

He turned to me, and I felt his gaze like fingers on my skin. A light shining on all the cracks. The hidden seams, smoothed by time, but still present.

"Is it the rain or the bus that scares you?" he finally asked.

I lifted my chin, ready to tell him that he didn't know what the hell he was talking about. That I wasn't afraid. But then I recalled him standing in the rain cupping my cheeks as he tried to coax me back from my nightmare with only his words.

"You're all right."

There was no use hiding now. He'd seen it all.

Tracing a groove in the upholstery, I slid my fingernail along the stitching. "It's not the rain." The weight of Logan's stare forced my gaze to my lap. "I mean, it's not *just* the rain."

Unspoken questions swirled between us like the winds of the storm outside. But instead of asking anything more, he just nodded. "Buckle up."

Logan's tone held none of the sarcasm I'd come to expect. And that was almost worse. I didn't need or want his pity.

After my seat belt was secured, he pulled out of the space with greater care than I would've expected. Being that I was a nervous passenger, I was grateful for that small favor, even if he wasn't aware he was doing it.

As he turned onto the side streets, heading north toward Sixth, I pulled my phone out. My unsent message to Taryn waited in the box, but I didn't have the will to send it. Screw it. We were ten minutes from the office. I'd explain when I got there.

Letting my head fall back, I closed my eyes, lulled by the hum of the powerful engine and the rain on the windshield. Moments later when the car surged forward, I jolted, swinging my gaze to Logan. "Why are we getting on the freeway?"

His eyes found mine for only a second before returning to the road. "How else you planning on getting to Oklahoma, princess?"

12

Logan

I hadn't thought this through. Not even a little bit. Shoot first, ask questions later. That was always my jam. Only this time, I was the one who took the bullet. Because here I sat, stuck in a car with a woman who, up until a couple of hours ago, couldn't stand the sight of me. Not that anything had changed in that regard.

Except that it had.

Something shifted the minute Tori let me behind her walls. It wasn't just the grief and desperation peering from the corners that struck a chord, but her mad strength and resolve. And also my guilt for putting her in this situation, even if she should've known better.

I couldn't just abandon her.

Only now, my decision seemed less heroic and more like the act of an impulsive teenager. Tori had a million people waiting in the wings to help her if that's what she wanted. She didn't need me.

Leaning on the gas, I put more distance between us and the raging storm. By the time we reached the northern tip of Williamson county, the clouds were a black smudge in my rearview mirror.

With nothing but blue skies and open road ahead, I eased off the accelerator and chanced a peek at my passenger.

Tori gazed out the side window, nervous fingers working the

fabric of the Caged T-shirt balled in her lap. The sun poured in from all sides, kissing her pale skin and the raven hair that fell in soft ribbons around her shoulders. There was no denying her beauty, but this messier version was far more alluring.

When her phone buzzed for the umpteenth time, I shoved my dirty thoughts back in the box.

After a brief look at the screen, Tori discreetly hit ignore and returned her attention to the scenery. Her frown told me I wasn't the only one with buyer's remorse. Thankfully, we were less than a couple of hours into our misadventure. Nothing we couldn't unwind.

I roughed a hand through my hair. "Listen, Tori—" A small gasp tumbled from her lips, and I whipped my head in her direction. "What?"

She blinked at me with wide, honey colored eyes. "The Little Czech Bakery. Can we stop?"

Her face glowed with excitement. *Over kolaches.* If I'd've known that puffed pastry filled with jam or sausage was the way to break through her rock-hard exterior, I would've brought a box to every meeting.

"Sure thing, princess."

She bounced in her seat when I slid the car into the right lane to exit. But her enthusiasm waned as soon as she got a good look at the parking lot. Packed didn't begin to describe it. Every traveler making the trek between Houston and Dallas/Ft. Worth was here. Or so it seemed.

"Maybe we shouldn't," she said, sinking back against the upholstery.

That was a given. The glorified truck stop, with its wall-to-wall people, was a recipe for disaster.

Ignoring the warning bells in my head, I pulled into a parking space as far away from the other cars as I could get.

"It's all good," I said, not really sure if it were true. Grabbing a Longhorns baseball cap from under the seat, I tossed it in her lap. "Put that on."

Running a finger over the frayed orange fabric stretching across the bill, she eyed me speculatively. "What about you?"

On any other day, I'd probably be the biggest celebrity in the joint. But the woman at my side had me beat hands down in the fame department. I was a star. But Tori was rock royalty.

I pushed the car door open with a chuckle. "I'll take my chances."

"Wait!" She caught my arm. "I've got something in my suitcase."

Yanking off her seat belt, she scampered onto her knees and then leaned into the back seat. Her blouse rode up, revealing the ink above the waistband of her jeans. I'd glimpsed the tattoo before, a large piece that took up most of her back. But I'd never had the urge to trace the lines with my fingers.

She wiggled her ass as she rooted around in her bag. Unintentional. But my dick didn't get the memo. And now I had a semi. Fucking perfect.

Shifting my attention to anything but that swath of skin, I muttered, "We don't have all day."

She plopped back into her seat, a TCU baseball cap in hand.

I wrinkled my nose. "Are you kidding me?"

Her tongue darted out as she secured her soft waves in the rubber band she'd pulled from her wrist. "Don't look at me like that, Cage," she warned as she yanked her ponytail through the hole in the back of the purple hat. "I'm probably a bigger Longhorn fan than you are. Which makes this an even more effective disguise." Propping her oversized sunglasses on the bridge of her nose, she smiled. "Don't you think?"

"It's fuckin' ugly is what it is." But she looked damn cute wearing it. Shoving the orange cap on my head, I slid out from behind the wheel. "Let's get this over with."

She joined me in front of the store, a pair of shorts and the Caged T-shirt clutched to her chest.

"What?" she asked, peering up at me.

"I never took you for the kind of girl who changes in public restrooms."

70

A laugh spilled from her lips. "Our first tour bus," she shook her head, smiling, "the bathroom had the most God awful smell. Nobody would use it unless they absolutely had to. I spent six months finding the cleanest restrooms in the country so I could dress without gagging."

A bell rang when I pulled the door open to the shop. "That's nothing. Our first bus was about a hundred years old, and the tour lasted a year."

Tori ducked under my arm, then smirked at me over her shoulder. "Ours was eighteen months. But six months in, our album went platinum and Taryn negotiated a better bus." Smug, she batted her eyelashes. But then someone strolled by munching on a berry and cheese kolache. "Oh my God, I want that. And a couple sausage and jalapeño too. And ..."

She moved toward the counter, but I cut her off. "Go get dressed. I'll take care of you."

Apparently, my tongue and my brain were on the outs. Otherwise, I never would've made that promise. But before I could take it back, Tori flashed a grin that lit up her whole face.

Was it really that easy to make the girl smile? And if so, why didn't everyone do it?

Taking my place in line, I tracked her movements as she weaved through the crowd. Gazing up at the menu, I couldn't decipher any of the items on the board. I'd been here many times, but always left the ordering to someone else.

Ten minutes later, the waitress shuffled over, and when I made eye contact, I saw the spark of recognition in her eyes.

"What's good here, darlin'?"

Tilting my sunglasses, I peered at her over the rim, just to confirm what she already suspected.

"Oh my God. It's you! You're Logan."

I managed to grab her hand before anyone investigated her shriek. "Let's not draw any attention, okay?"

A blush spread from her chest to her hairline. "Sure. What can I get you?" I rattled off a half dozen items, and when she handed me my receipt, she whispered, "Can I get your autograph. Pretty please?"

"Sure." Tossing her a wink, I scribbled my signature on her notepad.

With her prize in the pocket of her apron, she scurried off to fill my order while I scooted in front of the register. The cashier took my money, too busy to acknowledge me with more than a harried smile.

With the treasures in hand, I slipped out the door. My good mood evaporated when I spotted Tori hovering by the bumper of my Mustang. Clad in a pair of cutoffs with frayed ends that barely peeked from the bottom of the Caged T-shirt, she squinted up at some douche nozzle in a cowboy hat who didn't know the meaning of the word boundaries.

Scowling, I marched in their direction, wondering why she didn't just get into the car.

When I clenched my fist, my keys dug into my palm, answering the question.

"You sure you're married, darlin'?" I heard him ask as Tori turned to make her escape. And then he did it. His beefy paw wrapped around her arm, and I saw red.

"Get your hands off her!" The command ripped from my chest, low and lethal. But the cowboy fuck was too busy leering to notice. Tori's gaze found mine, and she shook her head imperceptibly. Maybe if the douche wasn't still standing close enough to breathe all over her, I would've heeded the warning.

"Did you fucking hear me?"

Tori slid between us before I could get a hand around the dude's neck.

Palms flat against my chest, she smiled up at me. "There you are." My rage subsided as she brushed her fingers lightly over my pounding heart. "I thought I'd lost you."

"Not likely," I bit out before turning my attention to the cowboy doing his best to skulk away. "Where do you think you're going?"

His hands flew up in surrender. "Sorry, bud. I didn't ... I wasn't ..."

Normally, his stammered apology wouldn't mean shit. Hell, it

72

didn't mean anything now. But as I took a step forward to teach him a lesson, Tori pried open my fist and laced our fingers. "Let's go."

Whatever was left of my anger dissolved under the weight of her touch, the softness of her hand in mine. And without giving the cowboy a second glance, I followed.

13

Tori

"**O**klahoma, baby!" *Paige squealed as she bounced in her seat, pointing out the window of the tour bus. "We've officially left the Lone Star State!"*

Taryn jumped up from the table and joined her, snapping pictures with the digital camera she'd bought before we left Austin.

Sinking deeper into the well of Rhenn's arms, I hummed along to the old Garth Brooks tune bleeding from the speaker on the antiquated sound system. He nuzzled my ear, and I felt his lips curve into a smile. "We're on our way, Belle."

Gasping, I came off the seat with a start, knocking the box of pastries onto the floorboard. The memory receded, leaving me with a burning throat and tears lining my eyes. Gazing around, I took in the watery landscape outside the window.

"Where are we?" I croaked.

But I knew. Before I even asked, I knew.

Eyes on the road, Logan leaned over the console to retrieve the box at my feet. "Oklahoma."

His arm brushed my bare leg, and I drew in a sharp breath. A hint of rain lingered on his skin. In his hair. Maybe it was the last vestiges of sleep still clinging to my consciousness, but I reached down and brushed my fingers over the soft, golden locks. "Why did you cut it?"

I'd wanted to ask him ever since the moment I'd seen him back on the bus. But we didn't have that kind of relationship. We weren't friends. Except here I was, sifting my fingers through the soft strands that barely reached his collar.

Smiling, he settled back in his seat. "Didn't think you noticed." He tipped his chin to the box on my lap. "Hand me a blueberry, will you?" I recognized a diversion when I heard one, so I shut my mouth and sorted through the array of pastries. As I handed him the treat, he closed his hand around mine, pinning me to my seat with a somber gaze. "What were you dreaming about?"

I pulled away as if I'd touched an open flame. But instead of shutting down, I let my eyes wander from his impossibly high cheek bones to his full lips and the blond stubble dusting his jaw. "Answer me first. Why did you cut your hair?"

The muscle in his bicep twitched as he tightened his grip on the wheel, his eyes narrow behind the aviator shades. "It reminded me of someone I'd rather forget."

"Who?"

His lip quirked at the corner. "That's two questions, princess. Your turn."

Maybe it was the confines of the car. The solitude that came when there was nothing but the hum of the highway under the tires. Or it could've been that moment we shared back in the parking lot. But I couldn't stop myself. "Our first tour ... we followed this route. Played the same venues."

Avoiding the prying eyes that had already seen too much, I turned my attention to the scenery.

"Why would you want to follow the same route?"

It was my turn to smile. "That's two questions. Your turn."

For a long moment, Logan said nothing, and the air grew thick with the weight of our secrets. Just when I thought he wouldn't answer, he sighed. "Jake. My old man. I hadn't seen him in years. But now, he's ... um, back."

Logan was so caught up in his own thoughts, I could've left it right there. Instead, I let the words tumble free. "Mac booked our first tour—launched us after the debut album. At the time I ... er, we, thought it was because he believed in the band. But really, it was all upside for Metro. Benny Conner, the concert promoter, he'd already made an offer to take us wide. But Mac wanted the money for himself. To build Metro. We didn't mind, though. We were partners. Or so we thought."

My voice fell to a whisper as I reached the end of the tether linking my past and my present. Standing at the abyss, memories threatened to swallow me whole.

I jerked back to myself with a start when Logan placed his phone on my lap.

"What's this for?" I asked, brushing my fingertips over the Caged logo on the screen. The same lion on the shirt I was wearing. And the medallion hanging from the rearview mirror.

"Why don't you find something on there to play. I can't get shit on the radio." Slanting his gaze my way, he peered at me over the top of his shades. "No Leveraged. Or Revenged Theory. No Drafthouse either."

Biting down a smile, I opened his music library. "Someone sounds a little jelly."

I froze when he reached over and swiped the corner of my lip. "I don't get jealous, princess." Heat pooled in my belly as he licked the raspberry smudge from his thumb. "And no Britney either. That shit just hurts my ears."

When I realized I was staring, I shook my head and turned my attention to the phone. "Yeah ... um, mine too."

Finding a playlist marked "country," I hit shuffle, and Willie Nelson filled the silence, crooning about angels flying too close to the ground. And for the first time in a long time, I didn't cringe.

14

TULSA, OK.

Logan

I pressed the phone closer to my ear, the noise from the highway and the breeze making it difficult to hear. When Chase's growl raced across the line, I realized volume wasn't going to be an issue. "Where are you?"

Reclining against the hood of my car, I kept an eye on the bathroom where Tori had disappeared a moment earlier. "Rest stop outside of Tulsa."

Relief laced Chase's tone as he relayed the information to someone else. Taryn, I assumed. I shook my head, because really, what the fuck did he think I'd done, kidnapped their business partner?

"All right ... okay," he said, his attention back on me. "So you'll be at the Hard Rock in what, an hour?"

I kicked a stone, and the little pebble skidded across the uneven concrete. "Depends."

"On what?"

Dropping my head back, I gazed up at the cloudless sky. Was the sky this big in Austin? It didn't feel like it. "On whether we decide to rob a liquor store now, or after dinner."

Dead silence, followed by footsteps and a muffled apology to his girl. And then a door slammed.

"Did you lock yourself in the bathroom?" I asked. "Because if you did, you need to get your balls back from Taryn."

"Goddamn it, Logan," Chase spat. "This isn't funny. You don't have any idea what you've gotten yourself into."

Tori's amber eyes, fearful and desolate, floated through my mind. "Enlighten me then."

"You've never dealt with Tori's kind of fame. People follow her. They snap pictures and ask questions, and—"

"Yeah, I get it." I pinched the bridge of my nose, squeezing my eyes shut. "The princess is pretty popular."

"Dude, you have no idea."

But I did. Long before Caged had ever played our first gig—when we were still a garage band without a sound, an original song, or even a name—I'd seen Tori perform at some street fair with her first band, The Austin Dolls. I knew then ... the girl was a star. She just hadn't been discovered yet.

Shoving to my feet, I turned to watch the cars roll by on the busy highway. "Look, I'm just giving the girl a ride to our first show. The rain freaked her the fuck out. Y'all can decide what you're going to do with her when we get to Tulsa." Chase grunted something that sounded like agreement, and I sighed. "This really isn't my idea of a good time, bro. I've got to find a reputable transport to ship my car back to Austin before we head to St. Louis."

"I'll take care of it," he grumbled, appeased. For the moment at least. "I've got to talk to Taryn—calm her down. Catch you later."

The line went dead, so I shoved my phone in my pocket. Raking a hand through my hair, I turned and found Tori frozen in her spot three feet away, two Dr. Peppers nestled in the crook of her arm. From the look in her eyes, she'd heard it all.

My spine went rail stiff.

Apologize. Take it back. Explain.

But I couldn't find the words, so I flicked my gaze to the soda. "Is one of those for me?" She gulped, drawing my attention to the tiny scar at the base of her throat. Suddenly, I had the urge to trace it with my thumb, to ask her how she got it, why it was there.

Without a word, she held out the can, flinching when my fingers closed around hers.

"We better go," I muttered, flipping my sunglasses from the top of my head to hide my eyes. From the sun, or her wounded gaze. I wasn't sure which. "I don't want to run into any traffic."

Wandering to the window in my suite, I ran a hand through my hair, still damp from the shower I'd taken to wash off the long drive. A riot of purple, pink, and orange painted the sky as the sun made a last-ditch effort to stave off the night.

Taryn had booked the whole floor, but since nobody was due to arrive for three hours, it was quiet. Too damn quiet.

Snatching the half empty bottle of beer from the table, I flopped onto the sofa, my focus on the door connecting Tori's room to mine.

Yeah, that was all me.

Twenty rooms, and I'd asked the clerk to put me right next to Tori. Not across. Or down the fucking hall. Right on the other side of the door. Not that we'd be doing any socializing since the girl hadn't spoken a word to me since we left the rest stop.

Earlier, I'd heard music in her suite. But nothing for a while. She'd obviously gone to sleep.

My stomach rumbled, so I picked up the room service menu. A dry chuckle scraped my throat, because, who was I kidding? I couldn't read the damn thing. And nobody was here to see my lame attempt at pretending I could.

You need to get laid.

Burying myself in a willing body was a sure-fire way to get my mind off the mess I'd made of things today. Off of Tori and her silent treatment. Again, my gaze shifted to the door, and I wondered what the princess would do if she heard some random chick moaning my name all night.

Fuck it.

It wasn't like our agreement included a celibacy clause.

Hauling to my feet, I strode to the bedroom and got dressed. Checking my reflection in the mirror, I ran my fingers through my hair. The unruly strands barely brushed my shoulders. Not my style at all. And if I were honest, I probably looked more like my old man now than ever.

Shaking my head, I grabbed my key and wallet from the dresser and headed downstairs.

The casino was packed, and rather than wade into the crowd, I skirted the edge of the main floor. And that's when I saw Tori, standing motionless in front of the wall of memorabilia. Every Hard Rock on the planet had one. But from the way her hand pressed against the glass, she hadn't run across some random item of interest.

My stomach sank when I edged up behind her. Inside the case was a photo of Rhenn, a pair of worn combat boots, and a guitar propped in a stand.

"It's got a crack in the neck," she said softly, her eyes never leaving the guitar. "Rhenn banged it on the floor during a sound check when it wouldn't hold a tune." Her bottom lip trembled. "It's a piece of shit."

As I struggled for something to say, some way to ease her pain, a couple strolled up, hand in hand. I took a small step, just enough to shield Tori from their prying eyes. But the dude was too busy gazing at the guitar to notice us.

"Man, look at this," he said, tipping forward to get a better view. "Rhenn Grayson's guitar. Do you think it's real?"

His girl shrugged, uninterested. "I don't know. Let's go to the buffet, I'm starving."

Tori's lips tilted into a sad smile as she watched them walk away. "It's real," she whispered. And then drawing in a big breath, she straightened her shoulders and focused on me. "I better get back upstairs."

Turning on her heel, she headed for the elevators. When she rounded the corner, I shook my head and stalked toward the bar. Sliding a hip onto the first empty stool I could find, I pulled out some cash and ordered a shot of tequila. Before I could lift the glass to my lips a brunette ambled to my side. Cocking her head, she stared at my profile. "You know who you look like?"

When I slanted my gaze her way, her eyes widened just a fraction, and I smiled. "No clue. But why don't you let me buy you a drink and maybe we can figure it out."

15

Tori

"Ouch," I hissed, turning the knob on the faucet to add some cold water to my bath.

"What's happening?" Taryn's disembodied voice echoed off the walls in the bathroom. "Tori?"

I'd avoided Taryn's calls all day, but in a moment of weakness, after running headlong into my past, I'd answered the phone. The second my best friend heard the sniffle, she pressed me for details. And instead of keeping my mouth shut, it all poured out in a rush—starting with my freak-out in the parking lot and ending with Rhenn's guitar. But now I was embarrassed and I just wanted to soak the stain of the day out of my pores.

"I'm fine," I finally said. "Just setting the temperature for my bath."

With a softer but no less demanding tone, Taryn asked, "Did you do your stretches first?"

My guilty gaze shifted to the exercise bands tossed haphazardly on the floor next to the bed. "Yep."

The lie slipped out easily, with conviction. It was almost true, since I planned on doing the damn stretches before bed. *Maybe.*

I pressed my lips together to keep from groaning as I stood. Eight hours in a car and every muscle in my body was stiff. But I couldn't admit that to Taryn. She was already threatening to hop on a plane and put an end to this farce.

"Did you eat?" she asked.

Ambling to the living room, I popped open the box of leftover kolaches. Picking through the contents, I found what I was looking for—jalapeño, sausage, and cheese. Kind of dinner-like. I took a bite. "Yep."

She sighed. "What's with the one-word answers, Belle?"

I dropped the pastry in the trash. "What's with the third-degree, *Taryn*."

We'd perfected this dance over the past five years. Taryn would push as far as I'd let her. But when I was done, I was done.

Before I could unload and tell her exactly how done I was, a knock at the door drew my attention. The *interior* door. I froze, hoping that Logan had knocked something against the wood by accident. Then I realized that "something" was probably a warm body. Another knock echoed, louder and more insistent.

"Is someone there?" Taryn's voice rose in alarm as I padded toward the source of the tapping. "Belle, don't answer it. What if —"

Yanking the door open, I looked up into pale blue eyes. Confusion lined Logan's brow, as if he didn't know why he was here, standing at my door with a pizza and a six pack of beer. And neither did I. The callous words he'd tossed out at the rest stop rolled and spun and tumbled around in my head. A soundtrack for my weakness and his disregard.

Swallowing hard, I lifted my chin and said flatly, "It's nobody, Taryn. I've got to go. My bath is ready." Ending the call, I folded my arms over my chest and glared up at Logan. "Can I help you with something?"

His gaze dipped to my chest, lingering on the logo of the lion's head on my T-shirt. *His* T-shirt. I had the urge to rip the damn thing off and throw it at him. But I wasn't even sure why. And while I stood there, fists clenched at my sides, mouth twisted in a frown, Logan used his cat like agility and brushed right past me.

I spun around, incredulous as he slid the pizza onto the table. Grabbing a beer, he dropped onto the sofa. "You can help me eat this pizza, for starters."

A smirk hitched up one corner of his lips. It did nothing for me, that smile. Nothing but tie my tongue into knots and steal my words. The unmistakable sound of water meeting the tile floor snagged my attention. Sure enough, the suds were creeping toward the carpet at a steady clip.

"Goddamn it." I moved without thinking, but Logan was quicker. Jumping to his feet, he headed toward the disaster before I made it two steps.

"Don't move," he said, looking over his shoulder at me as he turned off the faucet.

Ignoring his order— because what the hell was that about?— I continued into the room. Breaking our stare, he glanced down at my feet, which I didn't realize were covered in bubbles. Repelled by the slick tile and slippery foam, I jumped back onto the safety of the carpet.

And that made it all the worse.

At twenty-one, I'd dived off a cliff in Hawaii. I'd swam with sharks, parasailed, and even bungee jumped. But now, the thought of what might happen if I fell the wrong way onto a hard surface turned my blood cold.

Arms folded over my middle, I dug my fingers into my sides. "I can do that," I offered weakly when Logan reached for a large bath towel.

Shaking his head, he went to work sopping up the mess. For some reason, I didn't move, my gaze roaming the length of his fit body. He was barefoot too, and he had on different jeans. Faded, with holes in the knees and frayed hems.

"You changed your clothes?"

"Yeah." Slanting his baby blues in my direction, he tipped his chin to the living room. "Can you scrounge up some plates for the pizza?"

He was dismissing me, and I wasn't sure how I felt about that, so I lingered for a moment. Once I was sure I'd saved face, I wandered to the small kitchenette for the plates.

Easing onto the edge of the couch, I glanced at the open door adjoining our rooms. When I spotted the guitar leaning against the chair, my thumb skated over my fingertips reflexively. The skin was smooth now, with no hint of the callouses that once marred the surface.

And when had that happened?

Logan flopped down beside me, rousing me from my thoughts. He loaded a plate with two slices of pepperoni, which I took with a frown.

"What's the matter, you don't like pizza?" he asked, grabbing a slice for himself.

"Pizza's fine. I just …" As I tried to think of an excuse, any reason to get him back in his room and out of mine, he handed me a napkin. I forced a smile. "Okay … thanks."

He slid a beer in front of me, the same one he'd already opened, then reached for another. "Did you get things squared away with Taryn?"

So that's why he was here. To make sure I had a plan that didn't include driving halfway across the country in his vintage Mustang. I drew my legs under me. "Yep. It's all handled."

Pausing with the bottle halfway to his lips, Logan side-eyed me. *Dammit.* He wasn't letting me off the hook, and after the shit show that was today, maybe I owed him an explanation.

"The rest of the bands are arriving tomorrow," I went on, peeling off a slice of pepperoni so I had something to do with my hands. "I'll catch a ride on the Leveraged tour bus."

Tipping forward, he set his bottle on the table, then turned to look at me. "With Dylan?"

Narrowing his eyes, he waited for my reply.

"Yeah. That's the best thing."

Nodding like he was mulling it over, he flopped back against the cushions, arms crossed over his chest. "Is there something magical about the Leveraged tour bus that'll keep you from, you know …"

As if he realized he may have cut too deep, he pressed his lips together. But I was in it now, so I tossed my plate on the table and threw his words from earlier back at him. "Freaking the fuck out?"

Something flashed across his features. Regret? From what I'd witnessed, Logan Cage didn't do regret. It was anger. I would've bet money that the fragile truce we'd shared during most of our car ride was about to end. That he'd get up and stalk out.

Instead, he licked his lips and then said, "I didn't mean it."

With my features schooled into a mask of indifference, I blinked at him. "Which part?" Watching Logan try to cobble together a half-assed apology was more than I could take, so I shook my head. "Never mind. It doesn't matter."

I picked up my pizza and dug in. After a moment, Logan did the same. We ate in silence and when I'd finished my first beer, he was quick to offer me another. I made a grab for the bottle, but Logan didn't let go.

His index finger glided over mine. Once. Twice. "I didn't mean any of it, princess."

The moment evaporated as quickly as it came, and he picked up the remote. "So what's your pleasure?" he asked as he turned on the TV. "*The Last Jedi* or *Thor: Ragnarok*?"

Logan

Pins and needles raced up my arm, jolting me awake. Clenching my hand to get the blood flowing, I looked around. The On-Demand logo swam into view on the TV screen, the only light in the dark room. Drawing back slowly, I peered down at the body pressed to my side.

Tori burrowed closer, warm breath skating over the exposed skin above the collar of my T-shirt. Her hair smelled faintly of cinnamon and sugar. Like cookies fresh from the oven. And though that shouldn't have turned me on, my aching balls didn't get the memo.

A smarter man would've taken the girl in the bar up to her room for a quickie before I showed up at Tori's door with my peace offering.

Was that what it was—a peace offering? Or an apology?

I cleared my throat. "Wake up, princess."

Stop calling her that.

In the dark, it sounded more like a term of endearment than a thinly veiled insult.

Irked, I gave Tori a little shake, but instead of waking up, she started to topple over. Catching her at the last second, I gently repositioned her in the crook of my arm. Her head tipped back, exposing the one-inch scar on her throat. And just like at the rest stop, I wondered what it was and how it got there.

Pushing aside the bigger question—*why the hell do you care?*—I brushed my thumb over the raised skin.

Tori's lids flew open like a vampire meeting the dawn, her lips parting on a gasp. "What are you doing?"

Since I'd already been caught red-handed, I had nothing to lose, so I traced the faded line again. "What is this?"

As the seconds elapsed, I waited for Tori to push me away. Instead, she sighed. "It's where they inserted the trach tube after the accident."

"What's a trach tube?"

She swallowed hard, her throat bobbing beneath my touch as I continued to brush my thumb back and forth over her skin.

"I was choking when they found me. Bleeding internally, and I had a collapsed lung. So the EMTs put in a tube so I could breathe."

A tremor shook her body, and her lids fluttered closed. My thumb dipped lower, ghosting over her collar bone and up the side of her neck, beckoning her back from that place in the past.

I knew I'd succeeded when her eyes popped open and she pushed herself to sitting. A second later she was off the couch, rubbing her arms like she had a chill.

"You should go. It's late."

With her cinnamon scent still lingering on my clothes, my mind jumped to places it shouldn't, like what it would feel like to steal some of her sunshine and taste it on my tongue.

I hauled to my feet. "Yep."

Tori gave me a wide berth as I headed for the door, but when I crossed the threshold she was on my heels.

"Night," she said quickly.

I didn't reply, just crawled into bed and waited for the creaking hinges and the snick of the lock. Twenty seconds. Thirty. A full minute passed, and it never came.

Sometime later when I finally drifted off, the door was still cracked, leaving a sliver of space between her world and mine.

16

Logan

There's a hierarchy at rock festivals. The more popular the band, the later their time slot. Bands just starting out played early in the morning on the outer stages in front of small crowds. As the day progressed, the more experienced groups got their shot. The audiences were bigger. Livelier. But still, they were merely a warm-up. A down-ticket band.

That's where Caged usually fit in.

But not today.

Today, and for the rest of the tour, we were one of the four headliners. That being said, the other three bands were substantially more popular. Which meant Caged would take the main stage first, and we'd never get to play under the stars. But that was all right. We'd made it. It didn't really sink in until we arrived at the venue.

"Jesus Christ," said Sean, jamming me in the ribs with his elbow when our caravan of SUVs rolled to a stop. "Are you seeing this?"

Looking up from my phone, I peered out the window at the sea of people. Forty thousand, if the estimates were correct.

My heart rate spiked. "Yeah."

I didn't have time to ponder our good fortune, or how we'd landed here, on the shiny side of the coin. Because the door swung open, and out we went, single file, straight into the tunnel created by the small army of security guards. Usually, we'd stop to sign autographs, chat up the fans. But it was too risky with this many people.

Keeping our heads down, we stayed in formation until we got to a group of tents behind the barricades. And then, as if by magic, the curtain of muscle surrounding us dispersed, and there was nothing but blue sky, thick fluffy clouds, and bright sunshine.

Cameron twisted to peek at the stages in the distance. "This is intense."

Swept into the large tent where our preshow press conference was about to begin, we were greeted by a petite brunette holding a clipboard. Elise Donnelly, assistant PR director at Twin Souls. She looked way out of her element, all wide eyes, with her bottom lip tucked between her teeth.

"We're going to begin in a half hour," she said as she led us to the long, elevated table in the front. "Have a seat and make yourselves comfortable. I'll be right back."

Dumbstruck, we did as we were told. It was only after I dropped into a chair between Sean and Cameron that I fully took in my surroundings. Reporters congregated next to the refreshments, eating finger foods from small plates while they chatted each other up. The journalists from *Rolling Stone*, *Alternative Nation*, and the larger news outlets stayed to themselves, avoiding the bloggers and tabloid press.

After a moment, Christian tipped forward and swatted my arm. "Where's your babysitter? Shouldn't she be here?"

Tori. I hadn't thought about her since we'd left the hotel. When I'd poked my head inside her room this morning, she was already gone.

"No clue," I said, scanning the knots of people for raven hair.

Cameron chuckled. "She's probably heading back to Austin."

Whipping my head around, I searched his face. "Why? What have you heard?"

The smile fell from his lips. "Nothing. I was just kidding. Unless ..." His eyes narrowed to slits. "Did you do something to run her off?"

Despite my apprehension at the thought of Tori leaving, I forced out a laugh. "I wish. The princess isn't going anywhere."

If I can help it.

Even more shocking than the wayward thought was the conviction behind it.

Cameron abandoned our stare off, and I followed his gaze to a roadie holding the tent flap aside to admit a group of fangirls. "Shit," he muttered. "We should talk to someone about that. It's not like we need any preshow entertainment."

"Speak for yourself," I shot back, my automatic response drawing a collective groan from my bandmates.

But as I looked the girls over, from their pretty faces to their scantily clad bodies, I couldn't muster up one dirty thought. I was too distracted by what Cameron had said about Tori.

Elise appeared out of nowhere and dropped a piece of paper in front of us. "Here are your talking points."

Since nobody else volunteered, Christian slid the document in front of him.

As casual as you please, I leaned in, snagging Elise's attention. "Where's your boss, darlin'?"

She cocked her head. "Taryn's in Austin."

"Your other boss."

"Oh ... you mean Tori?" Flushing pink when I nodded, she chewed the corner of her already pulverized lip. "Um ... she's around. Have you tried texting her? On second thought, she probably wouldn't hear her phone. It's pretty crazy out there."

Out there.

It took a second to digest that tidbit.

Tori was *out there*, not tucked behind the railings and surrounded by security. I pictured the cowboy at the truck stop yesterday, then my mind jumped to the next possible conclusion and I was on my feet.

Panicked, Elise scrambled to block my path. "Where are you going?"

Cameron shot out of his seat, dragging her out of the way before I mowed her down. "Dude, what's up?" he asked.

It took every bit of my self-control, but I kept it light. "I've got to piss. I don't really think it'll take all three of us." I smiled down at Elise. "But you can come along if you want."

Her mouth twisted, and she wrinkled her nose.

"He didn't mean that," Cameron mumbled.

But the look I gave Elise was convincing enough, because she couldn't scoot out of the way quick enough. Shrugging, I tossed her a wink and headed for the door. Once I was outside, I picked up the pace, all my attention focused on the horde of people beyond the barricades.

"Logan?"

Tori's voice rose above the din. Above the music. Above the chaos. And my own thundering heart. Relief swallowed me whole. And anger. That was there too. So I went with it, embracing the familiar. Because she deserved it, every single harsh word about what could happen to her, alone, *out there.*

But when I spun around, the sentiment caught in my throat. Because Tori wasn't alone. Dylan Boothe was with her.

Rooted to my spot as they strolled up, I glanced from Tori's tiny T-shirt, to the holes in her jeans, to the unlaced Doc Martens on her feet. The boots were scuffed, well-worn and out of fashion. Wrong in all the right ways. Just like her.

Dylan held his fist up for a bump. "Hey, man. Good to see you."

"You too," I lied, my gaze fixed on Tori. In the natural light, her eyes were more honey than amber, and laden with a different anxiety than the day before.

But why the hell was she anxious at all?

"What are you doing out here?" she asked, full lips curving into a smile. "Isn't the press conference about to start?"

If her tone were any indication, this was more of a personal inquiry.

I rubbed the back of my neck. "Yeah, I was just ..."

Looking for you. Thank fuck I left that part out because Dylan let out a laugh.

"I know what you were doing," he said, reaching into his pocket.

"Let me help you out." Smiling, he offered me a stack of VIP Passes. Not the fancy, laminated jobs we gave to family and close friends. These were made of paper. Disposable. Meant to be given to the girls who hung out by the buses or in the rope lines. "I don't need these. But I know you'll put them to good use."

His implication was clear; I was a dog, chasing anything that moved. And he was above it. Yeah, no. Dylan and I were cut from the same cloth. The only difference? I gave zero fucks about what people thought. Except maybe the woman at his side.

Tori quickly looked away.

Well, fuck.

Shaking my head, I took the passes, smiling at Dylan like I didn't know how to repay him. Except that I did. "Appreciate you looking out for me, bud." Freeing one of the cards from the stack, I tucked it in the front pocket of his T-shirt. "Better hang on to at least one, though. We both know you'll be looking for it later."

Dylan's eyes locked onto mine, the silver consuming the gray. "I said I was good."

And just to prove how very good he was, the asshole slipped an arm around Tori's shoulder. I didn't fail to notice her flinch. It could've been surprise. Or maybe she saw right through Dylan's bullshit.

While I was contemplating the best way to break every one of his fingers, Elise walked up and joined our awkward trio. "Hey, y'all." A nervous smile played on her lips. "Sorry to interrupt. But I need to steal Logan. The press conference is about to begin."

"Guess that's my cue," I said, and as I took a step back, my eyes shot to Dylan's hand, still resting on Tori's shoulder. "You coming, princess?"

The question came out of left field, and I hated the silence that followed.

"You go ahead," Tori finally said. "I'll see you later."

When she turned her attention to the crowd, Elise took that to mean the matter was settled. Looping her arm through mine, she tugged me in the opposite direction, rambling a mile a minute.

"*Rolling Stone* and *Alternative Nation* are in the first row on the right. Bloggers are in the second row. And refer all questions about Mac or the lawsuit with Metro to me."

My stomach flipped. "Why would they be asking us about Mac?"

She kept her mouth shut until we were inside the tent, then turned to me with a serious expression. "Don't you read your emails?" She rolled her eyes. "Of course you don't."

She'd hit a soft spot without knowing it, severing my already frayed nerves. "Well, you see, darlin', I've been a little busy preparing for a tour. Maybe you can fill me in, since you're the coordinator and Twin Souls is taking fifteen percent of my earnings."

Two spots of crimson stained Elise's cheeks. "Of course ... I'm sorry. I didn't mean to imply ..."

She looked down at her toes, and I kicked myself for being a dick. The girl was still finding her way. In a month or so, she'd be able to spar with the best of us. Or she'd throw in the towel and head home.

"That came out wrong," I said, roughing a hand through my hair. "Can you just tell me what the email said so I don't have to go digging around?"

Bringing her gaze back to mine, Elise forced a tight-lipped smile. "Mac is leaking stories to the media. He claims he's in negotiations with one of the headliners and they're about to jump ship. It's all bullshit. But I just wanted y'all to be prepared in case someone asks."

The knot in my stomach worked its way north. Mac had to be talking about me. That fucker.

When Elise cleared her throat, I realized I'd let my mind wander.

"We really need to start," she said. "We're cutting it close to show time."

"Right behind you."

"That was one long piss," Sean joked when I reclaimed my seat. "Do we need to call a doctor?"

"Keep it up and you will," I warned.

"Enough," Cameron hissed through his smile. "Let's just do this."

Since it was up to me to get the party started, I adjusted the microphone, and when Elise gave me the nod, the usual controlled chaos ensued.

Disregarding protocol, I skipped right over the reporters from *Rolling Stone* and *Alternative Nation* in favor of a blonde in a mini skirt in the second row.

Cameron's knee collided with mine under the table. "What are you doing?" he whispered, irritation etching his tone.

Honestly, I had no clue. Except that everything felt out of my control. So I'd take my victories where I could get them.

Smiling at the blogger, I drawled, "Take it away, darlin'. I'm all yours."

Tori

"Princess?" Dylan scoffed, glaring at Logan's retreating back. "What the fuck is that about?"

Unwilling to have this conversation out in the open, I spun on my heel and headed for the barricade.

"Belle." Dylan's tone took on an edge that he rarely used with me. "You want to tell me what's going on?"

I didn't *want* to tell him shit. But I found myself rounding on him. "Stop! Just ... *stop*."

I couldn't look at him. Not here, with the music and the fans and the stage looming. Everything about Dylan reminded me of who I once was. And I hadn't counted on that. The visceral feeling of nostalgia that accompanied my every move since we'd arrived at the venue.

My gaze wandered to the media tent. To Logan. For some reason, when he was around my thoughts were my own, and not shaped by everyone else's expectations.

Dylan took me by the shoulders. "Jesus, Belle. You're scaring me."

I lifted my gaze, and it was there, the fear and the unease and the disquiet, painted on his features.

"Why?"

His brows drew together. "Why what?"

Why do you want me?

Neither of us was ready for that question. "Why do you worry so much? I'm fine."

Rather than take my little reminder as the happy news that it was, his jaw tightened. "If you're so fine, then why did you ride with Logan and not on the bus?"

I hadn't told Dylan about my freak-out, but I'm sure he suspected. Only there was a little doubt in his eyes, and I held onto that so I could do what I needed to do. For both of us.

Summoning my strength, I inhaled slowly. "Because he asked me to."

The lie passed quietly from my lips. And it worked, like I knew it would.

Dylan's hands fell away. "I need sleep," he said thickly. "Are you coming back to the bus?"

He didn't look at me, and that was for the best.

Wrapping my arms around my middle, I held myself together so my guts wouldn't fall at his feet. "I'm going to catch the tail end of the press conference and then watch the Caged show."

Dylan's eyes found mine, cold like slate. And then, for the first time in six years, he walked away without saying goodbye.

Jack, the security guard standing post in front of the makeshift dressing room gave me the eye when I ventured out. I didn't catch the end of the press conference like I'd intended, and I'd missed most of Caged's opening number. But now it was time to stop hiding.

Blowing out a breath, I swiped a hand over the wrinkles on my T-shirt.

"Do you want me to call you a car, ma'am?" Jack asked.

Ma'am? I was twenty-nine years old. Too young to be a "ma'am."

Maybe it was the clothes. They were at least ten years old. And the stupid boots. Nobody wore Docs anymore.

Slowly, I brought my eyes to his and forced my lips to bend. "No. I want to see the show."

Grimacing, he cast a nervous glance over his shoulder. "Yeah, sure. Let me just call it in." His hand curled around the device strapped to his shoulder. A walkie talkie, small, like the kind my dad used to wear when he was on patrol. "I've got Raven. We're headed for center stage."

Raven.

The alias was straight out of my past. A relic from the days when I needed a security detail to move around anonymously. I saw Taryn's hand in this, since she was the one who'd insisted that I have a body-guard while at the venue.

Jack took my elbow, his hold firm, but surprisingly gentle. "Okay. Let's go."

Amused, I let him take the lead. The guy was a tank, so resistance was futile. "Nobody is here to see me, Jack," I shouted over the music as we got closer to the stage. "You can relax."

His eyes darted around, a deep crease furrowing his brow. "I'm not so sure about that."

The roar of Logan's vocals, the wailing guitars, and the thundering drums made it impossible to protest, so I merely shrugged as Jack maneuvered me up the set of wooden stairs behind the stage.

My breath caught as I peered out from behind the curtain. Earlier today, when I'd taken a walk around the grounds, the crowd was equally dispersed between the three smaller stages. But now, every one of the forty thousand in attendance was spread out before me. Mesmerized, I took it all in. The sea of bobbing heads. The outstretched arms. All the bodies swaying in time.

And Logan.

Prowling the stage, he roared into the microphone, completely at home amidst the chaos and confusion. A thin sheen of sweat glistened on his arms and his face, his blond hair already a tangled mess.

When he turned in my direction, I glimpsed the word stamped across the front of his black T-shirt.

Damaged.

The letters were nearly translucent, blending into the dark fabric like a faded memory.

All of a sudden, I felt exposed, like a time traveler peering into a future that they weren't part of.

A pretty brunette had Logan's undivided attention now. And as the song wound down, he dropped into a crouch at the edge of the stage. The brunette reached for him, and he obliged, a wicked smile curving his lips as he touched her hand.

I knew what was coming next. Had seen it a million times.

Logan's gaze flicked to the wings, searching for a roadie to offer the girl one of those passes that Dylan had turned over. I tried to blend in with the amps so he wouldn't notice me. His blue orbs passed me by, and I sagged in relief, letting my head fall forward. But then a prickle of awareness danced on my skin, and when I looked up, Logan's gaze was locked onto mine.

A genuine smile formed on my lips.

And Logan smiled too. Only it wasn't at me. His focus had already drifted back to the brunette. He crooned the next number directly to her, a ballad with a hard driving beat, and before the song was over, a roadie had woven his way to the girl's side. She took the pass he offered, and it was like an arrow to the chest. Only I couldn't figure out why. Logan was nothing to me. We weren't even friends.

I tugged on the sleeve of Jack's T-shirt, and when he inclined his head, I spoke directly into his ear. "I'm ready to go whenever you are."

17

Logan

I pounded another shot of tequila, then raised my empty glass to get the server's attention.

"Thanks," I said, waving off the lime when she rushed over. "You can leave the bottle."

As soon as she left, Sean reached over and covered my glass with his palm. "Are you trying to piss Tori off the first night?"

Shoving his hand away, I poured my shot. "One—show's over. I'm off the clock. Two—Tori's not my keeper. And three—do you see her anywhere around?"

I motioned around the room without taking my eyes off Sean.

"That's not the point."

"It's exactly the fucking point. If the girl wants me to follow her rules, then she should be here to enforce them."

He cocked his head to the side. "I'm confused. Do you *want* Tori here?" Rather than answer his question, I tipped back my glass, glaring at him over the rim. He smiled smugly. "I know that look. You *do* want her here."

"Don't be stupid. If I wanted her here, I wouldn't have set up a date with ..." Sitting up straighter, I glanced around for the cute little brunette I'd left by the bar. When I didn't spot her right away, I pushed out of my chair to scan the crowd.

Sean snickered into his next sip of beer. "If you're looking for that chick you serenaded, she took off with Justin twenty minutes ago."

The fuck? I left the girl at the bar for a few minutes and Justin swooped in? My gaze darted to the table where the guys from Drafthouse were sitting, *minus* their guitarist.

Sean's smile withered, and he jumped to his feet, grabbing my arm when I took a step in their direction. "Dude, what are you doing?"

Prying off his hand, I growled, "That girl was here for me. And Dylan can't have her."

Sean looked as surprised as I did at the name that popped out of my mouth. "Don't you mean Justin?"

When I tried to push out a response, all I could picture was Dylan's arm wrapped around Tori's shoulder.

"You're either drunker than you look or something's going on with you," he grumbled, nudging me toward the door. "Either way, you need to get back to the hotel and sleep it off."

With traffic, it took two hours to travel the thirty or so miles from the venue to the hotel. Long enough for my buzz to wear off. But not the headache that followed. Fucking tequila.

I stepped off the elevator with Sean on my heels.

"You gonna tuck me in?" I asked, giving him the side-eye.

The question was rhetorical, since I knew damn well what he was doing. There were at least five "after" after-parties taking place on our floor. Not to mention the high-stakes poker game the roadies always threw together.

"Just making sure you don't take any detours," he said, confirming my suspicions.

I was too fucking tired to argue. That is, until I turned the corner and spotted the security guard propping up the wall in front of my door. Red painted my vision, and for the second time tonight, Sean grabbed my arm.

"Be cool."

But I wasn't cool. With any of this. Posting a rent-a-cop outside my door was never part of the agreement.

Yanking free of Sean's hold, I spun around, shoving him back into the hall. "Did you know about this? Is that why you brought me back here?"

When he used all his strength to push me away, I knew he was as surprised as I was. "Fuck no. How could you even think that?" Without waiting for me to answer, he sighed. "Look, dude, this is messed up. You can stay with Anna and me tonight. We've got a two-room suite."

My pride had taken enough of a pounding for one night, so I shook my head. "Nah. I'll take care of it. Go get some sleep." Sean moved in front of me, and I rolled my eyes. "I'm not going to clobber the guy for doing his job. But I might lay you flat if you don't get out of the way."

Undeterred by my threat, he crossed his arms over his chest. "Give me your word."

After twenty years of friendship, Sean knew what he was asking. I didn't make promises—or give my word. Not lightly, anyway.

Reserve the right to change your mind, boy. That's power right there. What you did? You just look weak.

That's what my old man had told me the night I swore I'd never return to his shitty trailer. Even though he was flat on his back at the time, bleeding on the gravel, he still managed to make me feel like I'd lost.

Banishing Jake from my thoughts, I sighed. "Fine. I give you my word. Happy?"

"Ecstatic."

After we bumped fists, I turned and strolled toward my room.

Rent-a-cop pushed off the wall as I approached. "Are you Cage?"

"Who else?" He was on me a second later, so close I detected a hint of cigarette smoke on his clothes. I held up my key. "I don't want any trouble. I just want to go to bed." He watched with narrowed eyes as I slid the plastic card into the slot. Once I got the door open, I shot him a smile. "If one of the girls from the party down the hall comes calling, make sure you let her in."

I was only half kidding, but the guy obviously had no sense of humor. Reclaiming his spot against the wall, he continued to glare at me until the door slid shut.

Shaking my head, I flipped the lock and then headed for the bathroom to shower so I could put this day behind me.

Soft music floated to my ears as I passed the door separating Tori's suite from mine. The voice was spot on, but the accompanying guitar was a little choppy. Curious, I peeked inside. The TV was on with no sound, casting the room in a blue haze. And on the floor, with my Martin wedged under her arm, sat Tori, her fingers fumbling over the frets.

An irritated sigh parted her lips when she tripped over an intricate chord change.

"You might want to try something simpler," I said. "That's pretty intense."

Sucking in a startled breath, she scrambled to her feet. "Shit …I'm sorry. I shouldn't have taken it without asking. I didn't think you'd be back tonight."

Swallowing hard as I closed the distance between us, she held out the guitar.

I dropped onto my ass on the carpet. "Where else would I be?"

She sank to her knees, still clutching the guitar. "I don't know. I just didn't expect you."

"You already said that." I tipped my chin to the Martin. "What's that you were playing."

I knew every Damaged song by heart. And even the stuff she'd done with the Austin Dolls. Whatever she was playing, I'd never heard it before.

Color flooded her cheeks. "Oh ... It was nothing."

"Sounded like something to me. Is it new?"

"Not really. I found some sheet music at home in Rhenn's ..." Pain flashed in her eyes, and just as quickly it was gone. "In my studio. I jotted down the notes, but I don't remember the chords or the key."

"If you sing it, I can probably figure it out."

Her brows scrunched. "How's that?"

I took the guitar from her hands. "I don't read music. But I can figure just about anything out." Setting the Martin on my knee, my thumb slotted the groove on the back of the neck, and I began to strum the opening riff for "Sweet Child O' Mine," the old Guns N' Roses standard. "It took weeks to get this one down."

Her eyes lit up as she watched my fingers fly over the frets. I stopped short of singing the opening stanza, and held out the guitar. She took it, confused. "Why did you stop?"

Don't.

But it was too late. The words were there, on the tip of my tongue, and I couldn't help myself. "I figured if you wanted to hear me sing, you would've stuck around for my performance."

There was no way to mask the bitterness in my tone. And if I were honest, I didn't want to. I braced myself for her snappy comeback, but there was only a smile.

"I was there." Shifting her focus to the frets, she ran through some chords without strumming. "I didn't stay because ..." She peered over at me, raven hair curtaining her face. "That was a really decent thing you did for me yesterday. So I thought the best way to repay you was to leave you alone. As much as I can, I mean."

"What about the guy in the hallway. Is he going to leave me alone too?"

She wrinkled her nose at the door. "Taryn hired him."

Then she went back to her chords like that explained everything.

"I'm not down for that, princess. You never said anything about hiring a rent-a-cop to stand guard."

Her head snapped up, and she blinked at me. "He's not here for you. He's here for me. Taryn's a little freaky about my safety, so she always hires a bodyguard." The light seeped from her eyes. "I still get threats every now and then."

Threats?

A million questions flooded in, but I didn't have enough air in my lungs to push out the words. Or enough room in my chest to contain my pounding heart.

After setting the guitar aside, Tori traced the smooth lines of the body with her index finger. And she looked so small. Not frail. Just delicate.

When she caught me staring, she tugged at the hem of her T-shirt. But there wasn't enough fabric to cover the rough patch of skin peeking from the bottom of her tiny sleep shorts.

"I need to stretch," she announced, her tone almost apologetic. "I didn't yesterday. And after that car ride, I really should have."

I rose to my feet and then took her hand, helping her up. "Are you saying my car is uncomfortable?" My fingers inched toward her wrist. "'Cause those are fightin' words."

"No. I just have a lot of ... um ..." She pressed her lips together and looked down. "I can't sit in one place too long. It's uncomfortable."

Had she been in pain?

I swept my thumb over her wrist, felt her strong and steady pulse. "Why didn't you tell me?"

Sliding her hand free, she lifted a shoulder. "You already witnessed the epic breakdown. I didn't want you to think I couldn't handle a day trip. I'm not, you know, damaged." She brushed her fingertips over the faded Damaged logo on my T-shirt, and I felt it everywhere. "Or maybe I am. But it's nothing I can't fix."

Brutal honesty colored her tone, and without thinking, I tucked a fallen lock behind her ear.

"Can I help?"

The question had no target. And no limit. Just an open ended, utterly inappropriate invitation. I expected her to laugh. Because it sounded ridiculous. But her eyes shone with nothing but curiosity.

"How?"

I shrugged. "We can start with the stretches. Don't you need a partner for that?"

She sucked her bottom lip between her teeth, contemplating. And then nodded, but it was more to herself than me. "Okay. Let me get my mat and a pillow."

Tori

I peeked at Logan through a crack in the bedroom door. What was I thinking, agreeing to let him help me stretch? I wasn't exactly nimble. *Shit.* He was taking off his boots. He really wanted to do this.

When he turned my way, I jumped back, wincing when pain shot through my hip.

"You all right?"

Hearing his footfalls, soft against the plush carpet, I limped over to the nightstand to grab a band for my hair.

"Fine," I called, hoping that would be enough to get him to reverse his course.

It wasn't.

"You want to just do it in here?" he asked, and my attention shifted to the bed for a good twenty seconds. Long enough that he nudged the door open. He didn't come in though, just leaned a shoulder against the jamb. "I don't bite. And I won't try anything."

My face went up in flames I could feel to the tips of my ears. "I know that."

I wasn't Logan's type. He preferred them brainless. Or maybe just ... free-spirited? Like Paige. I smiled at that, because she would've been right up Logan's alley. Paige was all about the love, as long as it didn't include any strings.

He took my smile as an invitation and stepped inside. "What are you grinning at?"

I went to work arranging my hair in a top knot. "Paige." His brow twisted, and I cringed. Not everyone was comfortable talking about the dead. When would I learn that?

"What about her?"

His gaze dropped to my legs, and I jerked the hem of my T-shirt down. But there wasn't enough of it to cover the scar on my thigh. "Um ... you would've been her type, that's all."

Easing onto the bench at the foot of the bed, he crossed his legs at the ankles, holding me effortlessly with pale blue eyes. "And what's your type?"

My breath caught in my throat. Rhenn was my type. Since the day I'd met him, there was no other type. Except, now when I saw rich brown hair and eyes the color of the finest chocolate, the combination gutted me.

He cocked his head to the side, concern furrowing his brow. "Is that too personal?"

It was a struggle, but I forced my lips to bend. "No," I lied. "I just ... I don't have a type. Anymore."

Logan nodded, though his eyes weren't in agreement. After a beat of awkward silence, I stopped stalling and tossed a pillow onto the floor next to the rolled up mat.

"You don't have to help me with this," I said, and then as gracefully as possible, I sank to my knees. "I'm used to doing it by myself."

One effortless move, and Logan was on the floor next to me. "No need to go solo when I'm around, princess." He stared at me for a long moment, his lips flatlining. "It was a joke. You don't have to do that thing with your nose."

"What thing?"

A chuckle rumbled low in his chest as he went about unfurling the mat. "You look like you smelled garbage." Sinking back on his haunches, he gave me a tight-lipped smile. "You ready?"

Still reeling from his comment, I crawled over.

Once I was flat on my back, Logan slid his hand to my calf. "What are we doing?"

His tone no longer held a playful quality, and even though I couldn't see him, I heard the seriousness in his voice.

Resisting the urge to call the whole thing off, I willed my muscles to relax. "So, first take my right leg." His hand moved north to my thigh, and I froze. "No ... uh ... my ankle. Put it on your shoulder. And then ..." Before I'd even finished with the instructions, my leg was elevated, and my foot rested an inch from his ear. He tipped forward slightly, and I felt the first tug at the back of my leg. Panicked, my fingers dug into the carpet. "Easy."

It came out in a strangled gasp.

Curving his hand around my calf, Logan inched forward at a snail's pace. "Don't worry. I'll go slow." A few seconds later, and he was above me, tranquil blue eyes roaming over my face. "Is this too much?"

When I shook my head, he bent my knee, his palm sliding over the top of my thigh as he pushed forward.

"Hold it there for a second," I said, breathing through the pain as I willed my hamstrings to give. *Please give.* Something about the heat from Logan's body made it more bearable.

As if he knew exactly what to do next, his hand moved to the inside of my thigh and he exerted a tiny bit of pressure.

"It wasn't the joke," I blurted through a labored breath. "Before, when I made the face? It wasn't the joke."

Slowly, he lowered my leg, releasing his hold when my foot touched the carpet. My lids fluttered closed in relief, only to fly open a second later when his hands came to rest on either side of my shoulders. Even though our bodies weren't touching, he had me trapped, one knee slotted between my legs, and those eyes boring into mine.

"What was it then?"

"It was the name."

He smiled, almost wickedly. "You don't like princess?"

"I don't like Belle." The truth slipped over my tongue, surprising us both. "I know it's not the same. It's just ... I don't know. I'm a little too old to be any kind of Disney character, don't you think?"

His gaze dipped to my mouth, then lower to the column of my throat before making the slow trek back to my face. "I don't know. You look like a princess to me."

Before I could reply, he rose to his knees. Panic seized me when his hand coiled around my left ankle.

"Wait," I croaked, struggling to my elbows.

"What is it? What did I do?"

My injuries were the worst kept secret on the planet. But since I never spoke about them publicly, it was mostly just speculation. Only a select few people knew the truth.

Was I really about to let Logan into the club?

Resting my heel on his thigh, he waited. One beat. Two. Five.

I licked my lips. "I don't have good range of motion in this leg. My hip ... the joint was replaced. I have pins holding it in place. My pelvis was shattered, and the femur was broken as well."

I don't know what I was expecting. Shock. Pity. Revulsion. But Logan simply held my gaze, his palm gliding back and forth over the top of my foot.

"Just tell me what to do, and I'll do it."

Swallowing any lingering embarrassment, I lowered myself back onto the mat. "Same. Just, you know ... less. A lot less."

Clenching my jaw tight when he lifted my leg, I traveled to another place in my head as he went through each maneuver. When sweat soaked through my T-shirt, and I couldn't take a breath without wincing, I knew I'd had enough.

"No more," I managed.

Once both legs were flat on the ground, I melted into the mat, my lids fluttering closed in sweet relief. As the searing pain receded, the tension in my hamstrings and quads faded too.

"Thank you," I whispered hoarsely. To Logan, or the universe, I wasn't sure.

I nearly groaned when he began to knead the muscles in my calves.

"Does that feel good?"

So good. Since I was a pile of goo, I couldn't find the words, so I hummed my approval. His hands traveled north, long fingers digging into the tiny knots. I sucked in a breath when he grazed the skin graft on my upper thigh.

"What?" He froze, alarm etching his tone. "Did I hurt you?"

It was the absence of pain or any sensation that startled me. Meeting his gaze, I forced a smile. "No. It's ..." *Dead*, was the accurate term. "There's no feeling there. I had a skin graft."

Or five.

Expecting Logan to sneak a peek, I stayed perfectly still and prepared myself, but his eyes never left my face.

"I guess we're done with that, then," he finally said, leaving sparks in his wake when he pulled his hands away. "What's next?"

With more agility than I thought possible, I hauled myself to sitting. "Nothing. Thanks. I'm good."

Smiling, he jumped to his feet and then offered his hand. When he pulled me up, I rocked on wobbly legs, and his palms molded to my hips to steady me. Warmth spread to my limbs, and with nowhere to go, the heat settled in my belly. It was an odd feeling. Light, and heavy, and foreign. But good.

After a long moment, his arms dropped to his sides. "You should get some sleep. We're headed out early tomorrow."

I didn't want to think about tomorrow. Not the bus ride or the next venue. Or even what I was having for breakfast.

Following him into the living room, I rubbed my arms to ward off the sudden chill when the air-conditioning met my damp skin. "Thanks again."

"Don't mention it."

He didn't look at me, just grabbed his boots and strode to his room, leaving the door wide open. I thought about closing it, but instead, I wandered over to the small dining room table by the window.

Picking up the plate of half eaten pasta I had left over from dinner, I nearly jumped out of my skin when I turned and found Logan standing behind me.

"Jesus ... you scared—"

"I'm not taking the bus to St. Louis. I'm driving."

Sinking onto the brocade covered chair, I gaped at him. "What?"

"You should come with me." The invitation flew out in a rush. Hasty. Almost like he didn't mean to offer it. Grabbing his guitar, he headed for the door. "I'm outta here at seven on the dot. Be ready if you want a ride, princess."

18

Logan

Two coffees sat on the dresser, the green goddesses on the side of the cups mocking me. Those smug smiles followed me around the suite as I picked my dirty clothes up off the floor and tossed them in the suitcase on the bed. It's like the judgmental bitches could read my thoughts. Like they knew I'd been awake half the night with a hard-on, obsessing about everything from the freckles on Tori's nose—I counted seven—to the way her eyelashes fluttered when she was nervous, to the little humming sound she made when she was happy.

My gaze shifted to the clock. Almost seven.

Maybe Tori wasn't going to take me up on my invitation after all. For all I knew, she was already on the Leveraged tour bus. And that would be the best thing. We could arrive in St. Louis separately and go about the tour in much the way we started. Maybe a little closer. But there would be no more adjoining rooms. No pizza and movies. The more I thought about it, the more I warmed to the idea. It was for the best.

I'd just convinced myself when I felt a little tickle, like fireflies dancing under my skin. And something else.

Relief.

Because I knew Tori was there, hovering behind me by the door, all wrapped up in a cloud of cinnamon and sugar. The girl smelled like a cookie. And all I wanted to do was taste her.

Banishing the wayward thought, I turned to face her, and when I got a load of what she was wearing, my casual smile slid right off my face, along with any lingering hope I had of arriving in St. Louis without a massive case of blue balls.

Tori's cheeks pinked, and she tugged at the bottom of her cut-offs, but it was the red cowboy boots that had my full attention. Maybe you had to be born in Texas to appreciate the visual.

"Nice boots," I managed to say when I finally peeled my tongue off the roof of my mouth. "You ready, princess?"

Her nose barely twitched. And that was a good thing. Because the name suited her, and I wasn't going to stop using it.

She crossed her arms over her chest. "Why are we driving?"

We.

The added bit of assurance chased away any doubts about her intentions. She was going. That is, if I could convince her that my offer had nothing to do with pity. Instinctively, I knew Tori detested the emotion as much as I did. But it's not like I could tell her the truth either—that I wanted to lay her down in my backseat on some deserted road and fuck her stupid.

"You ever seen the world's largest ball of twine?" Tori's brow arched, and she shook her head. "I have. And yeah, it's as boring as it sounds. Anna and Lily mapped out a bunch of stops between here and St. Louis. In case you were wondering, I don't feel like visiting the thimble museum either."

She pondered for a moment, her brow scrunched with worry. "But what happens after that? Once you get as far as St. Louis, you can't just drive back."

I closed the distance between us. "We play it by ear. I was never planning on driving back anyway. That's what transports are for."

Her brow went up again. "You're going to put your car on a transport?"

"It's just a car." Somehow, I said it with a straight face. "Where's your suitcase?"

She mulled over my response for a good ten seconds before she relaxed and said, "It's in my room." When I took a step in that direction, her palm met my chest. "I can get it."

Why was everything with this girl a fight? And more importantly —why was my dick twitching?

She took off, and with a sigh, I followed. Cutting in front of her, I lifted the rollaway off her bed.

As soon as the suitcase was on the floor, she took the handle. "I got it."

This time, I knew she was serious and I figured something out from the exchange. Tori would let me help her but only if she really needed it.

I held up my hands in surrender. "Suit yourself."

On the way back to my room, she snatched a flannel shirt from the chair.

"It's going to be hot as hell today," I said as I scooted around her to zip my suitcase. "I don't think you need layers."

By the time I looked around to see if I'd missed anything, Tori had the shirt tied around her waist. Adjusting the fabric, she took great care to cover the scar on her thigh.

I realized I was invading her private moment when she blinked at me. And once again I found myself behind her wall. She pinned a small smile to her lips that I wanted to kiss right off.

Stalking to the dresser, I grabbed the coffees. "How about I get the suitcase and you take care of the important stuff?"

Slowly, her fingers unfurled from the handle of her rollaway. "Okay," she said quietly as she took the tray.

I wanted to tell her this wasn't a battle. There was no surrender. But I didn't think she'd listen. So I decided I'd just have to show her.

19

ST. LOUIS, MO.

Logan

I could hear it, like tin in my ear. Off key. We'd rolled through the
number three times, but no. It wasn't right. From her spot atop
the high, canvas chair tucked way back from the stage, Tori looked
up. It was brief, just a tilt of her head. But she heard it too.

I held up my hand, and the music stopped. "Something's off. Let's
do it again."

Cameron pulled a face and stalked over, boots echoing in the
large auditorium. "It sounds fine. Maybe your ears are still plugged.
Once we get thirty-eight thousand bodies in this place, you won't
notice one note." He patted my shoulder. "Besides, you need to rest
your voice."

Sean and Christian nodded their agreement. Because they
thought I was sick.

The lie started out innocent enough. I'd sneezed a couple of times
on the day we'd arrived. I knew it was allergies. But once I was in my
suite with Tori in the adjoining room, she'd heard a particularly bad
fit. And then she'd ordered soup. The soup had evolved into a movie.
And then dinner. And then breakfast the next morning, followed by
another movie.

I never got around to telling Tori I wasn't sick. But, in my defense, I didn't tell her that I was either.

She took it upon herself to tell Elise, who in turn told the guys.

"My voice is fine," I assured. "Let's take it from the top."

Ignoring Cameron's eye roll, I took my place at the microphone. In my periphery, I spotted Dylan and the rest of his band walking up the ramp. He broke from the group as soon as he spotted Tori. Before he got to her, she hopped out of her seat and headed for the exit. Persistent fuck that he was, Dylan followed.

"Dude," Cameron called from a few feet away. "You missed your damn cue."

Clearing the non-existent tickle from my throat, I placed the mic in the stand. "I think y'all are right. We're good."

I gave a nod to the guys from Leveraged to let them know we were wrapping up. Beckett set his guitar case down and took off, presumably in search of his lead singer.

Cameron grinned as he pulled the cord from his Fender. "You mind repeating the part where you said you were wrong?"

I gave him a bland stare. "I didn't say I was wrong. I said you were right. There's a difference."

Since I had zero fucks invested in the conversation, I punched him lightly on the arm and headed for the exit. I was seconds from a clean getaway when Christian fell into step beside me.

"Melody flew in this morning," he said. "We're all going to hit the town tonight and hear some blues. Are you in?"

I continued to inch toward freedom. "Nah, man. I'm still feeling a little under the weather."

Since Christian could smell a lie from a hundred yards, I didn't look him in the eye when I offered up the lame refusal. And I might've coughed a little for emphasis.

"You've never turned down a blues bar," he said, concern lacing his tone. "You must really be sick. Maybe you should see a doctor."

Guilt crawled up from my gut. "I'm fine. Just tired. Maybe after I get some rest, I'll catch up with y'all."

Lies. Lies. Lies.

Tori had mentioned something about renting a horror movie. And if she got scared and spontaneously jumped into my lap, all the better.

Christian nodded, looking appeased. "Okay, we're not leaving until nine. Call if you can make it."

"Sure thing." Relieved, I spun around and ran right into Christian's girl. Frying pan. Fire. *Shit.*

"Hey, Melody," I said with a smile.

Ignoring my greeting, she assessed me with narrowed eyes. "Christian says you're sick. What are your symptoms?"

I threw a glare to my buddy. "Just a little tickle in my throat. It's gone now. Almost."

Taking a step back, I shoved my hands into my pockets. Melody was a research scientist, so it wouldn't have surprised me a bit if she whipped out a portable microscope and demanded a blood sample.

The small distance I'd put between us didn't stop the girl from levering up on her toes and pressing the back of her hand to my forehead. "You don't have a fever." She tapped her finger to her lips. "Probably a virus."

"I'm sure it's nothing. I'm going back to the hotel to take some—" I wracked my brain for a name. Any name. "Imodium."

Mel's eyes bulged. "That's for diarrhea. Is your stomach bothering you too? Because that could mean—"

"No." I backed away. "It was. But I'm better now. Really. I'm going to go rest. See y'all."

Mel's mouth dropped open, but I was already gone, heading for the stairs at a good clip. But as soon as I reached the bottom, I got tackled by a Munchkin. Pinning on a smile, I ruffled Willow's auburn curls.

"Hey, Willow-baby."

She lifted her arms. "Pick me up, Unc Lo!"

Since she was the one person I could never blow off, I swung her onto my shoulders. No sooner had she settled than Anna marched up. And for once, the fury in her eyes wasn't aimed at me.

"Willow!" she bellowed. "You get down this instant!"

I tipped back when she reached for the kid. "Whoa. What's up?"

Her emerald gaze shifted a few inches south to meet mine. "You want to know what's up?" She pushed a wayward strand of hair from her face. "I've just spent the last five days in a hotel room with a five-year-old. She doesn't like anything on the room service menu but pancakes."

Sean sidled up, his smile dissolving when Anna threw herself into his arms. Over the top of her head, he looked at me with both brows raised in question.

Since I had no clue what was going on, beyond the breakfast food thing, I shrugged and shook my head.

Easing back, Sean cupped her cheeks. "What is it, baby?" Anna rested her forehead against his chest and mumbled something I couldn't hear. Apparently, he did because he nodded and stroked her hair until she pulled herself together.

"I'm done for the day," he said. "Let's go back to the hotel and take a nap, okay?"

Anna blinked up at him, bottom lip wobbling. "We can't. Willow's too wound up. It's all the damn syrup."

On cue, the child in question did a little bouncy thing, drawing her parents' weary gazes.

In the background, Dylan's voice floated through the air. And if he was here, he wasn't with Tori.

Before I thought better of it, I said, "I'll take care of the kid for a while. We'll go to the park or something."

Sean's brows drew together. "I thought you were sick."

"Nah. I think it's just—"

"I'll get her car seat from the van," Anna interjected. "Stay here. Don't move."

Walking backward, she leveled me with a serious gaze, and when I gave her a little nod, she spun around, dodging roadies and sound techs on her way to the parking lot.

Amused, I glanced over at my best friend. "For someone who claims to be exhausted, she sure can run fast."

He raked a hand through his long hair. "We're still getting used to road life." He smiled up at his daughter, who now had me in a mini-headlock. "Willow-baby has more energy than usual."

"She'll settle down." I reached around and pulled the monkey off my back.

When she started running circles around us, Sean and I looked at each other and, in silent agreement, we each took one of Willow's hands. And then we strolled toward the parking lot, lifting Willow off the ground every few seconds.

We made it to the van and found Anna waiting at the curb. "All set?" I asked.

Dropping her gaze to the car seat with the portable nebulizer strapped to the side, she chewed her lip, a myriad of emotions playing across her face. And I got it. Willow was severely asthmatic. But it had been almost a year since she'd had a bad attack.

Dipping my head to catch Anna's gaze, I said, "There's a park with a zoo less than five miles from the hotel. Five miles. Nothing is going to happen. Now, give me an inhaler so I can go."

Willow was wearing one of the cylinders around her neck, but her mother always had a spare. Or twenty.

"Are you sure?" Anna asked as she turned over the medicine. "I mean ... I don't know ... what if ..."

Sean hovered behind her, blue eyes darting between his girl and me, and then finally landing on Willow.

"I'm positive," I said with enough conviction to chase some of the clouds from Anna's eyes.

After mulling it over, Anna took a deep breath and knelt in front of her daughter to say goodbye.

Five minutes later, with Willow on my hip and her car seat dangling from my fingers, I headed across the blacktop to my car. "You want to go to the zoo, Willow-baby?"

She snaked an arm around my neck. "Depends. Do they have beaws?"

I laughed. "I'm sure they do."

With all my attention on the kid, I didn't notice Tori propped against the passenger door of my Mustang until we were twenty feet away.

"Hey," I said, setting Willow on her feet.

She turned to me with a smile that evaporated when she saw the kid peeking from behind my legs. "Oh ... Hi ..."

I fished the keys from my pocket. "Where did you get off to?"

"I ... um ... I had to make some calls."

When I set the car seat down, Tori took a step back like the contraption had teeth. I'd never seen her so uncomfortable. Weird. But then, some people didn't like kids.

The notion unsettled me since Willow wasn't just any kid.

"Do you need a ride?"

Tori shook her head, fingers digging into her thighs. "No ... no. I can wait for the van."

"Why?" I asked slowly, then followed her gaze to Willow. "She doesn't bite."

The she in question scooted in front of me. "Hi. I'm Wiwwo."

It took all of two seconds for Tori's sun bright smile to appear. "Hi Willow. I'm Victoria." Her eyes darted to mine, a nervous laugh bubbling from her lips. "I don't know where that came from. Nobody calls me that but my family."

Victoria.

I rolled the name around in my head. It suited her. Like the smile and the blush.

"I like it," I said. "Can you watch her while I fix up the car seat?"

Tori surprised me by easing onto the pavement. A few minutes later when I backed out of the car, Willow was on Tori's lap, their heads together.

Tori peered up at me and smiled, and it warmed me all over.

Scooping Willow up with one arm, I offered Tori my free hand. "Ready?"

She popped to her feet with surprising ease. I helped her with the stretches every night. Maybe they were working.

Once we were all strapped in, I turned to Tori. "How's your hip, princess?" My tone was a little gruff. But I wanted an honest answer.

She didn't notice, her attention on Willow in the backseat. "Fine."

"No pain?" I waited a beat, or five, but got nothing. So I placed my index finger under her chin and coaxed her gaze to mine. "Are you in pain?"

Irritation flashed across her features. "I said: I'm fine."

"Good." I shoved my keys in the ignition. "Then you won't mind if we make a little stop at the zoo."

20

Tori

I woke with a start, a heavy weight on my chest. Willow. I blinked down at her, burrowed to my side, her small fist coiled in the fabric of my T-shirt. She was so small. A perfect little human.

Burying my nose in her soft auburn curls, I breathed her in. Sunshine and cotton candy lingered in her hair.

"I'll take her," Logan said gruffly.

"N-no," I managed, but he lifted her off me anyway. Rubbing the spot on my chest where her head had been, I watched through heavy lids as he carried her across the room.

When he disappeared into his suite, I willed my legs to work so I could follow him. But no. So I closed my eyes and let my head fall forward. Minutes later, when I felt the couch dip, I did my best to push myself to sitting. But I couldn't quite manage, so I ended up lopsided.

"What time is it?" I rasped.

Resting his elbows on his knees, Logan looked down at his feet. "Nine."

Nine ...

The fog lifted a little. Not much. But enough to push a heavy hand through my hair. "Sorry." I cleared my throat. "I ... uh ... guess I fell asleep."

Logan searched my face with narrowed eyes. "You weren't asleep. You were *passed out.*"

He spit the words like an accusation. And since they were true, I didn't respond. Which only seemed to agitate him more.

Making a clumsy grab for the water on the coffee table, I misjudged the distance, and decided the effort was too much, so I slumped back against the pillows.

Logan snatched the bottle from the table and pressed it into my hand. "You want to tell me what the fuck happened?"

I didn't know. Couldn't remember a thing after we'd left the elephant exhibit. I was having such a good time. And I just wanted it to last. But nothing ever lasts.

I took a sip of water. "I took a pill. A pain pill."

Admitting it made me feel weak. But I'd told Logan more about my injuries than anyone but my closest friends. What was one more thing?

When he didn't respond for a long moment, I lifted my gaze. Whatever I expected to find on Logan's face—sympathy, pity, understanding—it wasn't there.

He was mad.

Why was he mad?

"You have a prescription?"

The suspicion in his tone conspired with the chemicals in my brain, loosening my tongue just enough to let it fly. All the tiny truths I hid in dark corners and buried in deep holes.

"I have five. Muscle relaxers too. But I don't take any of them. Since they make me ..." I looked down at my legs, which I could see but not feel. "Like this. But I do take a low dose hormone to keep my one good ovary from shutting down." I laughed, and it was so brittle, I thought it might slice my tongue. "But it won't do any good. I'll never have a baby."

Shifting my gaze to the open door, I could just make out the small lump on Logan's bed. My hand crept up, and again I rubbed the spot where Willow's head had been.

This time when our gazes collided, Logan looked horrified. And I wondered what he saw. But really, I didn't want to know.

"You can go now," I said and, letting gravity work its magic, I slumped against the cushions and closed my eyes.

A minute or an hour later, the cushion dipped again. Something warm curved around my thighs, and when my lids fluttered open to investigate, Logan was on his knees in front of me.

"I'm sorry," he said, bowing his head. "I'm so sorry."

I made a clumsy attempt to push him away. Because I didn't want his sorrow. I had enough of my own.

"Don't ... don't feel sorry for me."

He caught my wrists. "*I don't.* That's not what I meant. Will you let me explain?"

I stopped fighting. "Go ahead."

Even with the medication dulling my senses, I felt his thumbs sweeping slow circles over my skin.

Looking down to where we were joined, he sighed. "My sister's an addict. You probably already know that. When I saw you like that, it reminded me of her ... before she got help."

He looked up with earnest blue eyes, ready to take all the blame. But even with the way he reacted, part of it was my fault. "I sh-should've told you about the pill ... I don't ... I don't have any toler-ance because I don't take them as prescribed."

Confusion lined his brow. "Why?"

A smile curved my lips. At least it felt like a smile. "There's this feeling. This moment that ... uh ... you're not here."

Turning around, he rested his shoulders against the edge of the couch and his head on my knee. "So that's a bad thing?" he asked. "That feeling?"

Maybe without the pill, I'd never tell him. Or maybe I just wanted someone to know, finally.

"No. But it's tempting. Or it used to be. So I stopped taking them regular ... regularly."

He looped an arm around my calf. "What was tempting?"

123

He shifted slightly to see my face. And when our eyes met, I felt the tug as he coaxed the word to my lips. "Oblivion."

21

Logan

The friend zone was an actual place. I knew it, because I lived there. With Tori in an adjacent room.

Four weeks into the tour and we had our routine down pat. She worked from the suite while I did band shit during the day. The problem was, the nature of festival tours dictated that I only had actual commitments three days a week. The other four days I was on my own.

Normally, that meant hanging with my boys, partying, and as much pussy as I could fuck. But there was nothing normal about my life since Tori crashed into it.

I spent all my free time with her. We ate our meals together in the suite. Watched movies. Worked on songs. And every night, I took her through her stretching routine. I'd added a back massage. For therapeutic reasons, of course. It had nothing to do with the noises she made when I rubbed the knots out of her muscles. Or the way her skin warmed me through the thin T-shirts she insisted on wearing, even though I'd explained the medicinal benefits of massage oil applied directly to the dermis. I thought using the proper terminology might get Tori on board with the whole shirtless plan.

125

It didn't.

And that was probably for the best. It's not like I needed the extra stimulation. As it was, whenever we finished our sessions, I ended up in the shower, fucking my fist with thoughts of her in my head. And like a damned addict, as soon as I shot my release, I vowed to put a stop to it.

But then the next morning, I'd find Tori with her mussed up hair, sitting in front of the window overlooking whatever city we happened to be in, and I'd cave.

Because, truth was, I liked having her around. *Liked*. Friends. Friend zone. *Fuck*.

This week we were in Chicago. After two back-to-back record-breaking shows, things were heating up outside our tour bubble, which existed on an alternate plane. It's like the real world only pushed in the two days prior to our gigs when we did press events.

I was eating breakfast downstairs in the private dining room the hotel had set up for the bands when Elise shoved a paper into my hands.

"There's been some changes to the schedule," she said, distracted.

After giving the document a dismissive glance, I returned my attention to my breakfast. "I'm a little busy." I spooned some brown sugar onto my oatmeal. "Just tell me where I need to be."

Elise's lip pulled back into something resembling a sneer. *Entitled douchebag*, may as well have been flashing on her forehead. As I'd predicted, she'd turned into a decent coordinator. Tough. Organized. And she didn't take shit from anyone.

When it was obvious I wasn't going to budge, she chuffed out a breath and flipped through her paperwork.

"Radio interview at WKRV," she said. "The van is picking y'all up in front in a half hour. Then cocktails and a light dinner with the VIPs that bought the platinum circle tickets. That's right here, in the private dining room, at five."

The platinum circle VIPs spent three grand a pop on their tickets. In addition to the show, they got the privilege of joining one of the bands for cocktails or a meal. It was a huge publicity opportunity.

Without waiting for an acknowledgement, Elise spun on her heel and headed for the buffet line. I stared at the paper for a couple of minutes and then I followed.

"I thought Leveraged was doing the honors with the VIPs?"

Elise perused the items at the omelet station. "Not this time. Tori changed it."

While she placed her order with the chef, I glanced around the room, and my gaze collided with Dylan's. Seated at a back table, deep in conversation with Beckett, a ghost of a smile curved his lips. It wasn't warm. Or inviting. Still, I mumbled a goodbye to Elise and wandered over.

Beckett was out of his chair before I got there, headed for the door. I expected Dylan to follow, but he just crossed his arms over his chest like he was waiting for me.

"Hey, man," I said, dropping into the seat across from him. "Haven't seen you much lately."

He poked his tongue in his cheek, as if he were amused. "I've been around."

Stretching my legs, I slung an arm over the back of my chair. "Mighty kind of y'all to let us take over the VIP thing tonight."

Dylan's lips parted, but then his gaze shifted over my shoulder. There was no mistaking the warmth in his smile or who it was for. When I glanced behind me to confirm, Tori was there, frozen in her spot a few feet from the table.

"Hey, Lo," she said before slowly swinging her attention to Dylan. "You ready?"

Dylan was already on his feet, smiling down at me. "Have fun with the VIPs."

The knot in my throat precluded anything but a nod. I couldn't even return Tori's wave as the asshole ushered her to the door.

Sinking back in the chair, I pulled the phone out of my pocket when I felt the vibration against my leg.

The Metro Music logo flashed on the screen. Mac. Or maybe it was a member of his team. My thumb shifted from the red button to the green.

"Hello."

A rumbling laugh set my teeth on edge. "Logan ... how's the windy city treating you?"

I twisted toward the door where Tori and Dylan had disappeared. "Awesome. What do you want, Mac?"

"I want to give you a chance to reconsider my offer. Before it's too late."

"I'm on tour, in case you haven't heard. And besides, I'm not leaving my band. I already told you that."

He clucked his tongue, and I could picture his beady, black eyes. "There's always another band. It's you that's not replaceable."

"Nice try, but I ain't interested." From across the room, I made eye contact with Elise. She tapped her wrist, and I hauled to my feet. "I better not find out it's you planting shit in the press."

Despite the record breaking crowds, Mac's lawsuit cast a dark shadow over the tour. We were constantly dodging questions from the media about the bogus stories his team planted.

"You should be thanking me. There's no such thing as bad publicity."

Jaw torqued tight, I ducked around a few clusters of people in the lobby. Hot air rolled over me as I passed through the automatic doors and into the summer morning.

"I gotta go."

Ending the call before he could reply, I pocketed my phone.

Sean gave me the side-eye as I slid into the seat beside him.

"You're looking rough," he noted.

"I need to get laid." Sean made a big production of putting a couple of extra feet between us. I laughed. "You're pretty and all, but I wouldn't want to ruin our lifelong friendship. You know I never stick around after I get it in."

The truth spilled out unbidden, and Sean made a face, either from the bad joke or the truth behind it.

Turning my attention to the window so he wouldn't see my smile fade, I said, "Lucky for me we're having supper with a room full of women that I'll never have to see again."

Tori

Trapped between Dylan and Beckett on the couch in Dylan's suite, I stared at the screen on my laptop while Trevor explained the latest avalanche of legal paperwork from Metro.

In the corner of the screen, Taryn alternated between chewing her fingernails and batting Chase's hand away when he tried to stop her.

When Trevor finished spinning his tale of doom, he roughed a hand through his hair and said, "Given what just came to light, it might be time to start looking at settlement options."

Dylan, Chase, and Beckett all spoke at once while Taryn just stared into the camera. At me. It was my fight. I always knew it. But Mac had just brought it to my door.

"Hold on," I said, my voice razor thin and barely audible over the chaos. But Taryn heard it.

"Everyone, shut up!" she screeched, and it was like someone pressed the mute button. "Belle, what did you want to say?"

I cleared my throat, but the tears were still there. When I tried again, Dylan's hand found mine and Beckett wrapped an arm around my shoulder. But they couldn't protect me from this.

"Let me understand," I began in a shaky voice. "The masters to the unfinished Damaged album are Metro's property? And Mac can do what he wants with them?"

Trevor shook his head. "The masters are in Mac's possession. He's asserting that they're his. That Metro holds the distribution rights. That doesn't mean it's true."

"But they're Rhenn's songs," Dylan growled.

"Technically, they belong to the group," Trevor responded calmly. "At least that's how I'm going to spin it."

"Spin?" Taryn interjected, indignant. "They *do* belong to the group. And therefore, they belong to Tori."

"Well according to this," Trevor held up a piece of paper. "Miles Cooper has standing as well. Are you aware of what this is, Tori?"

I recognized the document I'd signed all those years ago giving Miles a stake in the Damaged catalogue. "Yes."

Trevor sighed. "Then Metro's right, Miles has a claim."

Taryn started to speak, but Dylan beat her to the punch. "What does Miles need to do to ... I don't know ..."

When he struggled to find the words, Trevor took the reins again.

"He can sign a document relinquishing his rights. That's not a problem. But Mac is going to offer him a shit ton of money to make sure he doesn't. I'll set up a meeting with him and find out where he stands."

Dylan and Beckett looked at each other, and as if by some silent agreement, Beckett said, "Don't do that. We're his friends. We'll talk to him. "

Once, we were. But that was before. The only friends Miles had now were his pills and his booze.

Your fault, the voice in my head admonished. And as always, I listened. Because it was true.

Shifting my attention to Trevor, I asked, "How long until we have to file an answer?"

"A month from Friday," he replied, tossing his pen on his desk. "We still have some time."

"All right," I said, slumping back in my chair. "I don't want to talk settlement yet. Let Dylan and Beckett talk to Miles. I'll fly home before we head to Europe, and we'll discuss it more then."

Trevor raised a brow. "You're still going to Europe?"

Of course I knew what that look was about. But I hadn't even spoken to Logan about the online classes or modifying his plea agreement.

I shrugged noncommittally. "Yeah."

Dylan's heavy gaze swung my way, and Taryn didn't miss the exchange either.

Before they started up with the questions, I sat up straight and addressed my attorney. "Is there anything else? Because I've really got to get back to work."

22

Logan

Never.

Not in all my twenty-eight years had I ever turned down a blow job. Admitting that probably made me a dick. But being a dick was kind of a given. Now I had bigger things to worry about.

Like, "*Will this become a pattern?*" or "*What the actual fuck is wrong with me?*" or "*Please don't step on the hem of my dress,*" because, apparently, I'd turned into a woman.

That probably happened about the time I'd refused the blow job from the willing blonde with the nice rack. And the pillow soft lips. At least they looked soft. I hadn't actually kissed her.

And why was that exactly?

Because you're a woman.

Since the whole exchange sounded logical in my inebriated condition, I started thinking about lesbians. Because, if I were a woman, I'd most definitely be a lesbian.

The random thoughts continued to ping around in my brain as I stumbled toward my suite.

Tori's body guard du jour cocked his head when he saw me coming.

What the hell was his name? Didn't matter.

"S-stand down a-asshole. D-don't make me hurt you," I slurred, glaring at him with narrowed eyes. "D-o you w-want me to hurt you?"

It was my standard phrase. And it always, *always,* worked. I was a scary guy. *Scary.* Only, he didn't seem scared. He just stood there, flicking his toothpick from one side of his mouth to the other. And then he laughed.

"Yeah, okay. Don't hurt me."

Taking a step, I tripped over my own feet, and bounced off the wall.

He rushed forward. "Do you need some help?"

"N-no, but you will." I waved my key at him, but it slipped out of my hand and fell onto the floor. It seemed like a good idea to reach down and pick it up. Until the ground came up and met the side of my face. "The f-fuck?"

The bodyguard lifted me off the ground by my collar. "Up you go."

Out of the corner of my eye, the door swung open.

Who the fuck is in my room?

But it wasn't my door. It was Toris'. Plural. Because there were two of her.

They both stepped into the hallway. "What the hell is going on?"

I pointed at the bodyguard because, maybe she was talking to him.

She wasn't.

"Jesus, you drunk-ass," she growled. The bodyguard offered to help, but Tori slipped her arm around my shoulder, muttering a refusal.

"I-I can walk, princess," I said as she dragged me through the door.

"Shut up," she hissed, maneuvering me to the couch.

I really thought I was standing on my own until Tori wiggled free and I fell onto the cushions like a sack of potatoes.

She backed up to survey me, crossing her arms over her chest. "Do you have any idea what time it is?"

As she looked me over, I did my best to puff out my chest. *That's right, princess, this is the real me. I party All. Night. Long. And drink. And turn down blow jobs.*

Wait ...

Scratching my head, I tried to rework my thoughts into something clever I could force past my thick tongue.

Exasperated, Tori tipped forward. "Eight thirty! Why the hell are you so fucked-up at eight thirty at night?"

Surely, she meant morning? I'd been out forever. It seemed like forever. Maybe not forever. But a long damn time. I shifted my gaze to the window. It was dark.

I was still trying to figure it all out when Tori spun on her heel and stalked toward the television. No, the mini-bar.

"I'll t-take a Jack," I said, tilting my head so I could get a better look at her ass when she bent over. "No Coke."

When the room started to spin, I closed my eyes.

"Drink this," I heard Tori say, a second before she pressed something plastic into my hand.

I cracked open one heavy lid. And she was there, kneeling in front of me.

Somewhat dismayed when my first thought glided right past blow jobs, *again,* I reached out and touched her hair. "F-fuck. You're ..."

Some of the irritation fled from her gaze, and she dipped her chin. "I'm what?" Her voice was soft. Hesitant.

She was so many things. But as I took her in, only one word pushed its way past all the sludge in my head. "Beautiful." I ran my finger over her jaw and down to the hollow of her neck. To the scar. And that was beautiful too. "And you smell like cookies."

She laughed. It was light, like soft rain against the glass. "Cookies?"

"S-snickerdoodles."

My heavy lids fluttered closed. But I knew she was still there. I could feel her. And smell her. And if I tried real hard, I could almost taste the sugar on my tongue.

23

Tori

There's a place between asleep and awake when your brain is still lost in a dream, but yet, you know you're conscious. That's where Rhenn lived. He owned that space in my head. That little sliver when the day was new—it belonged to him. I could always feel him in the foggy mist, like a ghost on my skin.

Only, today, when I drifted up from the deep water, the soft fingertips gliding over my calf ... they weren't his.

I knew it, even before I opened my eyes.

It was Logan, sprawled out on the other side of the couch, in the same spot where he'd passed out. Only now he was awake, staring out the window, one arm tucked behind his head.

My gaze shifted to his other hand, stroking my leg with long fingers.

I watched him for a good two minutes, maybe more. The man was gorgeous. He shone like the moon. A light in all the darkness that swirled around him. And there *was* darkness. But it didn't consume him. Just danced along the edges, framing him in shadow.

His gaze jerked to mine when I retracted my foot. We stared at each other for a long moment.

Then he cleared his throat. "Morning, Victoria."

I tried to muster up some anger. It should've been easy, considering his behavior last night.

And why was I surprised?

Obviously, he was feeling better. Whatever virus had lingered in his system for the last few weeks was gone. So naturally, he was back to his old ways. Getting drunk. Staying out all night. Or until eight thirty. I was too tired to laugh at that.

Instead, I propped up on one elbow and ran a hand through my messy hair, looking anywhere but at him. "Morning."

With the way I'd slept, wedged against the back of the sofa with Logan's leg pressed against mine, I should've been stiff. But I wasn't. Just a little sore from the time I'd spent in the gym.

I snuck down there every day when Logan was out doing press. I couldn't run. Maybe I'd never run again. But the elliptical made it feel like I was running. Weightless.

Logan's feet hit the ground with a soft thud.

"Hangover?" I asked, pushing upright.

"Not bad. I wasn't that drunk."

Snickering, I gingerly climbed off the couch. "Okay."

"I wasn't," he insisted. "I remember everything."

His tone held a trace of anger, so I looked down at him, confused.

Was he mad because he said I was beautiful?

Probably.

Holding my gaze, he sank against the cushions, folding his arms over his chest. "How was your date?"

Jesus, he was still drunk.

I tried for an indulgent smile, but it froze under his icy glare, shattering into pieces. "I didn't have a date. I don't know what you're talking about."

"Lunch, whatever. With your *buddy*, Dylan."

There was no love lost between Dylan and Logan, and I got that. Band rivalries were real. And to be expected with someone who had an ego the size of Logan's.

Squaring my shoulders, I placed a hand on my hip. "We had some business to take care of. But I changed the schedule so that Caged could take over the VIP lunch with the platinum circle ticket holders."

I didn't know what prompted me to add that last part. And I didn't like the way it sounded. Revenged Theory or Drafthouse should've been tapped to fill in for Leveraged. But I felt a little bad because Caged never got any stage time after dark.

I assumed the jackass in front of me would be grateful. Or gracious at least. But I saw none of that. Just a smirk ticking up one corner of his lips.

"What did Dylan eat for lunch?" Logan's gaze roamed the length of me before settling on my face. "Cookies?"

You smell like cookies.

My mouth dropped open when I realized what he was implying. "We didn't eat lunch."

He pushed to his feet, and I had to lift my gaze to meet his eyes.

"Whatever. You don't have to send me on an errand when y'all want to meet. Feel free to rattle the walls anytime you want."

I was too stunned to reply, which only added to his mounting frustration. After a moment, his face lost all expression.

"I've got a show this afternoon," he said evenly. "I'm going to go get ready."

He stalked to his room without another word, leaving the door open only a crack.

I waited until I heard the water running to pull out my phone. My finger hovered between the phone and FaceTime icons beneath Taryn's picture, and before I could think better of it, I hit the latter.

"Belle!" My best friend's smile was electric, but it was the window behind her that had my full attention. Clouds and blue sky and buildings I could draw from memory.

Home.

Swallowing past the pebble in my throat, I curled onto the sofa. "Hey, T-Rex."

We talked about everything but business for the better part of an hour, and only after the front door rattled in the adjacent suite did I say my goodbyes.

Hauling my backpack into my lap, I felt around for the papers Trevor had given me. The documents were self-explanatory, but still, I jotted down a quick message on one of the hotel notepads.

Logan,

Trevor says if you complete the online courses and fill out the attached documents, the judge will look into modifying your plea agreement. If it all goes according to plan, my name can be lifted from the bond and you can continue the tour without a chaperone.

Biting the cap on the pen, I deliberated on what else to say. *Thank you, best wishes,* or *go fuck yourself* all sprung to mind, but I settled on a loopy *V.*

And then I tiptoed to Logan's room and laid the documents on his pillow where he'd be sure to see them whenever he decided to come back.

24

Logan

A current of anger ran the length of my body as I jabbed at the keys on my phone. I never cursed being born. And I didn't have the destructive kind of depression that led to self-harm. I tended to turn rage inside out. I ranted. Raved. Broke things.

Like this motherfucking phone.

Ready to hurl the piece of shit at the nearest wall, I took aim, but my rational side seized control at the last second.

Break the phone, and then what are you gonna do, genius?

I let my head fall forward at the same time my arm dropped limply to my side. My sour stomach and lingering hangover precluded any serious drinking, but one shot would make it easier to unscramble the knots in my parietal lobe. And yeah, irony was a fucking whore. Because at some point I'd been forced to commit to memory the exact spot in my dysfunctional brain responsible for unlocking the mysteries of the written word. But I couldn't actually read.

Smiling bitterly, I unscrewed the cap on the mini bottle of Jack. "To Irony." I toasted the air in my empty suite. "You're one sadistic bitch. Say hi to your sister for me."

That would be Fate.

Because, the two had to be in cahoots. Fate put Victoria in my path. And now the girl was under my skin. Which was the reason I was sitting in a dark room, trying to decipher the papers she'd left on my fucking pillow.

There was a note on top as well, but fuck that—it was in cursive. However, I did fold up the scrap of paper and put it in my wallet for some unknown reason.

Rolling my head from side to side, I continued the painstaking process of typing the letters from the document into the text to talk app on my phone.

What else did I have to do?

I'd rushed back to the hotel after the show without bothering with the meet and greet. So there wasn't even anyone here to party with.

My head snapped up when I heard the door *whoosh* closed in Tori's room.

Be cool.

Yeah, no.

Cool went right out the window when her voice drifted to my ears. She was singing. And not just any song. The tune we'd been working on.

I jumped to my feet, only to skid to a stop at the door. It was open, just a crack. But if I knocked she might not answer. And if I barged in she might be naked.

No ... she was never naked.

Tori changed in her bathroom, and on the few occasions I'd been around, she locked the door behind her. Girl was shy. And why did that get me hard?

Shoving my depravity aside, I knocked as I entered, figuring that was the safest bet.

Tori spun around, and her water bottle landed on the floor. Clear liquid spread at her feet, soaking into the plush carpet.

I blinked at her.

Rosy cheeks. Wild hair falling out of her ponytail in damp

strands. Dewy skin. And the clothes—tight little shorts and an over-sized T-shirt.

The girl looked like she just rolled out of someone's bed, and Dylan wasn't anywhere in sight. Along with anyone else she knew. *Interesting.* But only in the way that made my blood boil and my fists clench.

I leaned a hip against the doorframe. "Where you been?"

Flushing a brighter shade of pink, she eased into a crouch to pick up what was left of her water. "Nowhere."

Cocking my head, I closed the gap between us. "Well, you weren't here. So you had to be somewhere."

She glared up at me through impossibly long lashes. "Obviously."

"So what's the big secret?"

Shaking her head, she wobbled to her feet, and out of habit, my hand darted out, curving around her wrist so she wouldn't fall. She was hot. And not in the way that made my balls ache. Her skin was warm.

With my free hand, I tucked a damp curl behind her ear. "You're flushed, Victoria. Wanna tell me what you've been doing?"

"I was at the gym." Two beats and those eyes met mine. "Don't look at me like that, Logan. I used to run five miles a day. I hiked and cliff dived, and I even bungee jumped once on my twenty-first birth-day. And I would've done it again, but, you know ..."

All that righteous indignation faded, and I saw her. The real Tori. Sad and strong, and beautifully broken. But it had nothing to do with her body.

Since I wasn't the right guy to fix her, I dropped her hand. "Time to stretch, princess."

"Yeah I was about to do that. You should go."

She averted her eyes as she unfurled the mat, and that's how I knew she didn't want me to leave.

Her gaze snapped to mine when I knelt down beside her. "I will. After I help you stretch."

She pondered for only a moment before taking her place on the mat. We went through the usual routine, until I got to the butterfly stretch. With her legs spread, so inviting, I moved closer until I was between her thighs and our faces were inches apart.

Bracing one hand by her head, I moved the other to the outside of her leg. "How does that feel?"

My question had nothing to do with stretching, and everything to do with my fingers digging into her flesh as I molded her thigh to my ribs.

Her eyes rolled back on a sigh. Taking that breath and the gasp that followed, my lips ghosted hers.

"How about this? You like this?"

Whatever self-control I had flew right out the window when she squeezed her legs together, trapping me against her warmth. My mouth crashed into hers, my tongue dipping inside. And I was right. She tasted like sugar and cinnamon and vanilla and ... Victoria.

The combination made me hard in all the right places and so fucking weak I couldn't hold myself up.

Her eyes popped open when I pulled away. "Wha ...?"

Sinking back onto my heels, I crossed my arms over my chest. "You want to tell me about your note?"

All those endorphins flooding my brain, my cock hard enough to cut diamonds, and *that's* what I wanted to know? Not how hard she wanted me to fuck her. Or which position she'd prefer when I ate her sweet pussy.

Yeah, this wasn't good.

Her brows drew together over lust-filled eyes. "I ... uh ..."

Suddenly the idea of facing her while she explained was too much. So I patted the outside of her thigh.

"Roll over. Your hamstrings are tight. You can tell me while I get the knots out of your back."

Nodding, she pushed herself up and then turned around. But at the last minute, she tugged her T-shirt off.

I didn't move, didn't breathe, my gaze fixed on the ink shading her skin. Dragon wings with sad eyes in the center spanned the entire width of her back. Between the wings sat a single letter, an *R* in bold font, with a crown on top. The tattoo had no color, except for some opaque strands weaved into the design here and there.

Mesmerized, I brushed a finger over one luminescent thread and froze. It wasn't ink, but a tiny scar. There were dozens of them. A web of pain she'd turned into art.

"I was in one of the bunks in the back when the truck hit the bus," Tori said after a long moment. "The impact knocked me through the window. Through the glass."

She glanced over her shoulder, a raven curl falling over her eyes. The same eyes from the portrait on her back

"It could've been worse, I guess," she said, smiling sadly.

My hand curved around her hip, and she flinched. "How?"

Turning back to the wall, she whispered, "I could've been facing the window."

Gazing over all the tiny threads, my stomach twisted. Every instinct told me I wasn't worthy of her trust. That I should leave. I leaned in and pressed a kiss to her shoulder.

It was meant to be a goodbye. Because I knew I'd probably fuck everything up in the end. But I couldn't stop, and my lips moved north along the soft skin of her neck.

"You're beautiful, Victoria." I ran my nose along the shell of her ear. "All of you."

It wasn't some bullshit line to get into her pants. The truth was, I hadn't needed to use a line on a woman in years. And even if I were inclined to pull one out of the archives, it would never fly with Tori.

She let out a sigh, melting against me. And though I wanted to fuck her more than my next breath, to show her how beautiful she was and look into her eyes when she came undone so she'd know it was true, I simply slid my arm around her waist and held her.

Her hand covered mine. And when her fingertips brushed lightly over my knuckles, we took our first shaky steps out of the friend zone.

25

NASHVILLE, TN.

Tori

Tennessee Welcomes You.

The sign flew by, blurred by the fine sheen of mist coating the windshield. Shifting in my seat, I tipped my head back to peek at the speedometer. A hair over ninety. And climbing. Just like my pulse.

"Can you slow down a little?"

My voice was steady. I heard it above the roar of blood pounding between my ears. But Logan didn't acknowledge me. He hadn't said a word since we'd left Chicago five hours ago. Not about last night's kiss. Or my awkward game of show and tell. Not about the anger management classes. Or his plea agreement.

It was like he was going out of his way to ignore me.

Panic stole my breath when he gunned the engine, sliding over the broken yellow line to pass a slow-moving truck. Tears blurred my eyes out of nowhere, and my fingernails dug into my legs with enough pressure to leave half-moon indents on my skin.

"Pull over!" I choked when we were safely back in our lane. "Now!"

As if he just realized I was there, Logan whipped his gaze in my direction. His brows drew together over confused blue eyes, and that hurt me even more. Only I knew I didn't look hurt. It was fear he saw.

And I *was* afraid.

But it had little to do with the road or the droplets of rain spattering the windshield.

I was afraid of Logan. Terrified of the way he pulled confessions from me like he tugged the threads on his frayed jeans. Effortlessly. And how he made my stomach flutter. But mostly, I was scared that he wasn't feeling it too.

His eyes darted back to the road a second before he found his voice. "What is it? What—"

"Pull over!"

I hated the panic lacing my tone. And the way the car felt too small. Or maybe it was my stupid emotions, running wild and taking up all the space.

He looked around frantically, but since I chose to have my breakdown in the middle of nowhere on a two-lane road with no shoulder, he couldn't comply with my wishes immediately.

What was it about this guy that brought out the crazy? It wasn't my usual brand, which I covered with a layer of bitchiness. This was the messy kind. The kind that builds and builds until it explodes all over your leather upholstery.

And just to make things interesting, the spitting rain turned to a steady drizzle.

Burying my head in my hands, I fought the torrent of tears.
Breathe.

A minute later the car coasted to a stop.

"Victoria."

Logan's voice was calm, eerily so, but I was long past consoling. I clawed at the door, and when it opened, I tumbled out onto the dirt. Scratch that—the mud. Because of course it would be mud. Dirt you could wipe away. But mud clung to your skin and your hair and your soul.

When I heard his car door slam, I hauled to my feet, my cowboy boots sliding on the silt. And I ran. Which was the stupidest thing I could've done. Not only was my gait unsteady, but I had nowhere to go.

He'd parked on a small patch of ground in front of a gate that lead to a pasture where cows and sheep and horses grazed twenty yards away. Except for one baby cow who'd found her way to the fence.

"Victoria ... stop!" Logan's hand coiled around my wrist just as I sank to my knees in the grass. Crouching next to me when I reached through the barbed wire to pet the calf, he said, "She's gonna bite you."

"No, she won't." My fingers slid over her pink nose. "See?"

When I turned to Logan with a smile, he wasn't looking at the calf. All of his focus was on me.

"I'm sorry," he said. "I wasn't ... I didn't think ..."

Guilt pooled in my belly since only a fraction of all this had to do with his driving.

My attention returned to the calf. "S'okay."

After a moment, he sighed and dropped to his butt in the mud. Surprise parted my lips. Because he had to be as crazy as I was. Crazier.

"No, it's not okay," he said, pushing wet strands of blond hair out of his face. "I feel like I'm always apologizing to you. Why is that, princess?"

I side-eyed him as I scratched behind the calf's ear. She didn't move, as if she were as interested in whatever he was about to say as I was. Only he didn't speak.

When he hung his head, it occurred to me that Logan wasn't the jackass everyone made him out to be. Or else why would he be sitting out here in the rain, struggling to find the words to explain why he'd tripped over some imaginary line?

Any other woman would've taken the fun he had to offer instead of trying to forge some deep connection. There were no more breath-less kisses after my confession. He'd just held me like any good friend would.

"You don't need to apologize, Logan. Just take the anger management classes and the test. I was planning on flying back to Austin in a couple weeks anyway."

Or a month. But that didn't matter. Whenever he finished the classes, I'd be gone.

Logan's head snapped up. "What are you talking about?"

"Just some shit Mac is throwing at me. I've got to deal with it."

"In Austin?" I nodded, and the furrow on his brow deepened. "How long will you be gone?"

I went back to petting Bessie. She was on the ground now, legs tucked under her body.

"Well, I mean, after you take your classes, chances are I won't need to be here." Banishing the frown tugging the corners of my lips, I swallowed hard. "I know the only reason you drove to begin with is because of me. I don't blame you for being frustrated."

A dry chuckle rumbled low in his chest, and when I looked over, his face was tilted to the sky.

"*Fuck!*" he growled into the air, and I jerked. Shaking his head, he pressed his lips together. "I'm sorry. I'm not mad. I'm just …" His eyes found mine, pale blue and stripped free of any guile. "I didn't have a chance to read your papers, so I don't know what that's all about. I drove because, well … whatever, that doesn't matter either. As far as my mood, that's what I was trying to explain." Taking my free hand, he looked down at his thumb as it glided back and forth over my wet skin. "Last year when I found Laurel, she was here … in Tennessee." His mouth twisted up like he'd tasted something sour. "She was working at a strip club. I spent a few months here looking for her. That's what I was thinking about. How much I hate this fucking place. And the closer we got … I don't know …"

His declaration ended on a sigh, and before I could process anything he'd said, he reached inside the fence and rubbed the spot between Bessie's big brown eyes.

"What do you imagine she's thinking?" he asked, his brows turning inward in contemplation.

I took the abrupt shift to mean we were done with true confessions. For the moment at least.

147

I shrugged, fingering the little tag on her ear. "Don't eat me."

He laughed, and the sound was like a melody. A song that spoke to a place deep inside of me that longed to hear music again.

"We should go," he finally said, shoving to his feet.

Bessie rested her chin on the wire between two barbs and I leaned in, pressing a soft kiss to the top of her nose before taking Logan's hand.

When he hauled me up, he didn't let go. "Where's mine?"

I looked up at him, blinking the rain from my eyes. "Your what?"

His free hand slid to the back of my neck, and I shivered, because I knew. And he knew I knew. Which is why he didn't hesitate to pull my mouth to his. The kiss was chaste and sweet and totally different from the one we'd shared in the suite. But I felt it in my toes and my fingertips, and everywhere in between.

He rested his forehead against mine. "You ready?"

The question tripped from his lips, filled with innuendo and dripping with dark promises.

He's going to wreck you.

It should've scared me, that voice in my head. But I didn't pay attention. Because I was already wrecked. Love had wrecked me a long time ago. And *this* wasn't *that*.

Safe in that assumption, I nodded and let Logan lead me to the car.

26

Logan

*"Rock and Roll Princess Moves On From Her Prince
Almost six years after the death of Rhenn Grayson in a tragic bus crash,
sources confirm that Tori Grayson, Rhenn's widow, has moved on with a
mystery man. While staying in Nashville to oversee the Six Street Survival
Tour, exclusive photos were obtained of ..."*

The reading software spilling the dirty details into my ear
stopped abruptly when I hit the link on my phone and four
pictures flashed on the screen.

It was Tori's suite all right.

Two Styrofoam containers of half-eaten Chinese food sat on the
coffee table next to a Dr. Pepper can and an empty bottle of Shiner
Bock. Nothing incriminating about that. But the men's boots—*my
boots*—tucked next to the couch weren't so easily dismissed. And of
course, there was the requisite picture of the unmade bed. A doctored
image, with the sheets bunched by the footboard and the comforter
hanging halfway off the mattress.

Whichever rag had commissioned the photos worked fast, since
we'd only been in town a day and a half.

The door between our two suites crashed into the wall when Tori rushed in, still dressed in the oversized T-shirt and tiny shorts she'd been wearing a half hour ago when she'd trotted off to the gym. Face flushed and eyes shimmering, she skidded to a stop in front of me and thrust her iPad under my nose.

"Someone was in my suite. Look."

Panic threaded her tone, a tear spilling onto her cheek as she blinked at the screen, then at me, like somehow, I could fix it. I didn't know whether she was more concerned with the story itself or the breach of security. And I guess it didn't matter.

Taking the iPad from her shaking hand, I set it on the table and climbed to my feet. "I saw them." Her face crumbled, and I whisked away the next tear as I cupped her cheeks. "They don't prove anything."

Because there was nothing to prove. I'd be lying if I said I didn't dream about doing some really dirty things with Tori. Filthy things that hadn't been invented yet. And sweet things. *All the things.* But we weren't there yet. And right now, I was more concerned with finding the person who violated her privacy and making them pay with bones and flesh.

Her shoulders sagged, and she took a seat on the sofa, bottom lip entrenched between her teeth. "Elise is on her way up."

Tori was too shell-shocked to realize how it might look—her being in my suite at eight a.m., with me wearing only a pair of gray sweatpants and shower damp hair.

"I need to get dressed," I said. "And you should go wait for Elise."

Honestly, I didn't care if Tori sat right here while every member of the Big Three walked in, but I knew that wasn't what she wanted. Taryn and Elise could spin this right out into the atmosphere as long as everyone believed it wasn't true.

Tori nodded, and I helped her to her feet. Sliding a hand into her hair, I tipped her chin with my thumb so I could look into her eyes. "Don't worry, baby."

Baby? Where the fuck did that come from? The word didn't exist in my vocabulary unless I was talking to Willow.

Tori released a shuddering breath, glossing right over the endearment. "Okay."

When she shuffled to her room, I followed, just to see if there was anything I'd left in her space. I grabbed a T-shirt from the arm of the chair, my boots—and how the fuck did my deodorant end up on the table? Shaking my head, I added the stick to my growing pile.

Tori froze when voices sounded outside her door.

When she looked at me, her face said it all. *Leave.* And though I expected it, I couldn't help the flash of anger that shot through me.

"See you in a bit, princess."

And then I went to my room. And for the first time since we'd started our little adventure, I closed the door behind me.

An hour later, a member of hotel security escorted me onto an elevator, instructing me to take my place in the back. I complied, even though I knew if push came to shove, I could handle myself much better than he could.

Meeting his gaze in the shiny metal doors, I tipped my chin. "Do you have any idea what's going on?"

He didn't blink. "We were instructed to take everyone downstairs so they can board their respective buses. That's all I know."

My back stiffened, and I pulled my shoulders back. "What about ... do you know where they took Tori, er, Mrs. Grayson?"

He shook his head, but his eyes told me he knew more. Since I was already at zero, I had no problem using any means necessary to convince him to change his mind and answer my damn question.

Before I could say a word—threatening or otherwise—the elevator door slid open, and I froze in my tracks. It was chaos on a level I'd never seen. Four uniformed cops held back the unruly crowd that spanned the entire lobby of the hotel.

Security guy called over his shoulder, "Follow me," and I forced my feet to move. Once we'd reached the periphery of the crowd, he handed me off to two additional cops who escorted me through the mob. Despite their presence, I felt hands on my body, grabbing and pulling and touching as we made our way to the automatic doors. If it were possible, there were more people outside.

Keeping my head down, I shuffled along behind a polished set of boots. A strong hand met the small of my back, guiding me to the open door of my Mustang. "In you go."

Heart pounding and T-shirt soaked with sweat, I dove behind the wheel. It took all of two seconds to realize that I wasn't alone. That Tori was already there, hunkered down in the passenger seat.

One dip into Tori's amber gaze quieted the riot in my head. The moment was fleeting, though, because a loud knock on the windshield drew my attention to the cop whose face was a couple inches from the glass.

"Go!" he ordered.

Red and blue lights flashed from the roof of the police cruiser parked in front of us. There was no time to ask questions, or worry about why I was here, instead of on the bus. I turned the key, slammed the car into gear. And I drove.

Tori

We rode in silence for fifteen minutes before my phone's GPS directed us to merge onto a secluded highway. Two-lanes, because why would anything go my way today?

Leaning forward, I peered through the windshield and up to the cloudy sky.

Awesome.

But unlike our drive into Nashville, Logan was totally in-tune with my mood, and his foot eased off the gas. We couldn't have been doing more than fifty-five. Which had to be killing him.

"You can go a little faster," I said as the gap widened between the Mustang and our police escort.

He took my hand, lacing our fingers tightly together. "I'm not worried about it. Tell me about this place we're going."

I racked my brain for all the information that Taryn had passed on about the Fontanel Inn. "Do you know who the Mandrells are?" Blue eyes cut to mine, and Logan raised a brow like I was nuts for asking. "Don't give me that look, they're country singers. It's not like I asked if you knew who Kurt Cobain was."

A smile curved his lips, a little gloomy, like the clouds pressing in on us. "My mama never listened to anything but country. George Straight. Reba. Willie. The Judds." He slid an appreciative gaze to my custom-made Luccheses. "Have I told you how much I like them boots?" he drawled, the light returning to his eyes.

My cheeks flamed, because, yeah, he'd mentioned it. And after that I'd worn them whenever possible. Always with shorts or a skirt. And that was odd too, since I usually covered my legs.

Tucking my feet as far back against the seat as I could, I continued, "Anyway, the Mandrells built the Fontanel Inn on the same property where one of the sisters had their estate. Barbara, I think. It's really exclusive. Taryn called one of her contacts in Nashville to get us in." Since I sounded like I was trying to sell him a time-share, I stopped with the effusive praise. "You don't have to stay if you don't want to. Elise can book you a room at one of the hotels downtown. But I don't want to chance getting sold out again at one of the large chains."

I felt his gaze boring into the side of my head. "Is that what happened?"

153

Shrugging, I chewed my lip. "It could've been a maid. Or maybe it was the bodyguard. I couldn't risk it, though, so I had to fire him."

Which brought us to the real reason I made sure Logan was with me. Protection. At least that's what I told myself. Only I didn't believe my own bullshit.

"So you've stayed here before?"

Nodding, I twisted my fingers in my lap, hoping against hope he'd leave that one alone. And for once, I got my wish.

Stroking his thumb over mine in a lazy circle, Logan asked. "And who else is going to be there?"

The butterflies in my stomach stopped flapping. "Nobody. There are only six rooms."

A slow smile ticked up the corners of his lips. "Sounds like my kind of place."

27

Logan

Phone pressed to my ear, I stepped out onto the private deck on the top floor of the carriage house. The Fontanel Inn was everything Tori had described. Secluded, with beautiful views and every amenity.

I should've been happy. But I wasn't. Because there was one thing the carriage house didn't have—a door connecting it to Tori's room.

"Are you even listening to me?" Sean growled.

Bracing my forearms against the wood railing, I took in the rolling mountains and green grass. And then I tipped forward and looked to the right, straight into Tori's window like a peeping Tom. Disgusted with myself, I turned around. But only because I didn't see her.

"Yeah, I heard you. I just need a few days to chill."

"You've never needed to chill before."

"I've never had someone babysitting me twenty-four seven either. It's exhausting." The lie tasted so bitter, I almost took it back.

After a beat of silence, Sean cleared his throat. Never a good sign. "So Tori was babysitting you in her room?"

"What makes you think it was her room? All the rooms look the same."

"*Ahhh ...*" Sean chuckled like everything made sense now.

Because, of course, Tori and me together was all kinds of improbable. "I should've guessed. I saw your boots and I thought ... I don't know."

Another chuckle, and now I wanted to reach through the phone and shake him.

"Nobody's going to take any pictures out here. This place is off the grid, and the princess is in a separate building. I'll recharge and then meet y'all on Friday for practice."

Sean blew out a breath, and I could picture him pulling a face. "You've been missing in action a lot lately. Cameron's getting frustrated."

"What about?" As if I weren't keenly aware that Cameron did his best composing on the road. And that he probably had a notebook full of songs for me to review. And by review, I meant play over and over until I'd committed every chord and every word to memory.

Cameron thought it was part of my "process," so he never questioned it. And I lived that lie, too proud or too cowardly to set him straight.

"He's got new material," Sean confirmed. "And you know it always takes us a hot minute to get that shit organized."

Us. He meant me, but he'd never say it.

"I'm working on some stuff too."

It wasn't a complete lie. Tori and I ran through songs almost every day. Of course, they weren't *my* songs. They were hers.

Sean perked up. "Like ... music stuff?"

"What else?" Stalking back into the carriage house, I slammed the door behind me. "I don't need to know how to read to play the guitar. Or the drums. Or the fucking bass."

I knew I was being an asshole, but I wanted Sean to stop with the Zen bullshit. To fight with me like we used to. It relieved some of the tension when I started obsessing over the crap in my head.

He let out a controlled breath. "So you're a one man show now?"

"That's not what I said." Dropping into the chair, I dug my fingers into my eyes. "Listen, I gotta go. See you Friday."

The phone landed on the table and I watched it spin in circles. Round and round. Like me. Yanking my laptop from the protective

156

sleeve, I set the computer on my knee. Instead of checking my email, or browsing porn, or any of the hundred other things I could do online, I directed my browser to a website I had bookmarked.

"Compensatory strategies can help people cope with severe dyslexia. Early diagnosis and support can lead to long-term improvements."

Improvements.

Not cures. And my window had closed on the whole "early diagnosis and support."

When I heard knocking a flight below, I slammed the lid shut and trotted down the stairs.

Tori backed up a foot when I yanked the door open. Her gaze dipped to my bare chest, and lower to my sweat pants. "I thought you might like some company. But then I heard voices."

She peered around me, and I stood back to allow her entry. "Nope. Come on in. It's just me."

And my talking computer.

Smiling, she brushed past me, her bare feet padding lightly against the reclaimed wood as she climbed the stairs.

I sank into my former seat while she wandered around, peeking in the bathroom and even the closet.

"Expecting someone to pop out?"

Her cheeks warmed to that rosy pink I liked as she plopped down into the matching chair next to mine. "I guess I'm still a little shook up after this morning. Plus, I forgot how remote this place is."

Crossing my legs foot to ankle, I rubbed my fingers over my stubble. "I thought you'd be used to it. Living out at Lake Travis and all. That's pretty remote."

Her lips fell into a frown. "You never get used to it." Shifting her focus to my laptop, she sighed and shoved to her feet. "Sorry for barging in. I'll let you get back to what you were doing."

I grabbed her hand. "Why? You got a hot date?"

She smiled down at me. "Hardly. I haven't had a date in years."

Looping our index fingers, I sank back. "What about Dylan?"

The question slipped out smoothly, like it had been sitting on the tip of my tongue.

Tori's gaze crashed into mine like a hurricane making landfall, all howling wind and flying debris. "There is nothing going on between me and Dylan. Jesus ... is that what everyone thinks?" Squaring her shoulders, she shook her head. "Never mind, I don't want to know."

She made for the door like the devil himself was chasing her. Appropriate, since I was on my feet and I had her caged against me before she made it three steps.

"Don't go," I said close to her ear. "Let's just hang out for a while."

Since it was too late to amend the offer to include fucking, I smiled sweetly when she turned around, like I didn't want to rip her clothes off with my teeth.

She nodded and walked back to the small living area, but instead of the chair, she eased onto the area rug in front of the dormant fireplace. "Dylan isn't pining for me, you know?"

Dropping down next to her, I reclined on my elbows. "You sure about that?"

After picking at a piece of fiber to avoid looking at me, she examined the small ball of fluff and then blew it off her finger. "Pretty sure, since Taryn had to pay off one of his girlfriend's last year to keep her from releasing a sex tape." Tori's eyes widened, and she gulped. "Shit. I shouldn't have said that. You can't tell anyone. Please, Logan. You can't."

As much as I wanted all the details of Dylan's sexcapade, I shrugged. "I won't say anything. Promise."

She blew out a relieved breath. "Thank you."

Since she was in a talkative mood, I pressed my luck. "So you and Dylan have never ... you don't ..."

Tori cocked her head. "Fuck?" I nodded, and that drew a light chuckle from her lips. "I've never taken things to the next level with Dylan because he reminds me too much of Rhenn."

"And that's a bad thing?"

The light seeped from her eyes. "I had the original. I don't want a copy. Not that Dylan's *trying* to imitate Rhenn. It's just something that's always been. Even before ... you know ..."

Before he *died*. She didn't have to say it.

Eager to pull the conversation out of the nosedive before we hit the ground, I ran a finger over her knee. "Maybe they're all trying to get your attention."

It seemed logical to me, but Tori shook her head.

"No. Rhenn was like a force of nature. He drew people to him."

Since I'd spent my entire career in his shadow, I couldn't disagree, so I nodded.

"You're like him in that way." It slipped out softly, like an inner thought she hadn't meant to reveal. "But different."

The voice in my head told me not to ask. That I didn't want to know. But my inner masochist seized control of my vocal chords. "How so?"

She hummed softly. "Rhenn had this energy, but you—" Her gaze shot to mine when I started to push to my feet. "What?"

"Figured I might need a drink before you tell me everything that's wrong with me."

I felt her eyes on my back as I strode to the kitchenette. When I returned, she took the Dr. Pepper I offered with a frown.

"There's nothing wrong with you. What I was trying to say is that ... Rhenn had this energy about him because he knew."

Cracking open my bottle of water, I wondered if it was too early to trade it for something stronger. "Knew what, princess?"

Tori's eyes flashed hot at my sarcastic tone. "He knew he had an expiration date. It's the reason he was able to do everything he did. Why he focused all his energy on being who he was. Because he knew."

I raised a skeptical brow. "He told you this? Like he had a premonition?"

"No." She scoffed. "He didn't have to tell me. I saw it. The singular focus. It wasn't the talent. Hell, Dylan has more natural talent than Rhenn did. So do you. But Rhenn was committed to the music above anything else. Or anyone else." Unshed tears glazed her words as they spilled from her lips, falling like rain on the expensive rug. "That was his true gift."

Tori didn't seem salty about the revelation. It just *was*. Like a blue sky or a bitter lemon or night following day.

But still, I had to wonder why she told me. Was it a cautionary tale or a guide to greatness?

Her shoulders sagged, and she looked down. "Rhenn was the one who approved the modifications to the bus," she said quietly. "So that we could do the acoustic tour in the short window before we had to record the next album. He didn't know ... I mean, he didn't think ..."

As she struggled to push the confession past her lips, I took her hand. No details from the accident were ever disclosed. And maybe that was for the best. "You don't have to explain."

She nodded, and I thought she was finished, but then she sighed. "Xtreme Modifications cut corners in order to comply with Rhenn's timeline. They didn't have the rivets inspected. Partly because they didn't use the right grade of metal on the panels. So when the semi hit the bus, it sheared it in two. Rhenn and Paige were in the front, close to the point of impact. Miles and I were in the back.

"Xtreme produced at least ten emails alluding to the fact that Rhenn was aware of what they were doing. But he wasn't. Not really. He just told them to get it done and threw a bunch of money their way. Xtreme should've stood up to him. Told him that what he was asking was impossible." She smiled then, and there was no malice, no anger, just lingering sadness. "But that was hard to do. Even for me. Like I said, he was a force of nature. Kind of like you."

Her gaze roamed over my face and then she leaned in and pressed a soft kiss to my lips. Unsure if she was lost in a memory, I tipped my head back before it went any further. Her eyes shone with lust. And on any other day, with any other girl, that would've been enough. But when I finally got Tori under me, I didn't want anyone else in her head.

I tucked a fallen curl behind her ear. "What do you say you put on those cowboy boots and let me take you to dinner?"

28

Tori

Easing onto the floor in the bathroom, I laid the tiny pair of black panties on my lap. Tracing a finger over the little bow on the front, I thought about wearing them to dinner. Skimpy lingerie wasn't normally my thing. That was Taryn. She spent thousands at La Perla and Agent Provocateur. But I was more comfortable in plain, white cotton.

I stood up and slipped the lace over my hips, just to see how they looked.

Scrutinizing my reflection in the mirror, I touched the thick scar under my left breast. My hand wandered to the braided skin around my hip. And then down to the uneven patch on my thigh.

My appetite disappeared along with any hope that I could hide all the devastation under pretty lace and soft silk. There wasn't enough fabric in the world for that.

With a resigned sigh, I returned to the bedroom. And once I was safely tucked inside a loose-fitting T-shirt, I picked up my phone so I could text Logan.

I'm tired. I think I'm going to turn in early. Raincheck on dinner?

My thumb hovered over the send button. What was my deal? It was only dinner. But even I didn't believe that. My insides were only as strong as the seams that held me together. And tonight I couldn't bear to count the stitches. So I sent the message.

Chewing my lip, I glanced over at my backpack and thought seriously about taking a sleeping pill. Before I could act on the impulse, a loud knock threatened to bring down the walls.

"Victoria!"

With a groan, I climbed out of bed. Once I made it downstairs, I plastered on a tight smile and opened the door. "Hey."

"What's the matter?" Concern threaded Logan's tone as he pushed his way inside. "Are you in pain?"

Surprise parted my lips as his fingers sunk into my hair. Tipping my chin with his thumb, his gaze roamed all over my face as if he could figure out the answer for himself. And maybe he could.

Shaking my head, I placed my palms flat on his chest. "I'm not in pain."

"What is it then?"

I couldn't think with him so close, so I stepped to the side, but he shadowed the move.

"This … *us* … it isn't a good idea," I said to his throat, since looking into those baby blues would only weaken my resolve. "I don't do one-night stands."

I cringed at the silence that followed my declaration. What if all Logan had in mind was a meal?

Reluctantly, I looked up and found him smiling. A wicked smile that made my blood heat and my heart pound.

Breathe.

Coiling a strand of my hair around his finger, he tipped forward like he was about to share a secret. "No worries, princess. We've got a couple months left on the tour. I'm sure I could pencil you in for a repeat."

Rocked from the force of his words, I tried to keep my expression neutral. I guess I didn't do a very good job because he cocked his head.

"That was a joke," he said, but I wasn't sure if he believed it.

I sure didn't.

This time when I made a move to scoot around him, he didn't stop me.

"It wasn't funny," I shot back as I climbed the stairs.

By the time I reached the landing, Logan was right behind me. "Come on, it was a little funny."

Ignoring him, I crawled onto the bed and focused on the television, hoping he'd take the hint and leave.

Scratching his head, he looked around at the mess I'd made. "What happened in here?"

"Wardrobe malfunction."

Pushing aside some of the piles of clothes, he plopped down in front of me and reclined on his elbow. "So, besides your aversion to one-night stands, what else makes this such a bad thing?"

Since he was blocking my view, I had no choice but to look at him. "I'm not your type."

Sadly, it was true. But then, I didn't think I was anybody's type.

He thought about it for a moment. "Fair enough. I don't usually go for the stick up your ass kind of girl."

Before we started hanging out, these kinds of barbs were commonplace. Now they just hurt. And I was over it.

"If that's the case, why the fuck did you come over here to begin with?" As my anger spilled over, my voice rose, and he sat up, surprised. But I didn't stop. "I'm trying to give you an out! Why don't you take it?"

In the blink of an eye, I was flat on my back, Logan straddling my hips. Planting his hands on either side of my head, he tipped forward. "Who says I want an out?"

"You would, if you knew ... if you saw ..." I closed my eyes. "My body ... it's ..."

Scarred. Damaged. Broken.

Easing on top of me, he ran his nose along my jaw. "Show me."

"Show you what?"

"You."

163

Logan

I wasn't sure Tori was aware she was rocking under me. That all of her soft was pressing against my hard with each tiny motion of her hips. "I can't show you," she said. "But maybe if you felt them. Then you'd understand."

She made a noise like clearing her throat, but not. More like she was choking on her words. Doubt etched her features, all consuming.

I nodded, afraid if I said anything, I'd screw it up, this gift she was giving me. Because that's what it felt like. A gift.

"Roll over," she whispered hoarsely.

I did as she asked, and she flicked off the light, plunging the room into darkness. My eyes adjusted quickly, thanks to the moonlight pouring in through the windows. The sky was big here, the stars bright.

Tori climbed on top of me, thighs molding my ribs. I could see the outline of her heart shaped face. And the silhouette of her body. She was so small, not larger than life like she appeared in the daylight. And so fucking soft.

"Give me your hand," she said, voice quaking.

My cock pulsed beneath my zipper when she guided me under her T-shirt. With second base so close, I resisted the urge to sprint. *Patience.* I prayed for it as we inched closer to her perfect tits. But she stopped just short.

"Do you feel that?" she asked.

Loosening her grip, she let me explore. Two fingers skated over a thick ridge that spanned—seven inches? Eight? And suddenly I stopped thinking about the warmth between her thighs.

Swallowing the lump in my throat, I continued to stroke her skin. "What's it from?"

Idiot. I knew what it was from.

Before I could amend the question to something more specific,

Tori said. "That's where they removed my spleen during the initial surgery."

After a moment, her hand was on mine again, and lower we went, just past the curve of her waist. She flattened my palm, her hand covering mine. Holding. Pausing. "I told you about all the damage to my hip. This is ... everything."

With some hesitation, my thumb glided across the braided rope that spanned ... *Jesus.* The scar ran from front to back in an arc, starting just above her mound and ending on her ass cheek.

"You've seen my back and my thigh," she said, voice dull.

And on cue, her hand found mine again, and she guided the exploration to the uneven patch of skin on her leg that I'd felt many times during our stretching sessions.

I could see her eyes now, faintly shining in the near darkness.

My palm glided over the art on her back, past her shoulder, and into the raven curtain of silk. Cupping her nape, my thumb stroked the little notch on her neck. "Victoria ..."

"There's one more."

She inched two of my fingers to the base of her skull.

"I don't feel anything," I said, my voice gravel.

She gathered her hair in her free hand. "They inserted a stent to keep the swelling down in my brain. There's a groove."

My fingers sank into the little divot, and she let her head fall forward. We stayed like that for a long moment while I took it all in. I think she expected me to bolt.

Instead, I gently pulled her against me. "You scared me for a minute, baby," I said. "I thought you were going to show me something really bad."

It was bad. We both knew it. But it was also her. And that made it beautiful. She searched my face, eyes roaming over me in the darkness. And then her lips parted, and I stole her words, and her breath. My tongue dipped inside her mouth, dancing with hers like a long-lost partner. And fuck, she was sweet.

Tori broke our connection when my hand moved to her waist. "I've only been with one man. I'm not sure if I can ... if I'm ..."

"Ready?"

She nodded.

The wet spot on my jeans begged to differ, but that was her body. I wanted more. I wanted it all. So I twisted a lock of her hair around my finger and gave her a smile. "There are other things we can do."

She tilted her head, so innocent. "Like?"

Rolling her onto her back, I pressed a kiss to her mouth. "Since you taste like a cookie," I nipped her jaw, "I thought I might eat you."

Her hands slid into my hair, and I knew ... she wanted this. Maybe not all of it. Not yet. And that was okay.

Working my way to her breast, I scored my teeth over the pebbled peak through her T-shirt. Her back bowed ... and the noises she made. *Fuck.* Continuing my trek, I went down and down. When I passed the target, her fingers gripped my hair so tight, I winced. And that said a lot, since I didn't mind a little pain.

I sank my teeth into the flesh of her inner thigh, and she moaned louder. "Lo."

Peering up, I hoped to find her eyes. But she was gone. Lost in pleasure. And I hadn't even started yet.

Six years.

I tried to take it slow, but when her hips came off the bed, I lost the battle. Her panties came apart in my hand, the delicate seams ripping as I tore them off. Her knees fell open in offering, and I couldn't resist. My tongue slid between her folds, and there was nothing but her sweet taste and her whispered words.

"Yes," and "more," and, "please." And then my name. "Logan. Logan. Logan."

When I knew she couldn't take much more, I slid a finger into her pussy. She gasped, her walls tightening around me. I felt the storm gathering at the base of my spine, but this was about her and not me, so I ignored the ache and continued to suck her sweet bud.

Adding another finger, I gazed up and found her staring at me. And it was so fucking hot.

"Come," I whispered against her slick heat.

And she did.

29

Tori

When I woke the next morning, I was alone. Like, really alone. There was no moment of disorientation. No fog. Just an empty bed and the lingering scent of Logan on my skin.

I didn't have much—or any—dating experience, but I was pretty sure that riding someone's face into five mind blowing orgasms, then rolling over and passing out without returning the favor was a breach of etiquette.

Groaning, I sat up, grinding the heel of my palm into my eye.

This was bad. *So bad.*

Out of habit, I reached for my phone to call Taryn. But I couldn't bring myself to do it. Because I knew that any sentence that began with "I almost slept with Logan Cage" would end with her at my door. And probably Chase too.

And for what?

Logan had done nothing wrong. I'd told him I didn't do one-night stands, and he'd assured me that he was down for a repeat. But he never offered to spoon me or stick around for breakfast. I'd agreed to the terms, so there was no use unleashing the wrath of my best friend. On either of us. Because she'd be just as pissed at me.

Sweeping the covers aside, I threw my legs over the edge of the bed and a scrap of lace fell to the floor. My panties. They were ripped in half. Beyond repair.

I tossed them in the trash with a shake of my head. "Better you than me."

After a shower that only ended when the water ran cool, I put on a little makeup and did my hair.

I *did* feel better. More relaxed. And hungry as hell.

Since it was after ten, I couldn't take advantage of the made-to-order breakfast.

If I were honest, I hated eating alone. Eating alone in a restaurant? I'd rather have a tooth filled. Still, I decided to try. I was trying a lot of new things.

After pairing a flowing tunic with some ripped boyfriend jeans, I shoved my feet into a pair of sandals and trotted down the stairs.

My heart jumped into my throat when I pulled open the door and found a burly biker type waiting on the other side. He spun around in time for the wood to meet his face.

"Ms. Grayson?" came his gruff voice.

Everyone knew my name. Most people knew my face. A warm greeting meant nothing.

Pulling my cell phone from my pocket in case I needed to call 911, I replied calmly, "Who are you and what are you doing here?"

"Daryl Creston. Taryn Ayers hired me. I'm your new bodyguard."

With a shaky hand, I tapped out a quick message to my best friend.

There's a Hells Angel at my door. Is there something you forgot to tell me?

While waiting for her reply, I peered out the peephole. "Not that I don't believe you, but do you have any ID?"

A second later he held up a laminated card with his picture. *Creston Private Security.*

"Yeah, okay." Peering down at my phone, I willed it to ring or beep or something. "Just a minute, please."

There was no way I was opening the door until I got a confirmation. A second later, Taryn's face lit the screen, and I turned toward the wall to muffle my voice.

"Taryn," I hissed.

"Oh God, Belle!" she exclaimed. "I'm so sorry."

My shoulders sagged. "I'm going to kill you. Seriously, I'm going to fly home, kill you, then eat some barbecue. Because I won't even feel guilty about killing you."

Ignoring the threat, she rushed to say, "His name is Daryl Creston. He's a retired cop. He works private security for all the big country stars and ..."

While Taryn fumbled over the dude's résumé, I flipped the lock and pulled the door open. Greeting Daryl with a smile, I held up a finger. He nodded, then wandered to the railing a few feet away, where he turned his back to give me some privacy.

"Thanks for the heads up," I growled when Taryn finished. "I've got to go."

"Wait!"

Wait was never good. "Yes?"

"Daryl's with you for the rest of the tour."

My stomach dropped. "*What*?"

"He's the best. And he's highly recommended. After what happened yesterday, I'm not taking any chances."

Taryn may have stammered through her initial explanation, but now her tone brooked no argument. I could pitch a fit. But it probably wouldn't do me much good. Daryl would continue to shadow me, popping out of the bushes when I least expected it. Might as well accept it now.

"I'm hungry," I said, cutting Taryn off when she went in for the kill. "We'll talk later."

Ending the call, I let my head fall forward.

"Everything cool?" Daryl asked.

Regaining my composure, I pinned on a smile and stepped outside. "Yes. Fine." I offered my hand. "Sorry, I'm Vic ... Tori." He gave me an odd look, and I felt my cheeks flame. "You can call me Tori."

His beefy paw wrapped around mine, warm and reassuring. "Nice to meet you, ma'am," he drawled.

He wasn't that scary after all. Except for the scar bisecting his brow. And the huge, bulging muscles. And the piercing brown eyes.

"Are you hungry, Daryl?"

"No, ma'am."

"Okay, well ... I'm going to go grab something at the café."

He smiled. I think it was a smile. It looked a little foreign on his face. "Lead the way, ma'am."

We made polite conversation as we strolled along, but Daryl was only half invested, his eyes darting from here to there behind dark glasses.

The smell of garlic and basil hung thick in the air as we stepped inside the restaurant. Daryl spoke to the hostess while I hung back and looked around. And that's when I saw Logan seated at a corner table with his arm slung over his chair. Smiling up at the waitress, he appeared totally enraptured as she pointed to items on the menu.

Reality hit me, a knife gouging my heart. *Casual,* I reminded myself.

When the waitress giggled, tossing her long, sandy brown hair over her shoulder to give Logan a better view of her boobs, I scooted behind Daryl.

"I changed my mind," I said when he shifted his gaze over his shoulder. "I'll just take something to go." Peering around his bulky frame, I smiled at the hostess. "Do you have anything already prepared?"

Her jaw came unhinged, and her eyes widened. She recognized me.

Fuck. Focus, lady. *Please.*

It took a minute, but she recovered. "We have pizza by the slice. Pepperoni. Plain cheese. Combination. And ..." Her excitement got the better of her and an unrestrained smile broke on her lips. "I'm sorry ... I just love your music. Damaged was my favorite band. I cried for a week when ..."

Tuning her out, I nodded. I knew this scene by heart. A sincere apology for my loss, followed by a request for an autograph and a selfie. When her mouth stopped moving, I took the notepad she offered and signed my name while I mumbled an order for a slice of pepperoni.

Once she was gone, I said to Daryl, "I'm going to wait right over there." His brows drew together as he followed my gaze to the alcove by the door with all the brochures for local attractions. Since I wasn't asking for permission, and it was only ten feet away, I didn't wait for him to reply.

As I gathered information about wine tasting tours and the distillery on the property, I stole glances at Logan out of the corner of my eye. He was alone now, staring out the window at the grounds.

A moment later, Daryl shuffled over, takeout bag in hand. "Ready, ma'am?"

Smiling so brightly my cheeks hurt from the effort, I nodded and let him usher me out the door.

Picking at my pizza, I gazed out at the pond while Zoe chattered away in my ear. I'd called to talk to Mama and Daddy, but my little sister had quickly commandeered the phone.

"... and then," she snorted, "Daddy chased the guy off the stoop and told him he'd whoop his ass if he showed up again."

Easing onto my back, I closed my eyes and let the sun warm my face. "Which guy was that?"

She sighed. "Don't you ever listen, Vic? The guy with that blog that draws dicks on people's faces."

"Zoe!" My mama hollered in the background. "Language."

Another sigh. "Sorry, *penises*."

I chuckled when I heard a familiar *thwap*, and I pictured Mama's wooden spoon meeting my sister's behind.

Zoe howled.

"You big baby," Mama grumbled. "You know that didn't hurt. Now give me the phone."

My sister mumbled something that could've been goodbye. Or maybe she was sassing our mother, because another howl nearly broke my eardrum.

And then Mama was on the line. "I swear, I don't know where she comes up with this stuff. What does she know from penises? She's fourteen!"

Pressing my lips together, I stifled a laugh. "Do you want me to tell you how much I knew about penises when I was her age?"

A shadow fell over me, and I moved my arm, squinting into the bright sunshine. "If she doesn't, I do," Logan declared, a sinful smile curving his lips as he plopped down next to me.

My mouth fell open, because what the hell was he doing here? The pond was nowhere near the carriage houses.

"Ma ... let me call you back."

Since my mother had a habit of ignoring my first request to end a call, it took me three tries to get her off the phone. By that time, Logan was stretched out with his legs crossed at the ankles, sucking on a blade of grass.

"Hey," I said, pushing a hand through my hair.

"Don't 'hey' me." He cut his gaze to mine and raised a pale brow. "Spill."

"Spill?"

He rolled halfway onto his side, his weight on one palm. "Penises. Tell me all about it." My eyes flicked over to Daryl, who was now standing a few yards away with his back to us. Logan looked over his shoulder. "Nice guy," he said of my bodyguard. "Met him this morning when I was doing the walk of shame from your place. Not really much of a talker." He brought his gaze back to mine. "So ... about the penises."

I laughed. Honestly, I couldn't help it. "Do you have questions about something? A burning sensation perhaps?"

Amused and maybe a little surprised by my comment, he snorted. "Nope. Just wondering how old you were when you tamed the one-eyed monster."

My cheeks ignited, burning with the heat of the sun. "No way. That's too personal."

Logan scooted closer, dipping his head to whisper in my ear. "I know what you taste like. And the sounds you make when you come. I don't think there's anything too personal at this point."

When I turned slightly, his lips were right there. So close I could feel his breath fan over me. "All right. But you go first. How old were you?"

His mouth curved into a shit-eating grin. "Fifteen." I blinked at him, and he chuckled. "It's different for guys. That's like number one on the bucket list. Find a girl and—"

"Fourteen," I blurted, biting down my own smile.

Logan fell onto his back, his chuckle turning to a full belly laugh. When he got a hold of himself, he tucked an arm behind his head. "No wonder Rhenn was always smiling."

For a moment there was only silence. Even the air grew still while I waited for the clouds to press down on me and the pain to bloom in my chest. When nothing happened, a bubble of laughter tripped from my lips. "Never thought of it that way."

Logan's palm trailed up my arm and over my shoulder, fingers twining into my hair. "I've got something for you. Hold out your hand and close your eyes."

My lips parted, but his thumb found that spot at the base of my throat and I reluctantly complied. "I hope I'm not going to regret this," I mumbled, holding my palm up.

He moved away from me for a second, and I heard paper crinkle. And then I felt something warm on my skin.

"Okay, you can look."

My lids fluttered open, and I tilted my head. "It's a cookie." I blinked at him. "You brought me a cookie."

"Oatmeal raisin. The chef swears it's fresh from the oven." He broke off a large piece and held it to my lips. After I took a nibble, he popped the rest in his mouth. "It's good. Not as good as you, though."

Warmth spread through me, and I looked away.

He tugged my sleeve. "Come here. Someone kept me up all night. I need to rest my eyes."

I scooted to his side, and his arm looped around me, pulling me against his solid frame. Soon his breathing evened out, but I couldn't relax. So I settled for eating the rest of my cookie and listening to Logan's heart beating a gentle rhythm under my ear.

30

Logan

Tori sipped from her shot glass, her fingers skating over the bottles of spirits as she strolled around the gift shop at Prichard's Distillery. Biting her lip, she levered up on her toes, reaching for a fancy private-label rum on a high shelf.

I pushed off the wall where I'd been watching her for the last half hour.

Sliding one hand to her hip, I used the other to pluck her selection from the ledge. "Is this what you want?"

She slanted her gaze to mine, amber eyes hooded from all the liquor we'd sampled. "Yes. Thank you."

Stupidly, I'd thought arranging a private after-hours tour of the distillery would be a easy way to steer us back into the safe zone. Because that's where we needed to be. I'd known it from the moment I'd woken up in Tori's bed this morning. We hadn't fucked. And that was a good thing. Because once my head was clear, I knew I couldn't be trusted with all the shattered pieces of her soul. I wasn't that guy. But damn, just being around her was enough for me to question my decision.

Slipping the basket from the crook of her arm, I added the bottle to her growing assortment. "I think you've got enough here. You ready?"

Tori pursed her lips, examining her haul. "I want a pint of the Cranberry Reserve for Taryn. Help me find it, and then we can go."

She scooted off to begin her quest while I loitered by a display on a big oak barrel, trying to interpret the labels.

"Can I help you with something?"

I jerked my gaze to Brooke, our tour guide, who'd somehow managed to sidle over without me noticing. Batting her eyelashes, she peered up at me with a tempting smile. Except, I wasn't tempted. Not by her big brown eyes, or her pouty lips, or even her smooth skin.

I took a step back when her arm brushed against mine. "Yeah. I'm looking for the Cranberry Reserve."

Extracting a bottle from the center of the display in front of us, she inclined her head. "You mean this one?"

Normally, I'd pour on the charm. Get her to recite every word from the label, just like I'd done with the waitress this morning when I was trying to decipher the menu at the café.

"Is there any other cranberry?" When she shook her head, I shrugged. "Then I guess this is the one."

Brooke caught my arm when I turned to find Tori.

"I'm a really big fan," she gushed. "My friends and I have tickets to your show. Do you think I can get a picture?"

Apprehension corkscrewed in my chest when I thought of how fast that selfie would end up on social media.

"I'm trying to keep a low profile this week. But I'll tell you what." I pulled my phone out of my pocket and punched in the security code. "How about I get you some backstage passes for the show, and you can snap all the pictures you want then?"

Beaming at me, Brooke bounced on the balls of her feet and clapped her hands. "Oh my God! That would be awesome!"

Since I knew better than to try and gather the information myself, I held out my phone. "First and last name and your phone number." When she made a grab for the device, I held on for an extra second. "But you can't tell anyone I'm here. I'm serious about that."

She nodded eagerly. "Of course. Yeah."

One eye on the phone to make sure it didn't disappear, I leaned a hip against the oak barrel.

"Hey, I'm ready whenever you are," came Tori's voice from behind me.

When I turned, and she saw our tour guide tapping away on my phone, the smile slid right off her face.

Well, fuck.

Before I could say anything in my own defense, Brooke piped up, "Do you want my address too?"

And that was that.

Tori was on her horse, cowboy boots kicking up sawdust with every step. Something about the sway of her hips or the curve of her ass, or the fire in her eyes had me grinning. And I knew I was done for. There was no safe zone. It was all heat and fire between us. And even my fear of burning us both to the ground wouldn't keep me from dancing in the flames with Tori.

Fucking stupid.

Brooke winced when the door slammed with enough force to rattle the bottles on the shelves. "Is she okay?"

Chuckling, I shook my head. "Definitely not. Let me help you bag this stuff up before she takes off without me."

Tori

How could you let him rile you like that?

Mentally, I slapped my inner-bitch right in the head.

She was all harsh words and recrimination *now*. But where the hell was she last night when Logan was working me over with his mouth? I'll tell you where. Moaning right along with me.

Come to think of it, the little diva had a habit of going dark every time Logan flashed one of his heartfelt smiles. Or touched my hand

177

in just the right way. And she purred like a kitten when he gave me that cookie, sucking down every crumb.

He's a douche. What did you expect?

I stopped pacing, let my head fall forward, and muttered, "Stop lecturing me. You know you ate the damn cookie."

Crunching gravel, and then a low chuckle next to my ear. "No, princess, I ate the cookie," Logan said, patting my ass as he scooted by. "Now, get in the car."

Crossing my arms over my chest, I glared at him as he stowed the liquor in the trunk of the Mustang.

"That's three hundred dollars' worth of booze, by the way," he said as he opened the passenger door for me to climb in. When I didn't budge, he cocked a brow. "It's freezing out here. What are you standing around for?"

Seriously?

I shook my head. "Will your friend be joining us?"

He bit down a grin. "You shouldn't say things like that. I mean, do you know how hard it is—" Another devious chuckle. "Yeah, you *do* know how hard it is. But anyway, that girl is *not* my friend."

For a moment I wished I were like him. So fucking casual. That thought, paired with the alcohol still numbing my brain, stole all the heat from my body.

"What is she then, Lo?"

He took a deep breath and then cut the distance between us. Long fingers sank into my hair, and I was up on tiptoe, my palms braced on his chest. "Give me a little credit, Victoria. Do you think I'd scope out another woman with you standing ten feet away?"

He looked surprised. Like he didn't know why he said it. Which made us even, because I didn't know why I cared.

I waited for him to kiss me—really kiss me— the butterflies in my belly threatening to crawl up my throat. But all I got was a brush of his lips against mine.

"Will you get in the car now?" His gaze flicked to the only other vehicle in the parking lot. Daryl's. "I think your bodyguard is watching us."

"It's his job."

"Perv." Smiling, he brought his eyes back to mine. "Him ... not you. I don't have any evidence on you yet. But you look kinda kinky." His hand slid to my ass, and I squirmed. "Yeah. You're definitely a little freak. And you're shaking. Are you ready to go?"

I shook my head. "I don't want this to ..."

He buried his face in the crook of my neck, and his lips curved against my skin. "End," he whispered.

I nodded, even though I knew it had to. Just not right now. And if I had to stand in a parking lot in the cold, I would.

But the choice was made for me when Logan broke our connection. Tucking a strand of hair behind my ear, he gazed down at me, contemplative. "So you're not ready to go back to the carriage house."

It was more statement than question, and I nodded without thinking. Something flickered in his pale blue gaze, and a bulb went off in my head.

"Oh ... I didn't ... I mean, of course we can ..." I stammered, my cheeks flaming. "It's not that I don't want to ... uh ..."

He entwined our fingers. "Good to know. We'll save that for later."

I wasn't sure if that was meant to be a threat or a promise, and since I couldn't form words, I just kind of shrugged.

"God, you're fucking cute," he said as he pulled me toward the car.

Once we were heading for the inn, my curiosity got the better of me. "You think I'm cute?"

The headlights from Daryl's Jeep shone through the back window, and I squinted as I took in Logan's profile.

His gaze shifted to mine for a second. "What's wrong with cute?"

I shook my head and focused on the road. "Nothing." The driveway for the Fontanel flew by. "Hey, you missed the turn."

"I didn't think you were cute when we met," he said slowly. "Beautiful ... for sure. I mean, you're fucking gorgeous. But cute?" He sucked air in through his teeth. "Not so much."

My thumb skated over the groove on my ring finger where Rhenn's golden promise had sat for so many years.

You're so cute, Belle.

179

Pushing the memory aside when we coasted to a stop in a nearly deserted parking lot, I looked around.

"Where are we?" I asked when Logan creaked open my door, offering his hand.

"You'll see."

Looping an arm around my shoulder, he guided us to a foot path that disappeared into the forest. Once we'd stepped under the canopy of trees, lanterns framed the winding course, and a faint beat whispered on the breeze, barely audible over the leaves and twigs crunching under our feet. "Is that music?"

Logan snorted, pulling me closer to his side. "Debatable."

As we approached the clearing, I squinted, the outline of a log cabin coming into focus. Neon signs touting sour mash whiskey and beer hung in the windows.

Confused, I slanted my gaze up to his face. "Is this a bar?"

He stared straight ahead, pale blue eyes glued to our destination. Even in the faint light, I noticed his ticking jaw and the lines bracketing his mouth.

"No, baby," he replied solemnly. "It's a honky-tonk."

31

Logan

I was in hell. The moment I'd stepped through the doors of the honky-tonk at the edge of the Fontanel property, I'd felt the hot embers charring my insides.

Definitely hell.

The TV in the carriage house advertised this place as a friendly bar. Bars I could handle. Clubs were all good. But this was a good old-fashioned, dyed-in-the-wool honky-tonk. The kind of place I'd avoided for years.

I tipped back another shot of whiskey, chasing the burn with draft beer. From his post a few yards away, Daryl threw me a disapproving glare. I smiled at the dude, because, zero fucks. That's how much I had to spare for his bullshit.

He got the hint, shifting his gaze back to the dance floor where Tori's latest partner, a good old boy that had to be pushing sixty-five, twirled her around. She was all smiles and perfectly sober now, while I was slipping farther into an alcohol-induced haze.

Upside?

None of the twenty or so patrons in the joint had a clue who we were. Probably because every one of them qualified for social security. But I wasn't looking a gift horse in the mouth. At the rate I was going, I could very well end up on the sawdust floor, and it was comforting to know that if I did, there wouldn't be a video to memorialize the event.

The waitress wandered over. Smiling wide, she placed my empty shot glass on her tray. "Anything else, sugar?"

I downed the rest of my beer and slid the mug in her direction before fishing a twenty out of my pocket. "One more."

She shoved the cash into the pocket of her apron. "How about the missus? Another Dr. Pepper?"

I shook my head. "She's not ..." Tori's laugher drifted from the dance floor. "Yeah. Bring her another. Make sure to add a couple cherries."

"Sure thing. Be right back."

Mercifully, the song ended. The clatter of boot heels on the weathered floor drew my attention to Tori. All smiles, she plopped into the chair across from me. "Dang, it's hot."

Blowing a strand of hair out of her eyes, she picked up her watered-down Dr. Pepper and went diving around in the ice for the last cherry.

"Having a good time?" I asked.

"I'm having a great time. Are you sure you don't want me to teach you how to two-step? I'm a good dancer."

My stomach rolled when the opening riff to "Chattahoochee" poured from the speakers. Because my trip to hell wouldn't be complete without a little Alan Jackson.

"I love this song!" Tori exclaimed, her smile fading when I rubbed the back of my neck. "If you hate country so much, what are we doing at a honky-tonk?"

Because I didn't hate it. Not even a little bit.

Shifting my focus from her honeyed gaze, I ran a finger over the rim of my mug. "Exorcising the demons, I guess. That's a thing, right?"

She slid into the seat beside me. "Wanna tell me what that means?"

Nope.

That's what I planned to say, but when I opened my mouth, an explanation coiled around my tongue. "I told you my mama used to listen to this music all the time. And she ... um ... she sang too. Not onstage. Maybe she wanted to. I didn't know her that well, since I was only eight when she ... you know ..."

In the midst of my garbled confession, a memory pushed in.

Pale blond hair and bright blue eyes. Painted pink toes and ratty carpet.

"Stop fussing, Lo. I learned me a new song. Sit down and tell me what you think."

Tori's hand covered mine, her touch sweeping away the faint voice in my head.

"So this reminds you of her? Your mom?" I said nothing, hoping she'd drop it. But then I felt something scratch the inside of my brain, and I realized it was Tori, probing around for an answer. "Your dad, then?"

I narrowed my eyes. "I don't talk about my dad, princess. The man is dead to me, so move on, 'kay?"

She sank back into her chair, frowning.

Silence swelled between us, and when I couldn't take it anymore, I hauled to my feet. "Come on."

Folding her arms over her chest, her gaze shifted from my outstretched hand to my face. "We're leaving?"

If that were an option, I would've taken it. But her pout told me it wasn't. So I pulled her to standing. "Not yet. Let's dance first."

Surprise flashed across Tori's features. But then she hesitated, and I wanted to ask what else she needed to make her happy. Maybe a kidney, because it would probably be easier to scoop one out than act like I was enjoying this.

She took a deep breath and then shrugged out of her short, denim jacket.

And holy fuck, if I would have known what she was hiding under there ... The little white dress molded to her curves perfectly, but it was only after she turned to lay her jacket on the chair that I got the full effect. The gauzy material tapered into a V, exposing her entire back. Miles of ink and skin and art. And pain that looked pretty.

I dipped my head to kiss her bare shoulder. "Nice dress."

She turned her head, and soft lips grazed my ear. "Thank you. Now dance with me."

32

Tori

I leaned forward to get a good look at the moon through the windshield. Dark consumed every inch of the sky without a hint of light coming from the east.

"What's the matter?" Logan asked from his position in the passenger seat. He brought my hand to his lips, pressing a kiss to my palm. "Besides the fact that you look weird behind the wheel of my car."

Eyes still focused on the heavens, I slumped against the upholstery. It was almost over. Our endless night. One dance at the honky-tonk had turned into twelve. And that evolved into finding a Denny's to eat breakfast at two a.m. when they kicked us out.

And now here we were, sitting in front of the carriage house waiting for the dawn to come crawling and the magic to end.

Logan shifted to face me, his back against the door, head resting on the glass. "Talk to me, Victoria."

I smiled. "It's so quiet. Isn't it?"

He flipped on the radio. Which was *so* like him. See the problem, fix the problem. For weeks, he'd been doing it. From the moment he found me in the rain outside the tour bus.

"You do that a lot," I said, digging my pinky nail into a crease on the steering wheel.

"What?"

"Fix things."

Snorting a laugh, he bit my knuckle. "No ... I really don't. Ask my sister." Facing him fully, I waited for him to elaborate, but he shook his head. "Too early for all that shit, princess. Ask me some other time."

Shifting my focus back to the vast expanse of nothing outside the window, my stomach churned. In four days, Tennessee would be a memory. Things would change once we reached New York. There might not be another time.

I cleared my throat. "Did you start those online courses?"

My heart slammed against my ribs when he looked away.

"Yeah, I'm all over it."

Of course he was. *This* was nothing to him. A "road thing," as Paige used to call it.

"Things happen on the road, Belle. You'd know that if you were single."

Was I single now?

Logan raised our joined hands, pointing toward a tiny sliver of light on the horizon. "Look ... sunrise."

The air left my body in a soft rush, that little piece of morning stealing my breath. And suddenly, all I wanted was a bed with a lot of covers I could hide under.

"I should go."

It came out like a question, and Logan answered without words, straightening in his seat and scrubbing a hand over his face.

The magic was gone.

I climbed out of the car, eager to get inside before the morning rays crested the mountains. Logan joined me on the sidewalk, his hands stuffed in his pockets.

"That was fun," I said sincerely.

He nodded, looking anywhere but at me. "Where did Daryl get off to?"

I hitched a thumb over my shoulder at the white Taurus parked a few spaces away. "That's his back up. Lukas something. Supposedly, Daryl only needs five hours sleep. He'll be around later."

Nodding, Logan toed the pavement, chewing his lip.

My thumb danced over the Mustang logo on the fob clutched in my hand. Reluctantly, I held out the keys. "Here you go. Almost forgot."

He smiled as I dropped the set into his waiting palm. "I've never let anyone drive my car."

I rolled my eyes. "Please. I didn't even put twenty miles on the beast."

"Beast?" His brow quirked as he took a step into my space. "She's a girl."

Twisting my mouth to one side, I fluttered my lashes. "Whatever you say."

The smile melted. "You're so fucking cute."

He swung his gaze to the horizon, his eyes warming to turquoise in the barely there light.

"I better go," I said.

If I thought Logan would stop me, I was mistaken. But I did sense him watching me as I walked away. Without my jacket, I felt exposed, even though the sky had yet to turn and I was merely a shadow.

Once inside, I leaned against the wall and pried off my boots. Groaning, I wiggled my toes inside the cushy socks.

My heart rate spiked when a soft knock echoed in the small foyer. I tiptoed to the door to check the peep hole, my breath trapped in my throat. Blond hair. That's all I saw. But I knew it was Logan.

I swung the door open. "Hey, what—"

He crashed into me with enough force to knock me off balance. Not that it mattered because his hands were on my ass, his rock-hard chest pressed against me.

"You didn't kiss me good night," he rasped.

I tipped my head back to meet his gaze. "It's morning."

Curving his hand around my thigh, he lifted me off the ground like I weighed nothing, and we were eye to eye. "Then kiss me good morning."

I smiled, because if Logan really wanted a kiss, he'd just take one. It wasn't like I minded his little sneak attacks. But then I realized, he didn't want to kiss me. He wanted me to kiss him.

For a good five seconds, I just stared. And then slowly, so slowly, with my eyes wide open, I pressed my lips to his. It wasn't a kiss, but an invitation. "Do you want to come upstairs?"

Logan's gaze roamed over my face, and that made me a little nervous. But then he smiled. "Yes."

Just ... *yes.*

His lips touched mine as he eased me to my feet. When he headed for the stairs, I felt a tug on my arm and realized our fingers were laced and I hadn't moved.

He looked back at me with questions in his eyes. And my answer was the same as his. *Yes.* To whatever he offered. As if Logan knew my legs were the only thing keeping this train from moving forward, he doubled back and swept me up.

"I can walk," I protested, secretly grateful I didn't have to.

He smiled, but said nothing. And then, because he was right there, our endless night lingering on his skin like an imprint, I kissed his neck. His fingers dug into my flesh, and he released a sharp breath. And I did it again. And again. Normally, it was all Logan moving us toward the finish. But not right now. Right now it was me. Because I remembered this from before. And I liked it. But now it was after, and I still liked it. And I wanted it. I wanted Logan.

Gripping his T-shirt, I held on tight when he tried to lay me down on the bed. And for once, he was the one off balance. The clumsy one. We toppled onto the mattress, all arms and legs. My hands on his belt, his mouth ... everywhere.

And the words. His: "Fuck baby, I want you," and "God, you smell good," and "Yes. Fuck yes."

And then mine: "Now ... *Please.*"

Everything got quiet and still. Frantic, but not. Because this was going to happen.

Did I want this to happen?

Logan's weight disappeared, and he was on his feet, looking down at me, the hem of his T-shirt in his hand.

"On or off, Victoria?"

His eyes were a darker blue than I'd ever seen, filled with desire. But still, the choice was mine. Another night of not quite sex, if that's what I wanted. A safety net.

"Off. Take it off."

And though I knew I could still change my mind, something clicked as I watched him slide out of his clothes. I scooted toward the pillow, and he smiled, eyeing me like I was prey. And then he was on me again, hands under my dress, tugging off my boy shorts.

I squeezed my eyes shut, the world shimmering around the edges as his tongue dipped between my folds. Not gently, like last time. But urgent.

"So sweet," he growled in between licking and biting and sucking. "Your cunt is so sweet." I stopped moving, and he peered up at the same time I looked down. "You don't like that word, princess?"

His voice was rough. Challenging. But his eyes were still soft. Still gentle. Still Logan's.

"I like it," I was surprised to hear myself say. And he smiled, like he knew it all along. And maybe he did. Because this, all of it, felt so right. I didn't have time to ponder, because his hot mouth descended again. One finger slid inside me and found that place on my inner wall that made everything clench.

"Logan ..." My fingers coiled into his hair, and the world splintered. And I was coming. And chanting. Writhing against him.

His free hand found mine, fisted in the sheets, and he pried my fingers apart, lacing our digits. Like he knew if he didn't, I might float away. His lips moved to my inner thigh as the last waves of my orgasm receded. And then ... nothing. My eyes flew open because he was kissing that spot on my skin where there was no feeling. Except that there was. In my head, there was.

Logan finally finished, and he rose to his knees. With our fingers still threaded, he pulled me up so he could tug my dress over my head.

"Wait," I said. His head cocked to the side when our eyes met. "No

... Not wait. I just ... I want to get under the covers."

He nodded, something creeping into his eyes. Disappointment? Maybe I'd imagined it, because he tossed back the comforter. When I scrambled underneath, he followed me and drew the blanket over our heads like a tent. I almost laughed, because it felt like we were hiding.

"Kiss me," he said, his fingers in my hair. And then his mouth crashed into mine, and I tasted myself on his lips. When he finally broke the connection, he rolled away, and out of the corner of my eye, I saw him rip the foil packet with his teeth.

God, I was such a novice. How did I forget about that part?

"What is it?" he asked, grasping my chin and coaxing my gaze to his.

I thought about lying. But this was Logan. "I'm so stupid. I forgot about condoms."

It was meant to be a joke. Self-deprecating. But his eyes flashed with something feral. Just as quickly, it disappeared. "Lucky for you, I didn't."

The post orgasmic fog had lifted enough to let all my worries creep inside, filling the space in our little tent. And of course, Logan noticed that too. He was above me now, his slim hips between my legs.

"Are you okay?" he asked, and when all I could manage was a jerky nod, he pushed the covers off. His eyes narrowed, gaze roaming over my face. "Baby, you look scared. Tell me what's wrong."

"No, I'm fine." I slid my arms around his neck and tried to pull him back to me. Back to where we were just minutes ago.

But he didn't budge, shifting his weight to the side.

"Why are we stopping?" I asked, even though I feared the answer.

"We're not. I'm just waiting." I cut my gaze to the side and found him smiling. "I want all of you, Victoria. When I'm here," his fingers dipped between my folds at the same time his lips brushed my temple, "I want to be here, too. Inside your head. So tell me what it is."

Before I completely ruined the moment, I took a deep breath. "I

190

don't know how this is going to go. My body could let me down."

Let *you* down.

He grinned. "I don't think that's going to be a problem considering all the orgasms."

I bit my lip. "You weren't ... you know ... inside, before."

Propping on his elbow, he looked down at me. "So you're worried about me, then?"

What really worried me was this conversation. The need for it. "You've seen the scars on the outside, but inside. My pelvis was crushed. What if ...?"

I couldn't tell him the real truth. That I worried something was wrong. Inside. That when they put me back together, maybe they missed something. It was an irrational fear. But I pictured the mesh that held me together. The fragile seams.

Logan eased on top of me, and despite my trepidation, I opened for him. "Tell me if I hurt you," he roughed out. And then I felt him at my entrance. Resting his forehead against mine, he sank in an inch. When I gasped at the intrusion, he stilled.

"I'm okay," I said. "I'm good." Another inch. And another. And then I was full. So full. "Oh ... God."

"Open your eyes, Victoria." My lids fluttered open and I met his gaze. So intense. The truest, bluest blue. "Are you still okay?"

I nodded, and unable to find the words, I wrapped my legs around his waist.

This time, he was the one who closed his eyes. "Fuck ... fuck ... *fuck.* Tell me you're good, because I want to move, baby. You feel so fucking tight. So wet. I can't ..."

Sliding my arms around him, my fingers threaded the soft strands at the back of his head, and I guided him to the crook of my neck. "Go," I whispered, close to his ear.

And he did. Slow at first. Then faster. Harder. All the while, he spoke softly against my skin. And then his lips found mine, and our tongues joined the dance. The rhythm. The song. And when I toppled over the edge, Logan was right there with me. Ready to break my fall.

33

Logan

I stumbled out of bed with the ringing phone in my hand. Evening light poured through the window, the rays barely touching the tip of Tori's exposed foot.

We'd spent all day in bed. Fucking. Eating. Talking.

Tori stirred, rolling onto her back with her eyes closed. And with the sheet tangled low on her hips, exposing her tits for me to feast on, I seriously considered letting my sister's call go to voicemail. Fighting off the urge, I snatched my boxer briefs off the floor and headed for the bathroom. With one last look at the heaven I was leaving in the bed, I closed the door behind me.

"Hey, Laurel."

"Lo. Where have you been?" Irritation threaded her tone equally. "I've called you three times."

I took a seat on the edge of the tub. "Sorry, I was ..." I drew a blank. Well, not really a blank since Tori's fine ass popped into my head. But nothing I could share with Laurel. "Really tired. I was up all night."

"You were partying ... in _Nashville?_ You hate Nashville."

Not anymore.

"I'm not really in Nashville. I'm north of there at the Fontanel Inn. Ever heard of it?"

She snorted. "Of course I have. It's a little rich for my blood."

Biting my tongue, I stopped short of telling her I'd bring her here after the tour. Keeping Laurel out of Nashville was high on my list of priorities.

I grunted noncommittally, and she moved on. "Listen, I was wondering if you could do me a favor?"

"Yes" danced on the tip of my tongue. Then I thought about Jake. "Depends."

"Okay ... I have a friend who lives there." My back stiffened when I thought of all the "friends" who'd kept Laurel hidden during the months I was looking for her. "I used to sleep on her couch when Timmy ... when he'd get mad at me."

Timmy. The owner of the strip club where Laurel used to dance. He'd paid for every bruise he'd put on my sister with one of his teeth. Good times.

"Anyway," Laurel went on, "she really wants to go to your show. Do you think, I mean, is there any way ...?"

"I can get her tickets," I said, digging my fingers into my eyes. "Text me her name, and I'll pass it on. They'll be waiting for her at Will Call."

"Thanks, Lo."

Silence swirled between us, the way it had every time we'd spoken since our fight. I was about to say my goodbyes and peace out the conversation when Laurel sighed. "Aren't you even going to ask?"

I gnawed on my thumbnail, a habit I'd given up years ago after Jake slapped me in the head one too many times.

"Stop chewing your nails, boy. You nervous about something?"

Dragging my shoulders back, I glared at my reflection in the mirror. "Ask about what?"

I knew.

We both knew.

But the sooner my sister got it into her head that I'd never willingly inquire about Jake, the better.

"Dad."

That single word set my teeth on edge. "Don't have one, darlin'."

"Why do you still hate him so much?" she hissed, her tone laced with venom. For me. Not the monster.

The truth lodged in my throat like a ball of cement. But after all these years, I couldn't call it forth. And even if I could, Laurel wasn't prepared to hear it.

"He's a shitty person, Laurel. He doesn't deserve your love."

"Everybody deserves love, Logan. Even Daddy. Even me." Her tone softened. "And especially you."

She sounded so vulnerable, all the fight left me. "I love you, baby girl. Isn't that enough?"

Her silence said it all. It wasn't. My sister took love where she could get it. Even the bad kind. Because she had no self-esteem. And that was Jake's fault too.

"I gotta go," I said. "Text me your friend's name. I'll hook her up."

I pressed end before she could reply.

At the sink, I ran a hand through my hair and splashed some water on my face.

Everyone deserves love.

"Yeah, right," I mumbled to my reflection.

Shaking my head, I wandered back to the bedroom where I found Tori with her back propped against the headboard, staring out the window.

She whipped her gaze in my direction. "You're here."

For a moment, I didn't move. "Yeah," I said slowly as I walked to the bed. "Where else would I be?"

She looked down at her hands. "I don't know. I thought you left."

I stopped in my tracks. "Do you want me to go?"

After last night and today, I'd never thought about it. But obviously she had.

"Not at all."

Relieved, I climbed onto the bed. Onto her. Nudging her legs apart, my lips found that spot on her neck that I loved. But she didn't respond.

Tipping back, I looked down my nose at her. "What is it?"

Her lashes fluttered, a sure sign I wasn't imagining things. Something was up.

"Was it good?" she asked in a small voice.

And I knew she couldn't be talking about the sex. There was no way. But when she lifted her gaze, the doubt was there. How could she not know?

Sighing, I laced our fingers together and rolled onto my back. "Come here."

She pulled a face. "I'm right here."

I gave her hand a tug, and reluctantly she scooted down. When I shifted onto my side, she followed suit.

"How was it for you?" I asked, and surprisingly, I wasn't entirely sure what her answer would be.

Maybe the metric ton of orgasms I coaxed from her body wasn't enough.

A shy smile broke on her lips. "Good."

Cocking a brow, I slid my hand to her ass. "Just good?"

"Really good."

Slotting my leg between hers, I pulled her closer. Flush against me. Skin to skin. "What did you like the best?"

She pondered for a moment. "Promise you won't laugh." Right on cue, I did just that. She responded with a scowl. "I'm not telling you now, jackass."

Heat flashed in her gaze, and not because I was rocking my leg against the warmth between her thighs.

"Come on." I rocked a little harder. "Tell me."

A sigh and a great big eye roll. "The kissing, all right?" After a long moment of stunned silence on my part, Tori tipped her chin stubbornly. "What did *you* like best?"

Her knees fell open when I eased her onto her back, and her soft thighs molded my ribs. "This."

She looked disappointed. And honestly, I felt like a dick for lying. Or misdirecting. Because it wasn't her pussy that I liked best. It was the feel of her legs around me. Her warmth. Everything. All the things.

Before Tori could pull the rest of the truth from me, I kissed her. Long, slow, and hungry.

She broke the connection and blinked up at me with hooded eyes. "Can I be on top?"

The words barely left her lips and I had her above me, straddling my waist. My hand came to rest on her hip, right over the braided skin, and dread swam up and clouded her pretty gaze.

"Is this hurting you?" Stupid question. Anything that had to do with the accident caused Tori pain. From her memories to her scars to the void that might never be filled. "Physically? This position?"

"No. I just ... I didn't realize you could see everything if I was like this." Her shoulders sagged. "It's not sexy."

For all her confidence, and the girl had a bunch, it didn't translate to whatever she saw in the mirror. What I saw when I looked at her.

"You're sexy, Victoria." Her eyes locked onto mine. Holding. Searching. "You think this—" I ran my thumb along the scar below her breast— "makes me want you less? You're more than the fucking scars, baby. More than the stories they tell. You're just ..."

Everything.

She didn't see it because her pieces were scattered. And one day when she was whole, this would probably be over. Until then, I'd take what she offered.

"I'm what?"

Twining a hand in her hair, I brought her lips to mine. "Perfect the way you are." Snatching a condom from the nightstand, I winked at her. "Now ride me like it's your fucking job."

34

Tori

Logan stepped onto the private balcony, blue eyes roaming over me from tip to toe. Dressed for the gig tonight, he wore his favorite jeans—faded with holes in both knees—and a black T-shirt that fit like a second skin.

His hair had grown out since we started the tour and fell over his eyes, messy in all the right ways. And he hadn't bothered to shave. All and all, he looked every inch the rock god. And suddenly, the thought of thousands of women checking him out did things to my stomach.

Bad things.

Painful things.

Dropping into the chair beside my lounger, Logan frowned as he continued his slow perusal of my body. Even though we'd been naked together for the majority of the last three days, this was different. Stretched out on my stomach under the unforgiving sun in just a bikini, I felt more exposed than I ever had when we were in bed.

I was about to sit up and pull on my robe when he said, "You're going to burn, baby. How long have you been out here?"

I smiled. "Not long. And I won't burn."

He picked up my foot, and I almost purred as he began to rub small circles on my instep. "I'm not so sure about that. You look a little pink."

My eyes drifted closed. "Trust me, I never burn. I'm half-Mexican."

He stopped rubbing. "Really?"

"Um-hmm ... on my mother's side." When he didn't say anything, I twisted to look at him. "You seem surprised."

And how could I blame him? My bronze glow had faded years ago. With the exception of my yearly trip to the Guadalupe River in the spring, I never got any sun.

"No, I can see it," he said, returning to his task. "I was just thinking about Zoe. I assumed your mom was blond, since your sister's so ..."

He squirmed, and I smiled. "Fair?" If there was a politically correct term for "white," that was it. But I hated mincing words. "Chalky? Pasty? Kind of like you?"

One brow quirked high. "I'm not chalky, princess."

I laughed, resting my cheek on my folded arms. "Whatever you say. But ... Zoe ... she's adopted. Kind of."

"How is someone 'kind of' adopted?"

"She's a foster child." My tone turned wistful as I thought about my sister, the way she'd looked the first day I saw her. "She's been with my parents since she was four. Courtney, her birth mother, is in prison, but," I heaved a sigh, "she hasn't given up her rights."

Logan's heavy gaze found mine. "Why?"

He'd done it again—unearthed something so personal. Without even trying.

"Because of me, I think. The first Damaged album hit right after Zoe was placed in my parents' care. I'm not sure, but I think Courtney might be looking for a payday when she gets out."

"And when will that be?"

"Soon. Trevor's on it, though. He says we don't have anything to worry about."

But I *was* worried. And I think Logan sensed it. Because he didn't say anything more.

After a long moment, I felt the cushion on my lounger dip when he dropped a knee onto the side.

"Come to the show tonight?" He tugged on the string holding my bikini bottom together and, sweeping the fabric aside, pressed a kiss to my ass cheek. "Please."

"I don't know."

Slipping his hand around to my stomach, his fingers dipped lower, finding the slick heat between my thighs.

"Come ..." he roughed out, nipping the back of my neck. "Can you?"

"To the show?"

He smiled against my skin. "Sure. That too." Two fingers slid into my core, and he pumped hard, eliciting a harsh moan. "You look so fucking hot right now, Victoria."

I loved the way he said my name. It sounded so sinful on his lips. But then I remembered where we were.

"What if someone sees us?" I panted.

"Nobody's going to see us unless they have a helicopter."

It sounded logical. And honestly, I was too far gone to argue. It was like all the years without sex had turned me into some wild thing. Or maybe it was Logan. I wanted him. All the time. His mouth. His fingers. His cock. His dirty words.

Lost to the rhythm, I squeezed my eyes shut, grinding mercilessly against his hand.

"Fuck ... Lo ... God ... I'm going to come."

His teeth grazed my earlobe, and I felt him smile. "So do it. Let me hear you."

I flew apart, his name spilling from my lips like a prayer as he pressed open mouth kisses along my spine. Before the final spasm wracked my body, I heard his jeans slide down his hips, followed by the crinkle of the condom wrapper.

"Up, baby," he rasped as he pulled me onto all fours. And then he was inside me, buried to the hilt. "Am I hurting you?"

Every time. He asked me that *every time.*

I pushed back against him. "No. Please ..."

"Please what?" he growled. "Fuck you? Tell me you want me to fuck you."

My eyes rolled back. "I do. Oh, God. I do."

"Then say it." I gasped when his hand came down on my left ass cheek. Not hard. Just enough to sting. "Say it, baby."

"Fuck me, Lo ... Please."

He cursed and then pulled all the way out. Panicked, I whipped my head around.

Sunlight framed him, and I couldn't make out his expression. But his voice was demanding. "Roll over."

In this position, with my pussy bared to him, I couldn't have been more exposed. Unless I was on my back. In the sun. With nowhere to hide. Gripping the towel beneath me, I did as he asked.

"Don't hide from me, Victoria."

It was a standoff. And one I couldn't win. So I took a breath, and shoved the terry cloth aside.

He stepped out of his denim and then climbed on top of me.

"Why this way?" I asked as he pushed inside me again.

His lips ghosted mine, and he smiled. "Didn't you say kissing was the best part?"

35

Logan

Security met me in the parking lot at the venue. Before I'd made it two steps, Elise shouldered her way into the wall of flesh surrounding me.

"You missed the pre-show press conference," she accused as we shuffled toward the tents.

"Traffic."

And Tori. Between the fucking and the shower that followed, I'd kept the driver waiting for almost an hour.

"The driver said—"

"Traffic," I repeated, and when I cut my gaze her way, she pressed her lips into a firm line.

I wasn't in the best mood. Tori had refused to come to the show. And while I couldn't blame her—we were less than a week from the tabloid incident, and the press still hadn't let it go—I wanted her here.

Head in the game.

Taking my own advice, I pulled my shoulders back. "I'll do an extra couple of interviews in New York," I said as we reached the barricades. "Set them up."

Elise rolled her eyes. "Because there's going to be so much press coverage in the Catskills?"

Busted. Our next stop was upstate New York. Remote, with a laid-back vibe. The kind of place I used to hate.

I smiled. "Hey, I offered. If you line something up, I'm there."

Otherwise it was long mountain drives. Picnics. And as much sex as I could talk Tori into.

Fuck, I had it bad. The "it" everyone always talked about.

I'd been inside Tori's body over a dozen times in the past three days. And no matter what the tabloids claimed from the women who'd shared my bed, that was a lot. And yet, the mere thought of Tori made me hard, left me wanting. Because I did want her. Every soft piece. Every slick hole. All of it.

Elise mumbled a goodbye, heading in the other direction when we got to the media tent. I was so wrapped up in my thoughts, it didn't strike me as odd that no voices rang from inside the canvas cocoon.

"The prodigal son returns," Cameron said as I pushed my way through the flap.

I smiled, genuinely happy to see him. It felt like we hadn't spoken in … shit … I wasn't sure how long.

Maybe going in for a bro hug was overkill, but I would've done it. Except for the look on his face that said, "try it and you might lose a limb."

He was pissed. Pissed enough to make sure that whatever he had to say wouldn't be overheard. Because we were alone. Really alone. No Sean or Christian. No roadies or security. And since there were enough people roaming around outside to fill two stadiums, that couldn't be an accident.

Treading lightly, I closed the distance between us and shrugged off my backpack.

"Dude," I said, hand on my heart as I smiled down at him. "This is really romantic. But I hope you're not planning on proposing. Because, you know, I don't like you in that way. But we can still be friends, right?"

Cameron's hazel eyes flared, but I thought I detected a little amusement. "Sit down, jackass."

I flopped into the chair, still smiling. "What's up?"

Cameron tipped forward. "Really?" he hissed. "You begged off rehearsal yesterday. You didn't show up one time to the hotel to go over the new arrangements I'm working on. You haven't returned my fucking calls ... and you're asking me what's up?"

I scratched the back of my neck, "Yeah ... well ..."

My lungs refused to expel enough air to push out any excuses. Because I had none. I'd called off band practice yesterday because I didn't feel like going. But I couldn't tell Cameron that. I couldn't tell him anything. If he was pissed now, finding out about my fling with Tori would send him straight into orbit.

"Sorry, bro. It won't happen again."

Cameron looked as surprised to hear the apology as I was to offer it. But I meant every word. I needed to manage my time better.

"Sorry doesn't cut it."

Straddling the line between irritation and "I want to punch you in the face," Cameron waited for my reaction. The inevitable blow-up. And the revelation. Until that moment, I didn't realize I had a pattern.

I held things inside, then I hit something. And only after I let my temper take me for a ride, leaving devastation and destruction in its wake, did I finally cop to whatever I was hiding.

"Sorry is all I got, dude. Take it or leave it."

Please, please take it.

I may have been trying to do better, but I was unsteady, like a toddler learning to walk. Apply the right pressure, and I'd topple. I wouldn't say shit about Tori. But I might hit something, or someone, and since Cameron was the only one here ...

He blew out a breath. "Is there something I don't know?"

There were so many things he didn't know, I couldn't force out a response. Not even a shake of my head. But there must've been something in my eyes, because Cameron softened.

"Is it Laurel?"

Fuck. Fuck. *Fuck.*

"No. She's fine."

Spilling my guts about Jake would be simpler. An automatic get-out-of-jail-free card covering any and all indiscretions. But I couldn't do it.

Before Cameron could dig any deeper, Christian popped his head in the tent. "Is everyone alive in here?"

Cameron contemplated for a second before waving him in. "Yeah, we're all good."

It didn't feel that way, but who was I to argue? I was off the hook for the moment.

Christian joined us, feigning surprise as he looked me over. "Logan, right? I've heard of you."

Shaking my head, I ignored the goofy bastard and made eye contact with Sean as he strolled to the refreshment table. "Shiner," I mouthed.

"Where's your babysitter?" Christian asked. "I thought she'd be in here."

My anger rolled in like the tide. And I couldn't figure out why. It's not like Tori and I could wander hand in hand around the festival. Neither of us wanted that kind of attention.

Except when I spotted Dylan entering the tent with his boys, I thought maybe I did. I wouldn't mind it one bit if he saw me coax that smile Tori wore when she was thinking dirty thoughts. Because he sure as fuck had never seen it.

"She isn't here," I replied, taking the bottle from Sean. "Too many people."

Cameron's mood had vastly improved since everyone arrived, and he threw a smile in my direction. "Well, if you're lucky, you can find someone here and blow off a little steam." I looked anywhere but at him as I took a swig of my beer. And of course, he picked up on my discomfort. "Wait a minute ..." Cocking his head, he glanced me over like he could smell the sex on me. "You ain't suffering any. Let me guess, you found a little cutie out there in the sticks?"

"What cutie?" Anna cut in as she slid under Sean's arm.

"Logan's," my best friend replied, brushing a kiss to her hair.

Anna's brows turned inward. "I thought you were with Tori this week?"

With Tori.

Anna's question, coupled with the emerald gaze that had been able to see right through me since high school, stole the denial straight from my lips.

"He's not with Tori," Cameron scoffed. "They're just stuck together. Speaking of." He pointed the neck of the bottle at me. "A little birdie told me that you're about to get sprung."

I blinked at him. "Sprung?"

Cameron rolled his eyes. "Chase said that all you have to do is complete some online courses and they'll modify your plea agreement so Tori can head home."

Shifting my feet, I took another drink. "Uh ... yeah. I'm all over it." If all over it meant not even a little bit, then I was.

Anna's eyes locked onto mine, her lips parting with a question. But Sean pulled her a little closer and dipped his head to whisper in her ear. I took the opportunity to guzzle what was left of my beer.

"Be right back," I said to the group, shaking my empty bottle.

As I made my way to the refreshment table, I felt a pull on the back of my shirt. "Logan, hold up."

I turned to face the only woman I wouldn't rip apart for pressing the issue. "S'up, Anna-baby?"

She crossed her arms over her chest, frowning. It wasn't an angry frown, but the sympathetic kind that made my skin crawl. "Is that why you've been keeping to yourself? The classes?" Her soft tone elicited the same gut twisting response. "I can help you, Lo. You don't have to try and figure it out—"

Her gaze darted to my left, and she pressed her lips together. Reluctantly, I turned just enough to find Elise hovering a few feet away, trying to get my attention. She had a brunette with her. A pretty little thing with dark hair and eyes to match.

Seizing the opportunity to get away from Anna, I said, "We'll talk about this later," not caring one bit if she got the wrong impression. At least it would buy me some peace.

She patted my arm. "Sure, Lo."

As soon as Anna was gone, the brunette left Elise in the dust and strolled over.

"Hi," she said, peering up at me through her lashes.

Spotting the VIP pass around her neck, I gave her a smile and then shifted my focus to our coordinator. But Elise was too busy glaring a hole in the back of the brunette's head.

"It was nice to meet you, Jenny," she said in the most sarcastic tone I'd ever heard her use.

"It's *Ginny*," the brunette corrected with a dramatic eye roll.

"What. Ever," Elise shot back through clenched teeth. "Have a good time, y'all. I've got to get back to work."

Confused, I sidestepped Jenny or Ginny, or whatever the fuck her name was. "Wait," I hissed. "What is this?"

Elise inhaled a controlled breath as she turned to me. "*This* is your VIP. Full platinum, just like you requested." When I continued to stare at her, dumbstruck, she pinched the bridge of her nose. "You forwarded me her information a couple of days ago. Ring any bells?"

Laurel's friend.

Shit.

Roughing a hand through my hair, I sighed. "Yeah, right. Sorry. I mean … thanks."

Elise shook her head, muttering to herself as she marched away.

I nearly plowed right into Ginny when I turned around. And because she was my sister's friend, someone who'd showed Laurel a kindness when I wasn't around to do it myself, I forced a smile.

"So, Ginny, is it?" I wasn't completely sure of the name until she nodded. "How about I get you a drink and then we can find a good spot so you can take in the show?"

Tori

Technology can suck a dick.

I took another sip of wine, contemplating something worse.

The shriveled dick of a ninety-seven-year-old man.

Glaring at my laptop, I muttered, "Yeah, I'm talking to you."

But it wasn't the shiny silver computer I was mad at. It was myself. I should've known that once Logan was away from this little bubble we'd created, it would burst.

And it had.

Not seven hours after he'd left me, pictures popped up on social media. Photos of Logan with the brunette glued to his side. He'd asked me to go to the show with him. But being his first choice gave me little comfort. I wanted to be his only choice. Not his forever choice. But was it too much to ask for him to be satisfied with only me for one day?

He's a rock star, Inner bitch singsonged, like that was an excuse.

"Fuck that," I said to no one as I poured another glass of Pinot. "*I'm* a rock star. Rhenn was a rock star."

Guilt crawled over me. Rhenn wasn't Logan and Logan wasn't Rhenn. The comparison wasn't fair to either of them.

Rhenn and I had taken vows. And he'd never cheated. Logan was a fling. So technically, he wasn't cheating either. Which left me with no good reason to be angry.

Except that I was.

Stewing, I turned on the TV, since there was no way I was getting near the computer again.

And I drank.

Over the next four hours, I finished the bottle of wine and cracked open a pint of that cranberry whiskey Taryn liked.

I wasn't drunk. Just comfortably numb.

Pouring another shot, I gazed around at the clothes strewn on the chair, the dresser, and the floor. Logan's and mine. Comingled.

What a joke.

Infusing steel into my spine, I dragged my rollaway from the closet with every intention of packing. But then a rerun of *The Bach-*

elor diverted my attention. By the time the rose ceremony came to an end, I decided that I needed a reality show of my own.

Maybe I was a *little* drunk. And pathetic, since I'd stayed up all night obsessing about Logan and what he was doing.

Making use of the cabanas the venue provided, I assumed.

With the brunette.

Just before sunrise, a car door slammed outside. Creeping to the window, I peered out the shutters. Logan, looking totally disheveled as he walked the well-lit path to the carriage house.

Not his carriage house.

Mine.

Hell no.

Smiling smugly, I crossed my arms over my chest and waited for Daryl to tell Logan to get lost. Nothing.

The fuck?

I heard the beep as the lock disengaged. Surprised, I jerked my gaze to the nightstand where one of the plastic keys was missing. And then Logan was climbing the stairs.

Grabbing a handful of clothes from the floor, I stalked to my suitcase and tossed the items inside.

"Couldn't sleep?" he asked after a moment.

Anger expanded in my chest. Invisible. Noxious. Turning to unleash my wrath, I found him staring at me. With a damned smile. Pushing off the banister, he crossed the room, crooked grin firmly in place.

Stunned, I froze when he gathered me in his arms, breathing me in like I was his air.

Some of my anger dissipated from the contact. *No.* Sliding my palms to his chest, I ignored the heat and the sparks igniting under my skin, and I shoved. Well, nudged. It barely fazed him. All I got was a weird look when he tipped back.

"What are you doing here?" I asked, not at all pleased with the softness in my tone.

He cocked his head to the side. "Where else would I be?"

I felt my eyes narrow and registered the surprise on Logan's face when he noticed. "At the venue."

With the brunette, and screw that chick, I wasn't going to mention her. Give Logan that kind of power. But then I realized, he'd probably already screwed her. And the only power I had was flight. I could leave.

Logan's gaze shifted to my laptop. He stared for a good twenty seconds before bringing his eyes back to mine.

And then he pressed a napkin into my hand. "I got this for you," he said as he toed off his boots. "They didn't have plain sugar, so you'll have to settle for chocolate chip."

Sinking onto the side of the bed, I blinked at the cookie while he tugged his shirt over his head.

"Just tell me, Lo," I said softly.

He tossed his wallet on the nightstand. "Tell you what?"

When I met his gaze, he didn't shy away. "Who's the girl?"

"A friend of my sister's. I got her a VIP pass." He took a step toward me. "Would you believe me if I said I didn't fuck her?" Another step. "That she didn't blow me and that I didn't even kiss her? And that I sat in a car for four hours in traffic, just so I could get back here and bring you that fucking cookie?" Tucking his knuckle under my chin, he nudged my head back, blue eyes digging into mine. "Would you believe any of that, Victoria?"

He sounded sincere, but more than that, why would he lie? He didn't have to. We weren't committed.

I sighed. "You don't owe me anything, Lo. We're not ... we haven't ..." I licked my lips. "I just want the truth. Is that the truth?"

His hand slid to the back of my neck. "I wouldn't lie to you."

Please don't let me be making a mistake.

"Then ... I believe you."

He blinked like he was surprised. Like I'd given him a present. And then he smiled, thumb stroking my cheek. My lips. The curve of my jaw.

"If you don't want to go to the shows with me, that's cool. But I'd

209

hate to come back one night and find you out with some dude. So why don't we keep it exclusive until ..."

Until.

The proposal dangled between us, open ended. We could end tomorrow. Or next week.

Or never.

I smiled at the hopeful girl whose voice echoed somewhere deep inside. She was still in there. Broken and small. But still around.

With her urging, I leaned into Logan's touch. "Until is good."

36

NEW YORK, NY.

Logan

Standing outside the Good Morning America Studio in Times Square, I toed the black *X* taped to the stage while we waited for our segment to be announced.

Beside me, Cameron fiddled with his guitar strap. "I can't believe this," he said out of the corner of his mouth, his eyes shining with excitement as he glanced over the crowd. "How did we even get here?"

I cut my gaze right, zeroing in on Tori. The tiniest of smiles curved her lips, and I knew her eyes were locked on mine behind her dark shades.

"No clue, bro," I replied, smiling back at her.

But I knew. I was in bed with Tori when she got the call from Taryn informing her that Justin had a sore throat and Drafthouse had to beg off the charity show in Central Park.

Did I feel bad that Tori gave Caged the nod? No. Did it drive home the point that we had to keep our casually exclusive whatever-the-fuck-we-had-going-on private? Absolutely.

Honestly, it was getting harder to do. In the two weeks since we'd left Tennessee, I'd made an effort to manage my time better. I owed it to my band, my music. But dragging myself away from Tori was difficult.

Maybe once we got home ...

I didn't want to think about home.

I was happy just being out here on the road, experiencing all this shit with my girl.

My girl.

Slowly, I felt my brows turn inward, because when did that happen?

Contemplating, I chanced another peek to my right just as the host bounded onto the stage. The crowd erupted into applause, but all my focus was on raven hair, honey-colored eyes, and the sun-bright smile directed solely at me.

Tori *was* my girl. A piece of her anyway. Maybe that's all she had to give. A piece. Maybe the lingering sadness in her eyes was the one fragment she could never give anyone. The piece that died with him.

And maybe I'd have to be all right with that.

For now.

Tori

THE SUN POURED through the fortieth-floor window, casting a glare on my iPad. Even with the spots dancing on the screen, I could clearly make out Taryn's snarl.

"I'm going to kill him, Belle."

I nodded wearily, my attention divided between our conversation and the phone resting next to me on the couch. Elise was already at the next location upstate, leaving me to handle some of the logistics for this event. Not that there was much to handle. The free show in Central Park wasn't a Twin Souls production. Caged was one of half a dozen bands slated to perform at the concert to raise money for the New York Endowment for the Arts.

"I can't believe you're so calm," Taryn huffed, suspicion threading her tone. "Why?"

It was hard to get worked up with a steady dose of oxytocin flowing through my system from all the sex. I'd looked it up because I thought there was something wrong with me. Ever since Logan and I started hooking up, I stayed in a perpetual state of near bliss. I vaguely recalled this feeling from my youth, the all-over body glow I had when Rhenn discovered how to give me an orgasm. But this was different. More intense. Maybe because I didn't know back then that life was fragile. Happiness was fleeting.

Nothing lasts forever.

Shaking that thought away, I refocused on my best friend. "What's the use in getting upset? Mac's going to do what he's going to do." It was the truth. Mac wasn't trying to get my attention. Or make me see reason. He was greedy. But he couldn't exactly take me down without doing serious harm to his own image. So why not destroy mine?

Taryn chuffed out a breath. "We'll see. When are you coming home?"

"After the Florida show."

She marked it on the big ass planner she kept on her desk. "Are you flying out with the boys?" My blank expression drew a frown. "Dylan and Becks? They're coming home to speak with Miles about signing over his rights to the unreleased tracks, remember?"

Pulling my legs under me, I traced a finger over the heart I'd drawn on the knee of my jeans in red marker. Was I in high school? All I needed was Logan's initials in the center.

"Yeah," I said slowly, smoothing a hand over the little doodle. "I won't be flying anywhere with Dylan."

A long moment of silence turned into two, and I could practically feel a piece of Taryn shrinking from the finality of my statement. The screw in my chest tightened, and I shifted my gaze to the New York skyline to avoid the discontent in her eyes.

Whether she wanted to admit it or not, Taryn held onto the hope that someday Dylan and I would get together. Like he could be inserted into Rhenn's spot in all our framed pictures and the evolution would be complete.

I couldn't fault her. Hell, a year ago, I *was* her. When Taryn decided to leave her ex behind and pursue a relationship with Chase, it was like something shifted in our world. Like the door to the past was closing, sealing our memories on the other side.

"Why?" Taryn finally asked, her voice almost child-like.

Sighing, I met her stormy blue gaze. "I'm trying to move on." The truth spilled over my tongue, bitter and sweet in equal measure. "Dylan ... he'll never be more to me than a friend. One of my best friends. But that's all." A knock echoed off the high ceiling in the suite, saving me from any further explanation. "Someone's here." I smiled. "I'll call you tomorrow, okay?"

Taryn cleared her throat, holding me tight with unblinking eyes. Like if she didn't let go, I'd change my mind.

After a moment, she finally relented. "Yeah, okay." My finger hovered over the end button, waiting. Hoping. "I love you, Tori."

I released the breath I'd been holding. "I love you too, T-Rex."

She cut the connection before I had the chance, and a background photo of Rhenn populated the screen, superimposed over my reflection. Gazing into his rich, chocolate brown eyes, I waited for the searing pain to take me whole. But all I felt was a dull ache in the place where he'd always live.

A second knock brought me back to the present, and I struggled to my feet.

"Coming!" I called as I padded across the plush carpet.

Popping up on tiptoe to check the peephole, my stomach did a flip when I spied the redhead standing in the hall. Anna. I smoothed my hair—why I didn't know—then opened the door, offering a cautious smile. "Hey, uh ... Anna."

She blinked at me, her mouth slightly agape. From what Logan had told me, Anna was a fan, so I waited patiently for the awkward moment to pass. Within seconds, Willow surged forward, throwing her arms around my legs. "Vitoria!"

214

She beamed up at me with a gap-toothed smile that melted my insides. I'd steered clear of Willow since our outing in St. Louis, the longing that hummed beneath my skin more pronounced when she was around.

"Hi, Willow." I sifted a hand through her curls while her mother sputtered an apology and tried to peel her daughter off me. "It's fine, really." Even though I had no idea what brought them here, or if I really wanted to know, I shuffled back to allow them entry. "Come in."

"We don't want to intrude," Anna said, looking around as she stepped inside. "We were just wondering ... I mean, Willow was wondering ... and me too ... if you'd like to go to the park? With us?" A blush detonated on her pale skin. "Would you like to go to the park with us?"

It took me a second to decipher the rambling invitation. "Oh ... I ..."

"Pweese, Vitoria. Come to the pawk." Willow peered up at me with expectant blue eyes.

What choice did I have?

"Yeah ... sure, that sounds like fun," I found myself saying with a gesture toward the living room. "Y'all have a seat, and I'll find my shoes."

Anna took Willow's hand and they sat on the couch while I did a quick sweep of the room for anything incriminating. Logan had been pretty careful about leaving his stuff lying around since the Tennessee incident, but that didn't mean there wouldn't be some trace of him here since he stayed in my room every night.

"Make yourself at home," I said. "I'll be right back."

As discreetly as possible, I snatched my phone from the sofa cushion. Once I was in the bedroom, I fired off a text to Lo.

Did you know Anna was coming by?

The message was delivered, but after a moment, I abandoned hope I'd get a return. Logan was terrible about responding to texts. He didn't even look at his phone half the time.

Growling in frustration, I plucked my sneakers from the floor and retraced my steps.

215

Perched on the edge of a sofa cushion with her hands clasped in her lap, Anna looked less than comfortable when I returned. "We didn't mean to bother," she repeated. "I thought since the guys were going to be busy all day, you might want to get out."

There was a familiarity in her statement that caught me off guard. Did she know about Logan and me?

Reeling from the implications, I eased onto the sofa, my Converse landing on the carpet with a soft thud. "I usually work during the day," I said weakly.

I wasn't above using my position as the bands' manager to throw her off the scent. Not that it did much good. Anna slowly redirected her gaze to one of Lo's discarded T-shirts draped over the arm of the chair, and she smiled.

Shit.

Since I didn't have an excuse for that, I shoved my feet into my shoes and then pushed to standing, eager to get out of here before the redheaded bloodhound found something really incriminating.

I pinned a smile to my lips. "Y'all ready?"

An hour later, with Daryl standing sentry at the edge of the playground, Anna and I took a seat on the bench facing the sandbox where Willow was playing.

"Is that weird?" Anna whispered, gesturing to my bodyguard. "Having someone follow you around all the time?"

I shrugged. "I guess it should be, but I'm used to it."

Her green eyes dimmed slightly, and I wanted to kick myself. Even a veiled reference to who I was inevitably circled back to the tragedy.

"I loved your music," she said, out of the blue. "Damaged was like ..." She shook her head and looked away. "*Everything.*"

I never knew quite how to handle that type of comment. Should I commiserate? Thank her? Shrug it off? In the end, I merely nodded.

"Yeah."

"It must be hard to move on after something like that." All her focus shifted to me like a laser. "Have you? Moved on?"

A response twisted around my tongue, but I trapped it behind tight lips to make sure I didn't blurt out something I'd regret. Every day, my feelings for Logan intensified. Not love. That would be stupid, since we were only playing around "until." But ... something.

"I'm trying," I conceded, hoping she'd drop it.

Anna squared her shoulders, suddenly serious. "Logan's a really good guy. I've known him since high school."

A flush rose from my collar, burning a path to my face, because that look she was giving me—she knew. Jesus. There was no doubt.

Anna touched my hand, and I realized I was telegraphing my panic. If she didn't know before, I'd just confirmed it. Which made her an evil genius or me a dumb ass.

"The guys don't notice things," she said gently. "But I do. And Logan is special to me."

She slipped that last part in so casually, but her tone was one step from a warning.

"Special?"

It was out there before I could reel it in, and my tone had an edge as well. A razor sharp edge that elicited a small smile from the redhead.

"Sean is Logan's best friend. I mean ... they're all best friends. You know how that goes." She rolled her eyes, but I remained stoic. Watchful. "We were roommates after high school—Sean and me, and Logan." I tilted my head to the side, and I know my mouth was open because I felt the air on my tongue. Anna turned a shade of red that matched her hair. "No ..." She grabbed my arm. "Oh, God no. Not *that* kind of roommate. Shit ... I'm messing this all up."

Pressing my lips together, I watched her squirm for a moment while I tried to figure out an appropriate response. I finally gave up and opted for direct. "What exactly are you trying to say, Anna?"

She sighed, looking more than a little uncomfortable. "I just want Logan to be happy. He deserves it. If you only knew ..." She shifted, eyes back on her daughter. "Just don't hurt him. I don't think he's ever ... well, I know he's never connected with anyone. He doesn't let people get close."

"But you're close," I pointed out.

She nodded. "Do you know anything about what happened with Sean and me?"

I'd heard rumors. A year and a half ago, Sean was the biggest player around, second only to Logan, and then one day, boom, he was off the market. And then Anna was there, his high school sweetheart. With a kid no less. And one look at Willow and you could tell she was his.

"Not really."

She brought her gaze to mine, and this time, I saw something else. Pain.

"After the accident ...your accident ..." she began hesitantly, "Mac offered Caged their first contract. Sean, well, both of us, we were so young. Invincible, or so we thought. And so in love. But I had my own plans that didn't include chasing my boyfriend around the world. I would've done it, though. Especially since ..." Her eyes drifted to Willow, and I just knew what was coming. "But Sean made a terrible mistake. We both made mistakes. Anyway ... when Sean and I split, Logan chose Sean. No divided loyalties with that one. He's not built that way. So Logan and me, we didn't talk for almost three years. But then he emailed me. I don't know what I'm trying to say, except that Logan doesn't always come right out and say how he feels. He's more an 'actions speak louder than words' kind of guy. So, if you care for him, you might have to be patient."

Her tone was raw, infused with sincerity, and I couldn't help but respond in kind. "I don't know what Logan told you, but—"

"Nothing," she was quick to interject. "He wouldn't say anything. He might not even realize what's going on. But I see it. I can read him." She looked down, shaking her head. "Poor choice of words, I guess."

Anna was all over the place, and I had no idea what she knew or didn't.

"I like Logan," I said with a smile. "He's different than I thought he was. But, still kind of the same. He has his life and his goals. But he's honest. And that's all I want from him."

All he can give me.

Anna looked me over, dubious. "Are you sure?"

No.

"Yes." She nodded grimly, and I took a deep breath. "If you could keep this to yourself ... I don't want anybody to think ..."

All the warmth drained from her emerald gaze. "You don't want people to know, is that it?"

"Yes. No." I shook my head. "I don't want people to think that I'm playing favorites. It would only hurt the band. And my reputation. I have some other things going on ... legal stuff."

She relaxed a little. "Yeah, I know about that. Nothing specific," she added when my gaze darted to hers. "I'm a law student. I keep up with stuff like that. Especially when it affects the band."

Willow came trotting over, Daryl a step behind. He was smiling, a genuine smile that stretched across his whole face. I didn't know that was possible.

"I'm huggry," Willow said to her mother.

Anna sighed and shoved to her feet. "Let's see if we can find one of the pretzel guys around here. Then we need to get back to the hotel and get ready for Daddy's show."

"You're going?" I asked, pushing off the bench.

"Sure. Aren't you?"

Crouching in front of Willow with a Wet Wipe she'd produced out of thin air, Anna went to work on her daughter's hands. Did every mother have some hidden pocket where they kept all the things they needed to care for their child? I guess I'd never know.

"Tori?"

I shook my head, pushing the thought aside. "Sorry, what did you say?"

"Are you going tonight?" she asked. "To the show?"

Two sets of eyes, one emerald green and the other the bluest blue stared up at me. And I smiled.

"Maybe."

37

Logan

Becca, the rep assigned to the band for the Central Park gig, swept into the small building behind the stage. "We may have a situation," she announced, a tight smile frozen on her lips. "Nothing we can't handle, though."

Something in Becca's tone told me this wasn't as casual as she wanted us to believe. Christian must've thought so too because he was the first to react. Setting aside his bass, he tipped forward in his canvas chair. "What kind of situation?"

Becca twisted her hands in front of her. "Nothing to worry about."

If that were truly the case, issuing not one, but two disclaimers in as many minutes probably wouldn't be necessary.

Cameron went to speak but I cut him off. "Why don't you just tell us what's going on?" My tone was light, my smile nothing but casual.

"Well," she began, then bit her lip and sank onto the futon. "You see, last night ... I mean, early this morning, when we made the announcement that Caged was taking over for Drafthouse, we didn't anticipate ..."

My stomach sank when she paused her stammered explanation. If the fans were demanding refunds, it was their loss. Caged was prepared to put on the show of our lives. And fuck anyone who didn't believe we could do it.

Crossing my arms over my chest, I fought the frown with everything I had.

"It's the damnedest thing," she continued, brows drawn together. "People started lining up at twelve thirty a.m. And as of a few minutes ago, tickets were being scalped for seven hundred dollars a piece."

I could almost hear the collective breath the guys released.

"So what's the situation?" Cameron asked, taking his place beside me.

"We weren't prepared," Becca admitted. "When we agreed to the substitution, we thought we were trading down." A nervous laugh bubbled free. "It's not like Twin Souls offered up Leveraged or Revenged Theory."

At the mention of Leveraged, the warm glow in my chest evaporated. Side-eyeing Cameron, I could tell he wasn't happy about her comparison either.

"You still haven't told us how this is a problem," he said, irritation coloring his tone.

"We had to bring in extra security," Becca said. "It's going to cut into our budget." Her forced smile was back. "But, that's not your problem. I just wanted to let you know we did some shuffling, and Caged is anchoring the show. That'll give us time to beef up security." She pushed to her feet and brushed off her hands on her slacks. "You guys sit tight. It's going to be a little while."

Once she was gone, Christian jumped out of his chair. "Holy shit. What just happened?"

I smiled. " We moved up a rung, that's what."

Sean fished his phone from his pocket. "Anna's going to be here any time. She's bringing Willow. I'm going to tell her to stay at the hotel for a bit."

Angling for a better view of the crowd, I headed for the door.

"Careful out there," Cameron warned as he sank back into his chair.

At least he spared me the usual speech: *Don't start any trouble. Be cool. Don't take off with one of the fangirls and make us go looking for you.*

Just to keep him on his toes, I shot him a sly smile over my shoulder, waggling my brows. He scowled but said nothing. And why would he? I'd been toeing the line, showing up at his door semi-regularly to go over the arrangements.

Once I was out of sight, I put on my earbuds so I could listen to my texts.

Victoria 11:41 a.m. *Did you know Anna was coming by?*

Victoria 3:07 p.m. *I was thinking about coming to the show.*

Victoria 4:53 p.m.: *You've got a nice butt. Even if you suck at returning messages.*

Smiling, I scratched the back of my head as I beat a path for the side of the building. There were still a few people milling around since this was the only entrance for the VIPs, but at least I could hear myself think. I'd just lifted the phone to my ear when I spotted Mac heading straight for me, a tall, model-type tucked close to his side.

Since it was too late to avoid the bastard, I stowed my phone and squared my shoulders.

Mac held out his hand as he approached. "Logan."

In case there were any nosy photographers around, I slid my palm against his. But then I squeezed with enough force to let him know just what I thought of him. After overhearing bits and pieces of Tori's conversations over the last few weeks, I knew what kind of shit he was putting her through, even if she wasn't inclined to share the details.

"Why are you so far from home, Mac?"

"Just doing my part to support a good cause. You didn't think Twin Souls had the market cornered on that, did you?" The woman at his side gave a derisive snort, drawing my attention. And Mac's too.

"Sorry, babe," he said to her before returning his focus to me. "Logan, you know Harper, right?"

Mac's smile was sly, his eyes assessing.

"No."

But her name shook something loose in my memory. *Harper Rush.*

Her debut album was everywhere.

Chuffing out a breath, she looked away and muttered, "I'm not surprised."

Mac squeezed her shoulder. "Don't worry about it, babe." His tone was unmistakably loud, leaving no doubt that he wanted me to hear. And then his eyes found mine, and he added, "You don't need Twin Souls."

I was too busy trying not to throw up in my mouth, since the girl looked young enough to be his daughter. But then it hit me —*Twin Souls*?

"You're with TS?" I asked, my gaze fixed on Harper and not the lech at her side.

She rolled her eyes. "I was. I mean, I guess I still am."

Something didn't add up, so I dug a little deeper. "Then why aren't you on the Survival Tour?"

Her jaw hardened, but then her gaze flicked over my shoulder, and she froze. Mac was already focused on whatever caught her eye, and he said with a smirk, "That's a good question, Logan. Maybe you should ask your manager?"

Awareness rippled over my skin, and I turned, already knowing Tori would be there. She wasn't looking at me, though. I don't even think she registered my presence. Her gaze volleyed between Harper and Mac, a fury in her amber orbs that I'd never seen.

Cutting the distance in four quick strides, she stopped right in front of Harper. "If you're fixin' to break your NDA, let me know. I'll call my attorney right now."

Her rage brought out her drawl and a tone so venomous, Harper's eyes widened to double their size. Catching Tori's wrist when she inched forward, I stroked my thumb over her pulse point. "Easy, princess."

Mac blinked. First at Tori, then at me, then at my hand, still coiled around her wrist. And he smiled. "Still a spitfire, huh, Belle?" He shook his head and *tsked*. "Always trying to control the situation. How's that working out for you? It didn't have to be like this. Anyway, the show's about to start. If you'll excuse us."

When he brushed past us with a stunned Harper in tow, Tori turned to watch them leave, glaring daggers into their backs.

"What just happened?" I asked once they were out of earshot.

Tori dug her phone out of her pocket and took off down the path. I hung back just a little, but when she lifted the device to her ear and said, "Dylan. Call me. I need to talk to you," I saw red.

I was standing right fucking here, but instead she called Dylan. What the actual *fuck*?

Without thinking, I closed the gap between us and took her elbow.

"Are you crazy?" Tori asked, her eyes darting around. "There are too many people around here."

What did she think I was going to do—kiss her? Sink my fingers into her hair? Run a hand up her bare thigh and find out which panties were under that skirt?

Forcing myself to focus, I veered us off the path.

"Really, Vic?" I growled. "You almost took that girl down in front of God and everyone and you think *I'm* going to draw attention?"

I barked out a laugh and the anger brewing behind her amber gaze found a new target. Me.

Ignoring her death glare, my hand slid lower, past her wrist, and I laced our fingers. She grunted as I dragged her behind a deserted New York City Parks trailer abutting the wall separating the venue from the rest of the park. I continued to advance until we ran out of room and her back was against a plastic storage container that came to her waist.

"Are you crazy?" she hissed. "What if someone sees us?"

"Get over yourself. Nobody's paying attention." I wasn't sure if it was true. And I didn't give a fuck. "You want to tell me what just happened? And why you were calling Dylan?"

The last question slipped out from some unknown place.

She swallowed hard. "I can't."

I cocked my head so far to the side I felt the bones in my neck crack. "Why?"

"Because it doesn't concern you."

My hands came down hard on either side of her, fingers digging into the weathered plastic bin. "And what exactly *does* concern me?" My thumbs skated over the thin fabric at the curve of her waist.

"You just ... you don't understand."

My gaze flicked to her taut nipples, the flush rising on her chest, and finally her mouth. "I think I understand just fine." Sliding my hand to the hem of her skirt, I smiled bitterly when she squirmed. She wasn't going to tell me, but this—my fingers inched higher and her breath hitched—*this* she'd give me. A consolation prize.

Peachy.

And the worst part? I knew I'd take it.

"Turn around." I leaned in, my mouth so close now, I could feel her breath. "Turn the fuck around or I'm leaving."

She had the power. *Always.* The choice was never mine.

Slowly, she turned.

My palm skimmed her smooth thigh, up and up until I reached her panties. They weren't the tiny bikinis she usually wore, but some kind of boy shorts.

Cupping the back of her neck, I bent her at the waist. "Hands flat on the bin, princess. And don't move, or I won't fuck you." My fingers dipped inside her panties, over her slick flesh, and I leaned close to her ear. "You *do* want me to fuck you, right?"

I needed the words. All the words and all the thoughts. But I'd settle for just one.

"Yes."

She groaned when I plunged two fingers inside her sweet cunt. "I can make you come this way. But you want more, don't you?" My thumb grazed her clit. "Tell me you want more."

"Yes ... Yes ... I want more."

I pulled away, my lower half pinning her in place while I dug out my wallet from my back pocket.

Her head whipped around, lust-filled eyes locking onto mine.

"Turn around, Victoria."

I don't want to see you. As true as it was, I kept that part to myself.

She searched my face for a long moment, then did as I asked. My jeans hit the ground. And with her skirt bunched at her waist and her ass in the air, I stroked myself hard until my stomach coiled, and then I slid the condom over my shaft.

I planned to fuck her hard and fast. To tip over the edge and leave her wanting more. The way I did. But the minute I slipped inside her body, I knew I couldn't do it.

Fisting her hair in one hand, I kept the other flat on her back as I thrust.

She fought to find her rhythm, whimpering as she writhed against the plastic bin. "I want ... I want ..."

That voice ... it chipped away at my anger. And my resolve.

"What do you want?" When she didn't answer, I pulled all the way out. She jerked to standing when I tugged her hair. And then I spun her around and looked into her eyes. "Tell me."

She laid her palms flat on my chest, her touch searing me through my T-shirt. But she didn't speak.

Banding one arm around her waist, I lifted her onto the bin and she opened for me. Inviting me in.

Every instinct told me to go. Because this ... *her* ... it was too much. And too little.

Her fingers followed her gaze to my mouth. And then she kissed me. Softly. So fucking softly.

"Please ..." she whispered against my lips.

Curving a hand around her thigh, I pushed inside her warmth. "This?"

She groaned, resting her forehead on my shoulder. "Yes."

I fucked her slowly, deeply, my thumb tracing lazy circles over her clit. I knew she wanted more. The punishing rhythm. The relentless beat. But I refused. Because this ... *this* I could control. And I'd get her there on my terms.

When I felt her walls tighten around me, I tilted her head back. Her chin tipped forward, and I sank my teeth into her bottom lip. She came undone with a gasp, but no words. A bittersweet surrender filled with unspoken truths.

38

Tori

Tucked against the stone pillar in front of the hotel, I watched the pedestrians hustle down Park Avenue.

Jerking my attention to Logan when he picked up my rollaway, I said, "You don't have to do this. I can catch a cab."

He didn't say anything, just turned and strode toward the Mustang idling at the curb. We'd barely spoken since last night's show. After everything that went down, I was surprised he'd slept in my bed. And even more shocked when he woke me at dawn, pressing kisses to my shoulder and nudging my legs open.

But then, it came to me. This was our "until." And Logan was trying to tell me without words that we'd be okay. Friends. No hard feelings.

I knew it was silly to mourn the loss of something that never was, but I did. So when he left the suite an hour later, I decided to move up the date on my trip to Austin. Give myself a little time to adjust. Three days, and then I'd rejoin the tour upstate.

Wiping my shaky hands on the front of my jeans, I turned to Daryl with a forced smile. He pushed off the wall where he'd been trying not to watch the awkward exchange between Logan and me.

"Sorry about the last-minute changes," I said. "You can stay here or head up to Bethel. It's up to you."

Daryl thought about it for a moment, rubbing his chin. "You sure you don't need me to go with you?"

Surprised and more than a little touched by the offer, I shook my head. "No. I'll be fine in Austin. But thank you for asking."

A rare smile curved his lips. "Call me if you need anything." He patted my shoulder, a clumsy gesture that led me to believe he didn't offer this treatment to everyone.

Before I could think better of it, I levered up on my toes and pecked his cheek. "Thank you again."

He grunted something that sounded like goodbye before shadowing me to the curb.

Sliding into the passenger seat, I blinked against the tears stinging the back of my eyes as I fumbled with the belt.

Everything about this felt like the end.

"Ready?" Logan asked once I was strapped in.

I willed him to look at me, but he didn't.

"Yep. All set."

Moments later, as we crossed the Queensboro Bridge, Logan laid a little bag with a fancy label on my lap.

Le Pain Quotidien, Columbus Circle

Peeking inside, the smell of chocolate wafted to my nose. "Little cookies." I smiled over at him. "You bought me little cookies."

"I thought you were well traveled, princess. Those are macarons."

"French little cookies, then." As I broke a tiny piece off of one of the treats, it dawned on me. "Is this where you went this morning?"

"While you were planning your escape?" He spared me a glance. "Yeah."

Fingering the serrated edge on the bag, I chewed my lip. After a moment, Logan reached over and freed the abused flesh with his thumb. "Don't do that. I like your mouth the way it is."

Laying his hand on my knee, palm up, he wiggled his fingers until I got the hint and linked our digits.

"I wouldn't have left without telling you," I said, tipping forward

229

to get his attention when he didn't acknowledge me. "You know that, right?"

Inhaling slowly, he shook his head. "I don't even know *why* you're leaving. So, no, I can't give you that."

"I wanted to make things easier." It sounded stupid now, but he deserved the truth, so I pushed through. "I thought, after last night, that you wanted to move on."

Traffic ground to a halt, and with nothing to distract him, Logan finally shifted his attention my way. "Do you always think the worst?" As if the answer were written on my face, he smiled. Not a bitter smile, or a happy smile. Reflective. Like he could see straight into my head. "Yeah, I guess you do."

It was more of an indictment than an observation, and I thought about protesting, but I really couldn't. Because it was true.

I blew out a breath. "Do you ever think about balance?"

He quirked a brow at my abrupt change in topic. "Balance?"

"I don't mean balance like you're balancing something. What I'm getting at is ... you know how people have bad things happen to them? A fucked-up childhood, and then they become, I don't know, a rock star?"

Trying to make this personal wasn't a good idea, because Logan's jaw hardened to granite.

"Okay ... what about ..." I snapped my fingers. "JK Rowling. She's a good example." He went stone still, so I added, "Harry Potter? You've read Harry Potter, right?"

His nostrils flared, and he pulled his hand free. "Is there a point coming anytime soon? Or are you just trying to redirect the conversation so you don't have to tell me what's really going on?"

There was something different about his tone. An edge I'd never heard, not even when we used to spar.

Sinking back into my seat, I swallowed hard. "I was trying." My gaze dropped to my lap, to the little bag of cookies. "Never mind. I guess I'm not explaining it right."

Moments passed with only the sound of the traffic on the interstate and the hum of the engine.

230

"I didn't read Harry Potter," Logan finally said in a tone that sounded like he was confessing to a crime. "I'm not much ..." He rubbed the back of his neck. "I don't read."

I laughed. "A lot of people don't read."

He nodded, pressing his lips into a thin line. "So are you going to finish your story?" I shifted my gaze to the side window and a second later I felt his hand on my leg again. "Tell me, Victoria. I want to know."

Resting my head against the glass, I squinted into the sun. "I've read your bio, Lo. I know you don't like to talk about it, but your childhood was bad, right?" His reflection nodded. "And then it took five years for Caged to make it out of the dive bar scene. And JK Rowling ... she was on welfare. And she got rejected I don't know how many times before someone took a chance on her book."

A lump formed in my throat. Only Logan's hand on my knee, his thumb tracing lazy circles, calmed me enough to continue.

"See, I had a perfect childhood. My parents ... they're amazing. I never tried out for anything I didn't get. I won my first talent show when I was eight." I shook my head. "I don't even remember because it was only a blip. One of many. And then my first band, the Austin Dolls, we got discovered in a fucking mall."

Chancing a peek to my left, I found Logan smiling. "You're the full package, princess. What's the problem?"

"The problem is, there's always a price. But I didn't know that. Things came so easy. The perfect career. The perfect marriage. Money. Fame. And now I'm just trying to find my balance."

I cursed the tear racing down my cheek, but didn't have the will to wick it away. So Logan did it for me.

"I still don't know what you mean by balance," he said gently.

"It's that place in the middle where all the good things that happened are equal to all the bad things that came after. And I can start at zero again." I swallowed hard. "Maybe when I find that place, I won't expect the worst. And about last night. That woman—Harper?" He nodded. "She was the star of Dylan's sex tape. I should've just told you. But he doesn't even know I know."

Logan's eyes darted to mine. "What?"

"It's a long story. And we don't have time right now for me to explain. Maybe after I get back ..." After I got back everything would be different. There would be no more talking. Not like this.

Logan didn't say anything, just took my hand and pressed a kiss to my palm.

We rode in silence for a half hour, the whirr of the jet engines overhead increasing in volume the closer we got to the airport. When the GPS signaled our exit one mile ahead, Logan slid into the right lane. But something didn't look right.

"This isn't the terminal," I said as we made the turn into long-term parking.

Logan never squirmed. Not in all the time I'd known him. So the slight shift in his posture was noticeable. "I've got a couple things to take care of at home, so I thought I'd tag along. Unless you got a problem with that."

Another choice. But this one had consequences. Because Austin was home. Roots. Memories. Whatever vague notion I had of us didn't exist there. My lips parted, a refusal dancing on the tip of my tongue. But then I looked down at the bag of cookies in my lap. And I smiled. "No problem at all."

39

Logan

Tori fumbled with the keys outside the double doors to her mansion. The third time she tried to find the lock, I covered her hand with mine. "Let me help."

I knew it would be hard, coming here. But I didn't think it would be this hard. Not until the sedan pulled up to the gate with the big *G* entwined in the wrought iron bars. I remembered seeing it in the news reports after the accident, when the media laid siege to Tori's estate.

But this was different. *Real.* Tori once lived here with someone else.

Jealousy had always seemed like a dangerous emotion, one that I didn't inherit from Jake. But as I pushed through the door and into the grand foyer, that's exactly what I felt. Jealous. For a life that didn't exist anymore. And for the dead man who shared that life with Tori.

Brushing past me, she headed for a security panel with blinking lights while I freed my phone from my pocket. I was still waiting for the Lyft app to find my location when she appeared in front of me.

"What are you doing?" she asked, glancing at my screen.

I never told her I'd be staying, but still, I couldn't look her in the eyes. "Setting up a ride. But I can't get a bead on the location."

She didn't say anything for a long moment, and I had no choice but to lift my gaze.

A frown tugged her lips. "Service is poor out here. You're going to have to hook up to the signal booster. Let me get you the code. It's in the kitchen."

She reached for her bag, but I outmaneuvered her hands, cocking a brow at the massive marble staircase. "Really?"

She shrugged. "I probably won't sleep upstairs anyway."

Before I could ask why, she was off, her boots echoing on the polished floors. "Come on. I'll get you the code."

We passed room after room. Elegant spaces with high end furnishings and expensive art on the walls. But none of it looked lived in. Or inviting.

Once we got to the kitchen, Tori pulled open the door to the Sub-Zero. "Want a beer?"

"Sure." Retrieving two Shiners, she pressed a bottle into my hand. "You don't drink beer," I said as I twisted off my cap.

Shrugging, she looked down at the label. "I'm from Texas. Of course I drink beer. As long as it's the right brand." Leaning a hip against the counter, she took a long pull. And something about the way her mouth formed around the bottle ... *fuck.*

I shifted my feet, my cock twitching behind my zipper.

Maybe she'd agree to come to my place. Or maybe I'd just fuck her right here on the island.

"Logan ...?"

The beer caught in my throat, and I coughed. "What?" Wiping my mouth with the back of my hand, I cursed my one-track mind and her short skirt. And those boots. "Sorry. Did you say something?"

She arched a dark brow as if she knew what I was thinking. "I said: you don't have to get a Lyft. You can drive my car if you want."

"The Shelby?"

Smirking around her next sip, she rolled her eyes. "I was thinking the Mercedes, but sure. That's fine." Suddenly serious, she set her bottle on the counter. "Do you have time for dinner before you go?"

Hedging wasn't my style, so I plopped onto the barstool. "I do. But you seem uncomfortable having me here."

I watched her over the rim of my bottle, gauging her reaction.

She looked confused. "I didn't mean to come off that way. Besides Taryn, and ... um, a couple other people, nobody's ever stayed out here."

Guessing that one of the "others" was Dylan, I dug my thumbnail into the yellow label. Jealousy. What the fuck?

"You're welcome to stay, Lo." She sidled closer. "I have room."

Taking her by the hips, I pulled her between my legs. "Do you, now?" It was a stupid question, considering the size of her mansion. But then, I wasn't talking about the house. It was her life I was interested in.

She smiled so sweetly. "I do."

"Then I guess you better show me where I'll be sleeping."

The house was enormous. Seven bedrooms and at least as many bathrooms. And five living areas if I counted right during the tour. But I didn't see it all. The third story remained a mystery, along with whatever was behind the double doors at the end of the hallway on the second floor.

Once we'd finished with the show and tell, I'd excused myself and retreated to the guest room to shower just so I could get a handle on all the emotions pushing in on me.

Anger I could deal with, but this wasn't anger. I wasn't mad. Still, I wanted to tear things apart with my bare hands, or maybe just back

Tori against the nearest wall and plunge inside of her until she screamed my name loud enough to rattle the ghosts from the house.

But I couldn't hide out forever, so I made my way down the stairs. At the bottom, I took a left and wound up hopelessly lost. On my way out of the maze, I passed a circular room with a domed ceiling, and in the center sat a Steinway grand piano. Black lacquer beckoned me, gleaming under a pair of art lights. Following the call, I wandered inside, easing onto the matching bench as I tinkled the keys. The sound was rich, enhanced by the acoustics in the odd shaped room.

I'd just launched into a simple tune when a picture in a polished silver frame snagged my attention, knocking the wind out of me like a punch to the solar plexus. Tori with her sun-bright smile, nothing but promise in her eyes, standing next to the man who'd built her this house. I could try to pretend the last part wasn't true, that I didn't imagine Rhenn pouring over blueprints and making sure that every detail was just so. But there were too many things in the house that weren't Tori. Not the Tori I knew.

The jealousy crept back, stabbing through me like a sharp blade.

"There you are."

I snapped my attention to Tori's sweet voice, and the riot under my skin subsided, my heart expanding at the sight of her decked out in a yellow bikini. She didn't hide from me anymore, my girl.

My girl.

I'd just gotten used to the idea of it. And outside these walls, it was true. Maybe. Or was that an illusion as well?

Pushing to my feet, I raked a hand through my hair. "Hey."

My voice was huskier than usual, and what the fuck was that about? I'd already vowed to keep my hands to myself. Not that I had much choice. The room where I'd be sleeping obviously wasn't hers. But my cock didn't get the memo.

Tori glided toward me, a bottle of beer in her hand. I took it, eager for the distraction.

"Where's yours?" I asked in that same husky tone.

Tori didn't drink often, but when she did, we had some of our best

236

talks. Followed by mind-blowing sex and a sleep so peaceful I woke feeling drugged.

"I'll have some wine by the pool." She took my hand, and for a minute I forgot where we were. I wanted to kiss her. Fall on my knees, tug down her tiny shorts and bury my face in her sweet cunt.

"I can order a pizza," she said with a hopeful smile, totally oblivious to my lurid thoughts.

"Sounds good."

Cold marble chilled my bare feet as she led me toward the back of the house. Though I'd glimpsed the grounds during our tour, now that she'd opened the accordion windows and welcomed the outside in, the view took my breath away.

Tall trees of different varieties lined both sides of the property, stretching all the way to the lake. Unlike Sean's house, which sat right above the shore, Tori's estate was built on a bluff. A cliff some fifty yards away that went straight down into deep water.

Sinking onto one of the chaise lounges on the pebbled deck surrounding the swimming pool, I stretched my legs. I watched as Tori dipped a toe into the water. Her raven hair glistened in the fading light, a soft black curtain spilling over her shoulders. And her skin. She looked every bit the angel with those wings on display.

Tossing me a smile, she said, "Why don't you come in?"

I glanced down at my jeans before meeting her gaze. "I'm not exactly dressed for the beach, princess."

She eased down onto the first step, the water gently caressing her calves. "You know what I love about this place?"

"What?"

She pulled the string around her neck and her bikini top slipped off, freeing her tits. "It's really private." Biting her lip, she rolled one of her nipples between her thumb and her forefinger.

I took a sip of my beer, enjoying the show.

Disappointment etched her brow, and she stopped the sensual assault on her nipple. "You really don't want to come in?"

Reclining on my elbow, I palmed my thickening cock. "I want to watch." Tori blinked as if she didn't know what to do next. Which was fine. More than fine. "Touch yourself, baby." Hesitantly and with her eyes on mine, she dipped her hand inside her bikini bottoms. "What does it feel like?" I asked.

She licked her bottom lip. "Warm. Slick."

"Are you wet for me?" Her lips parted, and she nodded. "Say it."

Dropping her gaze to my hand squeezing my denim-clad erection, she swallowed hard. "I'm wet for you."

For me.

I wanted to believe it, but I wouldn't know for sure until we were face-to-face. "Come here."

She stepped out of the pool, achingly slow and so graceful. And then she was in front of me, amber eyes hooded, lithe fingers toying with her erect nipple.

Dropping a knee between my thighs, she leaned forward, brushing a kiss to my lips. And fuck ... she tasted so good. Like sugar on my tongue.

Her touch traveled south to the brass button on my jeans. Catching her wrist, I brought her hand to my mouth and licked her taste off her fingers.

She watched me with rapt attention, just a hint of her pretty pink tongue peeking out from between parted lips. "What do you want, Lo?"

My free hand cupped her nape. "Your mouth. On my cock."

Oddly enough, blow jobs from Tori weren't high on my list of priorities. I preferred the feel of her tight pussy. But tonight, I wanted those lips around my shaft and my hand on her throat when she swallowed me.

She tugged at my zipper, then hooked her fingers into my belt loops and dragged the denim just low enough for my erection to spring free. I guess if I'd really intended to keep things PG, I would've thrown on a pair of boxer briefs. But whether I wanted to admit it or not, sex with Tori was never off the table.

Threading my fingers into her hair, I guided her to where I wanted her. Eyes locked on mine, she slid down until her knees were on the deck. And then she lowered her head and swirled her tongue around the bead of pre-cum on my engorged tip.

"Suck, baby." And she did. Curling her hand around my base, she took me to that heaven in the back of her throat. "Fuck ... fuck ... fuck," I hissed as my fingers unfurled and I found that spot on her nape. "More."

My thumb glided back and forth along her throat, over the smooth skin and the tiny scar. And when she swallowed, I felt myself there. It was so fucking hot. Too hot. Too much.

"I'm going to come," I warned, and those eyes flicked to mine, a smile evident in the amber hue.

Even as the frenzy built, my stomach coiling and my balls tightening, I held back.

"No," I managed to grunt. "I want to fuck you."

Releasing me with a pop, she pushed to standing, and it was so quiet, just her gaze on mine as she stripped off my jeans. I managed to yank my shirt over my head before she climbed on top of me.

I froze when I felt her slick heat against my bare cock. Tori didn't notice, her hot mouth on my neck.

"I don't have a condom."

Tipping back, she blinked at me, and time stood still.

Telling her I was clean, that I never fucked without protection, sounded too much like begging. "I've got some upstairs," I said. "Be right back."

Her palm molded my shoulders, holding me in place when I tried to shift her body off me. "Have you been with anyone else since ... you know... us?"

She stumbled over the words, and I fought to keep from lashing out.

How could she even think?

"Nobody."

Snagging her bottom lip between her teeth, she nodded like she already knew. "Okay ... and how long before that?"

Really? We were doing this now?

I sighed. "About a week."

She searched my face, her gaze everywhere at once. "Before or after the health screening?"

"What?"

"The health screening for the insurance waiver? Twin Souls set it up."

"Oh ... before."

Admitting to my manager that I put off the tests until three days before we left for the tour probably wouldn't do me any favors. But right now, Tori wasn't my manager.

"You got a certificate of good health," she said. "I saw it in your file. No drugs. No diseases. And I'm on the pill."

"I thought you couldn't ..."

My jaw clamped shut when she winced. And this time when her gaze found mine, there was something else. A different pain.

"Physically, I can." She shrugged. "Maybe. I only have one ovary. But I can't carry ... I'll never be able to ..."

My mouth crashed into hers, stealing the words. And the pain. And her breath. She cupped my cheeks, pulling me closer.

When I finally broke our connection, there was lingering sadness in her eyes. And it gutted me. Threading my fingers into her silky locks, I touched my forehead to hers. "Shhh ... it's okay."

She nodded, resigned. Because what else could she do? And then she slid forward, and I felt her slick heat like an invitation. She rose slightly, allowing me access, and my hand found my cock, guiding the head to her entrance. And when she eased down on top of me, there was nothing in the world but her.

A vague notion took hold as she began to move. A tear raced down her cheek, and I kissed it away, tasting the salt and the sweet. And I knew then what it was—the glow spreading from my chest, owning every part of me.

Love.

40

Tori

In the morning, I followed Logan out to the garage to make sure the Shelby would start. A wistful smile curved my lips once the tarp came off.

"Candy apple red, and sexy as fuck, just like you."

Rhenn's voice receded quickly, leaving only a warm glow. No mind-numbing pain.

Logan knelt to check the undercarriage and cocked his head at my license plate. My cheeks ignited. "It's because of my nickname," I said of the "Beauty" vanity plates.

He nodded, then ducked his head and peered under the bumper. "Yeah ... 'Belle,' I get it."

I laughed. "You mean 'Beauty.'"

Pushing to his feet, he wiped his hands on his jeans, glancing at the plate again. "That's what I said. And I'm sure nobody'll disagree once I'm behind the wheel."

Slanting my gaze to his smiling face, I arched a brow. "You think you're prettier than me, don't you?"

He shrugged, and I tried to pull away in mock indignation, but he hauled me against his chest and said seriously, "Nobody's prettier than you, Victoria." Lifting me off my feet with lightning speed, he hoisted me to eye level. "Nobody."

Pushing the hair out of his face, my gaze traveled over all his fine features. Despite my teasing, I wasn't far off the mark. He was prettier than me. I traced a tiny scar right above his left brow. "What's this from?"

That familiar frost touched his eyes, and I could tell he was fighting to keep his smile. Cursing my stupidity, I blurted, "I'm sorry. I didn't—"

"I did a swan dive off the kitchen table when I was four." He rubbed the tip of his nose over mine. "Not everything in my life was tragic, princess."

He brushed a kiss to my lips, and his breath became my air. Sweet and hot and necessary. Before he could dive in for another kiss, I rested my forehead against his. "I'm having an early supper with my parents if you want to meet me there." When he blinked at me, I slowly tried to shake off the bear trap I'd stepped in to. "I thought you might like a home-cooked meal. No worries if you're not down."

One corner of his lips pulled into a half smile. "What time?"

"You're going to laugh." He shook his head even as his grin widened. "Four."

"Four?"

I sighed. "My dad used to work this weird shift where he got off at three, so my mom started serving supper at four. I'd skip lunch and dine with the fam. Then I'd eat my real dinner around nine. You can put me down now."

He tightened his grip. "What other weird habits are you hiding?"

I thought about it. "I put salt on my watermelon."

He wrinkled his nose. "Ugh. That's—"

"*Delicious.* And I'll order a melon from the grocery store and prove it."

Pulling a face, he eased me onto my feet. "You order your groceries? Why?"

I laughed. "Because I hate getting cornered in frozen foods while I'm trying to find my favorite ice cream."

He swept a curl behind my ear. "What *is* your favorite ice cream?"

"Blue Bell."

That half smile was back. "What flavor?"

"It's Blue Bell. Does it matter? Tell me your favorite, and I'll order some."

Dipping his head, he slicked his tongue over my bottom lip. "I don't care. As long as it goes well with cookies."

Sean's ringtone pierced the air for the fourth or fifth time, and I bit my tongue to keep from asking any questions. The lines were all blurry. If it were band stuff, didn't I need to know?

Logan's hand cruised through his hair as he took a step back. The loss of his proximity bothered me more than I liked to admit. "I'm going to take off so I can get finished by four."

Nodding, I pressed my lips together. "I'll text you my parents' address. Don't worry if you can't make it, though."

One beat turned in to two. And then five. "How long have you known me?" His tone held the frost he usually carried in his eyes when he was irritated. "A year and a half?"

I crossed my arms over my chest to ward off the cold. "Your point?"

This time when he pulled me close it was rough. His gaze snagged mine and held. "I don't do anything I don't want to do. And if I say I'm going to be somewhere, I'm there."

My teeth grazed my bottom lip. "I'm—"

"Giving me an out. I know." His features softened. "Am I that much of a dick?"

My gaze dropped to the polished floor. "No."

"Then what is it?"

Someday when this was over, Logan and I would still be friends. I'd still be his manager. So keeping my inner thoughts to myself was probably the best plan. But then his hand was in my hair, his thumb nudging my chin to meet his eyes.

"When I was eighteen, there was this girl who worked as a wardrobe consultant on our first tour. We used to talk. But then she sold a story about me to the tabloids. After that happened a couple more times I stopped being friendly with everyone, and I think I lost something. Because now I tend to order people around. I'm trying to get better."

His thumb skated over the column of my throat. "It's kind of cute that you think you can order me around, but ... *no*. If I don't want to do something, I won't do it. I won't even offer. So four o'clock?"

His words should've put me at ease, but they didn't. Because inside, I knew they were true. When Logan was done, he'd be done. And where did that leave me?

"Yep."

I managed a smile when he pulled away and strode to my car without a care in the world.

Balance.

He had it.

Shielding my eyes from the sun when the garage door slid open, I stayed rooted to my spot until he was gone. As I turned to walk back into the house, my gaze coasted to the other side of the garage, where another vehicle sat that no one would ever drive. I shuffled over and pulled the tarp back, revealing the bumper of Rhenn's Ford F150 Lightning.

Plopping down on my ass, I brought my knees to my chest and traced the letters on the vanity plate—Beast.

You're the Beauty to my Beast.

When I felt the clouds roll in, I pushed to my feet. On my way to the door, I spotted an empty box just sitting by itself in the corner. I didn't know why it was there, or where it had come from. Glancing over my shoulder at the truck, a knot formed in my throat.

"Thank you, baby," I whispered to no one but him.

Then I grabbed the box and headed upstairs, past the second floor to the studio.

"Belle?"

I nearly fell off my step stool when Taryn's voice rose up behind me. Whipping my head around, I found her hovering at the door to the studio, looking around at the mess I'd made.

I hadn't actually packed anything, which was discouraging, but many of Rhenn's personal belongings were now in piles.

"What are you doing?" she asked, her voice quivering with emotion. "I thought you were going to meet me at the office?"

For all Taryn's talk about me moving on, now that she was faced with the possibility, uncertainty etched her features. And sadness. So much sadness.

"Hey, babe," I said gently as I found my footing on the carpet. "Sorry, I lost track of time. Come in."

Taryn blinked at me as I moved slowly toward the couch. Normally, she'd have me in a hug by now, but she just continued to watch me with a wounded gaze.

"It's okay," I soothed as I sat down, patting the cushion beside me. "I'm glad you're here."

She licked her lips and stepped inside, glancing around like she expected Rhenn's ghost to jump out.

"What are you doing?" she repeated as she eased herself down next to me.

I'd often thought of how this would go, what it would be like to finally move forward. And in every scenario, I pictured Taryn pushing me. But if I were honest, this was better.

"Just packing some stuff." I smiled. "Are you going to give me a hug?" She scooted closer, banding her arms around me tight when I pulled her into an embrace. "Don't be sad, Panda Bear."

Shuddering involuntarily at the name Rhenn used to call her, she sniffled. "Why now?"

I stroked her hair. "Because it's time."

The rest we'd get to. In a minute, or an hour, or a day. At some point I'd tell my best friend about Logan. But not until she was ready.

Pulling away, she wiped her soggy cheeks with the back of her hand and sighed. "So where do we start?"

For two hours we worked, sorting through the piles, but I only managed to pack one box. The carton I found in the garage. Taryn knelt beside me as I laid Rhenn's shirt on a stack of old sheet music.

"Here's some tape," she said, brows drawn together as she glanced over the treasures. At the last minute, she grabbed my arm, frantic blue eyes catching mine. "Are you sure you want to pack that shirt?"

I sank back onto my heels. "I don't want to pack any of it." Tears blurred my vision, and I pressed my lips together to keep my chin from wobbling. "Remember when my mom used to talk about miracles?" Taryn nodded. "I prayed for one. Every day, I prayed and prayed that he'd come back." I looked around at the pieces of Rhenn scattered throughout the room. "But he's gone. And this is just stuff. I don't need stuff to remind me of him, T-Rex. He's with me." Pressing my fist over my heart, I smiled. "Right here."

By the time I got around to sealing the box, my hand wouldn't cooperate, so Taryn did the honors. Flinching at the snap of the tape as she dragged the spool over the cardboard, I reclaimed my seat on the couch.

A moment later she joined me, her eyes clear and focused. "Are you going to tell me why you're here? Is it Logan? Did he do something?"

He did a lot of things. Most of which I couldn't share.

"Logan's ... with me."

We were so in tuned, I expected Taryn to catch on. She didn't. "Oh, God." Her face fell. "Is it Laurel? Is that why he came with you?"

"No. No. Laurel's fine."

I think.

Logan said he had to take care of some stuff, but I wasn't sure what that entailed.

Taryn cocked her head. "Then why is he here? And why are you here?" Confusion threaded her tone, along with panic. That was there too. So telling her not to freak out was a moot point.

"Logan and me ... we're ... seeing each other." I hated the way that sounded. So formal. So wrong. "We're together," I amended. "For now."

Sinking against the cushions, her mouth hung open. "Together?" Her eyes slowly scanned the room. "Is that why—"

"No." Technically it was true. But I couldn't say that having Logan sleep one floor below while I kept a shrine to my dead husband didn't play into my decision to box up some stuff. "It's time for me to move on."

"With Logan Cage?" She spit out his last name like it left a sour taste. "He's our client."

Anger bubbled up. And indignation. For me. For Logan.

Crossing my arms over my chest, I dug my fingers into my sides. "You're going to marry Cameron's brother," I bit out. "Who happens to be our partner. And you were engaged to Beckett for years. So crossing lines doesn't seem to be a problem for you. And I'm guessing that if it were Dylan I was sleeping with, you wouldn't have an issue with it."

"You're sleeping with him?" she spluttered. "And you didn't tell me?"

"The way you told me about Harper Rush?" Taryn blinked, her jaw coming unhinged. "That's why I'm home. Because Dylan's little fuck buddy showed up at the Central Park gig. *With Mac.* We can skip the part where you've kept this from me for a year and tell me how much trouble we're in."

The column of her throat bobbed as she swallowed. "How did you find out about Harper?"

I sighed. "You signed her to our company. And yes, she has an NDA. She showed it to me when I paid her a visit in California. Obviously, she didn't think that applied to me."

Taryn shuddered. "Did you see it? The tape?"

I snorted. "No ... why would I ...?" Something about how she was looking at me was way off. "What's on the tape, Taryn?" The longer the silence stretched, the deeper my feeling of dread. "Did Dylan ... do something to her? Or did she do something to him? What are we talking about?"

Picturing Harper in some dungeon strapped to the ceiling, or worse yet, Dylan up there, I braced myself while Taryn struggled to find her voice.

"He said your name." Guilty eyes found mine. "During ... when they were ... He said your name."

My name.

My. Name.

Anxiety churned in my belly. For years, even when Rhenn was alive, we'd laughed off rumors about the nature of my relationship with Dylan. The way he looked at me. Smiled at me.

"That's why you signed Harper? Because of the tape?"

Taryn looked down at her hands. "I couldn't tell you, Belle. Dylan ... he was out of his mind with worry. He just wanted it to go away. So I made it happen."

I nodded. "I get it." I really did. Not that I agreed with the cover-up. "What are the chances that Mac doesn't know?"

She peered up at me through a fringe of heavy lashes. "Zero."

All the air left my body. A bargaining chip. Now I just had to wait for Mac to cash it in.

"It's a good thing I was there, then." I tried to reclaim my breath with little luck. "We need to get ahead of this thing, T-Rex. Set up a meeting with Trevor for tomorrow."

41

Logan

Precisely at four, I climbed the steps of the modest, two-story brick house.

"*What are you doing here?* an inner voice demanded, as if the question might get me to turn tail and run. Just like I had this afternoon when I sat in front of my sister's building, gazing up at her window from the driver's seat of Tori's Shelby.

Instead of going inside and facing my real family, I'd sped off. And now I was here, dressed like an imposter in my best jeans and a long-sleeved button-down, holding the bouquet of flowers I'd bought to impress Tori's mother.

It would take more than roses if the woman was anything like her daughter.

Blowing out a breath, I rang the bell before I lost my nerve.

A moment later, the door swung open, and I met Tori's smile. "You made it."

That scent I loved so well, the sugar and spice that clung to her skin, wafted to my nose, chasing away the doubts I had about coming.

"Yeah, I would've made it sooner, but you told me to keep it under ninety," I said as I stepped over the threshold and into her space.

She peered up at me with a bemused smile. "How about you leave five minutes earlier so you don't have to go ninety?"

Dipping my head, I pressed a feather light kiss to the corner of her mouth and whispered, "What fun would that be?"

Her pretty pink tongue darted out, slicking her bottom lip, like she was daring me to taste her. I leaned in again, only to be interrupted by thundering footsteps on the stairs.

"Is that Logan?" Zoe asked as she bounded into the room. Shouldering her way past her sister, she smiled up at me. "I knew it was you."

They may not have shared DNA, but the sisters had the same furrowed brow when something didn't sit well with them. And it was on full display when Zoe noticed the bouquet. "You brought flowers?" she asked, wrinkling her nose for good measure. "That's kind of lame."

Jabbing her sister in the ribs, Tori hissed, "*Zoe,* what's the matter with you?"

The kid didn't flinch, just assessed me with pursed lips like I'd committed the unforgivable crime of being uncool.

Fishing the velvet bag out of my pocket, I bounced it in my hand, which immediately caught Zoe's attention. Her blue eyes narrowed, zeroing in on the little pouch. "What's that?"

"Something I picked up for you at one of the shops at the Arboretum." Tossing the bag high, I snatched it out of the air. "It's probably lame though."

Shifting my focus to Tori, I found her smiling. Not her regular smile. But the one that softened her features and melted my heart.

"You bought me something?" Zoe asked, all her bravado gone. "Like a present?"

Pressing the bag into her waiting palm, I smiled at the kid. "Don't get too excited. It's not much."

Zoe loosened the drawstrings while I rocked back on my heels, waiting for her reaction. Lifting the rose gold and leather bracelet, her eyes widened. "Oh my God!" She ran her finger over the sterling silver heart engraved with the *Z* in the center. "Look, Tor. It's got my initial."

Leaning over Zoe's slender shoulder, Tori examined the trinket like it was fine jewelry. "It's beautiful. Let me help you put it on."

After securing the bracelet to Zoe's wrist, Tori said to the kid, "That's really cool."

Zoe glanced at the bouquet. "Better than your flowers." Blinking up at me, her mouth opened and closed like a guppy. "Sorry."

But she wasn't, and that's why I laughed. "These are for your mom."

Zoe's pale brows drew together. "So you didn't get anything for my sister?"

"Oh ... I did." Shifting my focus to Tori, I winked. "I'll give it to you later, 'kay?"

A flush spread from Tori's chest, crept north and settled in her cheeks. "Yeah, sure. That's fine."

Zoe looked between us and feigned a gag. "Gross. I'm going to tell Mom."

And off she went, blond ponytail swinging behind her with Tori in hot pursuit.

My girl was right. This house was filled with love. Affection lingered in the space like a living thing. Warm. Inviting.

Following the laughter, a smile ticked up the corners of my lips. But as I ambled down the hallway, another feeling took hold—*dread* —and my feet stopped moving. I'd experienced déjà vu before. Everyone had. But this was different. In another life, or another time, I'd been here. In this exact space.

My head swiveled to the right, my chest constricting when I found the photo of the woman I'd met on the worst night of my life. I knew it would be there. Because when my father had come to collect us the morning after, I'd stood in this very spot. That's what the lady in the fluffy robe with the kind eyes and the soft voice had told me to do.

"Don't move, sugar. Everything will be okay." I forgave her that lie. Because she'd believed it. So much that she'd stood up to my father. And the policeman he'd had with him. And all the while, I'd stood

there, *here*, memorizing her photo. Because I knew my dad would win. He always won. And when he did, I didn't want to forget the lady. What she looked like.

Back then, I wasn't tall enough to reach the picture. And there was a glare that bounced off the glass from the single bulb in the hallway. Maybe that's why I'd always believed her to be an angel.

But now, I had to look down to see the familiar amber eyes staring back at me from the photo. It wasn't Tori. But the resemblance was uncanny. Same raven hair. Same straight nose. The mouth was a little different, and the eyes more cognac than honey. But still, why didn't I see it before? A door slammed, catapulting me into the present. Only I didn't feel present. My knees were weak, my palms sweaty, and the pain in my chest threatened to break me in half.

Stumbling forward a couple of steps, I braced my hand on the table and tried to catch my breath. But I couldn't. It was like my lungs were reduced to the size of walnuts, so small no air could get in.

"Logan?"

That soft voice from long ago and a warm hand on my arm. Only it was now. And when I turned to the sound, she was there. Older, yes. Twenty-one years older. But the face was the same. And the smile. Full of sadness and pity.

I took it then, that smile. Because at eight, I didn't know what pity was. I only knew that the lady was kind. And her house smelled like cookies. And she made me macaroni and cheese and let me cry silent tears for my dead mother at her kitchen table.

I pulled my shoulders back. Somehow, I did it. And unlike then, I looked down at her. Because she was small, like her daughter.

"What's your name?" I heard myself ask.

"Tessa."

I really appreciate this, Tessa.

Blocking out the officer's voice, I swallowed around the thick lump in my throat. "Do you know who I am?"

My voice was rough, my questions rudimentary, because I couldn't hold a thought. My mind was too consumed with images of that night.

Tessa's thumb swept back and forth over my arm, a soothing touch I could feel through the fabric of my shirt. "Yes, honey. I do."

"And Victoria ...?" My voice cracked, the rest of my words falling into shards at my feet.

"No," she said, shaking her head. "That's your private business."

There was so much I wanted to ask. But then the door slammed again, and I heard Tori's voice. And I realized, I couldn't be here. Not like this, with my stomach turned inside out and my guts exposed.

"I have to go." The thought raced from my lips at lightning speed.

Tessa blinked at me, brow pinched with concern. But she didn't protest.

She simply nodded, that smile frozen on her lips. "Okay."

I headed for the door. "Tell Victoria ..."

The rest of the sentiment was lost to the humid summer evening when I stumbled onto the porch. Adrenaline flooded my veins, and though I'd never run from anything in my life, that's exactly what I did now. I ran. From Victoria. And the house that smelled like cookies but reminded me of nothing but death.

42

Tori

The storm came out of nowhere. Dark clouds dogging me as I made the drive from my parents' house just after nine.

In the cup holder, my phone sat idle, and the words from Logan's one and only text battered the inside of my skull.

I'll make it up to you.

No apology.

No explanation.

That was three hours ago. And I hadn't heard from him since.

By the time I pulled up to my gate, rain fell in sheets. Blinking against the downpour, I punched in my security code and then sped up the drive, my heart fumbling when the headlights picked up a glimmer of red paint. As I got closer, and the Shelby came into focus, the driver's door open with no one inside. And then I saw Logan, perched on my front steps with his head bowed and his elbows on his knees. Water dripped from his nose. His chin. His fingertips. But he didn't seem to notice.

For a moment, I forgot why I was mad at him. And that's all it took, one moment, and I was out of the car, calling his name over the driving rain.

He didn't look up. Not until I was so close our knees touched. And then slowly, he lifted his gaze, vacant blue orbs roaming over my face. "Victoria."

I cupped his cheek, and he leaned into me, ignoring the rain threading his long lashes and spilling onto his face.

"Lo ... you're scaring me." My voice cracked. "What is it?"

He let his head fall forward. And a second later when a shiver raced through him, I felt it all the way to my bones. I took a step back, ready to run to my car and get my phone so I could call for help, but he grabbed my hand.

"Don't go," he implored with pale blue eyes that spoke of a cruel winter but warmed me like the summer sun. So I nodded and sat beside him, fused from shoulder to knee while he held my one hand between both of his.

The rain eased, leaving only tiny tears staining the fallen leaves and other casualties of the storm.

Us ... we were the casualties. Logan and me. But in that moment, I saw nothing but a shiny new world illuminated by the moon peeking from behind heavy clouds. Hope and warmth and promise spread from the place we were joined.

And for the second time in my life, I fell in love.

43

Logan

The rain passed, but not the storm. I felt the hurricane gathering force beneath my skin, and even Tori's fingers, laced with mine, mooring me to my spot, couldn't stop it. She spoke to me without words, but it was another voice, a louder voice, that beckoned.

Jake's.

"You're worthless, boy. Always have been. Prove me wrong, why don't you?"

And I had, over and over.

His face was the target of every punch. And it was his blood that stained my fists after every fight. But it didn't matter, because the voice remained.

Jerking to my feet, I headed toward the Shelby, heavy boots splashing the shallow puddles on the flagstone path.

"Lo?"

My name on Tori's lips was like a lasso around my heart.

I skidded to a stop but didn't turn around. Because seeing her there, in the shadow of the life a better man had built for her ... that was too much. "What?"

"Where are you going?"

Tori's tone held nothing but concern I didn't deserve. But when I spun around to tell her so, the wispy clouds stretching across the moon parted just enough to illuminate her face. The blue tinging her lips and the soft chatter of her teeth snapped me out of my downward spiral.

I cut the distance between us and crouched in front of her, my fingers flexing with the need to warm her. But not before I calmed the fuck down. "I'm just going to lock up the car. I'll be right back."

Nodding, she rubbed her arms. "C-can you grab my keys. And there's some s-stuff on the passenger seat, too."

I pressed a kiss to her forehead before I stood. "Sure."

Blowing out a breath, I made my way down the path, regaining my focus with each step. Guilt replaced any lingering anger when I noticed the standing water pooled on the seat of Tori's classic car. It didn't matter that I could fix it, whatever the cost. It mattered that I broke it in the first place. I yanked off my shirt, doing my best to wick the moisture from the floorboard.

I was five minutes into my clean-up project when my gaze shifted to Tori, shivering on the steps with her eyes on the heavens. Her lips moved, and I wondered if she was praying. To God? Rhenn? Paige?

With one last look at the mess I vowed to clean in the morning, I locked up the Shelby and jogged over to the SUV where a pink bakery box waited on the passenger seat. I peeked inside, and the kernel of guilt threatened to choke me when I saw a quarter of a cake with *Happy* scrawled at the top in burgundy icing, buttercream roses in shades of pink nestled into the white frosting.

With a sigh, I slung Tori's worn backpack over my shoulder, grabbed the box, and headed up the walk.

"Whose birthday was it?" I asked quietly.

Tori took the keys with a trembling hand. "Mine."

Dumbfounded and rooted to my spot, I blinked at her retreating back as she pushed her way through the door.

"Yours?" I managed when I finally stepped inside.

She nodded as she set the alarm. "It's not for another ten days,

258

but since I'm going to be on the road ..." A small lift of one slender shoulder. "My parents surprised me. I didn't know about it."

Shivering in earnest now, her toes curled into the unforgiving marble as she looked anywhere but at me. I'd ruined her party.

I'll make it up to you.

I didn't say it, but it was true nonetheless.

Closing the gap between us, I took her elbow. "How about a warm bath?"

She smiled, gazing up at me through her lashes. "Okay."

Up the stairs we went, but instead of turning into the room where we'd slept last night, Tori headed straight for the double doors at the end of the hallway.

She gripped the knob, but then her head fell forward. I felt her turmoil, tasted it on my tongue as she hovered between her new life, the one with me in it, and the broken fairy tale that still lived on the other side of the door.

I pressed a kiss to her shoulder. And I waited.

Long moments later, she turned the knob and stepped over the threshold. Fighting to maintain the small smile pinned to her lips, she twisted her hands in front of her.

"This is my room."

But it wasn't. This was *their* room. I took the invitation and followed her into her past. The space was large, with a masculine four poster bed facing the floor to ceiling windows overlooking the grounds. Two couches and an overstuffed chair cupped the fireplace in the corner. But it was the wall of framed photos I gravitated toward. While Tori shuffled to the adjoining bathroom, I glanced over the memories from her prom, the first Damaged tour, and her wedding. Not a single picture from the years following Rhenn's death. And I wondered if she realized that.

With a knot in my stomach, I followed the sound of the running water and found Tori perched on the side of a marble soaking tub. Some of my tension eased as I looked around, because this room, this oasis, it was all her.

As if she could read my thoughts, Tori gazed up at the crystal

259

chandelier. "I designed this room myself. All the fixtures, and this tub." She ran a hand over the snow-white marble. "I imported it from Italy." Her eyes caught mine and held. And she smiled. "There's plenty of room for two if you'd like to join me."

Water sloshed over the side of the tub when I tipped forward with a bite of cake on the plastic fork. "Open."

Tori's lids fluttered, and she shook her head. "Ugh ... no more. I'm so full."

I popped the tidbit into my mouth. "More for me."

She smiled when I settled back and started massaging her foot again.

"You never wear shoes," I noted. "Must be a rich girl thing."

Tori pushed herself up, curiosity twisting her brow. "What do you mean?"

I shook my head and shrugged, a little embarrassed that I'd let the thought slip out. She splashed water at me.

"Tell me," she said.

I dug my fingers into her arch. "Anna doesn't wear shoes either." Tori's smile wilted around the edges, and I chuckled. "I told you we were roommates. You notice shit like that when you live with some-one." I realized how that sounded, like *we* were living together, Tori and me, so I quickly amended, "Or spend a lot of time together."

She hummed. "Okay ... but I still don't understand the 'rich girl' comparison. My dad was a cop. Not much money in that."

"He probably made more than a part-time bouncer. And as far as

260

the shoes go, in the trailer park where I grew up, you couldn't walk around barefoot. There were no lawns, just dried grass and broken bottles. So you wore shoes, even if they were two sizes too small with holes in them."

I forced my lips to bend as I offered the small confession. Maybe if I revealed enough of the shit that floated to the top, Tori wouldn't want to deep dive into the cesspool for more details.

Eager for a change of subject, I asked, "Did you see Taryn today?" Sealing her lips around her wineglass, Tori nodded. "Was she happy you were back? If there was kissing involved, don't spare any details." I waggled my brows.

"No kissing," she said with a small smile, placing her goblet on the tub ledge. "We packed up some stuff in Rhenn's—er ... the studio." When I cocked my head, she pointed to the ceiling. "Upstairs."

Rhenn's studio. The mysterious third floor. It all fit now.

I re-focused on her foot. "It must be hard, living someplace with all these memories."

Moments passed, each one heavier than the last. And then sighed, scooting farther down in the tub. "You know ... one day I added it all up. Rhenn and I only spent twelve nights under this roof."

My hand froze. "Twelve?"

She smiled, contemplative. "It took almost two years to build this place. And when we were in town, which wasn't often, we stayed on the boat."

"I didn't know you had a boat."

She nodded jerkily. "*The Belle*. It's docked at Volente Marina. I don't ... I don't ever take her out."

A shiver rolled through her like an earthquake, goose bumps rising on her skin despite the warm water. I nudged her with my foot. "Come here, baby."

She glided over and settled into the well of my arms, her back to my chest. I pulled her close, kissing her temple while she drew lazy circles on the top of my hand.

"You thought he lived here?" she asked. "Like, this was where we lived? Together?"

"Yeah."

Her head dropped back, and she slanted her gaze up to meet mine. "We lived in hotel rooms. And then on the boat. Rhenn built the house because I wanted to start a family. It was kind of a gift for doing the last tour." She laughed, a little bitter and a lot wistful. "Okay, I'm lying. He built the house because I threatened to leave him if he didn't." With that, her eyes unfocused, and she frowned. "Rhenn was a good man, Lo. But he wasn't perfect."

The selfish prick inside me wanted details on just how imperfect Rhenn Grayson was. But just knowing there were flaws was enough.

Another moment passed, and then out of the blue, she asked, "Did you go to your mom's funeral?"

It felt like she'd wrapped those dainty fingers around my throat and squeezed. "No."

"But you ... you knew she was dead, right? Like, as soon as it happened?"

The gunshot rang in my ears, and my heart stalled. "Yeah."

"You're lucky."

One hand curled around the lip of the tub, either to keep from sliding under, or to push Tori off me and bolt to my feet. I couldn't decide. "How do you figure?"

Lost in her thoughts, she didn't register my tension. Or the edge in my tone.

"Closure, I guess," she whispered. "You know how people wonder what it's like to be in a coma? I can't speak for anyone else, but I was in there sometimes. It was like a long dream. But I clearly remembered voices. Well, Taryn's voice."

Turning her head, she pressed her cheek to my arm, and tears spilled over my skin, burning hot and full of something deeper than sorrow.

"What did she say?"

"That Rhenn was waiting and I had to wake up. But when I did, he was gone. Buried. That's what I meant about closure. I knew ... *I know* ... he's dead. That Paige is dead. I know it. But one day I went to sleep, and they were there and then ..." I heard her swallow and it sounded like she was choking, drowning in a salty sea of tears. "Sorry."

I curved my body around hers, protecting her from the memories. And from the pain. "Don't apologize."

I tried to force out a hollow condolence, and I couldn't. Because even though I'd do anything to take away this horrible thing that had happened to her, without it, I wouldn't be here, in this very spot. I was still trying to figure out how many ways I'd burn in hell for my selfishness when Tori's hand found mine. Threading our fingers, she guided me down, between her thighs, and through her folds.

Nuzzling her hair, my lips grazed the shell of her ear. "Do you want to come, baby?"

"Yes ... yes ..."

My free hand cupped her breast, thumb gliding over her pebbled nipple as I fondled her clit. Her breath hitched when I slid a finger around her entrance, and she gasped when I gave in and plunged two digits deep inside her tight pussy.

Pumping her slowly, I ground my hard dick against her ass. "You feel that? It's all for you."

Groaning, she bucked against my hand. And when she came, clenching tight around me, it was my name that she sang up to the heavens.

44

Tori

Trevor sat back, contemplating. "The high road," he said, his gaze darting between Taryn and me, like he couldn't believe we didn't comprehend his shorthand. He tossed his pen on the table. "As in 'take the high road.'"

Pleased with himself, he took a sip of bottled water while Taryn muttered something under her breath that sounded like "arrogant fat boy."

"*What*?" I mouthed, to which Trevor laughed and said, "She called me an arrogant frat boy."

While this made better sense, as Trevor didn't have an ounce of fat on him, I was still surprised by Taryn's lack of professionalism. Until I noticed her eyes bouncing to my phone every few seconds and her nose twitching like she'd smelled something bad. She hadn't mentioned Logan since we'd walked into Trevor's building, but that didn't mean she wasn't still smarting over yesterday's revelations.

"How exactly do you want me to take the high road?" I asked.

Trevor mussed a hand through his hair. "Keep quiet. No scandals. Basically, you need to keep doing what you're doing. I'll hit Mac's team with a carefully worded letter. Warn them that we'll countersue for inducement if he even thinks about tempting one of your clients into breaking an NDA."

I sighed. "Okay. But what if he doesn't know about Harper's tape?" Trevor and Taryn exchanged a look. The one that said, "Isn't she cute?" Irritated, I snapped, "I know it's unlikely, but the bastard already has the gun. Let's not give him the ammo."

My phone buzzed, eliciting another series of facial twitches from my best friend.

Screw this.

Lifting my backpack into my lap, I said, "If there's nothing else, I've got a plane to catch."

Taryn didn't bother to hide her eye roll. She knew I was flying private, so I had no reason to rush. But honestly, I just wanted to get out of there.

"Wait," Trevor said, his brows diving together as he shifted his focus to Taryn. "Didn't you say that Dylan was coming by?"

My head whipped in her direction. "What?"

Taryn stopped shooting daggers at Trevor's head long enough to meet my gaze. "Dylan flew in yesterday. He's meeting with Miles this morning, or did you forget?"

Awkward silence swirled between us as Taryn pressed her lips together and went to work picking imaginary lint off her linen skirt.

"Well," Trevor drawled, pushing back from his desk. "Obviously you two need a minute. Can I grab something for y'all from the break room? Water, soda?" Smirking, he hauled to his feet. "Dueling pistols?" Taryn and I swiveled our heads in his direction and scowled. "Just don't get any blood on the carpets."

When the door slid shut behind him, Taryn held up a hand, one corner of her mouth ticked up in irritation. "Don't lose your shit, Belle. Dylan was coming anyway."

For the last year, since she'd returned from California, I'd been walking on eggshells because I was afraid of driving her away with my bad attitude. But, I was done.

Pushing out of my chair, I glared down at her. "Look, Taryn, whatever's up your ass, you'd better pull it out. You're the only one I've told about Logan. And I can't afford for this to be made public right now. It's not good for Twin Souls or Caged or me. So don't go getting it into your head that you're going to tell Dylan. He'll find out after the tour ends."

Her mouth fell open. "You think you're going to be together after the tour ends?"

Did I?

Sliding a hip onto the desk, I considered it for a moment. "I'd like to be."

Shock painted her features. "Shit ... you're in love with him."

It wasn't a question, but she scrutinized me carefully, waiting for confirmation.

"T-Rex ..."

"You are." Her voice rose, and I wasn't sure if it was concern or surprise. "I can see it."

I met her gaze, suddenly serious. "This isn't high school. You can't tell anyone."

A smile quirked her lips. "That you love Logan? And you want to have a million of his babies?"

She'd meant the joke as a peace offering, a way to ease the tension, but she'd hit too close to home.

Gripping the side of the desk for support as the air squeezed from my lungs, I tried to keep my features schooled, but Taryn caught on, and the light drained from her eyes.

"Belle, what is it?"

Clearing my throat, I shook my head. "Nothing."

Anyone else, it may have worked. But this was Taryn, and she was on her feet in an instant, her hand gripping mine. "It's not nothing. Tell me."

"I can't ... I won't be able to have kids."

Now that Taryn knew, it somehow made it real. Which is probably why I'd kept it to myself. But it was out there now, taking up space in the world. Another tiny tragedy.

Taryn dropped back into her seat, still holding my hand. "Are you sure?"

I tried to smile, but it didn't feel right. "The doctor said it's too risky."

She looked down, nodding. When we were younger, we'd always talked about raising our kids together. Taryn, Paige, and me. And now we had to grieve the loss of that dream as well.

But not today.

Today, Logan was waiting for me, and I didn't want to think about the bad things.

"I have to go," I said. "Give me a hug."

Tears lined her eyes as she wobbled to her feet, throwing her arms around me and holding on tight. "Are you sure you know what you're doing?"

I pressed my cheek to her shoulder. "Yeah ... I think I do."

I have to make a stop. I'll be there soon.

I sent the text to Logan, then took a deep breath and climbed out of my car. A gentle breeze smelling of fresh cut grass rustled my hair as I made my way up the sloping hill, willing myself to take the one-hundred-and-thirty-seven steps.

Sinking onto my knees in the shade of the oak tree, I laid the large spray of roses, lilies, and daisies in front of Rhenn's headstone. An offering to go along with the tears that were flowing freely now, and the note I'd scrawled last night.

Hugging my sides, I rocked gently and spoke directly to him.

"I wrote you a little poem." Sniffling, I placed my hand flat over Rhenn's name, then let my fingers glide over the Beauty and the Beast quote as I tried to find the words. "I wanted to tell you ... to explain ..." My stomach pitched, and I dug my nails into the stone. "I have to move on now, baby. It's time. I'll miss you every day." Blowing out a shaky breath, I straightened up and smiled. "Thank you for loving me. And for showing me how to love. Sleep well. I'll be back really soon to visit."

I kissed the scrap of paper with all the words and all the thoughts and all the gratitude I could never express. And then I carefully tucked the note inside the stems of the bouquet and placed the flowers in the urn attached to the stone.

Snapping off a stargazer that had yet to bloom, I rested the bud on the grass in front of Paige's memorial. "Take care of him, ladybug. Take care of each other."

As I wobbled to my feet, I committed every sight and smell to memory before pressing one final kiss to my fingers and releasing it on the wind.

I'd be back. Of course I would, but this was different.

This was goodbye.

"I love y'all. Always."

Tears blurred my vision as I raced down the hill. But for the first time in nearly six years, when I drove away, I didn't look back.

45

Logan

Tori curled in one of the big, cushy chairs on the private jet, legs drawn up to her chest and chin resting on her knee. Gazing out the window with a frown, she ignored her phone buzzing and jumping around on her tray table.

I thought things were okay with us, but maybe not.

Reaching over to silence her ringer, I snagged a piece of melon off the fruit plate that she hadn't touched.

"You're awfully quiet," I noted as I leaned back, stretching my legs. "Something going on I don't know about?" She continued to stare at the clouds. "Victoria?"

She turned to me, sunlight kissing her face and highlighting the dark shadows beneath her puffy eyes. "Sorry. What did you say?"

"I told the captain I wanted to reroute the plane to Fiji. You don't have any objections, right?" She blinked at me, top teeth resting on the bottom lip she'd been abusing since she got back from her morning meeting with Taryn. "I'm just kidding. You want to tell me what's got you so worked up?"

Unfurling her legs, she winced. "Nothing."

Pushing out of her seat, she twisted her body and then tried to touch her toes, but only made it halfway down before hissing out a breath. A stab of guilt corkscrewed through my chest. It was easy to forget about Tori's routine, to forego our nightly stretches, especially since I was usually consumed with thoughts of fucking her whenever she was on her back. Or on her stomach.

"Come on," I said as I hauled to my feet. "Let's get the kinks out."

She raised a brow as I took her hand, leading her to the back of the plane. "Kinks?"

"Get your mind out of the gutter," I said as I pushed open the door to the small bedroom. "I'm talking about stretching you." A smile curved her lips. "Not that kind of stretching, dirty girl."

Lifting her off the ground, I tossed her onto the thin mattress and her tits bounced in the most delicious way, leading me to believe she wasn't wearing a bra. Which in turn had me thanking God for private jets since she'd never head out for a commercial flight in a holey T-shirt and tiny shorts.

But I loved her this way. Casual. Fuckable. No makeup, and all that raven hair twisted in a knot on top of her head.

"Grab a pillow," I said and adjusted my semi-hard dick when she scrambled to do as I'd asked.

Her eyes found mine as I leaned over her, resting her ankle on my shoulder. "You're tight," I observed as I tipped forward just a little, trying to loosen her hips. Her cheeks flushed pink. "Your hamstrings, baby. Focus."

Jesus ... she's inflexible today.

"Breathe," I said, rubbing the outside of her thigh as I changed positions.

When we got to the butterfly maneuver, she tilted her pelvis, and with her legs spread wide and her eyes hooded, I knew what she wanted. And fuck ... I wanted it too. But her body was so rigid, I thought she might snap.

Placing a hand on her stomach, I gently nudged her back against the mattress and kept on working.

The leg I wasn't attending to slipped over mine, and she pulled me closer. "Logan."

Ignoring her breathy tone and the steel rod straining against my zipper, I fixed my gaze on anything but the juncture of her thighs. "Just a few more." Rather than slide my hands any closer to her center, I used my shoulder to apply gentle pressure to the spot inside her knee. She didn't budge. "Victoria, come on. This is serious."

Balling up her fists, she grunted, digging her knuckles into my pecs. "Move, Lo."

Confused, I rose to my knees while she scooted to the top of the bed, crossing her arms over her chest and glaring at me.

"What is it?" I asked.

That lip disappeared between her teeth once again. "You don't want me? Is that it?"

Falling back onto my heels, I stared at her. My dick was so fucking hard, it was punching a hole through my denim, and she had the nerve to ask if I wanted her?

I thought about flipping her onto her stomach, slapping that ass, and burying myself so deep in her cunt she'd never ask a stupid question like that again.

But I couldn't. Not if I wanted her to walk off this plane without assistance.

"What makes you say that?"

She scowled at me. An honest-to-goodness scowl straight out of our past. And fuck ... now I was thinking about all the times before we were together when I'd wrapped my hand around my cock with her image in my head.

I crawled up until we were face-to-face. "If I didn't know any better, I'd think you were trying to piss me off."

She thought about it for a moment. "Well that's fair, since you're pissing me off."

Her voice was huskier than usual with an edge that made my dick pulse with need.

"And why are you pissed off?" Pressing her lips together, she looked away. Yeah, no. Grasping her chin, I forced her gaze back to mine. "Answer me."

If I were honest, I was only half listening. I wanted to see her eyes flash with fire. Watch those lips curl. And then imagine her focusing all that intensity on my cock when she swallowed me down.

"I'm not made of glass," she spat. "It isn't up to you to decide when I'm capable of fucking."

"You're not a hundred percent," I bit out.

And maybe if my eyes weren't on her lips, I would've seen the intent and been prepared when she gave me another shove. But I wasn't, and she knocked me off balance with relative ease.

Grunting, my arm shot out and I caught her around the waist before her feet hit the floor. "You want to play?" I growled into her hair as I pulled her against me. "Say the word."

"I did," she shot back, clawing at my hand. "Now let me go."

She didn't want me to let her go. I was relatively certain. But my brain was too lust-filled to take any chances, so I said, "Think very carefully." Grinding my denim clad shaft against her ass, I pulled her closer. "Do you really want me to let you go?"

"No."

My hand snaked down, under her tiny shorts, and I pulled back the crotch of her panties. And ... *fuck* ... she was wet. So very wet. And warm. "You want me?"

Making Tori say it was a dick move. But then she wasn't exactly on her best behavior either.

"Yes," she spat.

Curving a hand around her throat, I whispered all my filthy intentions while I yanked down her shorts. After I pushed my jeans to my knees, Tori took over, kicking and squirming until the denim was a pool of fabric on the floor.

"You must really want to fuck," I whispered, rolling her halfway onto her stomach.

She pushed back against me, craving the friction of my dick against her ass. Squeezing the firm globe, I waited until she groaned and then gave her a sharp smack.

She gasped. "Logan."

In this position, I could just see her glistening cunt. Fisting my cock, I positioned myself at her entrance. "Promise me one thing," I said, my breath ragged.

"What?"

I tightened my hold on her neck. "If I hurt you, you tell me."

"I don't mind a little pain."

Fuck ... fuck ... *fuck* ...

This girl.

"And I don't mind giving you a little pain. But not *that* kind of pain." I bit down hard on her earlobe. "Are we clear on that?"

"Yes ... yes ..."

With my free hand molded to her hip to lessen the impact, I buried myself in one punishing thrust. And I didn't let up. I fucked her hard, my hand moving from her throat to her tit, where I pinched her nipple until she groaned and writhed. When her orgasm hit, she nearly dragged me down with her, but I held out until her body went still. And then I pulled out and, fisting my cock, rolled her fully onto her stomach so I could watch when I spilled my release onto her smooth skin.

With my balls drained and my head swimming, I pulled her against me. "Is that what you wanted?"

I prayed she'd say yes, because, truthfully, I had taken the game a little farther than I intended.

"Mmm-hmm ..." she purred, rubbing her cheek against my arm.

Once I could feel my legs again, I pressed a kiss to her shoulder. "Let me get something to clean us up."

Returning from the bathroom with a wet towel, I found her passed out on her stomach, clutching the pillow. I took her in, from her glorious mane of sex-tousled hair, to her ink, to the scar that ran from her front to back. And in the middle of it all, my cum, branding her. Claiming her.

She moaned when the warm cloth met her skin. After I'd finished, I scooted behind her, wrapping her in my arms.

"Thank you," she said, her voice dreamy and thick with sleep.

"For what?"

Humming, she burrowed closer and kept the answer to herself.

46

ORLANDO, FL.

Tori

"What are you looking at, baby?" Logan asked as he entered the suite.

Unable to tear my gaze from the spectacle outside the window, I settled for briefly meeting his gaze in the reflection. "Happily Ever After."

He chuckled. "That must be a pretty special window if you can see that."

I smiled, because ever since we'd rejoined the tour two weeks ago, I'd actually begun to think that happily ever after existed. And though I wanted desperately to believe that Logan could be a part of it, there were no guarantees. Trevor's warning about not drawing the wrong kind of attention precluded any kind of public acknowledgement of our relationship. So I settled for the possibility of us in some distant future. And I lived in the now.

"Haven't you ever been to Disney World?" I asked as Logan's reflection sank down on the bed to unlace his boots.

"Nope."

"Come over here."

He climbed to his feet, stripping off his T-shirt as he crossed the room. When he banded his arms around my waist, one hand slipping inside my robe to palm my breast, I almost forgot about the fireworks. Until one of the mortars shot up and lit the night sky directly in front of us.

"What is this?" Logan asked, his lips grazing my temple.

"It's the fireworks display they put on every night before they close the park. They call it 'Happily Ever After.'"

He took a deep breath and rested his chin on my shoulder. "So tell me about tomorrow. What kind of celebration is Disney planning for *Belle Grayson*?"

He never called me Belle, and the way he said it now, in a soft tone that wasn't soft at all, but cold and distant, sent a chill racing over my skin. All the while, he plucked my nipple, stopping just short of causing any real discomfort, but it wasn't pleasurable either. He was proving a point, but I'd yet to figure out what it was. I just knew it had something to do with my appearance tomorrow.

"I'm not sure."

Before another lie could spill out, Logan spun me around and, cupping my ass, lifted me to eye level so I couldn't avoid his gaze. "You must have some idea."

"It's for the Wishes Foundation."

I told him what he already knew, hoping it would be enough. It wasn't.

"And what's on the agenda?"

He slid the tip of his nose down the length of mine as another series of mortars went off, illuminating his face in reds and blues and yellows. And green. But that wasn't the fireworks. He was jealous. And while I should've felt some measure of warmth, there was only sadness for him and a little anger for me.

"Don't, Lo."

Sliding his palm to my thigh, he brought one leg to his hip, and I felt him, hard against my center. "Why? Is it a secret?"

"I don't have any secrets from you."

And damn, how I wished that weren't true.

"Then tell me."

Letting my head fall back against the glass, my eyes drifted to the ceiling. "Four interviews."

His hand slid to the back of my neck, thumb pressing against my chin, forcing me to look at him. "And?"

Outside, the whistle of several mortars filled the silence that swelled between us. "Dinner in the Beast's Castle in Fantasyland," I finally said, flinching as the night exploded into day, spilling harsh light into every corner of the room.

When the finale was over, and there was nothing but darkness, he eased me onto my feet. "Sounds like fun. Sorry I'm going to miss it."

He strode back to the bed where he undressed and climbed under the sheets in record time, turning his back to me. I thought about telling him to leave since this was my room. Or I could slip through the adjoining door to his suite and sleep in the bed that hadn't been touched in the four days since we'd arrived. Neither option sounded appealing, so I laid down on the couch.

Sometime later, strong arms lifted me from my spot, and Lo's familiar scent invaded my nostrils. Our fight filtered through my sleepy brain, and I forced my lids open. "What are you doing?"

He laid me onto cool sheets. "You're going to get stiff sleeping on that sofa. It looks uncomfortable as fuck."

Catching his arm when he tucked the comforter under my chin, I repeated the words he'd said to me the night I realized that I was in love with him. "Don't go."

He looked down at me, pale brows drawn together. "I wasn't planning on it." But instead of climbing into bed, he sank down on the edge of the mattress and released a heavy sigh. "About before ... I thought ... I wanted ..." He scrubbed a hand over his face. "Never mind."

And with cat like grace, he made to crawl over me to get to his side of the bed, but I stopped him, sliding my arms around his neck.

"Tell me, Lo."

Neither of us were very good at this part. The confessions fell from our lips in the dark or out of necessity. We were alike in that way. In so many ways. In all the ways that counted.

"It's your birthday," he finally said, his tone stripped of all bravado. "I didn't want to share it with ..." Pale blue eyes dug into mine, and it took a minute to realize where he was going. He didn't mean the kids from the Wishes Foundation.

I swallowed hard, pushing the hair out of his face. "With Rhenn?" A warm glow spread through me at the mention of his name. It wasn't longing. But it was love. A different kind of love. Evolved. And I knew it would always be there, that affection.

Logan nodded jerkily before rolling off me and throwing his arm over his face. "Yeah."

Burrowing against his side, I laid my cheek over his heart. "I agreed to do this before we left for the tour. It's for a good cause."

"You don't have to explain. I know—"

I rose up on my elbow. "You don't know."

Slowly, he tucked his arm behind his head, assessing me with a wary expression. "Okay."

My stomach knotted, and if I could, I'd skip this part. But, Logan needed to hear it.

So I eased onto my back with my head on his pillow. "When Damaged took off, Belle was born and Victoria slipped away. Rhenn and me, we became us. The couple everyone knew." Logan's hand found mine, and I took it, lacing our fingers together. "After the accident, though, she died. I'm just wearing her face. That's the reason I don't do interviews. I want Belle to rest in peace." I slanted my gaze to his. "I'm not her anymore. But every now and then, as a tribute to what we built, what we once were, I paint on her smile and I play the part. Does that make sense?"

Logan nodded, stroking his thumb over my cheek. "Yeah. I got it, baby."

Doubt shadowed his features. But then his mouth was on mine and I was on my back with his weight pressed against me. And I felt his love. Or maybe that was wishful thinking. But for now, it was enough.

47

Logan

The lady in the special events booth wearing the mouse ears and the scowl slid back the window when I approached. Before I could speak, she said in a monotone, "The Magic Kingdom is closed today for a private party. Mickey and his friends would love to welcome you at another time. Sorry for the inconvenience."

I nearly lost a couple of fingers when I tried to hand her my special ticket. "Wait! I'm here for the event."

Ignoring the gold leafed invitation, she cocked her head. "The Wishes Foundation event? For the children?"

A furtive glance around the area told me that Minnie was the only one on duty. It was either make nice or leap over the barricade and risk ending up in Disney jail. I pinned on a smile. "Yes. I'm a friend of Tori Greyson's. She's hosting the party." When she still didn't budge, I tipped my chin at the huge banner with Tori's picture and said through clenched teeth, *Belle* Greyson."

Dubious, she picked up the ticket and held it up to the light. To my surprise, there was a watermark.

"M'kay," she said, and then her gaze shifted to the little box in my hand with the Amorette Patisserie bakery seal. "I'm sorry sir, but there's no outside food allowed in the Magic Kingdom today. Mickey's rules."

Picturing an army of mice dressed like storm troopers descending on me to seize the petite cake I'd specialty ordered, I swallowed my pride and leaned forward as if to share a secret. "If you could help me out." I popped open the box. "It's, uh ... Belle's birthday today, and I got this for her. It's a surprise."

Biting her lip, Minnie peered down at the frosted treat, then up at me. "I guess I can make an exception." She attached a thin band to my wrist so I could enter the park. "That Belle is such a sweet girl. She made it a point to personally thank all of us before our shift. And what she's doing for the kids ... it's so awesome." She slid the ticket back to me. "It's a shame about her husband, though. Did you know him too?"

I felt my face fall right along with my stomach. "No, I never had the pleasure." My lips bent in a semblance of a smile. "Thanks for your help, ma'am."

I walked away with my head down so she wouldn't see the conflict brewing behind my eyes. One way or another, I'd been in Rhenn Grayson's shadow for years. First with my music, and now with Tori. Maybe that's the reason I hadn't pushed her to make this public. Behind closed doors, I could pretend there was no Rhenn. And that Tori wasn't with me by default.

I walked faster, trying to outrun my whirling thoughts. But when I looked up, I found myself on a tree-lined path that dead-ended into a lavender castle with gold accents and high turrets. Since this was Disney, there had to be at least a dozen castles in the park, and yet, my feet led me here. To Tori. She was in there, behind high walls of someone else's making.

"I want Belle to rest in peace."

More than anything, I wanted that too.

Just before sunset, Tori snuck out the side door of the castle, clutching the map I'd given Daryl to pass along to her with the little *X* marking my location. She'd left this morning before I woke up, so I stood back and admired the view as she strolled toward me wearing a dress I'd never seen before. Black, made of some kind of sheer material with tiny straps and a slit up the side that fell open with every step she took.

And now I was hard.

Resting my forearms on the stone bridge overlooking the pond, I watched her mouth curve into a smile when she saw me. Restraint was never my strong suit, so it took every bit of my willpower to keep from closing the gap between us and sweeping her off her feet. But I knew I wouldn't be able to stop. And though the park was nearly deserted with only a thousand or so people roaming around, we were far from alone. Anyone could see us.

And that made it even hotter.

"Hey. You came," she said in a lazy drawl as she approached. Twenty feet away, Daryl loitered by one of the tall trees, trying to be unobtrusive. I took a step with the intention of stealing a kiss, but at the last second, a couple scooted past me, their sights set on Tori.

"Oh my God," the woman with the mane of wavy blond hair exclaimed, shifting the toddler in her arms from one hip to the other. "It's really you. I'm your biggest fan. *Damaged* is everything." Her companion, a lanky dude in his mid-twenties who I assumed was her husband, placed a hand on Blondie's shoulder to keep her from encroaching any farther into Tori's personal space. "Sorry. It's just ...

your music means so much to me." Slanting an adoring gaze to her husband, she flushed pink. "To both of us. 'Lost and Found' was our wedding song." Turning her attention back to Tori, her eyes widened. "Oh, God, where are my manners? I'm Taylor, and this is my husband, Brett."

Brett reached out a hand for Tori to shake. "Hi, Belle. We're big fans."

Tori slid her palm against his and smiled her sun-bright smile. "Nice to meet y'all." Her amber eyes latched onto the child in Taylor's arms and she dipped her head to investigate. "And who is this little angel?"

"Ripley," her parents replied at once and then Taylor added, "She's turning four next month."

Four? She looked much younger. A lump rose in my throat when I noticed the little girls' spindly arms and the dusting of blond fuzz on her head. New growth.

"Are you a princess?" Ripley blurted, scrutinizing Tori with a serious expression. "Like the real Belle?"

Tori shook her head, and her smile turned wistful. "No."

Brett curved his hand around his wife's waist and as he pulled her to his side, he said, "We're so glad we got to meet you and thank you for this trip. We haven't been on vacation since ..." He looked down at his daughter. "It's been a long time."

Fighting to keep her smile, Tori said, "It was my pleasure, really."

After a round of selfies and some chitchat, Tori autographed their tickets and the three CDs that Taylor had sheepishly pulled out of her bag. During the entire exchange, I stood mere feet away, but the couple was so enamored with my girl, they never spared me a glance. Warmth spread through me, a mixture of love and awe and so many other things I'd never felt.

Once they were on their way, Tori edged closer to me. "What do you think she has?" she asked quietly, her gaze fixed on Ripley, waving at us over her mother's shoulder.

"I don't know, baby." My hand found hers for a brief moment, and I squeezed her fingers. "Come on."

We strolled down the deserted path in silence until Tori noticed the pastry box tucked under my arm. "What's that?"

Placing a hand on the small of her back, I guided her to the entrance of the one ride that no one was on. "You'll see."

A smile tugged at her lips. "It's a Small World? Really?"

"Yup."

The kid falling asleep on his chair snapped to attention when he heard us coming. Jumping to his feet, he blinked at Tori and then rushed over to steady the small boat with his foot so she could step in. He couldn't have been more than seventeen, but I could tell exactly what he was thinking.

Patting him on the back as I scooted by, I whispered, "Easy, son. She's mine."

The joke slipped out from some unknown place. And I wasn't sure what to expect when I tucked in beside Tori, but she snagged her bottom lip between her teeth to suppress her smile. "He wasn't even looking at me," she whispered.

"Oh, he was looking. And I guarantee, you gave him wood." Her mouth dropped open. "It's true."

Blushing, her gaze wandered to the kid as the boat glided forward. Placing my index finger on her chin, I guided that pretty face back to mine. "Right here, princess. Or you don't get your surprise."

It took all of two seconds for her eyes to dip to the box resting on my knee. She looked so cute, so eager, more like a child than a woman who just turned thirty. I took pity on her and pushed the lid back. Her eyes widened, and she blinked up at me. "You got me a cake."

I brushed a feather light kiss to her soft lips. "Red velvet."

Tori's body curved into mine in unspoken invitation. But I had plans. Ones I couldn't fulfill if I gave in to another kiss. So I pulled back and handed her a plastic fork.

"It's so beautiful," she said as she studied all the intricate details on the heart shaped cake.

As she dug into the frosted layers, I retrieved the small box from my pocket. Licking my dry lips, I shifted so I was facing her. "This is for you." She froze, the fork hovering above the cake as she blinked at the box. "It's not much," I rushed to add.

She lifted her gaze, and as she stared at me, I understood where beautiful melodies were born. Because I wanted to compose songs for this woman. Symphonies and endless verses.

Taking the box with a shaky hand, her fingers skated over the shiny wrapping.

"It's a cookie," I said, and I wasn't sure why. Maybe to lower her expectations.

Her chuckle died on a gasp when she opened the box. "Oh my God," she breathed, tracing the platinum filigree encasing the rose gold heart. "It's beautiful."

I lifted the trinket from the pool of velvet, and a faint chime tinkled, drawing another tiny gasp from her lips. "It's an Angel Caller," I said and, placing the pendant around her neck, fastened the clasp. "There's a little metal ball inside, and when you move, it calls your guardian angel."

Slanting her gaze to mine, she fingered the heart while I tried not to squirm. "I love it." Cupping my cheek, she tipped her chin up and pressed a kiss to my lips. "Thank you."

"I ..." The words were there—*I love you*—because I did. But I chased them away. "I'm glad."

When the boat emerged from the tunnel, bathing her face in the dying light, my heart swelled to twice its size. She could break me, this girl. Make me want things I knew I didn't deserve.

Pushing the thought aside, I helped Tori out of the boat.

Once she was on her feet, she peered up at me, amber eyes sparkling. "What's next?"

Sliding my hand to her nape, my thumb glided over the tiny scar on her throat. "Anything you want."

Tori's breathing picked up, and she let her head fall back, raven hair spilling over my chest like a silky curtain.

"Logan ..."

She was close.

Easing back into the chair, I let her take control, my hands resting on her hips and my gaze fixed on her reflection in the floor to ceiling windows. "Go, baby."

The first mortar burst in the night sky, illuminating every curve of her body as she rode me. And nestled in the valley between her perfect tits, the caged heart shimmered faintly against her pale skin. Over her moans, I heard the chime, calling to me like a sirens song.

Mine.

Mine.

Mine.

My hand snaked between her thighs, through her slick folds, and found her clit. Her orgasm claimed her just as the next round of fireworks exploded. The finale.

"Do you see it, baby?"

Her eyes fluttered open and latched onto mine as she rocked. "What?"

"Your happily ever after."

48

Tori

I should have seen it coming. But after Florida, something shifted, and I was so excited to head to Europe with Logan, I didn't think.

The hard part was over. I'd said goodbye to Rhenn. I'd moved on. That's not to say his memory didn't linger. I'd catch glimpses of him around corners when I'd tread on familiar ground, places we'd visited. But it didn't hurt. It felt more like a shimmer. Warm. Reassuring. A light breeze against my skin.

The first five days we spent in England, picnicking on the moors north of London and exploring tiny towns where nobody recognized us. Nights, we hunkered down in our hotel in the city, sampling fancy cheese and watching British sitcoms.

I was too caught up to see the clouds roll in. Too happy to feel the first droplets of rain. And by the time I noticed, I was down in it, lost in the storm. Adrift in a sea of depression.

It started ten days ago when we landed in France. *Paris*. Always Paris.

Of course, Logan didn't understand. And I couldn't explain. I tried to find the words, failing miserably. So I was left to watch the light in his eyes grow dimmer every time I flinched at his touch.

But he never sought distance.

Even now, he was here, beside me in bed, our joined hands spanning the ocean between us.

Scooting closer, my leg coiled around his, and I pressed a kiss to his shoulder.

I'll fix this.

As if he could hear my unspoken vow, he drew me into his arms, his breath fanning the hair on the crown of my head. But he didn't take it any further, thank God, because I couldn't. Not yet.

As soon as the first rays of light spilled onto the carpet, I crawled out of bed.

"What?" Logan said groggily, pushing up to peer at me through heavy lids. His gaze fell to the sundress balled in my fist. "Where are you going?"

A stab of guilt pierced my heart, and I tried a smile. But it felt wrong on my face. "I can't sleep. I'm going for a walk."

Roughing a hand through his hair, he nodded, looking disoriented. "I'll go with you."

"No. I'm good."

Cocking his head to the side, concern flashed in his pale blue gaze, quickly followed by irritation. Then the frost came, tiny cracks in the arctic pools of his eyes. He sighed heavily and dropped back onto his pillow. "Whatever, princess."

An explanation coiled around my tongue. But it felt like a betrayal, so I pushed it down and stepped into my dress. By the time I turned to find my shoes, he was on his side with his back to me.

I'll fix this.

I knew I could. But first I had to go deeper. Farther back. To the place beyond the grief for what I'd lost all those years ago.

I ducked out of the hotel, evading a group of paparazzi huddled by the valet station, drinking coffee and eating croissants, cameras dangling from the straps around their necks. Once I was safely across the street, I put my head down and walked the familiar path. At least I hoped it was familiar, and I was moving in the right direction. Everything about the time I'd spent here was a blur. But then I rounded the corner and caught a glimpse of the cross atop the majestic old church.

Moments later, with my heart pounding a staccato beat, I climbed the concrete steps and pulled open the heavy door. Morning light poured through the stained-glass windows lining the high walls, bathing the chapel in a warm glow. Nothing had changed. And yet, everything had. My hand went to my stomach. But unlike the last time I was here, there was no tiny bump.

"*Puis je t'aider?*"

Torn from my thoughts, I blinked at the priest. He was young, mid-thirties, with a mop of black hair and sparkling brown eyes. Clasping his hands in front of him, he waited patiently for my answer.

"Uh ... *Je ne ... Je ne ... parle pas français.*" Stammering through my reply, I hoped I hadn't just asked where the nearest bathroom was.

"English, then?" He raised his brows in question and, when I nodded, he smiled. "How can I help you?"

My pulse kicked up, and I looked around, feeling lost and out of place. "I ... I don't know."

He cocked his head, quiet concern painting his features. "That is okay. Why are you here today?"

"I ... I want to light a candle for ..." My fingers balled into a fist over my stomach. "My baby."

Understanding softened his gaze. "Certainly. Would you like to say a prayer first?"

I swallowed past the lump in my throat. "Yes. Thank you."

On wobbly legs, I followed him to a pew in the back. When he stepped aside so I could slide in, my mother's voice scratched the inside of my brain. Gripping the pew for balance, I did my best to genuflect, but with my hip, I couldn't manage more than a slight bend.

Once I'd settled on the bench, the priest took his place at my side and immediately dropped to his knees on the padded ledge in front of the pew.

"Oh ... sorry," I mumbled, easing down next to him.

"You are fine." A serene smile curved his lips. "Would you like to pray the rosary?"

My stomach cratered. "I don't ... I didn't ..." Gently, he took my hand and pressed the crystal beads into my palm. I nodded. "Thank you."

Finding the crucifix with my thumb, I gazed up at the words painted on the high wall above the alter.

Venite Ad Me Omnes ... Come To Me Everyone

"What is your child's name?" the priest asked.

A tear slid down my cheek, and I bowed my head. "He didn't have one."

49

Logan

"*Calculating route.*"

Stopping in front of the open-air market, I stared at my phone, cursing the universe for poor wireless connections, and myself for being a stalker, while I waited for the piece of shit in my hand to make up its mind.

Thanks to the oh-so-tempting app that Tori had put on my phone to track her whereabouts in case she ever turned up missing, I knew exactly where she was. But not how to get there.

"*Please proceed to the highlighted route.*"

Without looking up, I took a step into the street, and narrowly missed getting splattered by a passing car. The driver shouted something in French, his middle finger shooting out from the sunroof.

Even though I was dead wrong, my own finger went up in response.

Maybe the asshole would stop, and instead of following the yellow arrow to the girl who obviously didn't want me around, I could hit something. His car. Or his face. It didn't matter. But the little Fiat disappeared around the corner. So I trudged on, boots eating up the pavement as I tried to figure out exactly how my life had fallen to pieces in ten fucking days.

Playtime's over. She's done with you.

It made sense. The tour was coming to an end. Two more weeks and we were heading home. We'd avoided any talk of the future. I'd made a couple of halfhearted attempts, but Victoria had chased the words from my lips with soft kisses and gentle touches. Her mouth on my cock. Or her hands in my hair. So many distractions.

My palm went to my chest, and I rubbed at the tender spot. Was this really love? Because it felt like something was shredding my insides with a dull knife.

"You have arrived."

Scratching the back of my head, I looked from my phone to the massive stone structure with the statues of saints carved into the façade. A church. Switching the ringer off, I climbed the steps, the chord twining through my ribs and wrapped around my heart beckoning me to the door.

As I stepped inside, a calming scent wafted to my nose. Whatever lingered in the air, incense or holy water or hope … it centered me. And then I saw Tori, kneeling in front of a pew, shoulder to shoulder with a guy dressed all in black. A priest? I wasn't Catholic—hell, I wasn't anything—so I couldn't be sure.

But moments later, when he made the sign of the cross and pushed to his feet, the collar around his neck confirmed my suspicions.

Tori lifted her gaze to his, tears streaking her face. She nodded and tried to hand him something. A necklace? He shook his head, and his hand curved around hers. Then he helped her up, and together they walked to the alter.

I followed, keeping my distance, but the domed ceiling and stone walls didn't allow for secrets and a few of the priest's words drifted to my ears.

He is with God.

Honor him through prayer.

You will reunite with him in the kingdom of heaven.

The last one was like a punch to the gut. Tori wasn't mine. She'd never be mine. I could see the grief etched into her face, softened by the light that shone from the stained glassed windows. Agony that was as fresh and raw as it had been six years ago.

Dropping onto a pew, I landed with a thud that I was sure could be heard all the way to heaven. And I said my own little prayer. Not to God. To her.

Look at me, baby.

See me.

Feel me.

Want me.

But Tori didn't turn my way. She just continued to nod, clutching her beads.

A hundred years passed before the priest trailed a hand up Tori's arm and said goodbye. One final nod, and she shuffled to a little alcove where candles glowed beneath a statue of the Virgin Mary. Tori's lips moved as she lit a votive, and even in all her sorrow, she was beautiful. So fucking beautiful.

Maybe it was selfish to hold my ground, to make Tori face me when she was raw and vulnerable. But that's exactly what I did. If we were through, what better place to end it than here. In a church. In front of God.

A small smile lifted her lips when she stepped back, making the sign of the cross. And then she turned, and whatever solace she'd found evaporated into the ether when our eyes met. A better man wouldn't have been happy about that.

But it was something.

The statues of all the saints mocked me as I made my way to the door, a sinner, unworthy, the remnants of my shattered heart left like tiny stones at her feet.

Tori

Still clutching the rosary, I watched Logan's retreating back.

With every step, he took a little of my light and a little of my air and when the door slid shut behind him, I was in the dark, suffocating.

But I wasn't scared. And that's what frightened me the most. Because, this, *this* was all too familiar. The inky black void threatening to swallow me—*reclaim me*—was like a dark friend who wasn't a friend at all. Just someone I'd tolerated because they moved in one day and never left.

But Logan, he chased the darkness away and brought me into the light.

And now he was gone.

No ... *no, no no.*

I forced my feet to move, optimism propelling me into the crisp morning air. And then I was running—to the something better that Logan had promised without words, my Angel Caller swinging from my neck, chiming softly with every step.

Spotting Logan up ahead waiting for the light to change at the busy intersection, my heart leapt into my throat. "Lo!"

Warning bells went off when I heard the pounding feet behind me. And voices. But in that moment, I couldn't figure out why they were calling me. Confused, I whirled around, nearly colliding with a camera lens.

"*Très jolie* ... Tori ... make the smile!" one of the photographers said in heavily accented English. Several of his buddies surrounded me making similar demands.

Don't panic.

Fixing my gaze on their feet, I looked for any crack in the wall of bodies. "No comment. *Sans commentaires.*"

Finding a sliver of light, I made my move, but one of the bigger guys rushed to block my path, knocking a body out of the way in the process. A tussle ensued, and something hit my temple with enough force that I saw stars. Darkness crept into the corners of my vision as I crashed to the ground.

The crowd parted for a split second, and I saw a flash of blond hair in the sea of brunettes. Logan. The look on his face—murderous rage mixed with something else. Something I'd never expected to see. Terror.

He pawed his way through the worst of the throng, a caged lion set free, his eyes locked on mine. Pushing bodies out of his way, he ignored the shouts, the curses, everything, until a young guy—barely eighteen from the looks of him, stuck a camera right in my face. Instinct took over, my hand flew up, and I think I called his name. "Lo …"

And that's when the world exploded into chaos.

"Get the fuck away from her, you piece of shit!"

Logan's roar cut through everything, and the camera in my face swung around, colliding with Logan's chin. I tried to scoot back, terrified I was about to be crushed by the melee, when I saw the blood dripping onto Logan's white shirt.

As the kid's camera hit the ground, I knew what was going to happen, but I was powerless to stop it.

"You break my camera, you fuck!" the photographer hollered as he lunged, reaching for Logan's throat. But the paparazzo was too slow, and Logan's fist connected with his face, sending half the crowd fleeing. As I tried to scramble to my feet, a burly, older guy—close to forty—snaked an arm around Logan's neck.

"Stop! Let him go—"

Before I could finish the thought, Logan spun free. But then I heard a crack, and Logan's head snapped to the side, blood spurting from his nose. He barely flinched. In fact, he smiled. And with speed I'd never seen, he cocked his fist and let loose a bone-shattering punch straight to the guy's jaw.

The sirens cut through the din, but the two photographers were still trying to best this beast of a man who looked more like he belonged in a fight-to-the-death cage match than outside a Paris church.

"*Arrêter maintenant! Le Cessar!*" Two French police officers burst into the tiny circle, and the bigger one grabbed Logan's right arm, twisted it high behind his back, and kicked him in the knees, sending him straight to the ground.

"Lo!" I crawled forward, glass from the broken lens biting into my knees. A strong hand curled around my bicep, and another officer, a female, helped me to my feet. She tightened her grip when I tried to break her hold. "Let me go!"

"*Calmez-vous, s'il vous plait,*" she said firmly.

"I don't speak French! Let me go!"

"Baby ..." Logan's voice snapped me out of my haze. On his feet now, in the officers' hold, arctic blue eyes locked onto mine.

With one tug, I was free, and I stumbled forward. My gaze shot to the cop behind Logan. "Please ... it's not his fault. He didn't do anything." With a grim shake of his head, the officer removed the handcuffs from his belt. "No ... Please ..."

I continued to babble until Logan said calmly, "Baby, look at me." I jerked my watery gaze to his and a semblance of a smile curved his lips. "That's my girl." He rested his forehead against mine. "It's okay."

Flinching when I heard the metal cuffs snap into place, I fisted Logan's T-shirt. "No. Please."

The female officer appeared at my side, her hand on my arm again. "*Par ici, s'il vous plaît.*"

I didn't know what she said, but I shook my head and kept my gaze on Logan's. He pressed his lips together when the officers pulled him back with a jerk. And when they dragged him away, I shattered into a million pieces.

50

Tori

Daryl paced outside the back door of the police station, puffing on a cigarette. His presence only reminded me that all of this was my fault. If I'd told him where I was going, none of this would've happened.

When he spotted me on the steps, he flicked his butt onto the pavement and closed the gap between us in five quick strides.

"That's littering," I said, my hand braced on my forehead like a visor to block the sun. "Aren't you sworn to uphold the law or something?"

Placing his palm on the small of my back, he guided me down the steps. "First of all, I'm not a cop anymore. Second, even if I was, Paris is a little out of my jurisdiction. And third ..." Lip curled over his teeth, he slanted his gaze my way. "What the fuck were you doing out of your room?"

For a moment, he looked more like my dad than a guy on my payroll, and something inside of me warmed. But then I thought of Logan, locked in a cell in the hundred-year-old precinct, and my blood turned to ice.

"It was a spur of the moment thing."

Stepping around him, I headed for the SUV taking up two spaces at the curb. Daryl cut me off, reaching for the door. "We're not finished with this discussion."

Nodding, I let him help me onto the high seat, Logan's phone and wallet clutched in my hand.

Surprisingly, three or four of the paparazzi the cops hauled in to give statements corroborated my story. And once it was clear that Logan wasn't the aggressor, the sergeant had allowed me to see him for a few minutes. Despite the split lip and blood staining his T-shirt, Logan had appeared calm.

"Call Trevor. He'll know what to do. And don't worry."

I'd nodded, ready to profess my love right there in the dingy interrogation room. But the photographers had been right outside, perched on benches that faced our open door. So I'd settled for holding Logan's hand under the table until the guard had come to haul him away.

"See you soon, princess."

But would he?

As I gazed out the window at the Eiffel Tower, more gold than bronze in the midday sun, I had my doubts. The City of Lights had never been my friend. And she took more than she gave.

Daryl barked something into his Bluetooth and slammed his palm on the steering wheel. "Fuck."

Though I couldn't take more bad news, something told me I didn't have a choice.

"What is it?"

"Nashville is going to look like a walk in the park compared to this." My lips curved into a smile. Nashville was everything. Nashville brought me back to life.

"Glad you're amused," he muttered. "Because there are fifty photographers camped out on the sidewalk in front of the hotel."

My stomach sank even as my heart rate soared. "Fifty? Why?"

But I already knew. By now, the news of Logan's arrest had hit the wire. And there were pictures. And video. My phone had died at the station, and Logan's was suspiciously quiet as well. So I tapped the screen, confirming the device was out of juice.

I pinched the bridge of my nose. "Just get me into my room, Daryl. I have calls to make."

"What did I tell you about maintaining a low profile?" Trevor's exasperated voice bled through the speaker, loud enough to vibrate the glass covering the desk where the phone sat. "This is exactly the opposite of what I had in mind."

Burying my head in my hands, I ran my fingernails lightly over my scalp. In the past six hours, I'd consumed three cups of coffee and two energy drinks. Every nerve ending in my body was caffeinated—including my hair follicles.

Straightening, I rolled my head from side to side as I poured a glass of water. "Save the lecture and just tell me what to do."

Trevor sighed. "Come home."

I choked, spewing Perrier on the desk. "What?" Wiping my mouth with the back of my hand, I glared at the phone. "Be serious."

"I am."

Popping out of my seat, I shook my head. Which did nothing for the stabbing pain behind my eyes. "Why would you tell me to come home?"

Trevor blew out a breath. "Because this is exactly the kind of thing Mac is looking to exploit. He's going to try to make something of this —claim that you and Logan are together. *Romantically.* Do I really need to explain this to you? Hasn't Taryn told you that? She's the PR guru. You can't tell me it hasn't crossed her mind."

It had.

Over the past few hours, every time Taryn and I had spoken, she'd dropped little hints about what to expect. She'd never mentioned Mac though. Not that it mattered. There was no way I was leaving Logan.

Shuffling to the window, I glared down at the army of reporters lining the sidewalk and blocking part of the street. The police had set up a barricade, but it didn't help much.

"What do I care what Mac or the press say? I'm not married I'm a ..." pressing my forehead to the glass, I tried not to wince, "widow." The label conjured up images of older women dressed in black. Mournful. Pining. My hand crept to my belly. "I'm allowed to date."

Trevor inhaled sharply. "Wait ... Are you telling me ..." I didn't rush to fill the dead air, letting my silence do the talking. A moment passed before he sighed again. "Well, this is unexpected."

My lips curved into a smile. Unexpected, yes. And magical. And messy as fuck.

"Answer me this," he continued in a wary tone. "Is this just a friends with benefits kind of thing? Or are y'all ... *together*?"

Whatever Trevor's reason for asking, I knew it went beyond curiosity. Which meant I should answer truthfully. *I don't know.* But I couldn't bring myself to give my doubts a voice. Not here. If Logan and I were destined to end after the tour, we'd figure it out in Austin. Paris wouldn't take this from me too.

I pulled my shoulders back. "I'm not coming home, Trevor. I'm staying. Now tell me what I need to do to get Lo out of jail. A bond? Money's no object."

The attorney chuckled. "All righty, then. I guess that answers that."

I detected a smile in his voice and I hoped it wasn't sardonic. A grim warning about the man he'd known longer than I had. I pushed the thought aside, because I knew all I needed to know about Logan. He brought me cookies and he made me laugh. And I loved him.

"I've already spoken with the *Procureur de la République*," Trevor went on. "It was *combat mutuel*."

Frustration bubbled under my skin. "English! We didn't all go to law school."

Another chuckle. "I didn't learn French at UT. That came courtesy of summering on the Riviera." I was about to reach through the phone and knock Trevor on his entitled ass. Maybe he sensed it, because he rushed to say, "Logan won't be charged. The magistrate deemed it mutual combat. The stalking laws in France are quite favorable to celebrities."

It was my turn to laugh. More from relief than anything else. "Didn't seem like it this morning."

"Ahhh ... the perils of living in a free country. There's no law against taking pictures. Or gathering on a sidewalk."

Disgusted, I turned my back on the vultures in the street. "Tell that to Princess Di."

Trevor hissed air through his teeth. "Yeah ... Good point. It might be best to keep Logan out of their path if you can. This thing is going to be everywhere. The story will grow legs like no other, both there and here."

I let my head fall back, knowing he spoke the truth, but unable to reply with more than a nod he couldn't see.

"Mac will use it against you in the court of public opinion to justify all his shit," Trevor warned, the edge in his tone unmistakable. "Hopefully, I'll have some good news on that front by the time you get back."

I perked up. "News? On Mac?"

Trevor seemed to ponder for a minute as if he hadn't meant to reveal so much. "I can't say anything right now. You can't be a part of it. Hell, I shouldn't even be a part of it."

Well, that didn't sound cryptic at all. But honestly, I had too much on my plate to delve any deeper, so I blew out a resigned breath. "Okay."

I stopped short of telling Trevor I trusted him, because I didn't know if I did. He managed to use his contacts or his charisma or both to perform small miracles. And I wasn't sure I wanted the details.

"About Logan," he said, clucking his tongue. "I'm reading over this email from the magistrate. They need a copy of his passport. And that's about it. Unless you're planning on pressing charges against the photographers. If you are, it could hold things up a bit."

"No charges."

"All right, then. I've got a meeting and I need to mainline some coffee. Someone woke me up at two in the morning. Thanks for that, by the way."

With the amount of money I paid Trevor, I was entitled to a little after hours attention. "You're welcome. I'll call if I need anything."

"I'm sure you will."

With a snort, I headed to the bedroom to look for Logan's passport. Pain stole what little concentration I had, and I found myself perched on the mattress, glancing over the items on his nightstand. Throat spray. Loose change. And my tattered copy of *Wuthering Heights*. After I'd mentioned it was my favorite book, Logan took an interest, and occasionally I caught him thumbing through the worn pages.

Focus.

Hauling the heavy backpack onto my lap, I flipped open the side pocket. Jesus, he was a slob. Pens. Candy. His black Amex card. Really? Shaking my head, I plucked the piece of plastic from the mess with the intent of putting it back in his wallet. Where it belonged. But I stopped myself at the last minute.

Not your job.

Finding no passport, I sighed and then peeked into the main compartment. There was so much stuff, I couldn't see the bottom, so I started pulling out handfuls of junk and tossing it on the bed. A wrinkled stack of papers on the top of the growing pile caught my eye.

Snagging my bottom lip between my teeth, I stared at the Metro Music seal. Considering the state of the backpack, the documents were probably old. Right?

My inner bitch raised a skeptical brow.

Shaking my head, I resumed my search. By the time I found the passport, I was consumed. But was it curiosity or suspicion? Either way, I had to look.

And when I did, I wished I hadn't.

Artist Recording Contract

The following shall constitute an agreement between, Logan Cage (a solo artist) *hereafter referred to as the* "Artist," *and* Metro Music Limited, *hereafter referred to as* "us" *or* "we"...

The date of commencement was blank. But the contract itself was drawn just days before we left for the tour.

Logan was leaving Twin Souls? The band? Me?

"*Until...*"

That's all he'd ever promised. And now I knew why.

My stomach flipped as I pictured Logan sitting in the rain on my front steps in Austin. Did he mean to tell me then? And why hadn't he?

Slumping against the headboard, I perused the terms. Phrases like "*Artist shall provide any information not deemed proprietary with regard to current representation*" and, "*Artist agrees to sever all contracts with Twin Souls,*" jumped off the page. And so much more. It was obvious that Mac's legal team constructed the contract with one goal in mind: to hurt me. My company. My legacy.

I pushed to my feet, candy wrappers and postcards fluttering to the carpet. Staggering to the living room, I dropped onto the couch and gazed out the window at the Eiffel Tower, framed by a cloudless Parisian sky. Finding no beauty, only cold steel and heartless glass, I tried to muster the energy to be mad, but in the end, all I could do was hope to stay upright. And keep breathing.

51

Logan

Daryl inhabited his usual spot in front of the door to Tori's suite. He looked up when he saw me coming. If I expected any sympathy for my busted lip and the fourteen hours I'd spent in custody, I wasn't getting it from him.

Pulling the room key out of my pocket, I attempted a carefree swagger. Hard to do since the cops had taken my shoelaces, and my boots were sliding off my feet with every step.

"We need to talk," he rumbled, blocking my path.

Blinking slowly with heavy lids, I shook my head. "Not now, dude."

I needed a shower, a warm bed, and Tori. Maybe Tori in the shower. I smiled at that.

Daryl wasn't amused. "Did you see all those reporters downstairs?"

Glancing down at his fingers coiled around my bicep in a death grip, I raised a brow. "You want to remove that fucking hand, or you want me to remove it for you?"

Unfazed, he spat from behind clenched teeth, "What I really want is for you to tell me why you and Tori went for a sunrise stroll without informing me."

A stroll?

Images floated through my mind like snowflakes. Tori on her knees in the chapel. The small smile that lifted her lips after she lit the candle. Amber eyes filled with tears.

I inhaled a controlled breath. "She wanted to go to church."

It was the truth. Sort of.

A vein pulsed in Daryl's jaw. "I'm supposed to be protecting her."

Maybe it was the exhaustion or the strain of the day. Or maybe I was tired of pretending. But the truth uncoiled like a snake from deep in my belly. "No, man. *I'm* supposed to be protecting her!" I jabbed a finger at my chest. "*Me!* She's my ..."

Everything.

And when did that happen?

A memory of an awful night in an unfamiliar home when a little girl pressed a penny into my hand crowded my thoughts.

Then.

Tori was everything then and she was everything now.

Daryl's arm dropped to his side. "It's not your job to protect her."

I met his gaze. "Maybe not. But I want it to be."

It was more than I'd admitted to anyone. Even myself. Squaring my shoulders, I waited for Daryl to tell me all the ways I'd fall short of my goal. That I couldn't protect Tori, not from the reporters downstairs or the darkness that lived behind her eyes. Or from me.

But Daryl merely nodded and then reclaimed his spot against the wall.

I stuck the key in the lock, offering a small, grateful smile before the door slid shut behind me. Pale moonbeams poured through the window, the only light in the suite. Yanking off my T-shirt as I crossed the room, I wrinkled my nose at the dank sent of jail clinging to my skin. It was an odd mix of desperation, sweat, and hopelessness. And maybe a few tears thrown in from the kids who'd wound up behind bars because of one bad choice. That was me once.

Lost in thought, I failed to notice the closed door separating the adjoining suites until I was right in front of it.

What the fuck?

Pain shot from my bruised knuckles as I rapped against the wood. "Tori ... open the door." Getting no answer, I pounded with a closed fist. "Tori!"

The door swung open, and amber eyes locked onto mine. My heart swelled with relief, and I dipped my head to kiss her, but she scrambled back. "I can't. Just ... stay away, Lo."

A laugh fell from my lips, but it was all wrong. Like this scene. "What do you mean, 'stay away'?"

Despite the ludicrous request, I propped my shoulder against the doorframe with every intention of following her wishes. Until she rubbed her hip and winced.

She was in pain.

Dropping to my knees in front of her, I ran a hand up her outer thigh. "How bad is it? Show me. Do you need to go to the hospital?"

Tori shuddered, crossing her arms over her chest. "I'm fine. Just a little sore."

In my periphery, I noticed my duffel bag and my guitar sitting by the chair with my jacket slung over the top. "You want to tell me what's going on here?"

Spinning around, she stalked to the table and grabbed a handful of papers. "Why don't you tell me about this first?" She shoved Mac's contract in my face. "Or were you planning on waiting 'until' ..."

I sank onto my heels. "Where did you get that?"

Tori's face crumbled, and in that moment, I knew that she'd hoped for something else. Some kind of declaration to explain away the documents in her hand. Whatever it was that bound us, I felt it snap when she swiped a determined hand over the tear that spilled onto her cheek. "So you're leaving the band?"

"No." I shook my head. "Fuck ... no ... I just ..."

"You just what? Failed to mention that the man who wants to destroy me offered you a deal?"

Lifting my gaze, I pleaded without words. "I didn't know he was trying to destroy you, Victoria."

"What?" she croaked, incredulous. "You read the contract! It's all there. All the clauses about Twin Souls and providing information. What did you think Mac was going to use that for?"

My throat closed around the litany of excuses, denying them air. But my silence trapped the truth as well.

I didn't read it. I couldn't.

After a long moment, Tori straightened her spine. "I'm going back to Austin," she said, her tone flat and emotionless. "Trevor thinks it would be a good idea so the story won't hold any water."

I blinked up at her, confused. "What story?"

"Us."

52

Tori

Early the next morning, for the first time ever, I dined like a tourist at an open-air café on the *Champs-Élysées*. With Dylan. I'd never hear the end of it if I left without saying goodbye. So, despite my puffy eyes and the pain in my heart, I sucked it up.

"This isn't how I thought things would turn out," Dylan said as he traced a finger around the rim of his coffee cup. "I've spent less time with you during this tour than I do at home." Lifting his gaze, piercing gray eyes dug tiny holes into the wall I'd put between us over the last couple of months. "Why is that, Belle?"

Dylan knew about Logan. I was sure. Nothing in our "inner" inner circle remained a secret for long.

So I smiled and gave him the truth he could take. "I was trying to spread my wings and break away a little." I squeezed his hand. "But you're still one of my favorite people."

His lips parted, but he looked away when the waitress came by to fill my cup and drop off more croissants.

"You know," I mused, looking around at the people on the busy street. "I've never even walked the *Champs-Élysées*. Let alone eaten at one of these little cafés. This is like a major deal, right?"

Daryl stood sentry a few yards away, along with Dylan's regular bodyguard. But we were tucked so far back into a corner, nobody noticed us.

Sitting back in his seat, Dylan scrubbed a hand over his face. "You hate Paris. So I doubt this ever made your bucket list. Are you going to quit dancing around the issue and tell me why you're going home early? And don't give me some bullshit about the press. What did Cage do?"

He got a better offer.

"Nothing."

"Yeah right." He scoffed into his next sip of coffee.

I sighed, brushing off his rancor. "You were the one who pushed me to sign Caged in the first place. You never had a bad thing to say about Logan. Do you know why?"

"Because I didn't really know him," Dylan shot back with a bitter smile, saluting me with his coffee cup.

"You do know him, though." I searched the table for jam, unable to look him in the eyes. "He's a lot like Rhenn."

The knife with the strawberry preserves shook in my hand when Dylan tipped forward and growled, "How can you even say that? He's nothing like Rhenn!" I met his gaze, and his face twisted in disgust. "But then I guess there are things you know about them that I don't, huh?"

Of course, he would go there.

I set down my knife and folded my hands in my lap. "That's not what I meant. I'm talking about his ambition. That focus that Rhenn had. Logan has it too."

He snorted. "I don't see it."

Reminding Dylan that Rhenn, his best friend, had kicked him and Beckett out of the band and put Paige and me in their place was too painful to bring up. It wasn't an easy decision, but Mac had made it clear that he wasn't interested in signing Damaged unless there was something different about the band. Extra.

"You gotta bring something else to the table. Something to make the band stand out."

That "something else" turned out to be a smoking hot female

guitarist and a fairy-tale couple singing lead. And up until a few hours ago, I'd never thought about how much that must've hurt Dylan.

But if Dylan could forgive Rhenn, maybe I could forgive Logan too. Eventually. Even if he decided to take Mac up on his offer like I suspected he would.

"What time's your flight?" Dylan asked, tearing off a piece of my untouched pastry.

I gazed around the city I hoped I'd never have to see again. So much magic, but not a drop to spare for me.

"As soon as you can get me to the airport."

53

Logan

I poured another shot of scotch into my coffee cup and glared at the adjoining door in my suite. Someone was in Tori's room. Only it wasn't Tori's room any more. Not for the past forty-two hours and seventeen minutes.

Reaching for my guitar, I caught a whiff of something rancid. *Me.* I was rancid. Pickled in alcohol, sweat, and tears.

Tears ... really?

My head fell forward, and I tried to remember the last time I'd cried.

It came to me in dribs and drabs. Wilted petals from my mother's prized orchid strewn on the carpet under the window in the trailer. Me, on my knees, trying to glue the blooms back onto the stem. And the back of Jake's hand the minute before it came down hard across my face.

Now you've got something to cry about.

That was the last time ... until now.

A knock at the door snapped me out of my haze.

Tori ...

Struggling to my feet, I weaved across the room. At the last minute, my common sense decided to make an appearance, and I paused, the lock pinched between my fingers. "Who's there?"

"Me."

I rested my forehead against the wood. "Go away, Anna."

But she didn't. "We're worried about you, Lo. Please open the door."

Somewhat intrigued, I straightened up. "Who's we?"

"All of us."

Snorting, I pulled the door open and met the quiet concern painting her features. "Nice try." I leaned against the jamb to keep from falling over. "You want to hear the voice message from Cameron? He didn't sound worried when he threatened to beat the shit out of me."

Cameron knew better than to show up spouting that kind of nonsense. I wouldn't think twice about putting him on his ass. Or he'd land a solid blow and put me on mine. That would be almost as good.

Anna sighed. "Maybe if you hadn't kept your relationship with Tori a secret …"

I waited for her to bring up Mac. The meeting. The contract I'd ripped to shreds to prove to myself that I'd never entertained the notion of leaving the band. But I had. Drunk, I could admit it. Sober, I never would. So this little conversation was dangerous on many levels.

"You should run along," I said, failing miserably to control the edge in my tone. "I don't feel like talking."

Head cocked to the side, Anna seemed to contemplate for a moment. "Too bad." Brushing past me with a speed I didn't expect, she skidded to a stop a few feet from the door. "Oh, shit."

Turning, I took in the scene with bleary eyes. Overturned table. Broken laptop. Bed stripped free of all the sheets because I couldn't stand the smell of the laundry detergent. And Tori's note. I'd ripped it up and then taped the pieces back together. But I still didn't know what it said.

Without a word, Anna crouched down and started to clean the mess.

"Don't," I said, sinking onto the floor next to the bed where I'd left my bottle of scotch.

Anna eased down onto her butt in front of me. "Have you talked to her?"

Lifting a brow, a humorless laugh scraped my throat. "What do you think?"

She bowed her head, nodding.

And even wasted, I could sense that something was off.

I took another swig of scotch. "Spit it out, Annabelle."

"The media is saying that y'all are just friends. Twin Souls released a statement ... um ... confirming it."

Pain wracked my body, every nerve protesting the lie. "Whatever."

Anna's gaze snapped to mine. "So you don't care?"

"Of course I fucking care! I lo—" Swallowing that bit of truth, I cleared the lump from my throat. "It doesn't matter. Tori Grayson's in love with someone else. I never stood a chance."

Brows drawn together, Anna blinked at me. "Are you talking about Rhenn?"

"Who else?"

Looking away, I tipped the bottle. A few more drinks and I could sleep. Or pass out.

"Lo?" When I didn't answer, Anna dipped her head to catch my eyes. "Logan?"

With a weary sigh, I met her gaze. "Anna ... just stop, 'kay?"

She scooted closer, and for a moment, I thought she'd just provide quiet comfort. Commiseration, or whatever the fuck. But then she blew out a breath and took my hand. "I've loved Sean ... well, always." Her shoulders curved inward, and I knew she must've been thinking about the four years they'd spent apart. Leading separate lives. Suffering. "And if he died tomorrow, someday I'd have to move on. That's what he'd want, you know?" She paused, and I nodded. "But I'd never stop loving him. There would always be a

311

piece of me that belonged to him. And I couldn't love someone who didn't understand that."

A tear spilled onto her cheek, and I wiped it away, frowning. Rhenn didn't have a piece of Tori, he had all of her. "It's not the same thing. Tori doesn't ... she's not ready to move on."

"Have you ever thought that maybe it's everyone else that isn't ready to let her move on? Everywhere she goes, people ask about Rhenn. Stick cameras in her face just to see her reaction. And the only bit of emotion I've seen from her in the last few years was in front of that church. She was on her knees in front of all those people... crawling *to you*."

My hand began to shake, and I set the bottle down. Maybe ... *No.* I couldn't think like that. "It doesn't matter now. She left."

Before I could stop her, Anna reached over and plucked Tori's note from the floor. Chewing her lip, she glanced over the message and then carefully folded the paper into a square and held it out for me.

"I want you to remember one thing," she said, holding fast to the piece of paper until I met her gaze. "Tori didn't vow to love Rhenn for all of his life. She vowed to love him for all of hers." Confused, probably from the scotch, I blinked at her. "Think about it, Lo. You'll get it." Pushing to her feet, she smiled down at me. "Come find me when you're ready to hear what's in the note."

I'd never be ready. One goodbye from Tori was enough.

I stuffed the letter in the pocket of my T-shirt, right over my heart. "Okay."

Anna held out her hand to help me up. Reluctantly, I took it. And despite the warmth and the comfort and the unconditional love she tried to convey, I'd never felt so alone.

54

Tori

Six days after I returned to Austin, I climbed out of my Shelby, clutching the gift basket like a life preserver. Under the best of circumstances this wouldn't be easy. But doing it now, with my heart shredded to pieces, what was I thinking?

Closure.

With or without Logan, I needed it.

Reflexively, my hand crept to my heart. The heaviness in my chest felt a lot like mourning. Only not. Because there was hope. Logan had given me that. A promise that something brighter lived beyond the darkness. Even if he couldn't be a part of it.

A car door slammed, and I straightened my spine, shifting my attention to Daryl who was taking his sweet time walking up the long drive. Behind his sunglasses, I could see his eyes darting around, assessing for threats.

"How did it drive?" I asked, my gaze drifting to the truck parked behind the Shelby.

Daryl handed me the keys with a grim smile. "Like a dream."

Fingering the *R* on the fob, I shifted my feet. "I don't know how long this is going to take."

"No worries. I'm not going anywhere."

It was true. After the Paris fiasco, I couldn't shake Daryl with a stick. He'd insisted on coming to Austin to help me deal with the fallout from the press and all the extra attention. It had taken Mac less than twenty-four hours to launch an offensive. His latest tall tale involved me turning over the unreleased Damaged songs to Logan to use on his "new album." Though Mac had never come right out and said the word "solo," it was implied.

That was another reason I was here. To dispel the rumors face-to-face with the one person most directly affected.

You can do this.

My confidence wavered as I climbed the steps. Before I lost my nerve, I rang the bell. Slow, heavy footfalls sounded behind the door. And then he was in front of me, framed in soft light like an angel.

Miles.

Just seeing him brought me back to that night. And I guess it was the same for him, because he swayed in his spot.

"Belle."

Belle, where are you?

Rhenn's voice drifted on a breeze. And maybe Miles heard it too, because he cocked his head in that way he used to when he was poised behind his drum kit, waiting in the dark for Rhenn's signal to begin the show.

"Hey, Miles," I managed over the lump of tears clogging my throat.

He smiled, soft and wistful. And then he lurched forward, the brunt of his weight on his cane as he enveloped me in a one-armed hug. "It's about time you got here."

Miles smirked, fingering the little bow on my present. "A gift basket? Seriously? What's in here, like, crackers and—" He dipped his head, poking at the cellophane. "Olives? You brought me olives? What the fuck?"

Sinking back into the leather sofa, I glanced over the offering with a frown. He was right. It was stupid. Miles was like a brother to me, and after five years of distancing myself, this was the best I could do. Gourmet snack food.

"There's other stuff in there too," I said weakly. "I picked up some of those English shortbread cookies you like."

He perked up. "Walkers?"

I nodded and gave him a meek shrug.

"Fan-fucking-tastic! I love those things." He waggled his brows, and then in his best fake British accent, he said, "Let's have some, shall we?"

My heart throbbed painfully as I watched him tear open the wrapper. Why did I stay away so long? But I knew. Hell, we both knew. Even sitting here brought the most painful memories to the surface.

Miles handed me a cookie, and I flinched as my thoughts shifted to Logan. *You taste like cookies.* It was like my past and my present were locked in a battle for equal footing. Balance.

"Thanks."

Miles relaxed against the cushions, hauling his bad leg onto the coffee table. "You've been a busy little bee, haven't you?"

His tone held no censure, but still, I squirmed. "Yeah. It's been ..."

My tongue tied as all the adjectives found their way to my lips. Wonderful and magical and painful. And *everything*.

Miles nibbled his cookie. "Well, spill it. I'm all ears."

I longed to keep it superficial. To fall into an easy conversation about music and Europe and the weather. But that's not why I was here. I shifted my gaze to his leg, then over to the bar in the corner with all the empty shelves that once held every brand of liquor under the sun.

"You first. How's everything going?"

He shrugged. "Fair to Midland, as Paige used to say."

Her name slipped easily off his tongue, falling into the yawning cavern between us. Standing at the edge, my toes dug into the uneven ground.

"How was rehab?"

Brows drawn together in an angry slash, he spat, "It was fucking rehab, Belle. How do you think it was? If you want to get real, let's get real. Why are you here?"

Cheeks flaming, my gaze skittered away. But everywhere I looked, there were things I wanted to avoid. Photos and trinkets and pieces of our shared history.

"I'm sorry," I said softly as I met his gaze. "Really, Miles ... I'm so sorry ... for everything."

With some effort, he put both feet flat on the ground. I thought he might get up and leave me here, locked in this room with all his pain. And I couldn't blame him.

Instead he scooted closer and slid an arm around me. "Still carrying that guilt, Belle?" He drew back, looking down his nose at me. "Two martyrs aren't enough?"

I blinked at him. "Huh?"

"What are you apologizing for? You didn't *do* anything." He inhaled a controlled breath. "I told you to come and see me if you ever wanted to know the details about that night. But you never did. Instead you just ... disappeared. If you want to be sorry for something, be sorry for that."

Like me, Miles had never done an interview about the accident.

All of his recollections stayed locked up in his head. And every time he tried to speak to me about it, I shut down. Until one day, I just stopped talking to him altogether.

Snaking an arm around his waist, I held on tight. "Tell me. Start at the beginning and don't leave anything out."

His heart pounded against my ear, mimicking the sound of thunder that followed me into my nightmares.

"All of it?" he asked.

I nodded, and when I squeezed my eyes shut, I was there in the field, rain soaking my skin and smoke filling my lungs.

"The voices. That's the first thing I remember. Rhenn's and yours. Paige was ... she was already gone. The rain ... I'd never felt rain like that. And there was so much of it. I think it was the adrenaline, but I managed to push myself up. I was an equal distance between you and Rhenn. But I knew if I went to him first, he'd chew my ass for not making sure you were okay. So I made a choice." His voice cracked. "I couldn't ... I couldn't see anything, so I didn't know he was so bad off. I managed to get to you pretty quickly. You were babbling, but I thought you were going to be okay. I don't know why ... I just felt it. My leg though, it was hurting so badly by then. And I ..."

"You couldn't move." I slanted my watery gaze to his, my throat so tight I could barely get the words out. "And I asked you to. And I'm sorry. It's my fault that your leg is so fucked. If I wouldn't have begged you then maybe ..."

His eyes turned soft as he peeled back the hair sticking to my face. "Is that what you think? That's awful selfish of you." I hiccupped, my response coiling around my tongue, but Miles pressed a finger to my lips. "Rhenn was my best friend. You didn't have to ask me, Belle. I would've gone to him anyway. Even if it cost me a leg, or an arm, or my fucking life. I would've gone. And it was worth it," he gripped my chin, and looked deeply into my eyes, "to be with him at the end."

I heard the words, but my brain shut down. And then I was shaking my head. "But he was ... I thought he was ..."

Dead. I'd always believed it.

"He was pretty far gone by the time I got to him." Miles went on, eyes unfocused and tears falling freely now. "I told him you were okay. That you were going to be okay. And he smiled at me, Belle. It was so sweet, that smile. And then he said ..."

Sobs wracked Miles's thin frame, and I scooted closer, burying my face in the crook of his neck. "Please tell me. I need to know what he said."

Miles pressed a kiss to my forehead, and I felt his lips curve. "He said ... 'What a ride. I wish I could see how it ends.'"

55

Tori

"I don't mean to alarm you," Miles said as he handed me a cup of tea. "But there's a really scary dude wandering around outside."

I cocked my head and laughed. "Are you usually this calm when people show up in your yard?"

Shrugging, he plopped onto the sofa, displacing at least a dozen used tissues. "Well, usually I just invite them in. You're the one who was always so skittish about the fans."

"First of all, he's not a fan. He's my bodyguard." Miles lifted a brow like that proved his point. "Did you happen to see that little kerfuffle I got into in Paris? I don't just have a bodyguard to keep the fans away. The fucking press is at DEFCON-1."

"What the hell is a kerfuffle? Never mind." He plucked a shortbread cookie from the package. "And what did you expect? Your new boyfriend is a hot piece of ass. If you want the press to stay away, you should lower your standards."

Earl Grey flew out of my nose. "Boyfriend?"

"Don't even front, Belle. I've known you since you were fourteen." He wiggled his finger in front of my face. "You look at that dude the same way you used to look at Rhenn. All starry-eyed and shit."

I waited for him to pull a face. But he didn't.

Gazing into my cup, I lifted a shoulder. "We're not together anymore."

"Really? Do tell." Miles sat back, folding his hands in his lap. I chanced a peek at his face to see if he was merely humoring me.

"Are you sure? I mean, Dylan's head would explode if I even mentioned—"

"What do you expect? He's in love with you. Or he thinks he is." He snorted, then continued in his best Dylan voice, "'It's Monday, better pine for Tori now. Then flog myself for betraying my best bud.' He does the same thing every other day of the week, too."

I shifted uncomfortably, partly because I knew it was more fact than fiction. "Why do you think that is? After all this time, I mean."

Miles laughed. "Because he saw you first, of course."

"He did not. We were all in the cafeteria and—"

"Nope. Dylan scoped you out before that. He told us about you and even said you had a couple of friends. Rhenn and Beckett and I were supposed to play wingmen. Keep Paige and Taryn distracted so Dylan could make his move. But Rhenn took one look at you and it was all over. Nothing was going to get in his way."

Singular focus in all things. I smiled. "I didn't know that."

Miles patted my knee. "Well, you do now, so don't pay Dylan no never mind. What about Logan? What's his story?"

For some reason, it was always easier to talk to Miles. No judgment. Only love.

With a sigh, I told him about Logan and the tour. Our cross-country road trip. Glossing over most of the details about Paris, I only hit the high points.

"So you love this guy, then?" Miles asked when I'd finished.

So much it hurt. I fought everyday not to call him. Beg him to choose me. To choose us. But I couldn't admit it.

"Yes. But it's not that easy."

"Nothing is easy." He snorted. "When something is too easy, you gotta figure it ain't worth having or you'll pay for it somewhere down the line."

I nodded, smiling to myself. "Balance."

"Huh?"

"Nothing." I finished my tea and set the cup on the table. "Listen, I wanted to thank you for signing over your stake in the catalog. As soon as this is resolved, I'll give it back."

Miles let his head fall against the back of the couch. "I never cared about that. I have more money than I can spend, and those were your songs anyway. I'm not telling you not to fight for the catalog, but you shouldn't worry so much about the Damaged legacy." We sat in silence for long moments before Miles looked at me out of the corner of his eye. "So tell the truth. When you were out there on the road, did you ever think about performing?"

"A little."

He grinned wide and shook all over, the way he used to when he was excited. "Ah ... Belle, what I wouldn't give to be up there just one more time, the four of us."

"I know. Me too." For a moment, I felt that shimmer, and it was like they were there with us. Paige and Rhenn. And then it was gone. "I have to go. Big scary dude is probably hungry. Walk me to my car?"

Miles pushed to his feet with surprising ease. Now that it wasn't so painful, I looked him up and down. Tall and lanky, like always. And his arms were seriously ripped.

"You've got some guns," I said, squeezing his bicep as we walked to the door.

He flexed, waggling his brows. "Control yourself, woman."

When we got to the porch, the smile fell from Miles's lips when he saw Rhenn's truck.

"Do you remember when Rhenn got that thing?" I asked as I pulled the fob from my pocket. "I think you were almost as excited as he was." Finding his hand, I pressed the keys into his palm and then smiled up at him. "Do me a favor and take care of it for him, okay?"

56

Logan

The waitress came by while the band was in the lounge waiting for our early morning flight out of hell. Or Paris. Same thing. While the rest of the crew placed their orders for orange juice, I glanced over my shoulder at the pretty bottles of medicine. Which were really just liquor. Fuck Xanax when Jack and Jim and Johnny were available without a prescription.

When the waitress shifted her focus my way, I tossed the menu I'd been pretending to read on the table. "I'll take a Bloody Mary." Sean stomped on my foot, and like a whipped dog, I amended, "Virgin."

I was on thin ice and I knew it. Cameron still wasn't speaking to me. Christian was on the fence. Which left Sean as the odd man out since he had my back. Of course, he was the only one who knew my relationship with Tori wasn't some sleazy road hookup. Regardless, my best friend was going out on a limb, so I basically did the one thing he asked: I stayed sober.

During the day, at least.

At night I sucked down everything I could get my hands on ... but always alone. No bandmates around to give me dirty looks. No women, because every woman was Tori, and if I got drunk enough ...

Well, I didn't want to take the chance.

That's what jerking off was for, anyway. Unfortunately, whiskey dick was a bitch, and my hand got tired before I finished most of the time.

I could usually pull off a good wank in the morning. But only because I kept a bottle of Tori's body wash in the shower and, once the steam gathered and all that honey scented mist wafted to my nose, I was a goner.

"Sir?" The waitress was giving me a weird look, and I realized I'd spaced out, so I flipped my attention her way and raised both brows. Talking with a hangover was overrated. "So ... you just want tomato juice then?"

"Don't forget the celery," I replied with a bitter smile. "I haven't eaten breakfast."

Everyone went back to checking their phones or their iPads while I picked up Tori's worn copy of *Wuthering Heights*. She'd highlighted several lines, which I regularly, depending on my level of inebriation, fed to my text to speech app to decipher.

Willow sidled up, and since she was the one person I was never mad at, I gave her my warmest smile, which she returned with a wide-open grin that melted my insides.

"I got a book too, Unc Lo," she said proudly as she placed the little hardback in front of me. "The. Cat. In. The. Hat." She pointed to each word as she said it, then lifted her gaze to me. "You wanna read to me?"

I wasn't a really deep guy, but something told me this was my moment. That little stitch in time where I was forced to look at what my life had become and what this problem of mine had cost me. And what it would continue to cost me.

While I sat there and gazed into expectant blue eyes I'd have no choice but to disappoint, I could feel Tori's letter in my pocket.

"I ... uh ..."

Sean scooped his daughter up and set her in his lap. "Uncle Lo will read to you later. Drink your juice now."

Pity was the worst fucking emotion on the planet, and that's what I saw in my best friend's eyes when our gazes collided.

Fuck that.

I pushed out of my chair, and he made no move to stop me. And that was worse, since he knew where I was going—to find something to ease the shame. Dull the hard edges that came with being me. I'd used women for that. And fighting. But right now, I needed a drink. Just one fucking drink.

But what would happen when there was no more booze?

An image of my father popped into my head as I pushed my way out of the lounge. He's what I would become. A drunk. Bitter and mean and filled with rage.

My fingers clenched into fists when I saw the bar, but I willed myself to keep walking. And then I was at the edge of the terminal, facing a wall of windows. I'd run out of room. And out of time. All I had left was a dull ache in my chest and shame that I could feel to my marrow.

Staring at my reflection in the glass, I saw desperation. Need. And something so faint, it was barely visible. *Hope.* The one thing Jake had never beat out of me. But soon it would be gone. Unless I changed. But I wasn't even sure where to begin.

57

Tori

Trevor sat at the head of the conference room table, a "cat that ate the canary grin" on his face.

"This is just like *The Godfather*," he crowed, and when Taryn, Chase, and I blinked at him, his smile fell just a little. "You know, that scene where Michael Corleone says something like, 'Today I take care of all family business'?"

I'd never seen the movie, but Chase obviously had, because he tipped forward and gave Trevor a serious look. "So which one of us is Fredo? I don't want to be Fredo. Just sayin'."

"Why don't you want to be Fredo?" Taryn asked, her gaze volleying between her man and our attorney.

I was curious as well, but I wasn't about to give these two idiots the satisfaction of knowing that, so I just rolled my eyes and smoothed a hand over my T-shirt.

"Fredo gets whacked by his brother," Trevor explained, making a slashing motion across his throat. "And dumped in Lake Tahoe." And then in what I thought might be an Italian accent, he added, "Fredo sleeps with the fishes."

Taryn winced. "I don't want to be Fredo either."

"Fucking hell," I said to Trevor, fed up. "I'm going to kill you myself if you don't tell me why we're all here."

Chase muttered, "Obviously, she's not Fredo."

Trevor shook his head, widening his eyes as he picked up a folder. "Nope. She's Sonny."

I was hoping Sonny was some badass ninja chick, but that hope was dispelled when Chase looked over at me and said sympathetically, "Sonny was nuts. They whacked him at a toll booth. Sorry."

Taryn stifled a grin, the guys laughed, and for the first time since I shagged ass out of Paris nearly two weeks ago, I felt my lips curve of their own accord. It was a small smile, but a smile nonetheless. And then I wondered if Logan had ever seen *The Godfather*, and the ache was back, spreading through my limbs.

Baby steps.

When the laughter died down, I said in a somewhat more subdued tone, "This is fun and all. But I'm kind of busy, so why are we here?"

Taryn shot me a look. I hadn't been to the office since I got back, so I'm sure she was wondering what I was busy with.

"First of all," Trevor began, "what I'm about to tell you can't leave this room." Once we nodded our agreement, he pulled a document from the file in front of him, holding it up between his thumb and forefinger. "Have you ever heard of Sloane Ingram?"

"The reporter?" Taryn asked, sitting up straighter in her chair.

"Investigative reporter," Trevor corrected. "She works for the *Los Angeles Examiner*. For the past year she's been gathering information on Mac. We all know the guy is a sleaze. But this—" he shook the paper, "proves that he's more than that."

I reached for the document, but Trevor pulled it away. "No. I want your hands clean on this. Even I didn't have a copy of it until this morning. It's called deniability."

"Aren't people going to assume it's us anyway?" Chase interjected. "We have the most to gain if this Sloane chick does a hatchet piece on Mac."

Trevor laughed. "If this were a hatchet piece, I wouldn't be about to feed it to the shredder." He hissed air through his teeth. "This is going to get Mac indicted. He's been strong-arming his artists for years. The men ..." he sighed, shaking his head, "he just threatened them. But the female artists ... Well, let's just say the dude is a sick fuck who gets off on power."

Easing back, I stretched my legs and folded my hands in my lap. "So what if Mac ends up disgraced? What's that going to do for us?"

"Metro Music is a corporation," Trevor explained. "Yeah, Mac started it and he owns a good portion. But he's still beholden to the shareholders. And the board of directors makes the decisions. I've got an inside source who told me the board wasn't too happy about taking on Tori Grayson."

The muscles in my jaw tensed. I hated being referred to as a brand and not a person. "Why is that?" I asked, trying to keep my tone even.

"Because any suit against you is a loser," Trevor explained. "Even if you settle, which you won't, going after rock and roll's princess isn't good business."

Princess ...

I thought of all the times Logan called me that, and the ache in my chest swelled, doubling in size, taking on a life of its own.

"Anyway," Trevor went on, looking a little dismayed by my lack of enthusiasm. "My source tells me that as soon as this hits the wire, Mac will be removed by the board, and the second in command will drop the frivolous suit against Twin Souls." His smile widened, and two dimples appeared. "Probably even issue a public apology. That's what happens in these kinds of situations. Mac is going to be thrown to the wolves. And if you knew what was in here," he tossed the folder on the desk, his lip twitching in disgust, "you'd agree that it couldn't happen to a nicer guy."

Taryn blew out a breath. "I don't know, Trevor. Mac's been in some pretty tough situations. He isn't going to go quietly."

"Mac isn't going to have a choice. He's going to prison. For how long, I'm not sure. As far as the board dropping the claims against

Twin Souls—that's going to happen even if Mac cops a plea. I've seen the paperwork."

Digesting the news, my momentary elation cratered when I thought of Logan. I hadn't told anyone about his contract. It wasn't my place. Instead, I'd been quietly waiting for an announcement. And if I called him now, how would I ever know if he stayed with Twin Souls because he wanted to, or because he was out of options. And could I even handle hearing his voice? I'd avoided it for two weeks, letting his calls go to voicemail and only replying by text that one time.

I'm fine. Please don't call anymore. We'll talk when you get back.

"Tori?"

I snapped my gaze to Trevor. "Yes, sorry."

"That other thing we talked about? The concert?" His eyes drifted to Taryn and Chase, who were suddenly more interested in the patterns on the carpet. "I think it would be better if you put it off for a few months. The venue fee alone is two hundred and fifty thousand. Three weeks isn't enough time to make sure you don't lose money on this venture."

This was Taryn talking. She'd just enlisted Trevor as a voice of reason. So I turned in my seat and spoke directly to her. "This isn't about profit. I'm footing the bill for this on my own, so if we lose money it won't affect Twin Souls." I sighed. "I'm not going to strong-arm the talent, and I don't want you too either. We're better than that. If any band on the roster wants to participate, we'll make it happen. The proceeds, if there are any, go to Rhenn and Paige's endowment fund."

Taryn bowed her head, nodding. "We don't have to strong-arm anyone. This is going to be huge. I don't want to disappoint you, Belle. That's all."

Tears stung the back of my eyes, but I held them in. I'd cried more in the last two weeks than I had in the last two years. And I was over it. Not over the cause—Logan. I might never be over him. "You won't disappoint me."

Trevor broke the silence when he said, "I'll get the contracts drawn up. And Taryn can start working her magic."

She winced, and I took her hand. "No pressure, T-Rex. This is about the music. Music is fun, remember? Music heals." My gaze shifted to the window and the city I loved, and I smiled. "Music is everything."

Two hours later, the Cessna landed at Huntsville Regional Airport. Trevor hadn't spoken during the forty-minute flight, but as soon as we got into the waiting car, he turned to me.

"Have you ever visited someone in prison?"

Sweat broke out on my palms despite the air-conditioning. "No."

"Do you have any questions?"

Picturing a guard taking me to a back room and performing a cavity search, I cringed. But it didn't matter. I needed to do this. For Zoe.

"No."

Mouth twisted to one side, he scrutinized me. "Okay. Take off the earrings. And the necklace. And you should be set."

My hand shot to my Angel Caller. "Why?"

Since the day Logan put it on me, I'd never taken it off. It was stupid, but I liked to believe he could hear the chime. That it was our music. The music of us, and all that we'd shared. Because music went on and on. No beginning and no end.

"Because this is a prison," Trevor said, voice firm and expression serious. "And when you step inside a prison you have to follow their rules. If they decide to confiscate something, they can. And if they decide to ship it back to you in pieces, they can do that too."

With a nod, I undid the clasp.

Trevor cocked his head. "Is that a bell?"

Closing my fingers around the charm, I let the warmth flow through me. "No ... it's a song."

The woman across the table looked me over, her lip curled into a sneer. There was no denying that she was Zoe's kin. Same pale blond hair, pert nose, and big eyes. Only, there was no life in Courtney's cornflower-blue orbs. They were dead, like the skin on my thigh. No feeling.

"Let's get down to business," Trevor said, trying to draw the woman's attention.

It didn't work. She just continued to assess me. "Didn't 'spect you to come," she said in an accent so thick it was hard to understand her. "Someone like you ... I'da thunk you'd let your people handle the messy business."

"Zoe's my people," I said blandly. "And why wouldn't I come? After all, you sent me that nice letter."

I stopped short of calling it what it was—a ransom note.

For months, my parents had been waiting for the other shoe to drop. Every day they expected a letter from child services with a demand to present my sister like she was dry cleaning that someone forgot to claim. But that day never came. If Courtney actually wanted to *see* my sister, she would've sent that letter. Instead she wrote to me.

Because she wanted money. And since I had a shit ton, I didn't mind paying her off. We just had to negotiate the going rate for a fourteen-year-old. Which was why Trevor was here. Left up to me, I'd give the woman a blank check.

Courtney sank back in the metal chair, chewing her lip. "Since you came all this way, it must be real important to you."

Trevor's knee hit mine under the table, and I could almost hear what he was thinking. *I told you so.* He'd warned me that my presence would likely up the stakes. *Zero fucks.* Because I didn't care what it took. I was walking away from this table with a signed agreement.

"It is," I conceded. "She's my sister."

I shifted to the right to avoid another collision with my attorney's knee.

"Well..." Courtney drawled. "That's real special. But it's going to cost you."

Trevor went to speak, but I cut him off.

"How much?"

She seemed to think about it, rubbing her chin with grubby fingers. "I'd say, 'bout fifty grand."

Images of Zoe flashed through my mind. All her promise. All her potential. Her bright smile and her quick wit. And all this woman saw was fifty grand. Less, actually. Because I'm sure she thought I'd whittle her down.

"Done."

Trevor cursed under his breath while Courtney blinked at me.

"We do have some terms," my attorney said, exasperated. And I wasn't sure if he was talking to me or Courtney.

"What terms?" she asked, her focus on Trevor.

"Well, there is the matter of—"

"You sign away your parental rights today," I interjected. "And you never contact me, my parents, or my sister again."

Courtney cocked her head, gaze volleying between Trevor and me. "That's it? What about that other thing? I had one of my friends explain it."

Trevor sighed, tossing his pen on the table. "The nondisclosure?"

"We don't need it," I said.

She smiled then, like there had to be a catch. There wasn't.

"So you don't care if I tell people you bought my baby?"

I shrugged. "Zoe's not a baby. And I have a whole publicity team that can spin this around and around so people know what really happened—that you waited for almost eleven years and then you sold her. I wouldn't suggest you do it. But it's up to you. I don't have anything to hide."

As distasteful as it was, this was probably the purest deal I'd made in a long time. There were no hidden agendas. Courtney wanted money. Not power. Or publicity. And I wanted Zoe to have a clean slate. To be her own person.

Courtney snatched the papers, signing them without so much as a glance. "When do I get my money?"

"We could put it on your books or have a check waiting when you get out," Trevor replied as he stowed the documents in his briefcase. "Up to you."

"Put it on my books," Courtney said. "And don't pull no fast ones. I know people."

The threat was empty, but I let her have it.

When she got up to leave, a thought occurred to me. "There isn't a father listed on Zoe's birth certificate."

I let the statement dangle. Not really a question, but I was curious.

For the first time, I detected something in Courtney's eyes. A spark. "She don't have no daddy." Pulling her shoulders back, she lifted her chin. "He died 'afore she was born."

A lump formed in my throat for this woman. Once, she had feelings. I could see them, like an echo. Or the light from a star that was long dead.

I nodded, snagging her gaze and holding. "I'm sorry."

58

Logan

"This way," the nurse said.

Stifling a yawn, I followed her down the long hallway at Cedars Sinai hospital, trying to remember the last time I'd slept. Twenty-four hours ago, I was in Berlin, onstage for our final show. But everything after the concert was a blur of airport shuttles and customs declarations.

I didn't decide until the last possible minute to fly from Houston, where we'd landed, to Los Angeles. Which, of course, led to a scene when I told the guys about my plans. Probably because I didn't actually say much. I'd need to mend fences, but right now, this was more important.

Ushering me into a small room, the nurse pointed to a blue paper dress on the examining table.

"There's your gown. Everything off. And remove all metal objects." She smiled. "Jewelry *and* piercings."

And then, because I wasn't freaked out enough, she looked at my crotch. A long, lingering look she made no attempt to hide.

At first, I didn't get it, but when I did, I couldn't help but wrinkle my nose. Because who in the fuck would put a bolt through the head of their dick?

Apparently, someone who looked like me.

Easing onto a chair, I reached for my boot laces. "I don't have any piercings."

She looked disappointed, but whatever.

The weak smile slid right off my lips when she leaned a shoulder against the wall. Watching. Reluctantly, I peeled off my shirt, and still no sign of movement from Nurse Nancy. Fingers frozen on my belt buckle, I hopped to my feet when Doctor Patel strode through the door.

Thank fuck. Thank *fuck*.

Patel took one look at the nurse and quirked a brow. "You can go now, Cindy." The doc tried and failed to stifle a grin when the nurse scurried from the room. "Sorry about that, Logan. She's a little ..." Pressing her lips together, Patel looked down at my chart and shook her head. "Extra."

Reclaiming my seat, I hoped I hadn't jumped from the frying pan into the fire, because the doc looked like she was making herself comfy as well. Was this Cedar Sinai or Chippendales?

"Since you weren't able to fill out your forms, I'm going to ask you a few questions," the doc said, scribbling on my chart without looking up. "Then I'll leave you alone to finish undressing." A smile. "Sound good?"

My hand immediately dropped from my buckle. Not that I had any qualms about being naked. But discussing my deepest shame, without benefit of any armor? Yeah, no.

I exhaled a relieved breath. "That's fine."

"We're going to be starting with an MRI. Do you know what that is?" I nodded. "Good. There are different types of dyslexia. Traumatic —that comes from a brain injury. Primary—that's the most common. You're born with it. And developmental—that's caused by hormonal changes when you're in the womb, and it usually diminishes over time. Today we'll be scanning for brain injuries."

She paused with her pen hovering above the chart. "Do you remember any type of acute injuries you may have suffered as a child?"

"Acute?" I knew what it meant, but while she explained, I tried to decide how much I should tell her. When she finished, I cleared my throat. "I used to get hit in the head ..." Poking the inside of my cheek with my tongue, I tried to coax the words from where they were buried. "My dad used to hit me."

Patel nodded, but her demeanor never changed. No pity. Nothing. I relaxed a little more.

"Was this before or after you noticed your reading deficiency?"

"I've never been able to ... um ... reading has always been a problem."

"Did you noticed any marked change for the better, let's say, when you hit puberty?"

I shook my head.

Patel set the chart aside, and just when I thought I was home free, she crossed her legs and clasped her hands over her knee. "In your intake interview you said your mother died when you were a child. How old where you?"

Blood pounded between my ears, the steady *thump thump thump* making me dizzy. "Eight."

Shifting my gaze to the wall, I focused on all the charts. The head. The body. And then the other wall with a poster of a child, laughing.

"Logan?"

I snapped my attention back to Patel. "Yes?"

She smiled. Not a real smile. Just a slight curve of her lips. "Did your mother die of some kind of disease?"

Yep. Jake Cage. More dangerous than the plague and Ebola combined. "No."

Patel's brows drew together. "Would you like to tell me how she died?"

Pushing to my feet, I popped the button on my jeans. "No."

335

59

Two days after the tour ended, I showed up at Twin Souls for the first time since I'd returned to Austin.

Logan hadn't called. I tried not to read too much into his radio silence. After all, I told him we'd talk when he got back.

Sometime before ten, Taryn popped her head into my office. "The receptionist just buzzed ... they're here."

Heart racing, I stood before the mirror putting the finishing touches on my makeup. "Thanks."

She slipped inside, shutting the door behind her. "Do you want me to tell Logan to come back first?"

Meeting her gaze in the reflection, I raised a brow. "Because that wouldn't look suspicious at all." Her scowl did nothing to help my shaky fingers and sweaty palms. I took a deep breath. "Logan isn't a solo artist, T-Rex." *Not yet, anyway.* "I can't just invite him into my office for a chat without including the other guys."

Taking a seat on the arm of the couch, Taryn crossed her arms over her chest. "So you're going to keep up this charade? Logan's 'only a client.' I thought that was just something you were playing out for the press."

It would be easier to tell Taryn about the contract with Mac.

She'd understand then. But I couldn't trust her to keep the details to herself. Whatever Logan's choice, it was his to make. And I didn't want this to be any harder than it had to be. Because I loved him. Enough to let him go if I had to.

"Look," I said as I turned to face my best friend's frown. "Let me talk to Logan after the meeting is over. I don't even know what he's told the guys about us."

She chuffed out a breath, a response on the tip of her tongue, but I shook my head. "Taryn, please. He's got a lot to consider. How it would affect the band to come out publicly ... with me. Maybe he doesn't want the hassle."

Anger flashed in her stormy blue eyes. Indignation on my behalf.

Smiling at the gesture, I shifted my gaze to the window overlooking Sixth where a few reporters milled around on the sidewalk. "You can't blame him, T-Rex. It's not all unicorns and rainbows down there."

And it was about to get worse. The minute Twin Souls announced the upcoming concert, the press would go into hyperdrive. *A Damaged reunion at Zilker Park.* Even floating the possibility would be like pouring gasoline on an open flame. I knew I couldn't live under the media scrutiny for very long, which is why I'd opted for a very short window. Two and a half weeks. And then I'd give Miles what he'd asked for without asking. One last show. A final ride. And wherever Rhenn was, he'd finally get to see how it ended.

The butterflies in my stomach took a nosedive when I walked into the conference room. Christian, Cameron, and Sean sat on one side of the table, but Logan was nowhere in sight.

It was one thing to prepare for some far-off eventuality—a worst-case scenario. Isn't that why people bought raincoats? And had car insurance?

But it was quite another to face it head on.

Still, a tiny spark of hope lingered. So I forced a smile and took a seat.

"Hey, y'all. Glad you're back." I poured a glass of water just to have something to do with my hands. "Where's Logan?"

In the silence, I fanned the flame, hoping the tiny spark would catch fire. That by sheer will alone, I could change my fate. Change our fate.

But when Cameron's eyes found mine, I knew. Dammit, I did.

"He's in Los Angeles."

I tried to hide my shock. Because now it was real. Mac. The contract. The unwavering notion that Logan had betrayed me. Or he would, very shortly.

When Taryn walked in with the folder containing the agreements that Trevor had drawn up for Caged, I popped out of my seat, smile so tight, I thought my face would crack. "I just dropped in to say 'hi.' Taryn's got a business opportunity she wants to discuss with y'all. We'll talk soon."

My best friend's confused gaze followed me as I headed for the door. "Where are you going?"

But I didn't stop. In fact, I picked up speed, my Angel Caller chiming louder with each step. But that was a lie too. There were no guardian angels. And no happily ever afters. And sometimes a beast wasn't a prince in disguise. Sometimes he was just a man.

60

Logan

Sipping my third cup of coffee, I stood at the window in Dr. Patel's office. The door slid shut with a soft whoosh, and the doc's perfume wafted to my nose. "Why is there a statue of Moses in front of the building?"

Her reflection took a seat behind the desk. "Still can't sleep, Logan?"

I turned to face her, shoulders resting against the glass. "Does that mean there isn't a statue of Moses outside?"

I was only half-kidding, since it was entirely possible I was hallucinating. In order to give the evaluations my best shot, I'd quit using alcohol as a sleep aid when I got to Los Angeles. So now I hadn't slept in three days. I napped ... if I was lucky. Not always on purpose. Last night I'd fallen asleep in the middle of dinner. And when I woke up a couple of hours later, I was face down in a plate of pizza.

"Logan?"

Patel's voice snapped me out of my fog, and I found her motioning to the chair in front of her desk.

I took a seat while she put some images on a lighted board on the wall. "I've got some of your test results." Grabbing a file, she came around to my side of the desk, then slid a hip onto the wood. "Would you like to go over them?"

Patel also had a degree in psychology, I'd learned. So she did this thing where she made it seem like everything was my choice when really it wasn't.

I shifted uncomfortably. "Sure."

Folding her hands in front of her, she smiled. "You don't have a brain injury. That's very good news."

When her gaze shifted to my bobbing leg, I promptly clamped a hand over my knee to make it stop. My lack of sleep combined with the caffeine and being here had me ready to crawl out of my skin. "How so?"

"In the absence of an injury, then it is possible to learn to read."

I sensed a "but." It was something in her eyes. Slowly, she pulled out an 8x10 card from a stack on her desk and held it up. "What is this word?"

Three letters, none of them familiar. I looked away. "I can't read. Not having a brain injury isn't going to change that."

"Okay then, something simpler. Let's start with the letters."

I brought my gaze back to hers without bothering to hide my disdain. "I don't know what the letters say—" my tone started low and quickly gained volume, "—because I can't read them!"

Patel didn't flinch. Impressive, since I could feel my nostrils flaring and the scowl coating my features.

"This isn't reading. Try again." She tapped the card with a blunt nail. "Look at the letters."

Pushing out of my seat with enough force to make the chair wobble, I gripped my hair. "I don't need to look at the letters to know I can't read them."

The picture of control, Patel placed the card face down in front of her. "That's where you're wrong. We did an advanced battery of tests. You recognize symbols. Your memory is flawless. Your IQ, extremely high."

Somewhere in the middle of her speech I'd stopped pacing. "How can I have a high IQ if I can't read?"

"Problem solving. There's a formula we use. It filters out any reading questions."

This was almost worse. I wasn't stupid, but I couldn't recognize any letters. It didn't make sense. But then, it had never made sense. Flopping back into the chair, I rested my elbows on my knees and buried my head in my hands.

God, I was tired. So tired. I just wanted ...

Tori.

I wanted Tori. And sleep. I hadn't slept right since she left. She stole my sleep. My sanity. My control.

If I could just hear her voice ...

But she wouldn't answer my calls. So that was that.

Inhaling slowly, I pulled myself upright. "So what's my problem?"

Patel pondered for a moment and then held the card up again.

Tap Tap Tap, went her fingernail over the first letter. "One more time. What letter is this?"

Flinching, I shook my head. "I don't know."

Tap Tap Tap. "Right here. What letter is this?"

"I don't ... I don't ..."

Tap Tap Tap. "Concentrate. What letter is this?"

The card swam out of focus, but the tapping continued, like small caliber gunshots exploding inside my head.

And then another voice. Male, gruff. I could smell his cologne. And cigarette smoke. And coffee.

Concentrate, son. You want to help us, don't you? Just tell us what you saw. Give us a letter.

"I can't," I repeated, my gaze on the pavement. On his boots. And the blood spatter.

Son, if you want to help your mama, you need to concentrate and give us a letter.

"Logan?"

"*Logan?*"

Overwhelmed by images, flashing lights, and voices I couldn't place, I snapped my gaze to Patel.

341

"I can't." My voice was small. Insignificant. And I hated it. I hated her. Why the fuck wouldn't she stop with the tapping?

Patel's brows drew together and for the first time I noted pity in her eyes. She replaced the card on the stack, drew in a breath, then stood. "That's enough of that for a moment." She motioned to a sitting area. "Let's move over here and talk a bit."

Since I'd do anything to put some distance between her and the cards, I took a seat on the sofa while Patel opted for the chair.

"You have primary dyslexia, to be sure," she began, "but that isn't the reason you can't read."

I sank against the cushions. "What is it then?"

She sighed, shaking her head. "If I had to venture a guess, I'd say it's trauma related."

"But you said—"

"Not the kind of trauma resulting from an injury. Emotional trauma."

My skin prickled, all the warmth leeching from my pores.

Regarding me with a soft smile that offered no reassurance, Patel picked up a notepad from the table.

"Perhaps it's time we talk about your mother."

61

Logan

Ten days after I'd arrived in Los Angeles, and only seven days after my near breakdown in Patel's office, I got off a plane at Austin Bergstrom.

Everything looked different. Bigger. Scarier. Intimidating as fuck.

As I rode the escalator to baggage claim, I thought about turning around. Buying a ticket and skulking back to LA to my little hotel room across from the medical center.

But that would only undo the few steps I'd taken on the long road to wherever it was I'd end up.

God, I sounded like … someone other than me.

Since I wasn't sure who *me* was, that was okay.

At this point, I was flying blind. I'd been doing it for years, only now I was aware.

According to Patel, I'd reduced my world to something manageable a long time ago. Street signs, billboards, books, and even people were all just props. Things to be pushed aside and ignored when I couldn't figure them out.

But Tori had changed all that. She'd crashed into my life, a broken girl I wanted to resurrect. But instead, she was the one who'd opened my eyes. Revived me. She'd ripped back the filter on the world, and all the beauty and all the pain, the magic and the mayhem, it all flowed through her.

She was my conduit.

I dug my fingers into my tired eyes as I waited next to the belt for my luggage. Jerking when I felt something wrap around my leg, I looked down into the most beautiful little face.

"Unc Lo! You home!"

Scooping Willow up with one arm, I breathed in her baby scent. "Willow-baby. I missed you."

From a few feet away, Sean regarded me with narrowed eyes, blue like his daughter's, but not nearly as warm.

"Hey, bro," I said with a tip of my chin and a smile.

He shook his head, let out a sigh, and then strolled up like he couldn't believe he was here.

Despite his surly disposition, I pulled him in for a hug. "Thanks for coming to get me."

His back stiffened, but then he gave in and returned the embrace. "Shit, man. You had me worried. You haven't answered your phone in a week."

Releasing him, I lifted a shoulder, a little embarrassed. "I couldn't. Doctor's orders."

Sean's face fell. With his family history of losing loved ones to cancer, I should've been more sensitive, because he immediately went *there*. And in that moment, I knew how much he cared.

"Not that kind of doctor," I assured. "Patel deals with other stuff."

I tapped my temple and saw the understanding creep over Sean's features. And also a bit of surprise. I'd always subscribed to the notion that therapy was for those without the stones to deal with their own shit, and Sean knew it.

Surprisingly, he just smiled. "That's good. I hope it helped."

With a loud thump, the first bag tumbled off the chute and landed on the belt, precluding any further conversation. Which was a good thing since Sean looked a little overwhelmed by the new me.

Not that a person can change much in ten days, but my metamorphosis had started much earlier. With Tori.

The usual wave of emotions slammed into me as I thought of her. And I made no move to push them away, just let the tide roll over me and carry me out to sea.

"Shit," Sean muttered as I secured my duffel over my shoulder. "We need to get gone."

Following his gaze to the gaggle of reporters, I cocked my head. "Are they here for us?"

He snorted. "No, dude, they're here for you." He gave me the oddest look. "Haven't you been keeping up with the news at all?"

I shifted my feet, shrugging. "Not really."

Dr. Patel had insisted I unplug while I was in LA. No distractions. So I hadn't followed any gossip sites or kept up with my texts or emails. There were four messages I'd yet to open from Tori, and of course, her letter. I looked at the note every day, and it helped me focus on my goals. I wanted to "read" it, and to hear her voice in my head when I did. That was a long way off, though.

"This way," Sean said, scooping Willow into his arms. Falling into step beside him, I headed for the bank of elevators that led to the parking garage. Once we were safely inside the lift, he blew out a breath, looking anywhere but at me.

With a sigh, I leaned a shoulder against the metal wall. "Tell me what I don't know."

He met my gaze. "We're supposed to be doing a show in six days. I thought that's the reason you were back. It's going to be huge, man. Tickets went on sale last Monday and sold out in like, twenty minutes."

"Twenty minutes?" I scratched the back of my head. "How big is the venue? Who's on the bill?"

"It's at Zilker Park. I'm not sure about the lineup."

The door slid open, and I stepped out of the car, chuckling. "Dude, this has got to be some kind of publicity stunt. You can't sell seventy-five-thousand tickets in twenty minutes without announcing a lineup."

Our boots echoed off the stone walls, the only sound as Sean pondered his response. I was about to abandon my new-found Zen and shake the answer out of him when he swung his gaze in my direction.

"There's no mistake. The minute Tori announced she was coming out of retirement for a Damaged reunion, they couldn't print the tickets fast enough."

While I waited in the loft above the studio for the guys to show up for the rehearsal Sean had arranged, I placed a call to Tori. Straight to voicemail. And of course, the box was full.

For the first time in ten days, I plugged in my earbuds and opened my text to speech app. It felt like a defeat. Or a surrender. A silent admission that I was broken, and it would take me years, if ever, to do the things that came naturally to others.

"Fourteen percent of the adult population can't read, Logan. You aren't alone."

Patel's voice echoed in my head, providing little comfort.

Blowing out a weary breath, I went down the list of headlines.

Tori breaks the internet! Ticketmaster site goes down amid unprecedented demand for tickets to the Damaged reunion!

Sold out! Twin Souls announces lottery for last ten thousand tickets to the Damaged reunion!

Tori Grayson in hiding after announcing her return to the stage. Is the pressure too much?

And of course, the tabloid press had to get in on the action.

Rhenn Grayson spotted in Austin! Sightings of the iconic singer lead to speculation that Damaged front man faked his own death.

Where's Logan? Tori plans revenge concert after Caged frontman caught cheating in Berlin with supermodel.

Tori's heartache! Logan Cage undergoes treatment at Cedars Sinai for drug abuse. Click here for pictures!

Pictures? Of course there were pictures.

With a sigh, I hit the link and a photo of me exiting the outpatient psychology center at the hospital populated the screen. Stringy hair. Bags under my eyes. And a week's worth of scruff lining my jaw. No wonder they thought I was on drugs.

Had Tori seen these?

Gritting my teeth, I opened my messages.

If I waited to look at the texts until I could read them they wouldn't mean anything.

Just one.

I could listen to just one. As I glanced over the four options, I chided myself for playing these games. But then, up until a couple of weeks ago, life was a game. Now everything was real. Too real. Imposing a few rules to keep my sanity wasn't a bad thing, was it?

You're talking to yourself.

Jabbing the screen, I hit the last message from four days ago, and then sat back, imagining it was Tori's voice in my head.

"I know you have to do what's best for you. And I understand. I just wanted to say ... I'm sorry for the way things—"

A loud pop sounded in my ears when I yanked the headset off.

She was *sorry*? Sorry for what? That we'd gotten together? That she left? That she broke my fucking heart?

Closing my eyes, I let my head fall back. Even after everything, knowing how it all turned out, I wasn't sorry. Reluctantly, I picked up my phone and, scrolling to my music file, my finger hovered over "The Dance" by Garth Brooks. The tune had always reminded me of my mama, and lazy days spent in the trailer when she'd sing to me. But the lyrics, they were all Tori. And all me. *Us.* Messy and tangled, full of regret and lost chances. And love. So much love.

Replacing my earbuds, I settled back in the overstuffed chair, and let the music shred what was left of my heart. And when the song was over, I did it again. And again.

Sometime later, the door to the industrial elevator slid up with a loud crash.

"Just keep an open mind," I heard Sean hiss as I stuffed my phone into my pocket.

"The only thing I'm gonna be opening is a can of whoop ass," Cameron replied.

"Stop," Christian growled. "We're settling this shit today."

I pushed to my feet as they filed in. Before Cameron could land that punch he was itching to throw, I stepped up and enveloped him in a hug.

"I know you're mad," I said, close to his ear. "And I don't blame you. If you still want to hit me after I'm through, you get a free shot."

A beat of silence turned into two.

"Don't flatter yourself, son," Cameron finally grumbled, patting me on the back hard enough to knock the wind out of me. "I don't need a free shot to knock you on your ass."

Christian pushed Cameron out of the way. "Where's mine?" Pulling me in for a hug that could easily shatter a rib, he whispered, "You better make this right, bro. There are some rumors going around I'd like to ignore. But taking off to Cali like that …"

He broke away and then took his place on the sofa next to Cameron and Sean. It felt like I was in front of a firing squad. Not really conducive to rolling over and showing my soft underbelly, but oh well.

I reclaimed my seat. "I'm sorry I disappeared without letting y'all know where I was going."

"Where *did* you go?" Cameron asked impatiently, crossing his arms over his chest.

I guess the old me would have left it at a half-assed apology, so I couldn't really blame him for interrupting.

"California."

"I knew it!" Christian roared as he jumped to his feet. "You're leaving the band!"

He paced in a circle muttering to himself while Cameron just blinked at me. Shell shocked.

"I'm not leaving the band," I said calmly.

"Yeah?" Christian challenged, wrangling his phone from his pocket and shoving it in my face. "Did you read this? It's in the *Hollywood Reporter*. Not exactly a gossip rag."

Taking the device, I stared down at the screen. "I didn't read it, bro." Swallowing hard over the lump in my throat and the tears stinging the back of my eyes, I looked up. "I can't ... I mean, I couldn't. Because ..." *Say it. Say it. Say it.* "I can't read. I've never been able to read. That's why I was in LA."

The boulder attached to my back, the crushing weight I'd carried all my life, broke in two and tumbled to the ground.

Shifting my focus to each of my brothers, I offered a smile that almost felt ... peaceful. "This is going to take a minute to explain. Maybe y'all should grab a beer."

62

Logan

The following morning, just after sunrise, I found myself seated at the patio table on Sean's deck. I'd opted to take him up on his offer to spend the night, hoping the remote location and the proximity to Tori's house might help me sleep.

It didn't.

The back door creaked, and the birds scattered, except for one. The little dude stubbornly held his ground, eyeing me as he gathered the breadcrumbs I'd been tossing.

Anna slid a steaming mug of coffee in my direction. "You're up early," she said through a yawn as she took a seat across from me.

Tearing my gaze away from the bird, I smiled and picked up the cup. "I guess I'm still on European time."

Really, I was on Tori time. She always woke with the dawn. Shifting my gaze back to the water, I followed the shoreline west to the patch of trees on the bluff. To Tori's house. The media said she was in hiding, but I didn't believe it. The girl didn't run from anything.

Except you.

I frowned into my next sip of coffee.

"You still haven't talked to her?" Anna asked.

Was I that easy to read? Apparently so.

"I've been kind of busy."

She nodded a little too quickly, letting me off the hook. But, then isn't that why I said it?

Back off, I've been through enough. My mind's a little addled. Not quite right.

But that was a lie. I'd never been more clearheaded in my life. I knew exactly what I wanted—*Tori*. Any way she'd have me. But what if she wouldn't have me at all? What then?

I was about to come clean, confess my fears. But this was Anna, and she already knew.

"If you want to be with Tori, you shouldn't be afraid to tell her. What's the worst that's going to happen?"

A bitter laugh tripped from my lips. "She slams the door in my face and tells me to *git*."

That wasn't the worst. The worst would be if she told me she could never love me. But I couldn't admit that.

Anna nodded. "What if she doesn't, though?"

We could play this game all day. And she would, too. She'd wear me down until I admitted that I wouldn't know until I tried. That the reward was worth the risk. That even if the worst happened, I'd be okay. Eventually.

Grabbing a handful of breadcrumbs from the plastic bag, I tossed the tidbits at the bird who was now angrily pecking at the deck. "You're a persistent little fuck." And fearless too. But for that trait, he was like the rest of his buddies. Plain brown. A little on the small side. Bright, ebony eyes. "What kind of bird do you think he is?"

Anna dipped her head, and when he hopped her way, she smiled. "He's a wren."

Sweat trickled down my back as I trudged up the hidden path behind the luxury apartments. Once I reached the bluff overlooking the red bridge spanning the Colorado River, I eased down on a patch of dried grass under the canopy of trees and spread out the old wool blanket. After unpacking the dinner I'd picked up on the way, I sat back and took in the view.

When I was young, I used to bring Laurel here in the summer whenever we needed a break from the sweltering heat in the trailer. There was just enough level space in the clearing for a couple of sleeping bags. We'd eat our gas station burritos and watch the people on the opposite shore riding their wave runners and lazing by their pools. And for a few hours, we could steal a piece of their sky and pretend we were part of their world. Where everything smelled like coconut oil and sunshine instead of stale beer and desperation.

"Lo."

Laurel hovered at the edge of the clearing, looking around with uncertain eyes. Like she was still an outsider. It didn't matter that we'd made it. That I could buy her a place in this bright shiny world. She still carried the shame of the life we left behind. Just like me.

Pushing to my feet, I closed the distance between us and pulled her into a bear hug. "Laurel. I'm so glad you're here."

She tipped back, peering up at me with our mother's eyes. "Really?"

I could tell by the way her cheeks pinked that she hadn't meant to say it. But I'm glad she did, because I needed to hear it.

Tucking a blond curl behind her ear, I smiled. "Let's sit down."

Her gaze darted to the opposite shore. "What if someone sees us?"

"It's almost dark. Nobody's going to see us. And if they do, we wave." I laced our fingers. "Come on, your shake's going to melt."

A smile broke on her face when she saw the orange and white bags stained with grease. "You brought What-A-Burger. I love What-A-Burger."

Sinking to her knees on the blanket beside me, she tucked her hands between her thighs and looked around. "I remember when we used to come here on vacation when I was little."

I laughed because I thought she was kidding, but when our gazes met, her blue eyes were serious. "You thought this was a vacation?"

Taking the burger I offered, she shrugged. "It was the only vacation I ever had."

Easing onto my elbow, I toyed with the wrapper on my sandwich. "What about when you were with your foster family?"

Laurel never discussed her years in foster care. I wasn't sure if she was sparing me or herself, so I never pushed. But I wanted her to know she could talk to me about anything.

Shifting her focus to a speedboat pulling a group of kids on a large inner tube, she frowned. "I was too old for a foster family. At first, I was in a group home. It wasn't bad, but then I ran away ..."

Her sentence died when she picked up a french fry and dipped it in ketchup.

"Why would you run away if it wasn't bad?"

Peering at me through her lashes, she smiled sadly. "I just wanted to come home. So I ... um ... stole some money from one of the counselors and I bought a bus ticket."

My bite of burger turned to sawdust in my mouth. I chewed and chewed but I couldn't get it down. I finally reached for the chocolate shake so I wouldn't choke to death. "Where did you go?"

"Here. I was looking for you, but Daddy said you were already gone. He called the cops on me and they took me back. I ended up in another home that wasn't as nice."

I could guess the rest. Drugs. The strip club. All because of *him*.

The anger I'd been working so hard to push down roared to life. A firestorm, boiling my blood and charring my insides.

"Why, Laurel? After all that, why are you taking care of him?"

She opened the wrapper on her burger and peeked under the bun. "Same reason you are, I suppose. You hired those round the clock nurses. That can't be cheap. And that bigger apartment. Chase isn't charging me additional rent. You're paying for that too, right?"

A headache brewed behind my eyes, little flashes of blinding light dancing at the corners of my vision. "I'm doing that for you. Because you won't put him in a home. I don't want you alone with him."

She laughed then, a bitter sound that I could taste on my tongue. "What do you think he's going to do to me? He can't even hold a fork." Before I could stop her, she reached over and ran a finger over the scar above my eye. One of the many that Jake had put there. "I'm sorry he hurt you, Lo. But I hurt a lot of people too. When I was using. And still, you came looking for me. Even after you found out what I was, you forgave me."

I shook my head. "It's not the same thing. You're—"

"It is the same. I've done some terrible things. And this is like … karma. Maybe I'm supposed to take care of the monster because I used to be one myself. And when it's over …"

Tori's words came to me in the silence. "You'll be even."

A tear spilled onto her cheek as she nodded. "I knew you'd understand."

I didn't. But maybe I wasn't supposed to. This was about Laurel and what she needed. The unconditional love we were both promised, and never granted. And since my love for her was stronger than my hate for him, I trapped my objections behind tight lips. And we ate burgers. And watched the sunset. And we didn't speak about Jake again.

63

Logan

"Up," Chase said, taking me by the arm. "Now, Logan. I'm not kidding."

With the gaggle of press camped out in front of Twin Souls, there was no way he was kicking me out. Even if his girl put him up to it. Yeah, Taryn told me to leave. But I wasn't budging.

"I'm just waiting to talk to my manager," I said calmly as I shoved to my feet.

Anger flashed in Chase's hazel eyes. So much like Cameron's, but different. Crazier. Sure, Chase hid it all behind a calm exterior. But underneath, the dude had a fuse like mine, and from the vein bulging in his neck, he was about to blow.

"You did speak to your manager," he growled, his eyes darting to the receptionist who'd taken a keen interest in our conversation. "She told you to carry your ass home."

And wait.

But I was done waiting. I'd been waiting my whole life.

"My other manager." *Victoria.* The little thief who stole all my tomorrows when I was only eight. She'd been holding them in her pocket ever since. Even if she didn't realize it. I held up her copy of *Wuthering Heights*. "I've got something that belongs to her."

Rather than continue our chat in front of witnesses, Chase yanked me toward the hallway with the executive offices. My heart sank as we passed Tori's open door. The lights were off, and her desk was clear of any clutter. She wasn't here.

Chase gave me a shove, and I stumbled over the threshold and into Taryn's office. He closed the door, and for a minute, I was a little worried. His girl looked ready to rip my head off, and I wasn't so sure that Chase wouldn't let her.

Rounding the desk, Taryn headed straight for me, flames dancing in her stormy blue eyes. "What about 'go home' do you not understand?"

Chase cut in front of her at the last minute, steering her over to the sofa and urging her to take a seat.

Once she was settled, he tipped his chin to the chair, and I obliged.

"I need to talk to her, Taryn," I said.

"You and everyone else. Have you seen the press outside? I told you to wait. The concert's in two—"

"I'm not waiting. Her phone is off, and I want to know she's okay."

Chase's hand came down on Taryn's shoulder when her butt rose off the cushions. "Of course she's okay. Do you think I'd be sitting here if she weren't okay?"

I fingered the copy of Tori's note, tucked in the pages of the book. "Not good enough. I want to see for myself." I took a deep breath and softened my tone. "She left me, Taryn. Not the other way around."

Technically, it was true. But I hadn't given her much choice.

"And do you really think you two are going to ride off into the sunset after you went to LA to make that deal with Mac?"

My gaze flicked to Chase, and I didn't know whether to strangle the dude or commend him for his loyalty. He knew I was in LA, and more importantly he knew why.

Slowly, and with purpose, his gaze shifted to Taryn's office phone on the desk. A single light shone brightly on the panel below the keypad. It took me a second to catch on. I was on speaker and Tori was listening.

Releasing a controlled breath, I began, "I didn't go to LA to make any deals with Mac. I didn't even see Mac while I was there. If you don't believe me I'll call him right now and tell him to go to hell. *Again.* I don't want a solo career or a record deal with Metro. I want to be here. My heart is here."

With you. Always with you.

Staring at the tiny beacon on the phone, I willed Tori to answer. But all I got was silence. And when the light flicked off, my world went dark right along with it.

Tori

I stared at the phone, hanging on to Logan's every word. I could swear he was talking straight to me.

He wasn't leaving.

My heart is here.

He hadn't mentioned that in his voicemails, only saying he needed to see me. Which, of course, I took to mean he wanted to tell me in person that he was taking Mac up on his offer.

"Pride is one of those seven deadlies," came the voice from across the room.

My head snapped up, and I found Miles propped against the wall, ankles crossed one over the other. And I don't know why— maybe because I knew he was right—but I hung up. And then dismayed, I blinked at the screen.

A laugh from my drummer. "Jesus Christ, Belle. You are so fucking stubborn."

I set down the phone and ran a shaky hand through my hair. My heart raced as if I'd just run a marathon, and my skin felt too tight. Was I having a heart attack? I rubbed at the tender spot on my chest.

"Let's get back to work," I said thickly.

He sighed and then hobbled over while I jotted some notes on the sheet music I'd been working on.

Lost and found, you turned me around, and it all came down to you.

Our song, the one that Logan and I had composed on our cross-country journey. The lyrics blurred, shimmering under the canned lights in Miles's studio.

"So you don't even want to talk about it?" he said, taking a seat beside me.

"Nope." I scrambled to retrieve the paper when Miles plucked it from my hand. "Give it back!"

Settling sideways into the corner of the sofa, he glanced over the song. "Pretty sappy stuff here, Grayson." His gaze darted to mine, and all the humor left his face. "Are you still Grayson?"

My shoulders sagged, and in that instant, a little piece of me fell away. And I knew why I kept going back and forth with Logan. Yes, I was ready to move on. But who was I if I wasn't Belle Grayson? It went deeper than some persona the media had gifted me. It went all the way to my soul. To the memories shared with every important person in my life. It was much more than a name. It was *his* name.

Had I really let go?

I eased back against the cushions, frowning. "I don't know."

Miles tossed the sheet music on the table and scooted over. "Do you still want to be?"

I cut my gaze to his and shrugged. I fucking shrugged. Not from ambivalence. The answer held so much weight, I couldn't force the words from my lips.

If I said yes, did that doom my future relationships to fail? Consign all others to some secondary status? And if I said no, wasn't that giving up a part of me I wanted to preserve? The music and the memories and, yes ... the pain. The pain was part of me too, like my scars. There was beauty in those scars. A truth in the imperfections. Logan had helped me see that.

Logan ...

It all came down to you.

Minutes passed, and Miles didn't say anything. He was always the strong, silent type. Not one to impose his will through rhetoric. Unless it was really important.

"Belle?" I cringed without meaning to, and his gaze caught mine. I could see the wheels turning in his head. "You don't want to be 'Belle' anymore?"

He looked confused, and maybe a little crestfallen. And *that* was the problem. So many expectations. Even from those who had my best interests at heart.

"Nobody was supposed to know about 'Belle,'" I said quietly. "Belle was something between Rhenn and me. And when he died ..."

Miles nodded slowly. "It's painful, yeah?"

"Yeah."

"And the Grayson?"

"I don't mind the Grayson." I frowned. "Do you think that means I haven't moved on?"

He pondered for a moment and then lifted his shirt. Over his heart he wore the same *R* with the crown that was inked on my back. And above that, a flying guitar with a ribbon that simply read "Paige."

"Does this mean that I haven't moved on?" He shook his head in answer to his own question. "It's a tribute, Be ... Tori. Like this." Holding his wrist next to mine, the two birds etched in the far corner became four when they joined the ones inked on my skin. We all had them—Taryn, Dylan, Beckett, even fans. Everyone whose lives Rhenn and Paige had touched with their music, and their love, and their light.

An idea came to me suddenly, and I grabbed my guitar. "I want to make a change to the last song in the set."

Miles snagged his drumsticks from the table and then looked over at me with a smile. "Anything you say, Tori Belle."

Tori Belle ...

I could live with that.

64

Logan

My self-imposed dry spell ended with the first shot of Jameson. I didn't even like Jameson. But it was all I had in my loft. I looked around the place with a rueful sigh. *Home.* Except it wasn't. I'd felt more at home in every hotel I'd shared with Tori. And in the car.

After I'd left Twin Souls today, I'd considered dumping the Mustang in the lake. Everything in that rolling piece of metal reminded me of Tori. The chain she'd made of Big Red gum wrappers hanging from the rearview mirror. The two Goldfish crackers on the passenger seat that I'd looked at a dozen times but couldn't bring myself to sweep away. Her hair bands in the ashtray. And even the Dr. Pepper stain on the floorboard.

The Mustang wasn't a fucking car anymore. It was a time capsule. A roadmap of our journey. I could either stick the car in storage and never drive it again or learn to live with the pain. Sadly, there was no third option.

Another shot.

As the alcohol burned a path to my roiling gut, I wandered over and opened the window overlooking Sixth. What was it about this street?

Lost and found, you turned me around, and it all came down to you.

It wasn't the street. It was Tori. She was everywhere. In every face and every sound. Even the breeze held a hint of sugar and cinnamon. Sweet, like her. And so fucking bitter I could barely stand it.

The Jameson wouldn't wash it away. So why bother?

I held the bottle up to the light. "You took that away from me too, you little thief. I can't even enjoy this shitty fucking liquor. Are you happy now?"

A knock at the door drew me out of my thoughts. Pizza. I vaguely remembered ordering it. Stalking across the room, I grabbed my wallet from the table where small bags of Pepperidge Farm cookies in all varieties sat open.

Sweeping the crumbs off my T-shirt with one hand, I reached for the doorknob with the other.

And then Tori was there, standing in front of me.

She didn't say anything, and for a moment I wondered if I'd conjured her. So I did the only thing I could do. Threading my fingers through her silky hair, I pulled her mouth to mine for a kiss. Taking her air when she gasped, I claimed it as my own. Her tongue darted out, and oh my fucking God, thank you. Thank you for this. Whatever it was—hello or goodbye—if I kept her here, right in this very spot, I'd make it last forever.

"Lo," she murmured, and I tightened my grip. Her palms molded to my chest. "Logan."

Reluctantly, I pulled away and let my hands fall to my sides. It was a small victory, breaking the connection before she had a chance. Pride—I still had a little. It was in there somewhere.

"Hey, princess."

My tone was so casual that she looked up at me, confusion lining her brow.

Yes, I just kissed you.

Maybe if I didn't make a big deal of it, she'd forget about the last month. And we could pick up where we left off. But then I thought of her in that church, at the place where we ended, and reality crashed in.

"I wanted to talk to you," Tori said as she peered into the apartment. "Unless you're busy."

Did drowning in a pit of my own despair count as busy? Probably not.

"Nope. Not busy. Come in."

Standing aside to let her pass, I drank her in while she took a look around the place.

"This is nice," she said as she took a seat.

It wasn't nice. It was empty as fuck. Platinum albums propped against the wall. Boxes I'd never unpacked stacked up in the corner. A dead plant, leaves yellow and shriveled, sitting on the window sill.

That about summed it up.

Smiling, I plopped down next to her. "Thanks."

"So I guess you heard about the concert?" She flinched. "Of course you have. You're in it."

If I were smart, I'd ask why she was here. Put an end to this agony. But I was down for the pain if it meant a few extra minutes with her.

"Yeah ... I was a little surprised by that." When she cocked her head, I added, "The concert. It's not something I thought you'd be into."

Her gaze dropped to her lap. "I'm not, really. I'm doing it for someone else."

Her whispered words were like an arrow to the chest. Another reminder of what she was: the brightest star in someone else's sky.

"Miles," she added in a voice even fainter than her whisper. "I owe him that."

Miles ...

"He's not in a wheelchair?"

Tori's head snapped up. "No ... where did you hear that?"

I shrugged, my gaze darting to the Jameson. A few more shots might loosen the knots in my tongue. "I don't really know. But nobody's seen him in what, years?"

"He keeps a low profile. He's been to rehab a couple of times." She shifted her gaze to the window. To something beyond this conversation. "Things have been hard for him."

362

A knock shattered the silence, and Tori whipped her head to the door. "If you're expecting someone ..." She was halfway out of her seat before I could stop her. My fingers coiled around her wrist, and she looked up at me.

"I'm not expecting anyone. Nobody's ever been here except the guys. That's my dinner."

She sagged against the cushions. "Oh, okay."

I pressed a kiss to her palm and then dropped her hand and spun for the door without waiting for her reaction.

When I returned with the pizza, she was holding her copy of *Wuthering Heights*. "You had this?"

Lifting a shoulder, I dropped the box on the table. "You left it."

She hummed, and I felt it down to my balls, remembering every time I'd coaxed that little sound from her throat with my tongue, or my fingers, or my cock.

Stop.

But it was too late. My dick was now fully aware of her presence. *Painfully* aware. Forcing my brain to conjure thoughts of zombies and that killer clown from *IT*, I went about plating a slice of pizza. Mushroom and bell pepper. Her favorite.

"Here you go."

Taking the plate without looking up, her gaze remained on the pages in the book. "Did you read any of this?"

And I knew right then, Fate had intervened, giving me the perfect opening. I'd made my peace with the goddess, but I still thought her sister was a bitch. Yep, I was relatively certain that Irony was waiting in the wings to fuck things up.

Still, it didn't stop me. Sliding the book from Tori's hands, I gazed at the cover. "I didn't read it." I plucked the note from the front flap and looked her in the eyes. "Or this. Or the contract you found in my backpack."

With the connection we shared, I thought that might be enough for her to put some of the pieces together. But she just stared at me with a scrunched-up brow.

"I can't read, princess. Not a word."

363

That wasn't really true anymore. In just under two weeks I'd learned the alphabet. Simple words of the three-letter variety were jumping out at me now from everywhere. I'd also learned a name. Funny enough, it was Tori's and not mine.

"You can't read ... I don't understand." She scooted closer as if she could find the answer on my face if she looked hard enough. Maybe she could. With her knees pressed against my thigh, I wasn't going to stop her from trying.

"Illiteracy," I joked. "It's not just for inbred hicks anymore." My attempt at humor fell flat, and she frowned, concern etching her brow. No pity, though. I smoothed the wrinkles with my thumb. "That's why I went to LA. To meet with a doctor who specializes in adult dyslexia."

"But, I know people with dyslexia. Dylan has dyslexia. He can read."

After explaining to Tori about the three different types of the disorder, mostly to buy some time, I sat back with my arm behind my head. Easier to look at the ceiling for this.

"I have the garden variety brand of dyslexia. Except ..."

When I didn't finish the thought, Tori snuggled against my side, gazing up at me with her chin resting on my chest like I was about to tell her a bedtime story. Having her this close, it should've warmed me, but I was cold all over. I hadn't figured out how to relate the story without re-living it. So far, only Dr. Patel and the therapist she'd recommended in Austin had witnessed the telling.

"Remember how I told you my mom died when I was eight?" I felt her nod, and I took a last gulp of air, enough to sustain me for my descent into the murky depths of my memory. And then I closed my eyes. "I was there."

Logan

364

Mama gave me a little shove, and I stumbled onto the wooden steps in front of the trailer.

"Take your sister and get out to the car," she whispered, setting Laurel on her feet beside me. Peering around Mama, I saw Daddy sleeping on his chair. My lip curled back, and Mama grabbed my chin.

"Logan, baby, do as you're told. I'll be there in a minute."

I wasn't a baby, but I didn't mind it when Mama called me that. So I nodded. She kissed my forehead.

"Ugh ... Lo, stop pulling my arm," Laurel whined. "Lo-gan!"

I should've been paying attention. Should've made her be quiet.

But it was too late. The light flickered on, and my daddy's roar sliced through the night air. "Elizabeth! You hidin' from me, bitch?"

Laurel stopped dead in her tracks. "Daddy ..."

Turning toward the dirty window, I saw him. Daddy. He was out of his chair. And then he roared again. And Mama screamed.

Yanking Laurel's arm, I dragged her toward Mama's beat up old Mustang. "Shut up. *Shut up*," I pleaded. "He's going to hear you."

My hand slipped off the door handle. Once. Twice. I rubbed my sweaty palm on my jeans.

God, please, help me.

And the door opened. And then we were inside.

The window in the backseat was little. But still I could see. Mama was on the porch now. One of Daddy's hands around her mouth, the other in her hair. "Who are you going to see?" He shook her. "Huh? You cheatin' on me?"

Mama did that thing she told me to do when Daddy was angry. She just ... stopped.

It worked, and his hand slid off her mouth. "We're outta milk, Jake. I need some for the kids' cereal."

Maybe it was her voice—she had the voice of an angel—but he stopped jerking her around. "Don't you be leaving me alone with these kids very long, woman. You got ten minutes."

365

Mama's eyes jumped to the car for only a second, and I knew to get down. Daddy thought we were inside the trailer, me and Laurel. I shoved my sister on the floorboard so she wouldn't ruin the plan. She glared up at me. "Sorry, sissy."

"Go on now," Daddy growled, and he shoved Mama down the steps. She landed on her hands and knees. But it didn't faze her. She pulled herself to standing and, wiping her hands on her dress, she walked toward the car.

Run, Mama.

But she didn't. Her eyes locked on mine as she took careful steps, scooting around the empty beer bottles and soda cans.

Just a little farther, Mama.

I saw Daddy before she did. He burst out of the trailer, his wallet in his hand. "Where's my money, you whore?!"

And he was running. And Mama was running. She slid behind the wheel, and the engine fired up. "Logan ... stay down. Don't let him see you."

But as she pulled away, I peered over the backseat. Just my eyes, like an alligator. And Daddy was in his truck.

The car went all funny, the way it did that time Mama drove over the ice. I tumbled onto the seat, and we were going so fast. But I was happy. And Mama smiled at me in the rearview mirror. She was happy too.

"It's okay, baby."

It seemed like a long time passed, but I wasn't sure. Because my eyes were droopy, and Mama was singing that Judds' song about grandpas' and the good old days. The car pulled to a stop, and I blinked at the red light. Mama reached over to change the radio. And then I heard tires squeal and she looked up. Her eyes got real wide and she glanced around all quick like. A flash of blond hair outside the window. Mama's mouth barely moved when she said, "Be a good boy, Logan. Watch your sister."

The car door ripped open, and I dove onto the floorboard next to Laurel.

Pop. Pop. Pop.

I peeked over the seat and saw Mama on the ground. She was bleeding. She was bleeding so much. And then I noticed the car in front of us. Just for a second. There was a red glow around the license plate. I stared at it. Stared and stared until it sped away.

And then someone was leaning in the car. A man with blood on his hands. "Is this your Mama?" He was big, with a beard, but he sounded scared.

I nodded and looked back out the window. And the other car was gone.

"Don't move," said the bearded man.

I didn't move. But I hoped he'd come back. And he did. When he pulled the seat back and held out his hand for me to take, I saw Mama's legs. But her top half was covered with a blanket. A yellow blanket with a big, red blotch. The blotch looked wet. I didn't want to look at the blotch. Instead, I looked at Mama's legs. One of her shoes was missing. It was the red sandal with the little bow that fit between her toes.

When the bearded man helped me out of the car, he looked surprised to find Laurel clinging to my waist. Pulling her closer to me, I looked up at the man, and in my most polite voice, I asked, "Can you find my mama's shoe, sir?"

She needed her shoe. For when she got up.

The bearded man took my hand, and he grunted something that sounded like, "I'm sorry." And then he told me to sit on the bumper of a big truck. I did that too.

And then there were lights. Red lights. And blue lights. And the blotch was bigger.

The policeman knelt in front of me. He asked me questions. I told him about the car. I told him about the red glowy light. I told him everything.

And then there were two of them. Both on their knees, talking to me.

"Concentrate, son. You want to help us, don't you? Just tell us what you saw. The license plate on the back of the car. Give us a letter."

I tried. I tried so hard.

"I can't," I said and looked down at the pavement.

The policeman stood up, and there were spots of blood on his boots. And through his legs, I saw Mama. There were people around her now. And there was no more blotch. Just red. Red hair. Red dress. Red.

The policeman leaned forward again, his forehead all scrunched. He smelled like how Mama did in the morning. Like coffee.

"Son, if you want to help your mama, you need to concentrate and give us a letter."

And I knew what he meant. If I didn't give him a letter my mama would die. So I tried some more. And no letters came.

And she died.

By the time I finished my story, day had slipped into night. I was on my back now, Tori's hot, salty tears soaking through my T-shirt. Forehead pressed to my temple and lips a hair's breadth from my ear, she spoke in a faint whisper.

"*I'm sorry. I'm sorry. I'm sorry.*"

Over and over she said it, fingers digging into my shoulder where she held onto me. I wanted to tell her it was okay, that I was fine, but I couldn't form the words. My lids were too heavy, and I was so fucking tired.

Banding my arm around her waist, I took my last bit of energy and rolled us onto our sides.

Face-to-face now, I threaded a hand in her messy hair. "Stay with me, baby."

My voice was thick, the words slow and slurred. I was drunk on Tori and truth, and I hadn't slept in weeks. And it didn't even matter that she'd probably be gone when I woke up. Or that there would be no sex. Right now, she was here. And she smelled of warmth and safety and cookies. And I loved her.

And I might've said that too.

65

Tori

He'd said it. Not once, but twice.

I love you.

I love you.

It was like an echo. In the room and in my heart. And I so wanted him to mean it. I wanted the words to be true.

Tipping back, I peered down at Logan's face. Beneath the stubble and the faint shadows bruising his eyes, I saw an eight-year-old boy. Lost and alone. And in that moment, I felt our connection, the something that bound us beyond lust, love, or attraction.

We were the same, he and I.

Our lives had changed—not over months or years, but in seconds. Three shots and Logan's destiny was sealed. No matter what happened after that, he'd always be motherless. And me ... a minute later or a minute earlier on that rain slicked road, and I wouldn't be a widow. And Paige would be alive.

My copy of *Wuthering Heights* called to me from the table.

Whatever our souls are made of, his and mine are the same.

Pushing the hair back from Logan's face, I pressed my lips to his forehead. And I did something I'd never done for anyone. I sang to him. So softly it was nothing more than a whisper.

The logical part of my brain told me to protect my heart. That Logan's damage and my damage were too much to overcome. There wasn't enough left of either of us to survive if we crashed to earth. But I wouldn't think about that now. For a few more hours, we'd simply float.

The minute my eyes popped open, I knew it was late. Sunlight flooded the entire loft from corner-to-corner. If I had to guess, I'd say it was mid-morning. Which meant, I was in trouble. With the concert just over thirty-six hours away, I had a to-do list that could choke a horse.

Stupid.

Slowly, I stretched my limbs, stifling a groan when my hip protested. Once the pain subsided I pushed myself up. Logan shifted, and I chanced a peek at his face. So beautiful. The worry lines around his eyes had faded, and I was grateful for that. And then my gaze fell to his chest, and his shallow, even breaths.

Something metal caught my eye, and I tipped forward.

Smiling, I lifted the coin. Logan had a lucky penny.

Just like ...

My heart stammered, and then slammed against my ribs as I ran my finger over the stamping that covered the Lincoln Memorial. One word. LUCKY. All caps. The *L* was slightly lower than the other letters, and inside the stamp, most of the black nail polish had flaked off. But a little remained. Enough to let me know this was *my* penny. The one my dad had made me with his kit when I was six.

Just to be sure, I checked the date on the coin. *1988*. The year I was born.

Logan's fingers closed around mine, and I jerked. His expression was inscrutable. "Good morning, baby."

I blinked at him. "Where did you get this?"

But I knew. As I looked into those pale blue eyes, I knew.

Logan was the boy I'd given my penny to when I was nine. The boy who'd never offered his name. But that didn't matter, because I'd made one up: *Lucky*.

In my head, the boy was Lucky.

Lucky after the penny that was my most prized possession. Lucky because his dad had loved him so much, according to my mom, that he'd picked him up the day after his mother's horrific accident. Lucky because he wasn't a foster kid.

Just ... Lucky.

Logan smiled sadly. "You gave it to me."

"When?"

His thumb brushed over my knuckles. "The day you stole my heart."

66

Logan

I leaned against the counter in the kitchen while the coffee brewed, my gaze fixed on Tori in the living room. Holding the penny up to the light, she watched it spin on the end of the twine.

Me—I was that damned coin. On the end of her rope, spinning.

I'd meant to tell her about the penny last night—I'd meant to tell her a lot of things—but after all the stuff with my mom, everything got hazy.

I love you.

Had I said it aloud, or was that just a dream? I couldn't be sure, since I'd just slept for ten hours and the world was still a little fuzzy around the edges.

After fixing Tori's coffee, I headed back to the living room. "Here you go."

Taking the mug, she scrutinized me with a pinched brow. "My mom said that Lucky ... that *you*, had gone home with your dad." Tears welled in her eyes as she closed her fingers around the coin and brought her fist to her heart. "I didn't know it was you. How long have you known?"

I took a seat beside her, leaving a couple of feet between us. "That night at your parents' house."

"That's why you left?"

Ran was a more accurate description. I frowned into my first sip of coffee. "Yeah."

"Why didn't you tell me?"

Inhaling a controlled breath, I set my mug on the table. "Have you ever seen the movie, *The Reader*?" She shook her head. "This woman went to prison rather than admit she couldn't read. I've been carrying this secret my whole life, baby. You don't understand what it means ... how it feels ..."

She scooted closer. "But it's not your fault."

A brittle laugh scraped my throat. "Which part—not being able to read, or letting my mom's killer go free?"

I'd said it—admitted it—and now it was real. Shame pooled in my belly, coating me from the inside out, and I hung my head. In a flash, Tori was on my lap, straddling me, her hands in my hair.

"You did not let your mother's killer go free! Why would you think that?"

Curving my hands around her thighs, I chuckled. "Because it's true. I spent years blaming Jake. And even then ..." I shook my head. "I stayed in that trailer until I was seventeen. What does that say about me?"

Tears I didn't deserve spilled onto her cheeks. "It says you were scared. Are you sure it wasn't your dad? "

Tori spoke in a whisper, as if she might disturb the ghost in my head if she talked any louder.

"No. The car in front of us that night, it wasn't his. It was just dumb luck that we were there. Two robberies had been reported with a vehicle that matched my description. I found that out after Dr. Patel requested the police report. But I was the only one who saw a license plate."

My hands trailed up her thighs to her waist, memorizing the feel of her. Higher I went, to her nape, where my thumb found the little notch on her throat. Stroking the tiny ridge, I smiled. One inch, the difference between life and death. Without the scar, Tori wouldn't be here. So I leaned in and kissed the perfect imperfection with all the reverence it deserved. And then I pulled her against me, tucking her head under my chin.

"When I found out who you were, I took it as a sign."

"What kind of a sign?"

Stroking one hand up and down her back, I kept the other in her hair. "You're my redemption, Victoria. You're everything. On my darkest day, I found you. And I know it's not the same for you. You had your great love. And I get that." I brushed my lips over the soft strands on her crown. "I just want a chance. I want to make memories with you that are so beautiful they make you weep like you did in Paris. I want to be that for you, because you're that for me."

She turned to stone in my arms, and I felt my heart crack, falling to the ground in shards at her feet. I could never be that for her.

I was trying to figure out how to rephrase my plea so she wouldn't freak out when she said in a small voice, "I hate Paris. Paris is the worst place on earth." A tremor took her whole and she sniffled. "During the last Damaged tour in Europe, we played a gig in Paris. I was pregnant. Three months. After the show, I wasn't feeling well, but we had another date in London, at Wembley. Ninety thousand seats —sold out. I told Rhenn to go. I didn't think he would ... but he did. And while he was onstage the next night in front of all those strangers, I lost my baby in a hospital with a view of the Eiffel Tower outside my window. That day you found me in the church, I wasn't crying for Rhenn. I was crying for the baby boy that I never got to meet."

She lifted her gaze then, fat tears streaming down her beautiful face. "I loved Rhenn. I did. But maybe he was only meant to stay for a minute. To teach me what he had to teach me and be on his way." She cupped my cheek. "If my life were a song, Rhenn would be the first verse. But I think ... I think you're meant to be the chorus. The part that goes on and on. I love you, Logan. And it's so big ... this feeling, I don't know what to do with it."

Our confessions hung in the air, an overcast sky filled with tears, shattered dreams, and bittersweet memories. And a rainbow. I saw it in Tori's eyes, every color under the sun.

She loved me.

Jesus. How impossible was that?

I realized I hadn't said anything, and a furrow formed between her brows. Pressing my lips to the little spot, I whispered, "I love you, Victoria. Always you. Even before I knew it was you."

She tipped her chin, lashes fluttering. "Do you think ... I mean ... is it too much?"

"What, baby?"

"Us. I'm afraid."

I rose to my feet with Tori in my arms. "No. We're even now."

I wasn't sure if it were true. Because I had more than I'd ever expected. I had Tori. So I had it all.

Wrapping her legs around my waist, she buried her face in my neck as I carried her to my bed and laid her down on the uncovered mattress.

"Where are the sheets?" Lifting her hips so I could strip off her jeans, she raised her brows and waited for an answer.

Once I was undressed, I joined her. There was no place to hide. Nothing to cover us. "Ever since you left, I haven't been able to sleep. The sheets in every hotel smelled ... well, not like you. And when I got home, it was the same."

She settled against the only covered pillow. "What about this one?"

I sighed, easing on top of her. "That's not my pillow, it's yours. I stole it from the hotel in Paris."

A laugh tripped from her lips. "You stole a pillow?"

It seemed fair, since she'd stolen everything else. "Yes, and I'd do it again."

I pressed a kiss to her mouth, my tongue sweeping inside. So fucking sweet. Tori's fingers threaded my hair, and she sighed. A breathy little pant gave way to a moan as I worked my way to her pert nipples. She shivered as I ran my nose over the furled peak. Then she tightened her grip.

So impatient.

"You want me, baby?"

Her legs fell open, and I smiled, scoring my teeth across her nipple while my fingertips skimmed the length of her. All the skin I could reach. And when I made it to the heaven between her thighs, she gasped.

Parting her slick folds, I worked two fingers inside her pussy while my palm applied even pressure to her clit.

Lifting my gaze, I found her staring at me, lips parted and cheeks pink.

"I love you," she breathed, and then her eyes rolled back, and she was gone. She came undone a second later, surprising me with the intensity of her orgasm.

Before she'd even finished, my face was buried between her thighs. A guttural moan escaped from deep in her throat. And yes, yes, fuck yes, *give it to me.*

I wanted it all. All of her sounds, her taste, this sweet pussy. Mine. Finally, mine.

"Logan ... please."

When I managed to work my way back up, she peered at me with hooded eyes.

"What, baby?" I asked, brushing the hair out of her face.

Curving a hand around my neck, she pulled me in for a kiss, hips tilting at just the right angle for me to slide home. So I did. And somehow, I'd forgotten this part. The absolute contentment I found inside her body. I wanted to live here. Right here, in this moment. Forever. But we'd have plenty of moments. A lifetime. So I started to move. And an even more wondrous moment unfurled. Her eyes widened, and that honied gaze locked me down. And it was like staring into the sun. Blinding, but not.

"This is where forever lives," I whispered against her lips.

And she nodded.

And I nodded.

And we fell.

67

Tori

Daryl, along with four other hired guns stood next to the elevated table in the extra-large tent at Zilker Park where my press event was being held. The other bands had already completed their sets, leaving only my performance. The main event.

With less than a half hour before my show was scheduled to begin, my stomach churned. A quick glance in my direction and Taryn assessed my nerves. My inner turmoil. And thats why she was running the show and not Elise. Taryn knew me, all my tells.

She gave me a soft smile, then tipped forward to speak into her microphone. "We've got to get a move on, y'all. Last question."

Shifting my focus to a friendly face in the front row, I gave Ash Devonshire from the Austin Statesman the nod. He winked at me, a smile hitching one corner of his lips as he pushed to his feet.

And for the hundredth time today, tears stung the back of my eyes. But nobody could see them behind my oversized sunglasses.

Yeah, I was in full rock star mode. Clad in painted-on jeans, a barely there blouse, and sky-high boots, I looked nothing like myself. Which was only fitting. Because today, I was Belle Grayson. And I had a job to do. Something I should've done long ago. Not just for me, or Miles, but for the fans. Seventy-five thousand strong right outside the tent. Plus a million seven streaming live on Pay-Per-View. And the untold number who'd watch from the comfort of their homes when HBO aired the taped special next month.

All-in-all, this concert was slated to be the highest grossing event of the year, or the last ten years if the projections were on point.

"It's good to see you, Belle," said Ash.

I gave him a genuine smile, my first of the day. "Hey, Ash. Good to see you too."

Shifting his feet, he glanced down at the prearranged question. "Will this show signal your permanent return to the stage?"

His smile wilted just a bit in preparation for my answer, which he already knew. Ash had been covering Damaged since the beginning. So it was only right he'd be here at the end.

Clearing my throat, I took Miles's hand under the table. "Today marks my official retirement." Ignoring the shouts from the reporters who jumped to their feet to ask a follow up question, I tipped forward and smiled. "Sorry y'all. It's been an awesome ride. But it ends here."

Where it began.

Taryn fussed with the ties on my blouse.

"Make sure to reinforce those," I said, peering out of the curtain at the sea of people. "There's barely any fabric there as it is. One slip and the whole planet is going to see my goodies."

Deep in conversation with his boys some five feet away, I saw Logan snap to attention. Pale blue eyes, iridescent in the ambient light, shifted my way. Looking me over from tip to toe with a feral gaze, his tongue slid over his bottom lip. Still, he made no move to approach. Partly because of the camera crew shadowing my every move. But mostly because today, I wasn't his. Not completely. Today I belonged to all the girls in the crowd with purple and blue streaks in their hair. And to all the members of the bands who'd performed in tribute to who I once was. Today ... I belonged to Rhenn, Paige, and Miles.

But tonight, and every moment after, I'd be his.

I smiled, and he smiled back.

"You've got six feeds going live to the satellite locations," Taryn said in a shaky voice. "The screens to the right and left of the stage will pan in from time to time to give you crowd reaction."

I swept a lock of chestnut hair out of her face. "And where will you be?"

Chase was going to take in the show with Logan and the guys. But I wasn't sure about Taryn.

She pointed to a large group on the opposite side of the stage. Dylan was there, along with Beckett, and all the other members of the Big Three.

"It's only right," she said. "Full circle and all that."

A shadow appeared at the back of the stage. Miles. Though I barely noticed his limp, he was self-conscious about it, so he'd arranged to take his place behind the kit before the announcement was made.

Taryn sucked in a breath. "That's my cue. I'm heading to the other side."

As she took a step, I grabbed her arm, pulling her into my embrace. "I *love* you, T-Rex. Thank you for everything."

And I meant *all of it*. From kindergarten to now. And whatever would come in the future.

She hung on for a long moment before breaking our connection. "I love you back."

And then she was gone. And I was alone. Seventy-five thousand people, and I was by myself, staring out at three *X*'s on the stage.

A single spotlight pierced the darkness, and then Dylan was

there, in front of the microphone. It took a good few minutes of cajoling for the audience to settle enough for him to speak.

"I'm Dylan," he shouted when he got the chance. "And I'd like y'all to help me welcome the original Sixth Street band, Damaged!"

The stage shook as the audience roared, and instinctively, I took a step back.

But then Rhenn's voice drifted through the massive speakers, and the world went quiet. So still. Everyone hanging onto the edge of their seats.

"You know, we're just a little old band from Austin. We never expected all of this." A beam of light shot from the rafters, and his hologram appeared. So handsome, with his long dark hair and his favorite guitar hanging low on his hip.

And then Paige's voice, gentle as a breeze. "We love coming out to play for y'all. Isn't that right, Belle?" Another flicker from the heavens and she was there too. Bright smile and long, red hair flowing in the non-existent breeze.

The sound and lighting crew had spliced together pieces from old interviews and shows to make this an interactive experience. And it was, because the sight of them mere feet away brought a torrent of tears I could hardly contain. But I did. And one last time, I stepped into the light of the Sixth Street Legacy.

To say goodbye.

Logan

An hour and a half into the performance, Tori stepped up to the organ. It was the first time she'd ventured very far from her mark. Since I knew what was coming, I inched closer to the stage. Just far enough for her to see me if she looked.

I'm here, baby.

And for the first time since she'd emerged into the spotlight, her gaze swung my way.

I nodded, lending whatever silent encouragement I could.

Tori nodded back and then took a deep breath, resting her fingers on the keys. I'd played in front of some monster crowds in my life. Watched from the wings as some of the biggest bands in the world performed in front of audiences of nearly a hundred thousand. But I'd never heard anything like the collective roar that rose up when Tori played the opening bars for "Free Bird," the old Lynyrd Skynyrd standard that was eerily appropriate for this show.

A second later, the stage went dark, but for the two holograms. And then the rest of the instruments fell away, and the song morphed in an acoustic version with only Rhenn and Paige on guitar.

Overcome by the weight of the moment, the audience grew so quiet, you'd never know there were seventy-five thousand people in attendance. Except for the sea of lights that went on and on for as far as the eye could see.

What they failed to notice was my girl, gliding toward the curtain with her head down. She walked straight into my arms, and nobody knew. It was as if she'd left Belle on the stage, and only Victoria remained. And that was fine with me.

Tucking her to my side, I headed for the private lot where my Mustang waited, our bags in the trunk. She didn't even flinch when the crowd erupted behind us.

"Where are you taking me?" she asked, as if the thought had just occurred to her.

I kissed her temple. "I don't know. Where do you want to go?"

I knew, and my GPS was already programed. But still, I waited for the words.

She peered up at me. "How does Nashville sound?"

And I smiled. "Like heaven."

EPILOGUE

Tori

Three Years Later

Eyes bleary, I padded down the hallway, two bottles in hand. The nursery was dark, and I shook my head and kept on walking. At the door to our bedroom, I paused to take in the scene. Logan was sprawled on the bed, back against the headboard, with Lizzy curled in the crook of his arm, and Lucky on his back on top of his daddy's legs.

"What do you think is going to happen next?" Logan asked, smiling at our babies as he turned the page of the picture book. "I think the little pig is in deep shit."

I bit down a grin as he continued with the story, adding little sound effects. There was huffing and puffing, and a loud crash when the first pig lost his house. Lizzy started to fuss, but Logan didn't miss a beat. He kept right on reading as he rocked her gently, and she quieted down.

We'd never planned on twins. But when it came to the sorcery that was in vitro fertilization, sometimes you got more than you bargained for. Plus, according to Logan—super sperm. He had it. He knew it. And there was no convincing him otherwise. He wasn't the least bit shocked when the doctor confirmed that our surrogate had two buns in the oven. Since I was sure that my eggs were faulty, I was worried enough for both of us.

But nine months after the first IVF treatment, and only fourteen months after Logan and I married in a little church in Nashville, Elizabeth Paige and Logan Sean made their debut.

Lizzy and Lucky.

Lizzy was born first. Dark blond hair that flirted with brunette. Amber eyes like mine. Face shaped like a heart.

I loved her at first sight. A deep, abiding love that I knew could never be duplicated.

Until Lucky entered the world two minutes later. Bright blue eyes like his daddy. A shock of black hair. He was the quiet one. Circumspect. Like a little old man in a tiny baby body.

I pulled myself out of my daydream when Logan noticed me standing there.

A smile curved his lips, and I wondered how he did it—made me feel sexy with spit up on my night shirt and my dirty hair in a top knot. But he did. His gaze followed me as I crossed the room and climbed onto the bed.

"Look who's here," he said to Lizzy who blinked up at him with adoring eyes. "It's Mama."

Gently, I lifted Lucky off his daddy's legs and my baby boy gave me a sleepy smile. I sifted through his hair, and his heavy lids fell to half-mast.

Scooting closer to Logan, I rested my head on his shoulder.

"What should we read next?" he asked Lizzy, and then took a moment as if she might answer. But at six months old, that wasn't going to happen, no matter how gifted my husband proclaimed our children to be.

"*Winnie the Pooh* it is," he said, reaching for another book from the pile on his nightstand.

Lifting my gaze, I peered up at the man I loved. And God, how I loved him. And our life. So much that it scared me sometimes, because how could I be this happy? How could anyone?

Logan smiled, looking down at me. "What's the matter, Mama, you don't like the Pooh?"

"I like the Pooh. Read me the Pooh."

He brushed a kiss to my forehead, snuggled a little closer, and then he did just that.

The End ...

Jayne Said

As we close out the Caged portion of the series, I thought I'd share the original idea for the Sixth Street Bands. I was in Austin one day in 2005 and I saw a bronze statue of Stevie Ray Vaughan at Towne Lake. In case you're not familiar, Stevie was killed in a helicopter crash in 1990. I started thinking about his family. His dreams. His legacy. And then I wondered —who came after to fill his shoes? Who was the next great Austin band?

Being a writer with a wildly active imagination, I answered my own question by making up a fictional band. But not just one. I envisioned a band family, all 6th Street originals.

At the center of it all was the lead singer of one of those bands —Logan Cage.

Although there are four books that came before *Down To You,* it was always about Logan in my head. He was the prize.

So, thank you Logan. In the end ... *it all came down to you.*

Thank y'all for reading. Until next time. :D

Acknowledgments

First ... thank you to all my readers. Y'all are the best. I can't express how grateful I am for your support.

Maria ... there are too many things to thank you for. Covers, teasers, reading every word I write. But mostly, thank you for your friendship. Love you.

Victoria ... I know you think you're too old to live at home. You are. I get it. But I still demand one night a week. Non-negotiable. To the moon and back, I love you.

Patricia ... you're the best editor. I'm not just saying that. I couldn't do any of this without you. Love you.

Marla Esposito ... thank you for accommodating my crazy schedule. I keep saying I'm going to get better. Spoiler alert: I probably won't.

Frost's Faves ... I cherish each and every one of you. Thank you for all your support. The posts and the pictures keep me going. Y'all are the best of the best!

Also by
Jayne Frost

MISSING *from* Me

A SIXTH STREET BANDS ROMANCE

JAYNE FROST

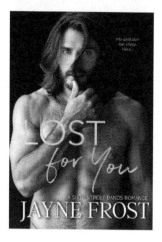

LOST *for You*

A SIXTH STREET BANDS ROMANCE

JAYNE FROST

About Jayne

Jayne Frost, author of the Sixth Street Bands Romance Series, grew up in California with a dream of moving to Seattle to become a rock star. When the grunge thing didn't work out (she never even made it to the Washington border) Jayne set her sights on Austin, Texas. After quickly becoming immersed in the Sixth Street Music scene...and discovering she couldn't actually sing, Jayne decided to do the next best thing--write kick ass romances about hot rockstars and the women that steal their hearts.

Made in the USA
Lexington, KY
04 May 2019